EVERYBODY SCREAM!

Also by Jeffrey Thomas

Terror Incognita
Punktown
AAAIIIEEE!!!
Monstrocity
Letters From Hades
Punktown: Third Eye (editor)
Boneland
Honey is Sweeter Than Blood

EVERYBODY SCREAM!

Jeffrey Thomas

RAW DOG SCREAMING PRESS

Everybody Scream! © 2004 by Jeffrey Thomas
All rights reserved

Published by Raw Dog Screaming Press
Hyattsville, MD

Hardcover Edition

Cover image: Mike Bohatch www.eyesofchaos.com
Book design: Jennifer Barnes

Printed in the United States of America

ISBN 0-9745031-4-2

Library of Congress Control Number: 2004094657

www.rawdogscreaming.com

Acknowledgments

Infinite thanks to the Raw Dog Screaming typing pool, who arduously transferred to type a manuscript written by hand in 1987-1988–most particularly to Jennifer Barnes, who did the bulk of the work. And thanks to Scott Thomas, for being Frankie Dystopia and my brother.

Smoke Circus

Licorice skies
Bend the lights
Of a steel skeleton horizon.

I spin in your vehicles
Cotton candy clouds
Popcorn teen faces
Scream the riders, loud.

Amass the delighted
Vibrant, excited
Is this where life starts?
Shooting gallery hearts.

Bumper car kisses
Who stops to idol?
The flax of humanity
Like a gold hero's title.

Flesh and metal
Neon and death
Flame the smoke circus
The purpose of breath.

-Frankie Distopia

In the colony city of Paxton, also known as Punktown, the current number one rock group was Sphitt, and the number one rock song this summer was their hit *In Your Face*. This song now played on Kid Belfast's music system–the third time he had heard it this morning. It had been background music previously but now he focused on it, listened to it.

As it was for millions of other young men right now, *In Your Face* was *his* song. It wasn't that he especially emulated the group physically, or their nearly indistinguishable kindred groups Flemm, Mhukas and Sputum (several of which had the same manager), as many of their other fans did. Sphitt's hair was snowy white fluffy lion manes overwhelming their tiny faces with their little chins and chiseled cheekbones and seemingly ceaselessly distended puckered pouts. Kid had short bristled hair, a nondescript light brown, and his lips were thin, their compressed lack of expression hardly sultry. When the members of Flemm and Sphitt did smile for the stills, their smiles were lazy insolent smirks worn like jackets tossed over their shoulders, and this was the unified smirk of most of their fans, as much a distinguishing badge as the explosive manes. When Kid smiled it was a shy, embarrassed grin like a fissure in his usual composure.

Also, Kid didn't spit much. Many boys now frequently punctuated their speech and activities with spitting, spit over each other's shoulders in greeting, at each other's boots in farewell, and at each other's bodies in hostility. Naturally he had done this to some obligatory extent, but he had seldom joined in the frequent contests of mucus launching of milling boys, and had only tried chewing tobacco once. He had almost vomited. It was, almost inconceivably, simply the music itself which appealed to him–its bombastic, melodramatic chest-beating, every song an overwrought epic of operatic emotion. Only their thundering exultant anthems seemed to rouse him from his near constant sullenness, but it was naturally their passionately unhappy, venom-spitting opuses that gripped him most. More than manes and kissable pouts with saliva loaded behind them, Kid Belfast embraced the *lyrics* of the songs by Sphitt, Mhukas and the rest.

He lay on his back in Noelle's bed, the sheet a stilled tide against the beach of his naked hairless chest, fingers laced under his head. It was his music system but it was here in Noelle's dorm room, a guest like he was, though it stayed while he came and went.

Noelle giggled with Bonnie Gross at the window, their bottoms presented to Kid, Bonnie's tiny bottom bare, tanned a darker color than Noelle's skin, although Noelle was partly black in extraction and predominately so in appearance. Bonnie was nude, as usual, Noelle wore an oversized men's white undershirt as a nightshirt. Somebody in a car, a male fellow student, was yelling back and forth with the young women. Kid was not a student; he had just slept over.

"Yeahhh, I'll be there!" Noelle shouted huskily. "I'll be there! I will *be* there!" The male yelled something back. "I don't know–I'll be there." His turn. Then Noelle. "I don't know where I'll be–everywhere!" Him. Then her. "All day!"

"Just be there!" Bonnie giggle-yelled down. Goodbyes were called. Noelle and Bonnie turned away from the window, Bonnie strutting past Kid on the bed, her back arched and shoulders so thrust back that her small tanned breasts aimed up at the ceiling. Kid might have been excited by her nakedness if he hadn't hated the idea of items as soft as bottoms and breasts being burnt to a leathery darkness. Noelle, on the other hand, was natural in her light darkness...soft...and Bonnie was *always* naked, always open, but Noelle had that shirt on, the points of her breasts teasingly nosing out the material, the hem falling just below her thighs. Noelle better understood her visual effect.

It took Kid a great effort to ask Noelle from the bed, as she bustled about with groggy animation, "Where is it you're going today?"

"The fair," she said, stopping at the cooking unit her mother had bought her to heat a mug of water from the jug in the mini fridge Bonnie's mother had bought her, so as to make tea.

"With who?"

"Oh, I'll be there with thousands of people."

"Including the person who was yelling up at you just now?"

"Yeah–including him–he'll be there. With thousands of people."

"And you'll be meeting him. Right?"

"Maybe. Maybe *not*." She gave him a look. Not a long one, but long enough.

Bonnie laughed at Kid, sipped her glass of cough syrup-thick, apricot-scented breakfast wine. "The Green Monster," she said in a horror movie voice, wriggling the fingers of her free hand.

"That should be a ride at the fair," Noelle Buda joked. Both women giggled heartily.

The bones of Kid's face worked under the skin. His eyes screwed themselves into the ceiling. Angry replies, counterattacks ground themselves against each other in his mind like his teeth, but couldn't pry their way out of his jaws. Bonnie had to be in his way, as always, throwing his strength off balance, an obstacle, one of Noelle's "buddies," a cancerous growth that Kid would have liked to slice off Noelle and ground under his heel.

"In your face," sang Chauncy Carnal, of Sphitt, "I want to shoot my gun,
Blow your brains out, now ain't that fun?
Seize you by your tresses, slam home my sperm
Rip off all your dresses until your lessons are all learned
If that's what it takes for you to look in my eyes
If I have to deafen you so you'll hear my cries
If I have to tear into your dreams to make myself real
Do I have to spit in your face to make you feel?
To make you feel, make you feel that I'm real?
Oh, oh, oh, in your face, you sorry little bitch
Yeah!"

EVERYBODY SCREAM!

Barnacle-like organisms clung, or rather were fused, to the insides of the damp tunnel, each one as big around as a large truck tire, projecting funnel-like, black and glistening but for the anemone-like translucent white tentacles which flowered at the ends. The tentacles glowed, attracting unwary moths and such and illuminating the tunnel, and slowly writhed as if in some underwater current, but Wes and Fen merely avoided them casually. Once this circular tunnel had conveyed water; the barnacle-things had fed on insect-like plankton forms, but had since adapted mindlessly to the plankton of the air. They were possibly a hundred years old, like this tunnel.

Wes and Fen were both nineteen. Their plastic sleeping bags still lay on the sheets of packing foam and the flattened-out giant cardboard box they had put down to insulate themselves further from the moist tunnel floor. Wes sat cross-legged on his bag pouring some black coffee from a thermos. Fen, who hated coffee, sat on a chair made from two cinder blocks and a board, smoking a cigarette. On their radio/chip player they listened to a chip by Sputum–but not too loud. They were in hiding. By Wes's knee on his bag lay his automatic pistol.

"Have a doughnut, spitter," said Wes, chewing, holding out a crinkly bag.

"They're stale. They were stale yesterday. I need some real food."

"All we can eat at the carnival tonight."

"All we can eat. Are you going to sit down and vote on the best quilt, too, while you're at it? We aren't going there to eat and play games, mucoid, we're going to make our move and get out of there. What if one of the enemy is there and spots us? Many people will be there, it's not impossible."

"The enemy," Wes echoed with a smirk.

Clack-clack. Fen's automatic was a foot from Wes's nose. Though Wes's identical Tikkihotto military sidearm was closer to him than his friend's gun, Wes didn't take the chance. "Yes," hissed Fen Colon, "the enemy. You can mock the fact that I was in the army for two years, but the sleeping bag you slept in last night is an army bag, the gun you carry is an army weapon, the coat on your back is an army jacket, the boots on your feet and the thermos you got your coffee from are army issue. And it's my army training that's kept us alive so far and that will see us through tonight, after which our lives will get a hell of a lot better. So mock me, mock the service...but the next time you do you're on your own. You can do things the civilian way, and walk right into the minefields and blow yourself to confetti."

"Oh yeah, if I left you on my own you'd really let me walk away alive." Wes wasn't so cowardly that he couldn't speak his mind with death poised in his face.

"You miserable little drooler." Fen spun away from Wes and off his chair, stepped further down the tunnel and then whirled to glare at his friend, cramming his pistol back into its holster. "You really got a high opinion of me, don't you? A soldier never betrays a buddy! Never! You'd do that to me in a second, but don't ever think I'm as low as you!"

"All I said was one stupid little thing!" Wes turned his head to spit on the wall to emphasize his exasperation. "Let's just forget it all, huh?" Wes sipped his coffee. You'd think that Fen's code of honor had been forged on the battlefield instead of at a military training station/vocational school on the outskirts of Paxton. Fen had acquired their gear mostly from army surplus stores, and much of it was of the Tikkihotto, not Earth Colonies, armed service. Wes bit into his doughnut. Stale. Too stale for poor Fen, the soldier.

"The enemy are soldiers," Fen grumbled. "You don't stand a chance against soldiers unless you yourself are a soldier. Being a soldier is a state of mind, a religion, and your gun is your Bible and your crucifix and your God. God won't keep me alive unless He's in the mood, but my gun is always there for me. The enemies think the same as me, mucoid, the same way. And they outnumber us a hundred to one. You haven't seen them, you think it's all a joke. I almost wish we would run into them tonight so you'd see."

"Alright, okay. I'll take it seriously. What if some of them are there buying when we make the move–do we wait and let them go or fuck them, too?"

"I want to avoid engaging at all costs. Only if we must will we engage them. They aren't yet aware of us; the less they know about us after the move the less far away we have to run to be safe."

EVERYBODY SCREAM!

"They won't wonder about that drooler we fucked? That won't put them on guard?"

"Moband was highly connected, highly involved in many avenues. They won't necessarily...won't be likely to associate his murder with LaKarnafeaux."

"Yeah, well just maybe to be on the safe side they'll have some gunners around keeping an eye on LaKarnafeaux. If I can think of that, then I'm sure these *soldiers* can." Wes stressed the word a little sarcastically.

Fen let it go by. "They know LaKarnafeaux can look after himself. He may be a little on guard, but I don't think he'll be too fortified. All should go well. But we aren't going there tonight to buy candyfloss. Remember that."

"You're the one who wouldn't eat stale doughnuts."

Fen fingered his pack of cigarettes out of his breast pocket. Two left. That was worse than only having stale doughnuts. He'd have to pick up a few packs tonight at the fair, along with a few *quick* bites. This pack, and the pen lighter (a writing instrument, red, with a lighting device at the other end) he now used to ignite his second to last cigarette, he had taken off Moband's corpse. Wes had done the actual killing, after they'd first found out who the big dealer of the drug purple vortex was, said to be working the fair. Only this lighter pen, applied to Moband's forehead, had finally elicited the information. Roland LaKarnafeaux. The "enemy," as Fen Colon referred to them, got all their vortex from him...hence Fen's insistence on caution tonight when he and Wes Sundry went to rob and kill LaKarnafeaux.

Wes preferred calling the enemy what they called themselves–Martians.

The next cut by Sputum started up...*I Am What You Eat*. Wes bobbed his head enthusiastically to the thumping beat, spit at a mammoth barnacle on the wall and then sang along to the words:

"Hey you squirmin' mermaid, wriggle on the beach
The water's so close and so far from your reach
Flap your fishy tail–spit, you smell fine!
Got my knife all set and I'm ready to dine
Here I go, lady, I'm casting my line!

The worm I've got for you is a good three feet
Swallow it all, baby, cuz I am what you eat!"

Yeah, maybe they could meet a few girls at the fair tonight, too, thought Wes, inspired. Fen didn't want to hang around long, but purple vortex might prove a quick bait. He hadn't had much time for fun with Moband, a surgical hermaphrodite; he'd had to close his eyes to climax–and not because Moband was dead, but so overweight and homely. Wes was determined to have a little fun tonight no matter how much Fen tried to hold him down.

"You can spit it out later if you don't think it's sweet
But invite me in for dinner cuz I am what you eat
What you eat, what you eat, bitch
Yeah!"

Dolly Horowitz lived in a fifty-third floor apartment in Robin Plaza, with an expansive view of lovely Plaza Park across the street, as safe an area as any in Punktown could be, but she wasn't happy with it. Her husband had moved them there from Miniosis last year to be near his work assignment with Tessler Bioplastics. She spent most of her time consoling herself in the inferior malls and art galleries of Paxton, or painting. She had already dressed for some painting after breakfast, in tight blue jeans and a powder blue work shirt open at the throat and rolled up to the elbows, white sneakers and no socks. Hair pinned up in back. She looked so great this way, as sophisticated casual as she was in an evening gown. Also, she had the girls to occupy her. Her husband's daughter by his first wife, Chana, was off for the summer in Caba; her eighteenth birthday present from her father. Fawn, Dolly's daughter, was home. Next week school would start, and though the summer would still be in effect by the calendar's reckoning, it would be officially over for all the kids. Fawn was going to the fair tonight as she had the past two nights, a last party before school. Tonight was the last night for the fair.

Fawn came scuffing into the kitchen in her furry white slippers and

EVERYBODY SCREAM!

pink satin Kodju-inspired robe, her long dark red hair mussed, sneering at her own grogginess. She was a pretty girl, turned sixteen a month ago, and her somewhat long nose gave her narrow face an intelligent refinement and a touch of ethnic character, Dolly was pleased to note. Dolly had chosen for Fawn her beautiful rusty hair and soulful hazel eyes through scientific artistic design when she had decided to become a mother (not carrying Fawn inside her either, due to her work with the museum in Miniosis at that time, though carrying one's child the natural way was coming back in the upper class, a "statement" some called it). Fawn was tall and slender–her mother liked to describe her as willowy. Though Dolly was kind and affectionate toward Chana, her resemblance to her own mother–short, dark and large-breasted–was bothersome and partly responsible for Dolly's design for Fawn.

"I'll make you some breakfast before I go paint," said Dolly.

"Ugh–no thanks. I feel like retching up everything I ate last night." Fawn plopped herself at the breakfast counter. Propped her elbows on the counter and her forehead in her palms. "I have a junk food hangover."

"And you want to go again tonight. You know, Miss Brain Damage, it isn't the money you waste going down there night after night or the poisons you put in your body–it's a dangerous and scary place for a sixteen-year-old girl to be, with just a few friends and no adults. This is Punktown! Even in Miniosis it wouldn't be smart! Look, Daddy and me went with you the first night and you had fun...why can't you wait and see if Daddy can come home early enough tonight to take you?"

"I promised Cookie and Heather!"

"Well I can unpromise Cookie and Heather. I don't like it!"

"I can't stay locked in a castle all my life!" Fawn whined, morose.

"Oh you poor little neglected thing. You don't care how I worry, though, do you?"

"There are security guards!"

"People *die* there!"

"Troublemakers."

"Wait until Dad comes home."

18

"Daddy said I could."

"You just want to meet boys, Fawn, and you can do that next week safe and sound in school."

"So what if we meet boys? Then it won't be us three girls defenseless, will it?"

"Such a smart, sarcastic mouth." Dolly marched into the bathroom off the kitchen, could be heard rummaging in a cabinet. Came back with a bottle of something to settle Fawn's stomach. The teenager raised her head dutifully to accept the offered spoon, which clinked on her teeth. Dolly said, "You're driving me crazy, you're killing your mother, but what do you care?"

"Oh–how am I killing you?" Fawn twisted her face.

"By wearing me down and upsetting my nerves. I hope you have children someday…you'll find out." Dolly spooned Fawn some more medicine as if in punishment. "Heather's asshole of a father had better not be late picking you up tonight like he was last night or I won't have her over in my house again. That understood?"

"Yes, Mom."

"Your stomach will be fine in a minute. I'll make you some toast at least." Dolly went to pour juice. So much of her previous artistic inspiration had been wrung out of her. Kids; they eroded you. But Fawn was the pride of Dolly's life.

After breakfast Fawn returned to her room to shower and call her friends, and Dolly got in a little work on the large panel that she had gained permission to hang in the hall outside her apartment, after much persistence and after inviting the owners of Robin Plaza to a dinner party. It was–by most anyone's standards, but for those of the highest tolerance and arrogance–horrible.

Even Dolly didn't seem too thrilled with the growing quagmire of red, blue and yellow this morning, and abandoned the painting, wiped her hands on a towel as she sought out her daughter. She opened the soundproofed door without knocking and wasn't surprised to see Chauncy Carnal of Sphitt standing before her in his characteristic broad stance wearing his white leotard with the crotch cut out, masturbating in the direction of her daughter while he serenaded her with a twisted pouting sneer, his white mane cascading onto his bare bony tanned shoulders. He was growling the surly/sultry ballad *Fall to Your Knees*, Fawn's current favorite song.

What distressed Dolly was seeing Fawn's willowy body naked, rocking and bouncing on what first might have looked like a strange black saddle she was strapped into, minus a horse. It was actually that damn "love bug" Chana had bought Fawn for her birthday and which Fawn had managed to keep secret and hidden for almost a month. It was furry and mindless, a genetically designed beetle play-thing, some of its legs locked around Fawn's white legs and waist, two of its gentle feelers stroking and coiling around Fawn's slight breasts. Her head thrown back and mouth open in abandon, eyes closed for the moment and music loud, she didn't know her mother was there at first, until Dolly made some noise in looking about for the remote control that would banish Chauncy Carnal's convincingly sweaty hologram. Fawn gasped, embarrassed.

"Don't you respect my privacy? Why can't you knock?"

"I'll respect you when you show a little respect around here, brat. Turn that disgusting hologram off. And get off that thing! I'm going to have your father take that stupid thing away! You have to be so damned preoccupied with sex!"

"I'm normal, okay? Do you want me to do it with real boys instead?"

"I want you to have a little taste!"

"Oh come on, I know you've tried Herbie, too–don't deny it!"

"Oh you little smart-mouth brat. Just wait until Daddy gets home tonight. And if you still think you're going out today you can forget it."

"Oh come on–what did I do?" Fawn wailed, but too late–the door had slammed shut. "Bitch!" she hissed to herself, sneering as she fought back tears, motionless astride her obedient pet. It continued caressing her breasts as if to console her. Chauncy Carnal, undaunted, bellowed out the ballad's tear-wringing crescendo:

"I love you so much
I just want one last touch

Just taste once my tears
They're the liquid of my fears
But you say I secrete
More than you can eat
Though I beg you please
You won't fall to your knees
I love you so much
I love you so much
I love you so much!
That I hate you, you spoiled little bitch."

"Oohh...shut the fuck up." Del Kahn reached out to the radio alarm like a drowning man to a life preserver of sanity, tendons straining, fingers wiggling, until with a final grunt of effort he touched the dial and gave it an emphatic click which banished the awakening assault of Sphitt's *In Your Face*. Del rolled away from the radio onto his back to groan. He couldn't have felt more jarred if he had awakened to the members of Sphitt shaking his bed, kicking it, and pursing their lipstick pouts down at him. Sophi listened to that station; he seldom did. They seldom played any of his own songs these days. Very seldom.

Rolling his head, he surveyed Sophi. The detonation of music hadn't pierced her thick dark tangle of hair, all that he saw of her. Funny, that was the first thing you focused on with her–the first thing he had, anyway, that body and those eyes aside. Thick dark hair, long, a lion's mane on a lioness. Del and Sophi had been married five years. She had never cut her hair short, never dyed or frosted it blonde or any other color and certainly hadn't shaved herself bald a few years ago when that was big. None of that would be Sophi. Other women could get away with that, with all of that. Their mutability was their identity. Sophi's identity wasn't dependent on the latest fashion or fad; bald-headedness, green frost. Sophi *was* her hair. If fashion had led her like a ring through the nose, she might have never married Del Kahn in the first place. Even five years ago he had been largely forgotten.

EVERYBODY SCREAM!

He stole out of bed stealthily so as not to rouse her, made it to the floor, padded out and through the parlor into the narrow kitchen. The bathroom was the last room, but for some low-ceilinged basement-like storage space below. They'd had the trailer three years, though for some of that time Del had briefly lived elsewhere, on and off, depending on moods. His moods to leave, or her moods which made him leave. They had talked about it and both agreed that it was this semi-regular leaving that kept their marriage intact, like steam vented off to prevent a total explosion.

Del finished urinating, flushed the toilet, ran a hand over his mirrored jaw. Yeah, it was cramped, you couldn't shave without bumping your elbow on the wall. But how about those tour buses, fifteen, seventeen years ago? Talk about cramped. At first he had loved the trailer for its nostalgic references to those tour days before he and the band became so big that they simply teleported to the gig and back home that same night. He still loved the trailer, it was home, but sometimes its closeness chafed him, and he had to leave. Today he was here.

Shaving could wait; coffee was the priority. In the low-ceilinged kitchen, its walls and ceiling turquoise plastic, the cupboards, counters and floor an imitation swirly pink marble, Del filled a pink mug that was made from a Tikkihotto sea shell. The smell of coffee—one of the little pleasures of life that mean so much but have so much else stacked against them. Del paced the narrow kitchen idly in his bare feet, wearing underpants and v-necked undershirt. Flipped though a magazine on the little table. Moved the pink blinds to gaze out the window at the activity of morning, people starting themselves up for work like machines, passing by with Styrofoam cups of coffee in hand, or cigarettes, which served them the same purpose. He'd have to get Sophi up soon, but he liked these few minutes alone with himself first.

He clicked on the radio on the kitchen table. It was a replica of a Sears Roebuck "Silvertone" from 1948, a child's radio, dark brown with an ivory cowboy on a horse on the side (*Silvertone* spelled out in his lariat), and the dial Del turned for a suitable station was an ivory plastic cowboy hat. The radio in the bedroom that had woken him was a replica 1938 Majestic "Charlie McCarthy," white, with a painted representation of a monocled ventriloquist's puppet projecting from the front, in top hat and tails. The hidden auto-alarm feature was not characteristic of the original. These were Sophi's, and she did have some original collector's radios, mostly Choom. Del had given her a few old Tikkihotto radios from a trip he'd made to their planet as one of his last performances. Sophi collected odd, quaint, bizarre knickknacks, most of which had once served very common day-to-day uses. Their furniture, refrigerator, their plates, lamps, their salt and pepper shakers were all from such older times as to be conspicuous, forming a unified crazy-quilt of the past. *Yeah*, Del had mused on it before, Sophi collected relics, once popular but passed over for newer fashions. *Like me.*

Nothing appealed to him. He shut the radio off, moved back into the parlor and inserted a chip in his modern music system. Forwarded to a particular cut. *Salon and Saloon.* Jim Croce, a twentieth century singer-songwriter. Let it never be said that Del Kahn would allow another artist's work to fade into the oblivion of the past, if that artist had something beautiful or meaningful to say. It wasn't that there was no beauty or meaning in today's music—not at all. In a place like Punktown, the versatility was such that any sort of music was accessible. And of course beauty and meaning were subjective, when it came to art; what to Del might be a sappy, corny, commercial-minded piece of ordure might be another's heart-rending ballad, and there were no doubt those who found a personal meaning even in what to Del was the most loathsome music, such as that of the snidely hip Child Beaters, Tongue Tongs, or Spectral Excrement...the favorites of some college stations, a nasty-hearted sort of post "fuck-sound" rock...and, of course, the music of groups such as Flemm and Sphitt.

Del liked a little of a lot. Classical, jazz, folk, country (very little, but still), pop, rock, even fuck rock, and a lot of other-world stuff. But he didn't like a lot, too. He didn't like to smell money in his music too conspicuously, or the oil of a factory machine, or the cigar smoke of some business meeting concoction. A lot of that was inevitable—he knew that well, did he ever. But it was something he had fought against, and only tolerated to its most necessary level. It had to be art. And not prop art, either, not a posture, not a bloodless hip fake. Sophi's trailer furnishings and decor made up from flea markets and antique shops were hip, funny, but it was a passion with her, nostalgic and sentimental and heartfelt, from her spirit. It had to be *real*.

After his song ended Del finished his cooling coffee and let the chip play out softly while he went to shower and shave.

With the water hitting him, he could see other trailers outside through a little window. Most were white to Sophi's turquoise, and most were of a less domesticated nature. Thick black cables snaked across the dirt path between them. There were strewn empty popcorn cups, soda and beer cups, half-eaten remnants of food, even here away from the carnival proper. Even as he started to become disturbed by the trash one of the maintenance kids scuffed along dragging his wheeled zapper, picking up the more salient refuse and dropping it into the disintegrator. He wore elbow-high black rubbery gloves to protect himself from accidentally getting his hands too close, and a Flemm t-shirt. You'd think they were the only fucking group on the planet Oasis, Del thought.

Last night for the fair. Del had mixed feelings. He had enjoyed the experience more this year than the first two that Sophi had run the fair, because this year he had barely allowed himself to participate in the organization and execution of it. It was Sophi's pet–why should he bang his head against a wall, keeping after the endless details and responsibilities? For once he'd had some real fun. He'd had a chance to meet people, and get to know the crew people of the fair and carnival themselves. Some people knew of his past achievements, many didn't–which was good, in a way, since his privacy had always been vital to him. Actually, maybe he'd had too much fun, met too many people, got to know others too well. Like any work community, this one was a jealous, gossipy bunch and he was sure that Sophi knew about his several summertime flings with crew members. She hadn't said anything overtly, though...just a few of her knowing sort of dry remarks, such as her familiar offer to have a new, inconspicuously flesh-colored wedding band made for him. Despite their arrangement, he kept things quiet. It was a silent arrangement, at this point. Sometimes, though, it felt like a silent volcano to him. Caution was best.

So, that crazy and dream-like carnival excitement would end tonight. The carnival's end was as sure a sign of the end of summer as was the starting of school after this weekend. According to the calendar, summer would continue on a few more weeks. But everyone else knew better. It was already autumn. The weather had already changed–the past few days had been gray and cool, chilly at night. Normally he loved autumn, but the closing of the carnival was always a bit depressing, as if again he felt that he had to return to school. He could empathize with the flocks of kids, squeezing what last summer juice they could out of this final night (though their too-great squeezing seemed to irritate him more each year, especially with all these arrogant swaggering louts dressed up like Chauncy Carnal).

Autumn wouldn't leave Sophi totally without projects, by any means. Some of the carnival (which she outright owned, initially purchased primarily through Del's resources, though the *fair* which featured the carnival was organized by the township with Sophi placed at the immediate helm) would break up and go south for the cold seasons, and other parts would teleport to tour some Tikkihotto towns (Del's coup, with the aid of the people who had promoted and helped facilitate his shows there previously). Last year the Kahns themselves had gone south with the carnival but this year, thank God, they were staying up here. He wanted to kick back, this year, just rest, while she did her buying and dealing and organizing for next year, and her long distance overseeing of the dispersed schism carnivals.

But what happened when he got tired of kicking back, just resting, as he knew he must? He had before. He didn't want to think about it but the water wouldn't wash away the question. His business manager kept urging him to produce, at least, and he kept saying that he wanted to some day, but he didn't feel the drive. His keyboard player, Rusty Scupper, was doing a second solo album, splitting the vocals with another singer (Rusty was a pleasant singer, with the right–light, bouncy–material) and had hinted to Del about doing a duet. Somehow Del had ducked his good friend's first album, but how could he do that again? The first album hadn't sold very well. Rusty, all friendship and fun aside, was actually asking his friend to help him make some money and strengthen his self-supporting projects. Del had been hoping that Rusty wouldn't be offended if he wrote a song or two for him instead. He just didn't want to put his voice out there again just now. He wasn't ready.

EVERYBODY SCREAM!

He'd try to push Rusty into recruiting some of the other members of the old band for guest appearances. They'd do it–they were all good friends. Del still saw them all, though not very often, and seldom more than one at a time. That is, except for Tex. Even the others all shunned Tex Plano now. Not that some of them might not still care for him, but they didn't dare aggravate Del. Tex, the percussionist, had been Del's friend and a band member from the beginning. That was why, when he found out that he'd been fucking Sophi for several months, he nearly wanted to kill him. Literally kill him. But he didn't, and he didn't even fire him, and that wasn't even why Del didn't want to reassemble the group. Del never went to Tex with his gun to threaten him, as he had fantasized, and he never had to speak to him–Tex backed off by himself like a naughty dog when Sophi told him that Del knew about them. Del was polite to him. The others were polite, but that was it. When Del admitted his feelings to his then-manager David Hellmich, Hellmich told him he should have followed through and killed Tex. No one would prosecute a star, they could make it look like defense anyway, and the publicity would juice up his drooping career. Del had fired Hellmich not long after that, and his new manager knew best to just concern himself with seeing to the royalties.

Ah, summer. The last drops from the faucet, tonight. No more blasting light, blasting music, blasting noise, blasting life. No more distractions from the things that nagged him.

Yet he didn't want to follow the carnival south this year. No, it would be too crazy to try to sustain the fun he'd had this season. But more than that, despite the uneasiness, he just didn't want to keep running. He didn't know what else he planned to do once he tired of resting, but...he was trying to open up to possibilities.

He shut the shower off, dried, stepped out, shaved. He heard the kitchen radio go on, but took his time in finishing. Tucking his damp towel loincloth-like around his waist, Del padded out into the kitchen. Sophi was there at the table. She was slumped over a steaming black coffee as if to unblock her sinuses, chin in hand, elbow propped, in a white terrycloth robe, a cigarette unfurling its lazy ghost serpents. Her eyes, a feline light green with naturally heavy lashes emphasized by makeup, appraised him, even after all these years making him uneasy until he knew what was behind them. Maybe alcohol, still, from the look of the weighted lids, but not necessarily. Her eyes were always a little narrowed, making them more piercing, though more so now with the smoke and the clouds of sleep still dispersing. Their heavy brows were peaked in the middle. Her hair was a thick tousled mass, rich and weighty even to the eyes. Del knew from the sight of it (let alone the feel) why women in some cultures were compelled to hide their hair from men so as not to distract and beguile them. Her nose was pointed at the end–no dainty upturned item–but not one of the big, mannish, asymmetrical "ethnic honkers," as Sophi called them, popular with models now (which some models even acquired through surgery). Her lips were tight and firmly drawn, sealed, the lower lip thrust out beyond the upper a bit, and her jaw was squared. When she smiled (though she didn't now) she seldom parted her lips to show her teeth.

"Good morning," said Del.

"Mm." Her voice was as dark as her hair; husky. She tipped her head back and squinted her eyes further as she blew out a stream of smoke.

"Rough night?" No reply. Del thumbed the buttons of an air filter system. He'd never been a smoker of anything, particularly the harsh crap Sophi favored–bad for the throat. "Want some eggs, toast, something?"

"I'm all set. What time'd you get in last night?" she croaked.

"Before you."

"Ohh–I guess that's why I saw you in bed when I came home."

"That's probably it."

"I know you got in before me, Del, you don't have to be evasive. I'm not grilling you.

I'm just making cheery breakfast conversation, like on VT." She sipped the black coffee.

"Evasive? I wasn't being evasive. I got in just after midnight, and read for an hour or so."

"You didn't have to put in that 'read for an hour or so,' Del. Christ, are we a little paranoid, or what?"

"Paranoid? I'm not being paranoid."

"Defensive, too."

EVERYBODY SCREAM!

"Anything else?"

"Testy."

"Who wouldn't be, after that diagnosis."

"Did you know a kid got killed on the Dreidel last night?"

"No–when'd that happen?"

"Right before shutdown, wouldn't you know. I talked to the kid who runs the ride and he seemed straight, he swears he always locks all the belts himself. The belt came open; it wasn't broken. We figure the stupid punk played with it himself."

"How old was he?"

"Seventeen."

"Oh God...man...this has been some season, huh?"

"It'll be okay, nobody will touch us. He was just some Choom kid, not some politician's son or anything.

"Boy. I hope for your karma that it was his fault."

"My karma's got nothing to do with it, Siddhartha–it was his karma."

"Has the town been told?"

"Yeah, always, don't worry, Maxie is handling it. I'm not trying to alarm you. Just making cheery breakfast conversation."

Del started out of the room to dress. "Most women talk about the curtains they want to buy."

"Oh yeah? On what planet is that?"

"VT, I guess."

When Del returned, Sophi was where she had been, though her coffee cup seemed to have refilled itself, the cigarette butts had multiplied in the ashtray (Del had won it for her in a carnival game) and she had dragged toward her the magazine Del had flipped through earlier. Her forehead was in her palm, hair a hiding mantle like a nun's habit.

Del stood watching her while he adjusted his black string tie and the clasp, like a silver belt buckle adorned with turquoise, a gift from Sophi, that held it. "For somebody who's trying so hard to further her career and better her life and go forward, you sure do a lot to weigh yourself down and go backward. So ultimately, where do you end up going?"

"You tell me, Mr. Success." Sophi didn't look up. "Where are you going?"

"Nowhere. But I'm not trying to, now. When and if I do, I won't let myself be my own obstacle and my own worst enemy."

"I'm not a fucking alcoholic, numb nuts. I don't have a drink to get rolling in the morning…"

"You have."

"I use it to relax. I work hard so I relax hard. Don't lecture me today, pal; you go relax your way and I'll relax mine. You have your own modes of escape, don't you? Aren't you a little too attached to yours?"

Del didn't respond. He'd known from his first words that sooner or later she would turn things around on him, and had known that it might not be a good idea to say any of this and expect her to agree with him. He wanted to say that she had her lovers too in addition to drink, but he knew she would reply–and correctly so–that her lovers had been outnumbered by his five to one. All he dared risk in conclusion was, "I don't like to see you poisoning yourself."

"What am I now, a snakebite addict? Am I really so pathetic, Del?"

"There are worse things. That doesn't make it good."

"I love it when somebody doesn't get drunk or drugged–all of a sudden they're God. As if there weren't other and worse ways to poison yourself."

Del took his silk jacket off the back of a chair. "I don't deny that. I'm not talking about that. Like I say, that doesn't make what you do good."

"Just worry about what you do, pal. I like myself okay. You had your revenge, you gave me *your* diagnosis. So go take your walk."

"Do we have to start out every day like this, Sophi?"

She didn't answer. She turned a page in the magazine to a spread of bright photographs showing the rooms of a beautiful country house that it was hard to believe anyone actually lived in.

Del sighed, slipped on his jacket, left.

"What do you care, anyway?" Sophi murmured belatedly, still not looking up.

EVERYBODY SCREAM!

Noelle didn't offer Kid tea, or even a cup of water–that bothered him. He hated getting out of bed in front of Bonnie in his underpants. "Cute little gut you're working on, Kid. Making a pillow for Noelle?" His stomach was a little soft. Sometimes it was a crack about his height (he was shorter than Bonnie) or his pale skin (she was nearly as tanned as a saddle) or the size of his nose (she liked her hard-bellied, tanned men to have straight little noses though she had the asymmetrical "ethnic" nose so fashionable now). At least Bonnie offered him some of her breakfast wine, though he wouldn't take it, not wanting to have to be grateful.

Bonnie had gone now. A knock, the door had opened, the head of a female Choom student had popped in, human in appearance but for the alligator grin stretching back almost to the ears, filled with multiple rows of square teeth, her hair cut short and bristling in the preferred Choom style. "Hey kids, there's a Golden Sunrise in Love's room. Ten munits at the door; that's only five more than the buffet breakfast at the *Kampus Kettle*."

A Golden Sunrise was usually a weekend luxury; someone would go out for doughnuts or pastries, and also pick up some gold-dust if they didn't already have it to offer. A little party to perk everyone up for the day, get things rolling from the start. On weekdays when things were more rushed but the need still there, people had their own personal Golden Sunrises. Anyway, Bonnie had jetted off but Noelle had hesitated, decided to stay. Kid Belfast wondered if she could possibly have felt guilty about leaving him alone, knowing he would be too shy, too antisocial to join the others.

They were alone, though the door was open and across the hall in the laundry a handsome, naked, tanned and hard-bellied male student was doing a load of wash. He glanced over a few times into the room but looked away finally under Kid's deliberate glare. Kid didn't know if the rich little bastard was displaying his glory for Noelle's benefit or for his. At a party last weekend given by the sophomores to welcome the incoming freshpersons like Noelle, a school tradition, Kid had been sitting uncomfortably on the arm of a sofa when someone began stroking his thigh. It was a boy slumped back in the sofa, smiling Choom-like up at him. Kid had gotten up and moved. Later he had left the party and Noelle after a witty, grinning, drunken boy repeatedly asked Noelle to go upstairs and take a shower with him. She had declined, but Kid couldn't stay and watch any longer. He had never liked schools anyway, all the smug groups, the rivalry. He'd dropped out at fifteen. Noelle had done well in school, and was already very much at home here. Real adaptable, Noelle had proved to be. She hadn't seen any naked boys in high school halls, but already she could ignore the tall soap opera Adonis in the laundry (if only, maybe, for Kid's benefit).

Three days after the party, Kid had slept over with Noelle after much hesitance on her part, it being a school night. He had crept out after she was asleep and with a spray paint can he'd brought had painted symbols he'd seen in a book about a frightening cult of Satan-worshippers who had been raided, captured or killed in Punktown thirty years ago, all over the hovercar of the boy who had tried to entice Noelle at the party. A security guard had appeared but Kid had escaped without being identified, though he couldn't return to Noelle. Thus she guessed it was he who had perpetrated the vandalism, and confronted him about it, but he had angrily denied it.

Last night she had finally relented and let him sleep over again, even though she didn't believe him about the car, and even though she had made it clear to him early in the summer that she only wanted to be friends with Kid now.

Kid had intended to shower off last night's sex at the men's shower room a few halls over (the coed showers downstairs were unthinkable despite the visual cornucopia) but now with Bonnie gone he had to make the time count. He had pulled on his old jeans, climbed into his black sweatshirt, embarrassed now to be so naked before Noelle. "Noelle," he said. She had been making a pretense of picking up around the room.

"What?" She straightened, moving from her face a curtain of her long and thick and curly black hair, a mass around her head like a soft material aura.

"Ah, look–if you're going to the fair tonight why can't I go with you?

EVERYBODY SCREAM!

You told me you don't want me coming around next week…I can understand that. This is your…"

"*Kid.*"

"No, wait, give me a minute, huh? I'm sorry I came around this week, I'm sorry…I won't…I'm sorry about that."

"Are you sorry about Mike's car?"

"Forget Mike's blasting car, will ya? I won't come around next week, alright? Or call you either."

"I don't have to bargain with you, Kid–I don't want you coming here next week no matter *what!* Come *on!*" she winced, turning away, tossing up her hands and beginning to pace. "How can I deal with this new experience and all my classes if you don't stop bothering me?"

"Bothering you."

"You don't *understand.*"

"Of course not. I'm a drop-out. I work in a warehouse."

"I just want air, Kid, can you understand that? Air?"

"Yeah. Like next week when I won't see you, like I promised. But what's wrong with you seeing me tonight?"

"For one, you'll want to stay again, and you can't. Mostly, I just don't want to keep encouraging you. I told you how I feel…"

"You want to just cut me away clean. Why? I'll back off. But why do you want to cut me off clean?"

"I *don't!* We're still friends, I told you."

"Friends. You're just ashamed of me in front of all your little college robots. You're just being everything your parents ever wanted and that you promised me you wouldn't become. Do you remember that? Things you said and promised me? Why can't I stop bothering you? Because you told me you loved me. *That* bothers *me!*"

"Oh, man." Noelle paced past him. Even upset, her voice was soft, sweet, breathy, gentle. It seemed almost teary even when she was cooing happily, and it was the most beautiful voice Kid had ever heard. It was as dreamy as her heavy eyelids, as sexy. It had cooed and groaned and moaned in his ear, so softly, murmured secret things in his ear, pressed out of her by his rhythmic weight. Now it pleaded, just as moaningly, "Can't you respect how I feel?"

"How about how I feel?"

"We *always* talk about how you feel, Kid. See what I mean? Is a person a villain just because they don't feel the same as another person?"

"You told me you loved me! You promised me you'd stay beside me no matter what your parents said. But they threatened you that they wouldn't pay for school, and *bang*–that's it for promises, right?" Kid was no longer soft, meek, afraid to upset her.

"That wasn't it, I told you! Do you think I'd give up a person I love just because of a threat about money? That hurts, Kid."

"How do you think I feel?"

"Look–I know what I said to you. Things change, people grow in different directions…sometimes you can't live up to promises, you can't foresee your changes. Other people aren't changing me. *I'm* changing me."

"Stools."

"I am, damn it!" Even "damn it" was a soft-edged moan. "I can't live up to what I told you, alright? A father can say he'll always love and protect his child and give his word, but what if a car hits him?"

Kid barked a hateful laugh. "That's an act of fate–not a decision. Don't give me that. You gave in, that's all. To everyone. That's easy. Staying by me, that would have been too hard." The boy in the laundry was on the periphery of Kid's vision again, looking in at them. Kid whirled and strode to the threshold, eyes blazing across the hall like twin machine guns, slammed the door. He almost locked it.

"Kid." Noelle was hesitant to say something, but did. "You got a lot of mileage out of being my first."

"Oh…"

"I said things…you heard me say…the confusion a person has…the first times are intense. I *did* care for you, and I still do, I always will. We had good times. But now I can see that I said things that weren't totally accurate."

"Okay, alright, this is all just stools. Bloody blasting stools." Kid was pacing now. His thrust jaw was a snow plow cleaving the air. "This excuse and that excuse. Change, sex, confusion. Why not face the truth, huh? I may not go to college but I'm not a *total* moron, Noelle, believe it or not. You just can't handle what I am. Same as your blasting parents..."

"Now *you're* talking stools, Kid. Don't start on me with that again because it's not true!"

"Oh no? No? Yeah–right." His pacing had sped up, electric, with abrupt turns, forcing her to stop moving about so as to stay out of his way. He kept his eyes off her, though. "You don't want to dirty yourself on an inferior being..."

"That's not it! That's not what upset me! It's because you're a liar!"

"A liar, huh? Why, because I didn't give you a copy of my family tree? Are you a liar because you never told me if your father is all black or if your mother is all white? And what kind of white? What do I care? Did I throw a fit when I found out your mother was white? Did I call you a liar?"

"I never hid or denied or misrepresented anything. You did. You wouldn't let me see your parents. Some proud son you are."

Noelle was struck by a lightning bolt of regret even a split second before Kid locked into his tracks, whirled and blasted her with his eyes, aiming the bayonet of his finger. "I love my parents! Don't ever suggest I don't love my parents! I never disowned them. It was just awkward, that's all. I introduced you finally."

"*After* the picture."

"So what? So what?"

"Kid, I'm not prejudiced..."

"Yes you are, like your parents."

"My father liked you. I think my mother even did a bit."

"They blasting hate me and you know it!"

"Only because you act like a jerk–calling me at three in the morning, throwing stuff at my window, following me everywhere to spy on me. *That's* what I'm prejudiced against, Kid!"

"Fool yourself. Fool yourself."

"Same to you."

Kid Belfast softened, took in deep droughts of air. "Think of the times we've made love. We made love last night. Why did you let me? And don't tell me you gave in, or you felt sorry for me."

"That was a lot of it, Kid. And I like sex. And like I told you, I do care for you. It wasn't making love, but it felt nice to be close, and I did like feeling close to you in the past and I'll always remember that."

"That's *love*, Noelle, can't you see that? You feel it! It's just that everyone has you confused, they turned you against me!"

"I don't love you."

"You do!"

"I *don't!* Maybe I did, I did, I don't know! I did, alright? But I don't, I don't want to, and you can't talk me into loving you!"

"They poisoned you with their hate and prejudice. Your parents. Your blasting worthless worm-friends. And you can't stand to touch me anymore. I used to see warmth in you eyes, a smile just for me, inviting me closer. Now I see the doors are shut and you're pulling away from me. Because of money and prejudice. You can't even see it, they have you so drugged. You lost your integrity, Noelle. Welcome to the robot club."

"That's all in your mind, Kid."

"Stools."

"Please leave, Kid. I'll call you next weekend, and maybe we'll go out to lunch if you grow up and learn to calm down and listen to what people are really saying."

"Oh yeah? Listen to this." With one jumping step to cover the distance Kid swung his leg in a powerful kick, flipping his music system off its table, the top of it slamming into the wall. Another kick caved in the front of a hip-high expensive alien floor-plant he'd given her last year, Mort they called it, a purplish veiny cylindrical thing. Snatching off her desk the glass angel he'd given her last Christmas (he called Noelle his angel), he cocked back his arm, aiming at a wall.

"...yourself, Kid!" he heard Noelle crying. "You're only hurting yourself!"

"Yeah? Yeah?" His voice shook. He straightened up, slipped the crystal angel in his pocket. "We'll see who I'm hurting."

Noelle was hugging herself, as if cold in her man's t-shirt. "You succeeded in scaring me, Kid. Is that the idea? Is scaring me your idea of making me fall in love with you?"

"Blast you, you little bitch."

"Good. Fine. Remember your words, Kid—I will."

Tears nudged up into his eyes, and they trembled there. "I love you. Remember those words." And with that, Kid Belfast left the room, shutting the door after him.

Noelle let out the air clenched in her chest. It shuddered out of her. Her eyes dropped to Mort. Poor Mort…

Kid glared into the laundry as he passed it, fists bunched. The naked boy was gone. Lucky for him.

It was a good thing, too, that Bonnie didn't chance upon him in the hall, to comment on his reddened eyes. Even without his gun he would have killed her instantly, he swore. Yeah, his stomach was soft, but he was muscular and strong, and he'd won plenty of fights with bigger boys in his life. He'd smashed a boy's jaw and cracked two ribs once for stealing a music chip at his old job. He'd read about the high percentages of males who would have murdered at least one humanoid by such and such an age in Paxton. Of course these things fluctuated—the depression had gotten very bad, until the munit system and other measures picked things up—but even today they estimated that three out of five males would have killed a person for whatever reason by the age of fifty. Kid was only twenty but he felt left out, a bit. He wasn't afraid to kill. He looked forward to it almost as much as he'd once looked forward to losing his virginity. The two were similar.

He drove. Two boys danced out of his path. They wore slippers without socks, extra-baggy drab-colored trousers, dark ill-fitting sweaters with white shirt tails bulging or hanging out from underneath, expensive colorful silk scarves, their short hair fashionably tousled, one boy with a spidery purple "birthmark" covering one cheek. Actually a tattoo or stencil—wine birthmarks were in. Blasting college worms. One in the rear-view monitor made a gesture but Kid left him alive, kept on driving. So many handsome, happy boys, so many lovely, glowing girls. His hatred made him nauseous. He checked out at the security gate.

The hatred rode with him. Hateful memories drove through his head. He saw Noelle, the photo in her hand. He'd left the room; she'd innocently found it in his top desk drawer where he kept other groups of photos he had shown her. He heard her cry out in horror. Rushed in. Saw her. Realized, as her horrified eyes lifted to his…to his face.

The photo was a school portrait of him, age twelve when toys meant more than girls, crew cut, his plaid shirt buttoned neatly to the top button. He was smiling shyly, the smile, even bashfully restrained, cutting back almost to his ears. Noelle had probably never been shocked before by the face of a Choom.

The music chip was inserted, advanced to a particular song. This was from Del Kahn's last recording, *Heroes*. The song was titled *Rust*. The only accompaniment was pre-colonial traditional Choom instruments, and at various points in the background a muted Choom chorus chanted hauntingly in the now little-used native language. The listener found the lyrics, which described a true incident and actual individual, stirring.

"Smooth bore musket
Forged before his birth
A proud family symbol
Before the guns of Earth
The barrel itself four feet long
Longer than the growing boy
Who stared at the black-wood carven stock
And went, inspired, to play with the gun toy
Carved by his father from the black-wood
Until the day his father summoned the boy Fen
And put the musket in his hands
To bind them both as men

The Earthlings came, a tide of machines

EVERYBODY SCREAM!

Small-mouthed smilers selling magazines
The pale soft village folk gave in to their perfumed bribes
But the Earthers were met with musket balls
When they came to push out the desert tribes
Mooa-ki Fen led his people high
In the jagged rocks to resist or die
For six months they eluded the colonist soldiers
Until finally the siege
At their castle of boulders
Fen resisted capture
Climbed ever higher
Til perched within sight of his clan and his foe
Drank death from the barrel of his father's musket
As hands reached out to catch him
Pulled the trigger with his toe

The sandy rocks turned sunset red
It dried to a bitter crust
Reverent clan folk scooped the sand into cups
Like hourglasses filled with rust
The Earth tribes moved in
As victors must
Fen was there buried
His pride turned to dust

The captain of the Earth soldiers
Awarded himself the long impressive gun
It went on the wall of his beach house
Not to a Choom chieftain's son
It had existed before Fen
It outlasted his corroded dust
But taken from the desert air
The gun began to rust."

At the first few notes of the next song, about a woman who was shot and wounded by a security guard while releasing the dogs and primates from a laboratory at night, Fen shut the chip off. He'd listened once to the entire chip but it was pretty boring. He'd heard the song *Rust* on the radio and bought the chip for that alone, though on the strength of that one inspiring song Fen thought Del Kahn was a pretty good artist.

"That was different," said the young woman driving the hovercar, next to whom Fen sat, having played the tune on her system. She had been asking him what kind of music he liked, and he had demonstrated.

"I like Sphitt, Flemm, the Saliva Surfers," put in Wes Sundry, from the back seat where he sat beside another young woman.

"What're your names?" asked the driver.

"I'm Fernando Colon."

"Fernando." The driver rolled the word on her tongue jokingly. "Can I call you Fern for short?"

"Yeah, but not for long. Fen, they call me."

"Fen. Oh, like in the song?"

"You got it." Fen smiled.

"I'm Wes…but you can call me Wes." Wes grinned at the woman beside him. He had her charmed already. Wes was tall and baby-faced, with eyes that were twinkly squints when he smiled, his apple cheeks bunched up; he had cultivated a light growth of beard to make himself look older, however. His Outback Colony drawl was ingratiating, also. The women were dismissing the odd smell from the tunnel, assuming it was from a factory or something. "Come on, go to the fair with us," Wes persisted to his riding companion.

"Sorry, we can't. I wish we could, really."

Fen twisted around in his seat, looked into Wes's eyes meaningfully. "We got things to do anyway, Wes. Remember?"

"Yeah, I remember." Wes folded a wad of chewing tobacco into his mouth. His new friend smiled, smitten.

Man—Wes and his goober charm. Fen wasn't too jealous, though—he knew that the higher quality females who would appreciate his sophisticated superiority over Wes were naturally fewer in number. He untwisted to face forward. He didn't seem to be doing too badly, anyway, with the driver, though she wasn't very pretty and dark hair was boring.

"Can we stop for smokes somewhere?" asked Fen. The girls didn't smoke. It would save them time at the carnival, tonight, to stock up now.

"You eat breakfast?"

"Doughnuts."

"We'll stop somewhere and have some. Alright? You can buy your smokes there."

"Great," said Wes, chewing, twinkling at his companion.

"When do you guys wanna get to the fair?" asked the driver.

"Not until night," said Fen. He and Wes had just wanted to get out of that tunnel and closer to the fair once those giant barnacles began emitting that strange, choking greenish gas. Wes had thought that he'd seen one of them slide a few inches down the wall.

"Oh really? Want to come over our place for awhile? We have to run a few errands first, though."

"Yeah–love to," said Wes.

Fen twisted around again. His dark eyes were hot. "Do I have a say in this, mucoid?"

"Sorry."

Fen faced forward again. This was the comrade he might have to entrust with his *life* tonight? God forbid Wes should have to choose between saving Fen's life and flirting like a goober with some pudgy giggling fourteen-year-old near a candyfloss stand.

"Thanks," said Fen at the invitation. Maybe blasting these two would be a good idea–it would get it out of Wes's system at least a bit, to keep him purer for tonight. And Fen, of course, was only human, too.

The rides were empty, quiet, still, dormant–a factory waiting to be thrown into crashing, clanking, slithering, spinning, whirring movement by its many bored operators, the conveyor belts and cages bearing along people, however, rather than bottles and boxes, and the final products were excitement, exhilaration, nausea. Del glanced at a few as he strolled past on his usual morning walk. Like a red-light street of the deep city lined with shops and strip joints, ablaze at night with colorful lights and colorful people, the carnival was drab and melancholy at dawn, gray, the brightly painted surfaces showing their blisters and true fadedness. Trash. Dropped prizes proudly won. Shuttered games and concession stands. People came here for awhile to hide from reality inside the noise and lights, and then went back to their lives; but in actuality, it was they who brought that energy here. Without them, this place was as sad and lacking as their realities.

But melancholy can be beautiful, and Del liked the carnival all shut down. It was a fantasy people had, exploring an abandoned carnival, like the fantasy of exploring a shopping mall all alone, or being the last survivor of a war and having a city to yourself, because a carnival was a shopping mall *and* a city. Del heard the far off radio of one of the crew. The morose drawn-out low of a cow. He could smell the livestock. Birds waddled around, picking through scraps. Up ahead through the shiny plastic horses of the miniature carousel Del saw a ghastly, skeletal bluish hairless dog. A snipe. They could be dangerous, the more so because their minds were a bit more than animal, but they showed a healthy fear toward the carnival people because a number of them had been killed by security. Still, as this one proved, they weren't totally deterred, and Del almost hesitated, wishing he had his gun, but he seldom wore it. The snipe had seen him also, though, and bolted away out of sight, leaving the trash can it had knocked over. Del continued on. They were pack animals, and being caught alone on a quiet street or subway platform by a pack of snipes was one of the scariest things Del could imagine, but in the day they generally split up as lone scouts or scavengers and were as fleeting and peripheral as ghost hounds. Their blood, when they were wounded or killed, turned instantly to a noxious black gas when it hit the air–superstitious types said this was their souls fleeing. They were not native to Oasis and no one knew where they had come from or how they had gotten here. Mutants, thought Del, glancing sharply over his shoulder as he quickened past the quiet merry go-round. He wondered where their pack nested.

EVERYBODY SCREAM!

Over the tops of the central cluster of kiddie rides loomed the rides for older kids and adults, towering like abstract sphinxes and idols built of dark metal and bright plastic, blistered and rusty from careless workmanship though plastic, metal, and paint that could survive thousands of years unblemished was available. Oh well, it added to the melancholy, nostalgic character of things, and to the delicious fear that the machinery would come apart and hurl you to your doom. A few times it had. Rearing above some treetops on the edge of the carnival, in the distance, was the Dreidel, not one of the more dangerous rides but last night a murderer. They were gargantuan robots that usually tolerated the foolish swarming humans and other beings but would sometimes, irritated, swat them or ping them away or crush them like insects.

The rides fell behind, mostly; the aisles of games were long and still mostly shuttered. A few people; Del waved or nodded or exchanged a smile and a few words. He kept on. It was a second coffee he was in quest of. Finally, the sprawling central carnival proper behind, ahead lay the many food stands and little trailer and booth shops that sold cheap toys, buttons, clothing, hideous bright paintings on black velvet. A few trailer shop operators were now setting out their wares. Gypsy-like, they either followed Sophi's carnival when it moved or affixed themselves lamprey-like to another carnival or opened up on the side of a highway or blended into a large flea market.

"Mornin', Mr. Kahn," said a skinny old man with leathery, weather-blasted skin and sleeked-back yellowish-white hair, setting out the black velvet paintings painted by his wife and daughter.

"Mornin', Andy. Always getting an early start."

"I haven't gotten up later than six in forty-nine years, Mr. Kahn." Del had stopped to scan the paintings, hiding his disgust. Sophi, as a joke, had given Del a painting on black velvet by Andy's daughter for his last birthday. A portrait of himself. It hung in the bedroom, on the wall behind the door they left open. Paintings of tigers, of flowers, oriental dragons, huge-eyed hideously cute children. Several paintings of Lotto-ichi, the Tikkihotto hero Sophi had urged Del to write a song about on *Heroes*, but he had resisted, wanting to keep to more obscure subjects. Lotti, as they called him, sort of a cross between Elvis and King David, had started his career as a singer and in becoming a political figure had continued to spread his words in song. Naturally, like any good revered figure, he was assassinated. For the birthday before last Sophi had given Del a plastic bust of Lotti, again bought at the carnival, with realistic moving Tikkihotto eye tendrils, which played one of his songs like a music box. Again, hideous. But lovable, in its way. It was on a bureau in the bedroom. "See anything you like, Mr. Kahn?" smiled Andy.

"All of it, Andy."

"Where's your better half this mornin'?"

"In my pants."

"Oh–ah, hah, hah!"

"See you around, Andy."

Del crossed the dirt boulevard to a canvas-tented stand that sold coffee and pastries to raise money for missionary work on far colonies. The Canon nuns who ran it were here already to set up, their van parked behind. They wore secular clothes so as not to scare people off. A few of them Del found sullen and unpleasant, a few cheery and friendly. He said good morning to them all and bought a large Styrofoam cup of coffee with cream and sugar, and a large cinnamon-sugar doughnut on a napkin. He sat at one of the folding tables under their pavilion, where one of the friendly nuns was writing in a notebook, a tea by her elbow.

"Last day," smiled the nun, without looking up.

"Mm-hm. I'm relieved, but it's sad."

"Yes. Where to now?"

"I'll just kick back for a while. What about you, sister?"

"I'll be heading out to Arbor, in the Rothman System." Sister Brandy looked up now, glowing with enthusiasm. "It's a beautiful planet, almost one continuous garden...tropical at the equator, more like forest elsewhere. The natives are peaceful beings evolved from plants. They don't even have a word for 'war'."

"That might make it hard for them to understand parts of the Bible."

Sister Brandy raised a scolding eyebrow but maintained her good humor as always.

EVERYBODY SCREAM!

"Don't start."

"If their life is so beautiful why not leave them be? How are they going to relate to a religion that says man alone is made in God's image, and all the animals and plants are only things put as his disposal?" Del smiled, sipped his coffee.

"God has many images, Del."

"Says you, or the Bible? I've read most of it, and it seemed less generous than that."

"The Canon has adapted the old views to address space and dimensional exploration, Del. Also, we can't leave the Arbor beings alone—Earth industries are instituting lumber operations, other operations, and the Arbor beings are now exposed to humanity. Our presence will be relevant and vital to relations, to an understanding of human values and beliefs."

"*Some* humans' values and beliefs."

"Well, we could leave them to watch porno movies and drink beer with the lumber crews."

"Now that sounds better!"

"You *are* terrible, Mr. Kahn."

"I'm just trying to ruffle your feathers, sis. My wife would have told me to fuck myself by now."

"There have been those occasions I was tempted myself, Mr. Kahn."

Del laughed heartily. "You're lucky I'm already married, sister."

"I thank you for the compliment, Del."

Sister Brandy wasn't a real beauty but she had a round-faced ingenuous prettiness, a nice figure, and natural red hair–a rarity indeed. Del had never had a redhead, even for all his encounters, and would have loved to press his lips and nose into red hair. But more, he had never had a nun. Sure, it was that fantasy of converting a nun or a lesbian with your irresistible male power, as some women fantasized about enlightening a priest or gay man, but the fantasy was admittedly a potent one. Del would have loved to gently undress Sister Brandy, who would be stimulated but still a bit unsure, torn; kiss her breasts wispily as he tenderly uncovered them for the first time to a man's eyes, stare deeply into her scared and hungry and confused and yearning eyes as he slowly inserted one finger inside her. If only he had detected a sign from her, but he never had and didn't expect to, and he couldn't possibly make the first move. Bad karma.

He glanced at an older nun behind the counter, who seemed to be glaring at him but flicked her eyes away. A funny feeling. Was she a bit of a telepath or was his guilt simply squirming? Del decided to leave the nun to her work and bear his coffee along elsewhere. He rose and excused himself. "Have a good night tonight, sister. I'll try to catch you before I leave, but if I don't, good luck with the salad people." He shook her hand, gave it a warm squeeze. He really did like her beyond the fantasy.

"You have a good night tonight, too, Mr. Kahn."

"Del."

"Del. And thank you and your wife for letting us set up our stand."

"My pleasure. Hope to see you next year if you're around."

"I doubt it, since it's a four year stint, but...one never knows."

"Well, tell ya what, maybe we'll head out that way, if the Arborites prove to be fond of corn dogs and black velvet paintings. God forbid."

They both laughed, parted, waved.

Del strolled on, aimlessly drawn toward the distant livestock smell, knowing that here there would be more activity to observe, people to talk with as the animals were tended to, their canvas blankets unstrapped, their hay or feed shoveled. But someone behind him, a man, called his name.

The man, Mitch Garnet, was walking at him fast, bouncing in his white running sneakers. Mitch had an energized swagger. He was, like Del, only medium height at best but muscular without being bulky, though more athletic and restless physically. He had short, curly brown hair and a serious, handsome face, blue eyes under intensely lowered dark brows. He didn't smile much, his small mouth held with an almost arrogant solemnity. Even his words came over with a bitter, insolent edge. Del liked him, though–but didn't feel close. Garnet was the chief of security under Sophi. The town had its own uniformed crew–this year they were trying a new outfit after last year's last day riot. Sophi's personal crew consisted of just Mitch, a human woman, a Choom man, and the two KeeZees–whose greatest effectiveness

EVERYBODY SCREAM!

was as showpieces, but who still quelled a lot of trouble through direct action. They all wore street clothes to mingle, but for the black-garbed KeeZee duo. Mitch now wore faded jeans, a white polo shirt and a silver windbreaker.

Del sipped while he waited for him. "Mornin', Mitch."

"Mornin'." Garnet had reached him. Straight to business. "I've got a body in the morgue you might wanna see. We found it this morning behind the Screamer."

"Oh boy. How many does that make from last night? Four, now?"

"Yeah. This one was murdered. Real murdered."

"I thought we'd do better than last year." Del fell in beside Garnet and they walked off another way. "I'm waiting for a day in which we get away with not one fatality."

"That kid that fell outta the Dreidel last night got picked up already. Nobody called after this one, though. And we don't have any I.D. yet."

"Can we post a photo around?"

"Not of the face. We can describe the clothes."

"If this morning is any indication of the day to come I think I'll hide in my trailer until it's all over."

"Last night," Garnet consoled him. He was hard to keep up with.

With Garnet, Del had pretty much retraced his steps. One trailer toward the front of the trailer village was Sophi's formal office, and Garnet's large security trailer with its holding cells was beside it. Lost children, thefts, myriad problems were reported here. One of two secretary-dispatchers was always stationed, aided by a few unfancy robots. Next to this trailer was a large medical trailer, always adequately staffed, with two small helicars parked on the roof. The town also kept some vehicles on the site, plus a teleporter for real emergency cases having to be sent to a hospital without delay. The town security vehicles and temporary structure were here, and finally Sophi's security team's morgue, a large black trailer with the white-stenciled word MORGUE looming on the side. Sophi's med team turned over the cases they couldn't deal with on a long-term basis to the town med team, and her security crew turned over their arrests to the town, usually within a day or two, to deliver to

Punktown's police facilities. But the dead delivered even by the town's hired security crew and medical team remained at the carnival morgue pending pick-up. If not identified upon discovery, the bodies waited there to be claimed. At the end of the season the morgue turned over its unclaimed collection to the town. Those bodies not claimed at the Paxton morgue in six months were then separated into two groups: those killed or first handled by the town teams, and those killed or first handled by Sophi's staff. Thus were belongings and valuables distributed fairly. The town then disintegrated their bodies, but sometimes the carnival found innovative uses for their share...

Del waited for Mitch to tap the entry code into a small keyboard; the morgue door slid open. Del followed him inside. Mitch slid the door shut. No other living beings were in here. It was a little chilly, but much of that was in Del's mind and in the sickly greenish cast of the lights.

"I haven't been in here in a week," murmured Del, scanning about. He sipped his coffee.

"You've missed some good ones." Drawers with digital readouts for labels lined the walls; Garnet touched a master control and all the drawers slid open simultaneously (but for those containing victims of possibly contagious disease or radiation poisoning). Del hated when he did that. Macho indifference to death carried too far, flaunted. But after the initial shock he did feel his morbid curiosity kick in, and he stepped closer to one of the nearer drawers.

"What happened to her?"

"Raped and strangled two nights ago. No callers. She's twelve, says equipment. Maybe a runaway."

"She is pretty made up." Del agreed, taking in the ruffled mini skirt and red open mouth. So pretty–God what a waste, he thought. "Tall, for twelve." Her cheek looked so soft you wanted to touch it, her long dark hair straight and silken. Del looked away. "Terrible."

"This one smelled to hell when we brought her in–I almost passed out."

Tossing his empty cup in a zapper, Del shuffled to another plastic sarcophagus. The transparent cover had remained locked. Inside was a black shiny mask of hair-fringed tentacles, and poking up from them a mushroom-like head with a series of bright red gills underneath. Del leaned in closer. "Ha."

"What?"

"Did you know this is an animal, not a person?"

"No–are you sure? I never seen one before."

"It's not an Oasis animal. It's Kodju. It must be somebody's pet."

"Are they capable of extradimensional travel, maybe?" The Kodju people, of another dimension, were capable of this by a difficult but natural process.

"I, ah, I doubt it. An escaped pet, or maybe the spawn of a pet gone feral."

"Is it worth anything?"

"I'll look into it. Hang on to it–someone might come in, though I haven't seen any Kodju."

"Maybe it's not a Kodju's pet, but an Earther's pet."

"True." Del continued browsing, hands in pants pockets, as if searching among a jeweler's cases for an engagement ring. A few gang kids, killed by ugly ray wounds, and one missing its head, one arm and much of the upper chest, obviously eaten away by a weak plasma bullet. A good plasma wouldn't have left anything, but even black market dealers were careful not to allow into common hands ray or plasma weapons which left no body. Mitch himself was required to only use a mild explosive bullet so that enough would be left for a proper investigative report (when and if an investigation was called for–though Paxton hardly had the resources or time to investigate every killing in town). Mostly this was a precaution to keep him from misusing his power.

"Fucking gang punks," sneered Garnet.

"Well, they're trouble, but they buy lots of popcorn."

"The KeeZees iced that one," Garnet indicated one gang boy, whose remnant of a head lay a few inches apart from the ragged stump of neck. An explosive bullet hit to the throat. "Most of these bodies are ours, Del. That fucking bunch of potbellies from Fog are too busy flirting with girls and standing in line for corn dogs. When the heat comes up, the Fog disperses. So much for tougher town boys."

"I know–I'm surprised. It'll probably be another service next year."

"Sophi's gotta say something."

"Talk to her."

"I have been."

"She probably will."

"Well, anyway, we end up with more bodies."

"That's not much of a concern to me."

"Yeah, well, naturally people with a lot of money on them aren't likely to stay unclaimed long unless they're a dealer of some kind. Ever think of making a horror ride with some of these? You don't have a good horror ride anymore–that haunted house is pretty stupid."

"Come on, it's a town thing; the school kids made it to raise money. It's creative."

"Whatever, but you and Sophi really need one."

"Well, that's for her to figure, not me."

"What's a carnival without a horror ride or at least a fun house?" Mitch opened the jacket of a gang boy to better see the black-edged ray wound in his white chest.

"We've got more variety than some I've seen, less than others."

"I'm not trying to be a jerk," Garnet said earnestly, his face somber, suddenly concerned.

"No offense taken, Mitch." Del didn't worry about Mitch's loyalty. He was ever respectful of Sophi, and of him, although Del was not technically a manager despite his great money investment. Garnet was grateful to Sophi for taking a chance and hiring him after he had been discharged from the Paxton police force after too many citations for excessive violence.

Most of the other cadavers Del had seen before, some from early in the season. As yet unclaimed. A man with a lot of packets of snakebite on him–a dealer, no doubt, his skull bashed in and wallet taken. His killer hadn't known about the drugs, obviously. A number of derelicts, mostly very old or very mutated, though one was a good-looking young Earth man in ragged stinking clothes, underfed, wild long hair. Scavengers that got in somehow, like the snipes. Del had insisted that security go easy on their kind so long as they weren't hostile. Garnet's team were tough but they weren't utter monsters, and they complied. Otherwise the Kahns largely gave them free rein; they did what they had to do. Only one of these derelicts, a grotesque naked mutant with pinkish-purple folds of flesh and a huge lipless mouth of jagged teeth, had had to be killed by the team.

Mitch stared at this one a moment, in fact. From its lower jaw projected a much smaller, more twisted version of the grimacing head. Under that emerged two useless tiny arms like those of a baby.

Del didn't notice; instead stared at a huge-bellied naked black man with half-closed lids and open mouth, elbows and knees bent, toes and fingers curled unevenly. The skin looked like plastic, or wax. The dead could look so fake—movie corpses were more familiar and realistic. A snipe or smaller creatures had chewed off his nose and upper lip. Inhuman-looking.

"Where's the one you want to show me?" Del said quietly.

The little head had no eyes, and one of the diminutive arms was bent, the fist disappearing back into the jaw. "These guys would've been twins. Chooms, looks like," murmured Mitch. "Wonder how sentient the lesser twin was."

Now Del looked. "Couldn't be very. The big one doesn't look like it was too sharp, itself." Del hadn't known Garnet to get so philosophical over a dead mutant derelict before. "Where's the one from last night, Mitch?"

"Yeah—right over here."

A teenage girl. Tight black sweat pants, a rubbery transparent jacket over a black bra. The front of her face was mostly eaten away, as if it had simply caved in, the central nasal cavity enlarged to join with the mouth and eye sockets. Only the teeth of the lower jaw remained. The edges of the pit and inside the head still glowed a very soft violet, as if with a plasma that was still active.

"Vortex?"

"Yeah," sneered Garnet. "It reacted with the gold-dust she snorted, and something else...maybe just some prescription drug she was on, or a few buttons, or a few drinks. Vortex can do that, especially mixed with dust."

"I've never seen it this bad. I've seen Cokeheads—they mix vortex with cocaine, and their noses corrode. Stick those metal tubes where their noses were so they can keep snorting..."

"Mm. I ran into a few on the force. Dangerous, crazy. Vortex does that. This is our fifth death by purple vortex this season alone, Del."

"I know."

"Let me run that fat fuck out."

"It's our last night."

"Let me emphasize that he isn't welcome next year."

"We'll worry about it next year. I don't want a crazy scene like last year. Let's have a mellow night. I hate him as much as you…but face it, one of the big reasons kids come here is to buy drugs, get whacked. He's not the only dealer here."

"Of vortex, he is. He's so big on vortex I'm surprised the syndy hasn't either sucked him up or wiped him out."

"Well, he is getting too big for a renegade. They can't keep track of everybody, but he is pushing his luck. Maybe somebody else will take care of him for us."

"Del, don't imply that we *need* fucks like him selling their drugs to keep this place going."

"I don't like it, Mitch, believe me. But we do. We need the gangs. The psychos. Everybody but him." He gestured at the two-headed mutant.

"Frustrating," grumbled Mitch.

"Agreed. Can we get out of here now?"

"Might as well."

The restaurant was dark, sophisticated; Kodju cuisine. Incense vaguely creeping, beautiful wall hangings, soft tinkling of Kodju music. A few short decades ago the Kodju had been utterly mysterious beings, a race from another dimension as rare and fleeting on this side as visiting mythical gods, intense humanoid giants adhering to a strict code handed down from their warrior forebears. Now, while these things were not always inexpensive, one could purchase Kodju plants and decorations for their homes, wear Kodju silks, eat Kodju foodstuffs cultivated here. Kodju movies were big, the more violent the better. For all the great beauty of their culture, Hector Tomas was just a little tired of the Kodju.

But he hadn't eaten the food in awhile, and it was undeniably good–his favorite, though best reserved as a treat, so as not to become tiresome. He had come for a late breakfast. It wasn't a usual idea for a breakfast, but that made it more interesting. Mostly he had just been driving, seen this place, remembered the food was good, and come.

There weren't many other tables occupied, the five women seated at the table directly behind him outnumbering all the other patrons. Hector's towering, glowering obsidian-skinned demon of a waiter had just politely left his meal, and as he munched he idly absorbed scraps of the conversation wafting from the table behind him.

It was quickly obvious that they worked together. One told another that so-and-so had said she was cute. "Cute? Oh really?" the other replied, gratified, but with great nonchalance. They were out for breakfast before work. Some distantly curious portion of his mind strained to determine the nature of their work, while Hector's eyes followed another robed Kodju as it passed across the room. Once he had yearned to visit their dimension, had made it a goal for the future. Not any more. It wasn't the same as "crossing over," but there were still dangerous things that lived in the space between this realm and their realm, waiting to prey on the weak traveler. Anything like crossing over no longer appealed to him.

They worked at an animal hospital; Hector assumed it was the one not very far down the highway from here. Their giggling, their mocking humor and the topics of conversation now attracted his full attention…and as one discussion began to crystallize for him, Hector seemed to sit up straighter where before he had been languid. He was becoming disgusted.

From what he put together, a man had recently brought in his ten-year-old dog due to some problem Hector couldn't ascertain. The man was so attached to his dog that he was shaking when he left it in the care of the woman who laughed as she told the story. He was afraid he would never see it again due to its age. Another added that the dog too had whined as its master left, staring after him yearningly. Laughter. "…he should learn to be a real man," observed one woman with a touch of distaste. As it turned out, the dog was safely reunited with its owner, but the women wondered what would happen when it had to be put to sleep one day. "You can handle that, Jan," said one. Laughter. Jan said, "Thanks a lot."

Hector had only last year had his sixteen-year-old husky put to sleep due to growing painful ailments, at the very hospital he believed these women to be from–not that he expected human nature to vary much from one hospital to another. The dog had died in his embrace, and he had cried right there in front of the doctor, his tears falling and nose running. He'd found her as an abandoned puppy, had carried her home in his arms. Now he had borne her to death in his arms. Sixteen years. Much of that time she had been his closest companion in life. When he paid his bill at the desk, had one of these women taken note of his red eyes so as to be able to laugh about it with her friends at lunch?

Frightening. All it proved to Hector was that the man's love for his dog showed more compassion than all these women combined showed for him, unless some coward wasn't speaking up. Even the love of the *dog*, a so-called lesser animal, dwarfed the emotion exhibited by these benighted souls. Shortly after, one of them told the others about a cute metal canister filled with gourmet popcorn she'd seen in a store, which showed colorful cartoon versions of Choom prehistoric animals roller skating. It was so *cute!* But a dog yearning after its master was a joke for breakfast.

He should learn to be a real man, was the ultimate line. Unbelievable. Could women still believe that a real man didn't cry, didn't shake, didn't see an animal life-form as anything more than an expendable commodity? Hector didn't want to meet the men these creatures desired. That ten-year-old dog must put *their* puny souls to shame, too.

Was it just their constant exposure to animal pain and suffering? A defense? No, not necessarily. The head vet, who had put Hector's husky to sleep, had had tears in his eyes when Hector's mother sobbed over her dog which he had just put to death, and Hector's cousin had told him that the woman behind the counter at her vet had cried along with her when her dog didn't survive efforts to save it after a hit and run. It wasn't the job; it was the type of human.

EVERYBODY SCREAM!

Years ago, a friend attending med school had told him that doctors sometimes laughed behind the backs of some of their more amusing patients, trading stories. They were only human, the med student chuckled in their defense. It didn't sit so well with Hector, who didn't believe it was unrealistically idealistic to expect doctors to be ethical, professional and dignified.

Hector had once heard that at a burn unit for children much of the staff commonly referred to the children as "crispy critters"; this was said to be a defense mechanism to keep the staff from becoming too involved, too unglued. Hector had never forgotten it. Did he simply expect too much of people?

He wanted so badly, so *badly* to turn around in his seat and say to them that he would never bring his animals to that hospital again, and that he intended to write an editorial about this experience for a newspaper. But they would only laugh, sneer, tell him to fuck off. They couldn't possibly be made to feel ashamed. Hector said nothing, his attempt at a peaceful breakfast treat rotted.

Hector grew alert and watched them when they got up and left. He was really shocked at how pretty they were; he had expected this from their shallowness and smugness, but most of them were actually glamorous, could have been models, in tight gray skirts, long hair, ruffled blouses. Heels. Early twenties. Not one of them yet in her uniform. The money had to be good, was the only thing Hector could figure. He had shaken his head with disbelief during their story, but none had noticed him then or noticed him now as they filed out in a cloud of perfume. Hector was filled with a despairing contempt.

Hector drove his expensive vehicle on autopilot; as a Theta researcher he had made good money. He read the newspaper, a hard copy printed off his car's computer. It was, as always, an encyclopedia of horrors. On one page alone there was a father who had killed three of his children and wounded one, killed his ex-wife and his brother's ex-wife and her new boyfriend (he was distraught, poor father, that he had lost a custody battle for the children), another man who had stabbed his wife and sixteen-year-old son to death (there was "blood all over" from the struggle with the poor boy, who was found at the foot of the living room stairs), and a boy being tried for stabbing his grandmother with a knitting needle and beating her to death because she wouldn't lend him money (he gave his girlfriend some of his grandmother's rings to wear, sweet boy, as if they were heirlooms passed down to him). A single newspaper page often held even greater horrors, but it was notable that all three of these cases were linked by family violence. The hell of disharmony.

Hector could scarcely believe that there could still be a population in Punktown with all this violence. To think that one or two towns in this country, Duplam, had even higher percentages of violent crime. Why did he torment himself with the paper? He swore, one day soon he was going to lock himself in his apartment all day, read no papers, and watch no VT but for a children's channel or carefully selected vids. He would listen only to particular music chips. He'd take a hot bath and read in the tub. He'd keep the shades down all day...

Junk mail for his ex-wife still occasionally came to his address. She had liked receiving catalogs of sex-oriented merchandise (they had liked sex) and some had been extreme. Hector had gotten one yesterday. One of the more elaborate pieces pictured in the handsome, glossy pages was a kind of bed covered by a cylindrical plastic canopy, with two odd enclosed trays running along either side. Inside individual cells in these transparent trays one could seal bumbles, four on either side of the bed. Bumbles were a popular genetically engineered pet, the size and appearance of a large, floppy-eared rabbit, with alternating bands of black and yellow fur. A tube was inserted into each bumble, and their blood drained. Their panicky convulsions inside the tiny cells was an "additional stimulus," according to the catalog. Their blood was conveyed to an overhead sprinkler system and rained down on the human lovers in the narrow bed ("or the Scarlet Shower can be enjoyed alone"). It was more a device for people with money, jaded and bored and experimental, and bumbles weren't cheap either, though any small creature would do. Cats. Plain rabbits could be kept and bred freely for the purpose. But bumbles were so especially cute and colorful and beloved, a fad pet right now.

Hector had fantasized one day about flicking off the autopilot but still not piloting the car, except to accelerate on some forest-flanked highway late at night with no one else close. But he couldn't. Not after having remembered crossing over, which he tried not to remember. Hector was afraid to die. He was even afraid to sleep, because dreaming could be like crossing over, and he had dreamed about crossing over and what he had seen, what he had spoken with, and now he took drugs so he didn't sleep. Five months since he had been put on disability leave, and he hadn't slept a wink for the past three. The drugs got expensive, and they did strange things to you, and to be constantly awake could be the greatest nightmare, but whenever he was tempted to escape into sleep he grew too afraid.

Sedatives helped, though mixed with the anti-sleep drug did yet stranger things to his mind and body. Deep narcotic-like drugs were out of the question—the idea of being too lax, too unaware, too dreamy made him shiver. Too much like sleep, like crossing over. The sedatives were prescription, but the powerful anti-sleep drugs he took were illegal. He didn't have much left, and he had to stock up on them tonight, because he had found out last night that his regular dealer Moband had been killed. This morning over the phone he had arranged to buy them tonight directly from Moband's source, Roland LaKarnafeaux, who worked at the fair—but this would be its last night and Hector wasn't sure when or where he'd be able to get them again, so he would bring a lot of money.

Sophi Kahn wore a loose-fitting, oversized violet sweater with sleeves pushed up her forearms, a gift from last year's winner of the ribbon for best adult sweater in the craft competitions, very faded and very tight straight-legged jeans, and old white sneakers without socks. Her hair looked scarcely less tousled than it had upon her waking, mostly pushed over to one side, threatening to obscure one eye. A cigarette was like a constant sixth finger in her right hand. She narrowed her eyes up at the ride called the Double Helix.

Gooch Varvak, a Choom, had the standard Choom bristly short haircut but for one tight braid hanging down to the small of his back, a heavy tool belt slung low over his hips. Little red and yellow lights glowed or flashed on a few of the odd devices in its pouches. His hands grease-stained even at this early hour, Gooch pointed his Styrofoam cup of hot mustard up at the towering skeletal machine.

"There's no way I can get it to work tonight without a new crystal board, and nothing I have is compatible except the Whirlpool, and I don't have a spare for that. So it's a matter of choice...you can have the Helix disabled, or the Whirlpool."

"You can't run a cable or set up a transmission from the Whirlpool's board to the Helix, and run them both off one?"

"You're right, I can't. Not without an overload. You'd have to crank the power so low, if you did, that you'd have kids falling asleep on them."

"Fuck," Sophi muttered, glancing elsewhere; dragged on her cigarette. "The Double Helix is one of our best rides, and so it the Whirlpool...but the Helix does better."

"So switch?"

"Yeah, switch. If you get a chance you might as well start packing up the Whirlpool–that'll give you a head start on tomorrow. It'll also keep people away from it and asking about it."

"Right."

"Gooch, yesterday I read in a paper that they dug up some ruins in Baloom and they found sealed clay vases of wine and intact loaves of bread–almost two thousand years old. Two thousand year old bread, and we can't buy a new crystal board that lasts all summer."

"What's the big deal? My wife makes bread like that."

"Next year we buy a spare, whatever the expense." Sophi began walking away.

"I'll teleport one now, if you want!"

"And pay that for one night's work?" Sophi kept walking.

"We'll still have it around for next year, practically new."

Sophi stopped, turned to face her chief mechanic. "Do it, Gooch."

"Yes, ma'am. Right on it."

"Thanks."

Again Sophi walked. She felt rather stupid for not thinking of it first, and she didn't like to feel stupid about running her carnival. That was Gooch's department; naturally he should come up with the solution, she tried to tell herself logically on the one hand. On the other, she made it her policy to be harder on herself and expect more of herself than anyone. But her irritation decreased a few conspicuous notches anyway. Distractions, she justified to herself.

Almost nine o'clock. At ten the gates opened. It was still pretty dead around, considering. Sophi wondered where Del had made off to. She walked past the miniature merry-go-round. Her eyes were drawn to a knocked-over trash barrel. Fucking clean-up kids–probably smoking seaweed behind a ride somewhere…

A peripheral movement on her left, she turned her head and gasped. The KeeZee had come out of nowhere. It stood staring at her, down, as she might look upon a child. Its three black marble eyes glistened. Glossy blackish-gray skin almost translucent in thinner areas over the hard bones of the monkey-wrench head. Black hair flowed from the sides and back of the skull. The creature loomed six and a half feet in its black uniform, but was a foot or more shorter than the even more dreaded white-skinned northern KeeZee. It didn't speak.

"Thanks for the heart attack," said Sophi. She knew the names of the two KeeZee security officers but couldn't tell them apart.

Now came Mitch Garnet, catching up with his bouncy swagger. "Mornin', boss-lady."

"Just 'boss' will do."

"You're not a lady?"

"Sometimes, when I'm in the mood, but what I mean is there's no boss-gentleman."

"What's your husband?" Mitch smiled.

Sophi wasn't really joking. "An investor and a pain in the anus." She was trying to remind the security chief that she was the owner and manager and Del had no actual authority, but without seeming insecure about her position. It was a constant problem, and not really Del's fault because often she did rely on him to help her, but sometimes people consulted Del where they should have consulted her, brought their problems to Del first. Mitch was good for that, too often. It chafed her.

"Got a body this morning behind the Screamer. Care to see it?"

"Mitch, have you considered selling admission to the morgue? And you could be the barker. I'll even buy you a ringmaster's top hat."

"You'd make good money." Garnet didn't take offense, although Sophi was in reality criticizing him–she always had this sarcastic humor.

"I'd rather you just tell me what happened; I have a good imagination."

"A teenage girl, no I.D., her face totally caved in from a heavy intake of purple vortex and probably some other shit."

"Great."

"I asked your husband if I could run the fat man out but he said no, it's just one more night. But another kid or two could die tonight. And those fucking Martians that come around here make me edgy–that situation could always explode."

"A lot of situations could explode. You know you can get buttons from the guy who runs the corn dog stand? And iodine from about half the other shops?" She was exaggerating. "You can get anything here. They make good money on the kids. What can we do? If I really screened, if I ran a clean shop, a great portion of our crowd would be a lot less inclined to show. It's their choice, Mitch. I choose not to sniff vortex, but if some teenage nit-wit wants to cave in her face that's her choice in life. She'd do it elsewhere. How bad can I feel? You have to be a realist, ugly as it may seem."

"She didn't *choose* to cave in her face, Mrs. Kahn."

"She chose the road that *led* to the caving in of her face, Mr. Garnet. And call me Sophi, please, like I've told you–I'm getting tired of being Mrs. Del Kahn, like I'm just the female extension of him or something."

Now Mitch began to feel offended, as much as his gratitude and loyalty allowed. "With all respects to you and your husband, Mr. Kahn hasn't been too famous these past few years. I don't think anybody around here sees you as being just Mrs. Del Kahn. If anything, I think sometimes he's seen as being Mr. Sophi Kahn."

"Whatever, Mitch. Just try to I.D. that girl, alright?"

EVERYBODY SCREAM!

"Right." Mitch turned away, rather less buoyant than when he'd approached. The KeeZee lingered a moment, jagged jaws parted a few inches, gazing down at her; it hadn't once moved.

"Dismissed, handsome," Sophi told it, a little uneasy.

Mitch gave a whistle. The giant then pivoted to follow him.

Sophi walked in the opposite direction. She was fairly bristling now. Nerves, she told herself, flicking away her dwindled cigarette. Last night; an uncertain, long cold season ahead. Without a trip down south to look forward to, autumn and winter and much of spring united into one chill fog in her mind. There would always be work to tend to, but that was still a lot of time. Maybe she'd steal a week or two to catch up with that portion of the carnival which would split down south, just for a break from the staleness. No doubt Del would make the best of that situation, she joked to herself sarcastically.

Sophi lit a fresh cigarette.

Bonnie rode her sporty hovercar on autopilot, her parents, making good money, were able to afford such a high school graduation present. She had clothes on finally, but the convertible top was retracted and she and Noelle rode with the naked freedom of the open air flowing over them, laughing, blasting the hovercar's chip player over the whoosh of the wind.

They hadn't really planned to embark this early–they couldn't even remember if the fair opened at ten or eleven, and it was only ten now–but Noelle had been restless about remaining at school, anxious to get away. Although Bonnie had asked if Kid were the cause for this and Noelle had moodily evaded the issue, Noelle was in good spirits now, freshly showered and dressed and in the rushing air. She barked laughter at Bonnie's words.

"I can't *believe* I'm up and out at ten on the *weekend!*" shouted Bonnie. "It must be because I didn't blast anybody last night...and ask me to explain *that* on a weekend, girl!"

"Why, I can scarcely believe it myself, of you!" giggled Noelle. "Do you think the guys will show or get sidetracked?"

"I hope they don't, really. We can see them anytime. We might meet some sweet meat. Have ourselves a treat to eat."

"Neat." They both laughed heartily. Noelle turned her head to watch a building go by, brushing her lashing hair back with her arm. Her mood visibly transmuted. "I hope Kid doesn't try showing up."

"He probably will, the little worm. Can't you ever blow that moron off? He's as persistent as an STD. Get somebody to beat him up or something. I can arrange it for ya."

"It'll take time. He'll go away."

"Stools, girl. Not so long as you're still opening up your legs for him. You've gotta be cold."

"I feel sorry for him."

"I feel sorry for mutants but I'd blow their brains out if they put a hand on me."

Noelle wondered how much more strongly her roommate would disapprove of her ex-boyfriend if she knew he was really a Choom who had undergone cosmetic surgery to appear human, and had successfully kept this secret from Noelle for a long time. She hadn't dared to tell any of her new college friends for fear of looking duped, stupid, freakish. Everyone at school, particularly the worldly upperclassmen, seemed so chic, so sophisticated, so in control. It was an exciting, but intimidating, sea to swim out into gracefully.

"Oh, look at these winners, speaking of freaks," sneered Bonnie. A long white battered hovercar with a scorch-edged ray hole blasted in the passenger door was nosing up alongside their car in the left lane. The windows were open and three young Hispanic men were crowding out their faces and a few arms. One face made puckered air kisses, the other two called out to Bonnie and Noelle. Bonnie had already hit the button to close the convertible top, causing the boys to shout more loudly, gesture more emphatically. "This car has everything but what I need most–a rocket launcher," Bonnie observed. She might have sworn over at them except that only this summer a car of kids had pulled alongside her on the highway and sprayed her vehicle with bullets, laughing. Luckily she had had time to raise her windows (Noelle had said they probably allowed her this, meaning to frighten and tease rather than kill); fortunately the car was bulletproof.

"Ignore them, they'll get tired of it," Noelle said.

"Check this, you obnoxious fucks." Bonnie dabbed more buttons, and every one of her windows tinted itself an impenetrable black...even the front, lest they pull ahead of them to leer out their rear window. Noelle laughed again. Bonnie turned up the volume on her chip player. There. Now even if the car was strafed with bullets they would barely know or care. "You can't ignore losers like that when they harass you–you have to take decisive action," said Bonnie. "Hint, hint, hint."

"You're so subtle, Bonnie."

"It worked, didn't it?"

"They can still follow us."

"Then I'll deal with it. I mean it–you have to shut the door all the way, block him right out of your sight and your life. Don't chain yourself to a rotting corpse, girl. You have to have some pride and self-respect."

"I have to have a heart, too."

"God...I'd like to strangle whatever aborigine it was who decided that an organ in our chests pumps love instead of blood. Blood will keep you alive when love won't."

"You're on a poetic roll, aren't you?" said Noelle, subdued again.

"Yeah, you want some more? The organ you need isn't a heart, and it pumps something other than blood. You've got to realize that there isn't just one of these in the universe. He's still got you pinned on his prick, honey. Get another one in you; it's the best cure, I can't say it enough."

"What about Jackybuns?" Noelle replied, defensive.

"A good start, but not enough. It shows you have the spirit. *Free* it."

Noelle wondered what Kid might have done had he known that at a party shortly before they split, during their rocky final days, she had gotten very drunk and fellated her friend Jackybuns, whom Kid hated and had always insisted had a more than platonic interest in her. They had begun by kissing and he had freed her small breasts to squeeze and suck them, but the knocking on the bathroom door had grown too insistent and they hadn't gotten further than her briefly performing oral sex on him. Jackybuns had haunted her for a short while afterwards like Kid was doing now, but without the intense bitterness. Kid suspected that she'd had other lovers, accused her of it, but it was good that he didn't know about Jackybuns, because he had sworn to Noelle that if Jackybuns ever touched her he would shoot his eyes out.

With the windows blackened, Noelle and Bonnie didn't see the honking, shouting white car accelerate and rocket away ahead, nor did they see the iridescent black, horny *Scarab* buzz past them. Too bad; it was Bonnie's favorite car, the current fashionable vehicle for affluent young people. Inside, the young man driving it did so manually, scorning the autopilot the way a photographer-artist might scorn an automatic focus and light meter. A car like this was meant to be taken in one's hands and *driven*. Autopilot was like letting someone else make love to your girlfriend for you.

The young man inside the *Scarab*, the outer shell of which was the actual exoskeleton of a giant insect designed and raised for the purpose, was Bern Glandston. He was a senior at a school other than the one Noelle attended. His parents had selected his body like they had selected his vehicle for him. He was muscular and tanned, thick-necked and square-jawed, with the same face as a sports star his father had idolized years ago, pale blue eyes and dirty blonde hair. Blonde hair, dirty or otherwise, was a rare find in other than genetically-tailored individuals. His hair flowed long in back, over his collar, while it was swept back and held in moussed grooves on the sides, and on top it was parted to one side with a few cascading moussed spines curving down over his forehead. He wore all black, a sure sign of artistic sophistication–a loose black V-necked peasant shirt, very loose black pants, and black lipstick on his thin lips; a popular new look, competing with the wine birthmarks, one of which he'd had dyed on his lower back. He didn't have the cold white alabaster skin and pitch black hair favored by most of the black-garbed, black-lipped artistic types at school, but his blonde hair and tan had their healthy share of admirers. An even more distinctive, personal trademark were his shoes. His ex-girlfriend had bought them for him on a trip. They were laceless, almost like slippers, made from the skin of a Torgessi, the scales–which varied in size in odd natural patterns–being silvery white and metallic black. He got a lot of comments. They were his pride, and he wished

EVERYBODY SCREAM!

he knew where to get a spare pair around here for when these finally wore out. Wherever he walked, his Torgessi shoes preceded him, carried him, gave him the bounce of the confident.

Bern was the top student dealer of gold-dust at the Paxton Institute of Technology, where he was majoring in biotech business management. It was a position he had worked at diligently from his freshperson year, and now he was one of the most popular students at school whether his tan conflicted with his black lipstick or not. Of course, there had been a few bumps in the road; his room had been broken into three times, though only once was any gold-dust found and taken, and once at gunpoint a cool and masked trio of men with older-sounding voices had intercepted him on the way to a big deal, robbing him of a considerable chunk of dust and his money but without harming him. Hey, these things happened–it was part of the job. He carried a pistol. If he kept at it, he could continue his side career on into whatever biotech corporation eventually took him in. Staircases could be built from gold-dust.

Bern had built a palace of dust at school. In some rooms of the palace–bedrooms–women had stayed a while, coming and going. Though he had no real army, his palace had its walls to protect him, propped up by the loyalty of those who depended on him. No other students dared really threaten or cheat or attack him in any way face to face, due to the strength in numbers of his supporters, just as angry consumer groups can not harm a product much as long as the consumers embrace it. Sure, after this year at school it was doubtful he would see all but a few of these many women and friends again, but he would advance and enter a new world and gather up new women and friends, build a new and better palace brick by brick. Bern didn't have a fear of the future, there was no doubt about his destiny; his life road stretched out bright before his hurtling *Scarab*.

Which didn't mean he had to be happy with everyone he dealt with, and it annoyed him that tonight he had to deal with Pox, one of his suppliers, and that Pox had been very noncommittal about what time he was to meet Bern at the fair. "I'll be there tonight."

"But *where?*"

"Be around, I'll find you. It's not that big a fair."

"Why can't you give me a time?"

"Hey look, kid, I got things to do. You don't need to know my schedule. You want the gold, you be there tonight. That's the best I can do."

Arrogant bastard, but what could Bern do? He needed Pox, a dealer for the Tocci Brothers crime family. Nobody else at school had sources like that. His supply was depleted and he had already set up a half dozen big deals of his own for tomorrow. So he would go to the fair, what the hell, spend the day. Make the best of it. Ride rides, eat junk, play games, meet girls, buy a variety of other kinds of drugs. He had nothing better to do with his day and evening–it could be a lot of fun. But he didn't like Pox's arrogant, syndy-crude lack of professionalism.

Oh well, hardly a bump on the wide bright road. Bern Glandston inserted into his chip player the latest chip from the Tongue Tongs, and nodded his head and tom-tommed his control console to the music.

Traffic was congested, as if these suburban, tree-lined roads where deep-city streets. "We're close," observed Noelle, sitting up on the headrest of her seat, the convertible top again open, craning her neck as the patient autopilot computer urged the vehicle at a crawl. "I think I can hear it."

"This looks like it's gonna be a pretty low budget affair," sneered Bonnie.

"It's a fair, not Paradise." Paradise was a world-renowned circus-carnival-entertainment center-vacationland in the far province of Kai-hany.

An old Choom woman on the front porch of an aging wooden house sat watching the crazy slow parade of diverse vehicles, a large cat on her lap also watching. "Goober-land," said Bonnie, bulging her eyes back at the woman.

"Looks like a really nice spot to live," Noelle said. "Quiet. Trees…"

"You look awful young for a hundred-ten, girl," Bonnie remarked. "*Move*, for Chrissakes!" She pounded her palm on the horn's button. "Why stick this thing way out here? We're practically out of town."

EVERYBODY SCREAM!

"The only clear spot big enough," said Noelle.

"They could have had it on the roof of the Canberra Mall, right in town."

"And compete with the carnival *in* the Mall?"

"I'm just making an example. Here we go–geesh." They rounded a bend, and up ahead they saw the traffic was taking a sharp turn left where a traffic robot was waving its arm, a yellow light flashing on its chest. A sign announced: "WELCOME TO THE NINETEENTH ANNUAL PAXTON FAIR." A lesser sign went on: "Midway, rides, food, live entertainment, crafts, art, agricultural exposition and contests."

"Alright, so how much of this thing is cows and gourds?" Bonnie said.

"I don't know."

"There aren't any farms in Punktown."

"There's a few big farms on the outskirts I can think of. Two I know for sure–my dad used to take me to buy vegetables and pumpkins for Halloween."

"Yeah, but they're big business-type factory farms."

"There're farms out beyond Punktown, in littler towns. You don't have to live in Punktown to enter. It's just a convenient meeting spot. Probably hardly any of the agricultural stuff is from town."

"This should be positively Dark Ages."

"Nobody forced you to come, Bonnie."

"A *real* Punktown expo would have awards for the best gold-dust, best seaweed, best home porn-vid, best tally of customers by a prosty–they could have the people buy tickets to ride!" Bonnie laughed. "Now *that* would be a fun fair!"

"Come on, don't spoil it. You can go to the Mall anytime, but this is old-fashioned. It's quaint."

"Quaint. Is it a fair or a museum?"

"Maybe it is a museum a little, but people should stay in touch with the past...the old way of doing things, making things with your own hands."

Bonnie scrunched up her tanned face. "*Why?*"

Vehicles with wheels bounced and rumbled, dipped and crackled over the dirt and stones of the huge lot created for parking, its far boundaries bordered by trees. Bonnie had a hovercar which floated a few feet off the ground, but still cursed to see the dirt parking lot ahead on the right. A second robot stood at its mouth, waving and pointing. Some people, though, were parking in smaller grass lots on either side of the road or on the sides of the road itself, and filed in a pilgrimage on foot. Bonnie slammed her horn at a family walking directly in front of her car, received a glare from the arrogant teenage son and his girlfriend. "There's a spot," said Noelle.

"I want to get up close—I don't wanna walk all that way. Is the parking free?"

"Yup—I guess."

The impatient robot waved them into the giant lot, pointing down a particular corridor of vehicles. "Blast you," muttered Bonnie, and instead wormed her way closer to the path which rose ramp-like up a steep hill to the carnival. Above the crowns of the bordering trees on the hill reared a Ferris Wheel, and the Double Helix. Loud sounds, loud music.

"Good thing we came early," noted Noelle, taking in all the cars, and a few school-type buses.

"*Nyah!*" Bonnie cried, accelerating forward. Noelle screamed and fell into the back seat. The hovercar shot into a prime parking spot ahead of another vehicle, which slammed on its brakes to avoid hitting them. A group of Asians inside poked out their heads to scream in a language they didn't know.

"Blast *off!*" Bonnie yelled.

"You want to get us *murdered?*" Noelle whined, scrabbling into a sitting position in the back seat.

The car of Asians spun out its tires, raising a dust cloud, and moved along. A beer bottle was flung out in its wake but missed Bonnie's car by a wide margin. "Greasy slants," Bonnie snorted.

"They could catch up with us in the carnival," said Noelle, climbing out of the car.

Bonnie got out after raising the convertible top "Ease up, girl. We're here to have fun, right? Come on." And Bonnie started across the crunchy gravely dirt.

Noelle ran several steps to catch up with her. They started up the ramp, which was paved but cracked, weeds growing through fissures. Trash in the tall grass to either side. Louder sounds, louder music, a blended and blurred graffiti of noise, just ahead, just out of sight. For those sounds were a thing that could be seen; the noise *was* the carnival, all of the carnival one big sprawling noise machine, noise taking the visible forms of bright lights, bright colors, cotton candy and cheap teddy bears. A world built of solidified noise, like the deep city…all just over the hill.

At first there had been the intense dam-like build up of bodies, but after the gates were opened and the initial, anxious flood had burst in, the river flowed forward steadily at a more relaxed pace. The KeeZees were at the gate, to give potential troublemakers something to think about from the start. In fact, one of them had seized and tranquilized, already, a teenage Hispanic boy who had fought with a Choom boy when the gates first opened and elbows began to jab and shoulders to butt. A knife had come out, down by the boy's leg where he figured no one could see him use it clearly, and he cut the Choom boy's buttock deeply. The first arrest and first med patient of the day.

Mitch Garnet was there at the start also, with a large number of the security team the town had hired; big black-garbed, black-helmeted men with long black riot sticks that could give cattle prod-like charges of varying intensity. Most of these men were in their forties and big-bellied. The perfect men to chase a fleeing teenage mugger or brawler, Mitch sneered inwardly, watching the gathering of them glower meaningfully at the influx of varied fair-goers. They wore two guns each—one on the hip and one in a shoulder holster; one to kill, one to tranquilize. The tranquilizers worked fast, but some beings were immune, some punks took drugs that nullified the effect, many people wore body armor, jackets with bullet and ray-proof mesh sewn in. Mitch's silver windbreaker contained such a mesh. He would carry a clip or two of tranquilizer bullets, but mostly he stuck to the explosive shells. He'd rather make out all the pain in the ass forms to establish justifiable homicide than to risk being a homicide himself, or risk innocent bystanders becoming a background of targets.

Standing off to one side, a cup of icy soda in hand, Mitch scrutinized the people filing up to the gate, which was not charged now, although where it ran off to left and right as a high meshed fence it became charged, completely surrounding the fairgrounds, with a tell-tale hum and a distinct blue glow to dissuade the foolish. But not every fool would be dissuaded from trying to break in; after all, the charge had to be kept low in case small children free of their parents approached it. The town security boys had a video map in their trailer which showed the outline of the fence, and this would flash in an area where the fence had been cut or disturbed. They dealt with most of those incidents.

One by one the people would purchase their tickets at a booth, from a person behind protective clear plastic, and one by one they would be admitted through a narrow archway with a revolving subway turnstile. A door could slide shut to block the archway, operated from inside the booth, if need be. Inside the arch were the eyes of weapon scanners. However, these were not put to use. Mitch wasn't happy with it, but he wasn't running the fair. Yes, it would be a major pain to confiscate weapons, tag them, or make arrests for the possession of too conspicuous or threatening illegal items; yes it would make for many tense situations and would turn away many potential patrons, even discourage many from coming in the first place, but it burned Garnet to think that these gun-toting punks and scum could go anywhere they wanted unchecked, undisturbed. Only on extreme occasions could he approach a person for bringing in a weapon, such as when a young gang boy had a shotgun slung over his back, or an assault rifle in his hand. On the other hand, he'd been told to let bikies have their way, and whole troops of them sauntered in, fat and leather-coated, with slung shotguns and machine-guns, beers in their hands.

Mitch had been wanting to nab one of these new fucking Martians with their prominent guns all season, but either they came through with no guns visible and had them tossed over the fence, or they got over or under the fence themselves. Mitch had started to run after two of them who he saw with their big guns inside the carnival but one of the KeeZees grabbed his jacket and held him back.

EVERYBODY SCREAM!

One of the town security boys had been shot dead early in the season but no one had come forward to say who'd done it. The ray bolts that had obliterated the man's head had come from a gun such as those ridiculously over-equipped monstrosities toted by the Martians.

Now Mitch watched gang boys strut through the archway-turnstile one by one with pistols holstered at their hips or ribs, and could not step forward to stop them. His blue eyes were streaming ice cubes of frozen hatred.

Pulling the little string to ignite his cigarette, Bern Glandston watched the behinds of the two teenage girls ahead of him, one with a baby in a stroller. Their hair was frosted violet and blue, respectively, with a luminous dye which would show up better tonight. They had on tight transparent plastic pants with nothing underneath. Bern wished they'd turn around so he could see if their pubic hair matched their head colors. One went through the turnstile. Bern noticed the weapon scanners, and was glad he'd left his pistol in the *Scarab*. The girl with the stroller passed through, and then him. He pocketed his ticket, kept walking after the girls. They stopped at two thin, hard-faced gang boys in clear jackets made of plastic, an imitation of the clear rubbery leather taken from a huge amphibious creature that was quite popular now, but more expensive than plastic. Bern took his eyes off the girls, branched off past them on their left, but as he did so his eyes fell on a pistol holstered at the hip of one of the boys. His eyes darted to the other boy. A sawed-off double-barrel shotgun in a pouch buckled at his hip and tied around his thigh.

Removing the cigarette from his mouth, Bern halted in his tracks and turned around to watch a few people squeeze through the turnstile. The fifth person to come through was a Choom man in a t-shirt and cutoff jeans with a snub revolver holstered on his beaded belt. The weapon scanners said nothing about it.

Jesus. Now if he wanted to go back to his car he'd have to pay for re-admission, right? To hell with it. He turned to the carnival. The two gang boys in bogus clear leather, bony and mean-bodied inside, were looking at him.

"Pumpin' shoes, man," one of them said, spitting appreciatively on the ground by Bern's feet.

"Oh…yeah…thanks."

Jeffrey Thomas

The distant shouts, cries, exclamations, laughter had been almost frightening at first to Del on some deep level, as if he feared that when the near-empty corridors of the carnival suddenly flooded with people he would be trampled. It was almost enough to make him want to seek shelter or higher ground. It was a scary thought, like the scary thought in years past of what it would be like to suddenly fall off the stage into the masses of his fans, like a man who can't swim falling into the sea. He didn't hate the sea, he loved it, but he'd rather love it from a ship. A big, high, unsinkable ship. There had been a time when Del–who wasn't even a very distinctive, interesting-looking man–couldn't walk a city street to browse the stores, couldn't go into a fast food restaurant for a burger. He didn't have that problem anymore, but it had taken a while to feel comfortable among the masses, and to hear these distant voices like the great murmuring he had once heard from backstage now gave him a brief shiver, as if thousands of people would be pouring in after *him*, to grab at him and in crazed possessive love tear his body to pieces. Funny, Del thought, how he had sought both to evade the masses, out of fear and a sense of jealous privacy, and how he had sought to draw the masses to him and hold their attention with all his strength.

But there was no mad animal stampede–the turnstile only allowed one at a time, and there were many corridors of the carnival maze to disperse the flood quickly, and only a few children ran frenziedly past him, exhilarated. Del now stood at a candyfloss booth, chatting with the woman inside, Toovish Oga. Too, as they called her, was a Tikkihotto, who were human in appearance but for the swimming translucent nests of tendrils that grew from their eye sockets in place of eyeballs. Too, however, had had her tendrils cut down to stumps which hid inside cosmetic human eyes, gazing out of them, although her vision was thus limited for her kind. She'd had eyelids made, and eyebrows implanted. She was very tall, shapely, with long fluffy brunette hair, and very funny and friendly. She was quite pretty but wore too much rouge, lipstick and eye makeup for Del's taste. One night after work

EVERYBODY SCREAM!

Del had taken her out for a late night snack at a highway restaurant stop, and afterwards they had kissed and embraced in his car. He'd fondled her breasts and started slipping his hand into her sweat pants but she'd squirmed free shyly. Del was married; she didn't feel right. Del was surprised, in light of her great friendliness toward him, her sexy makeup and hair and rather showy clothing. But it wasn't that she had been teasing him, he knew. Though disappointed, he was impressed to see that all along she hadn't just been flirting with him, flaunting her attractiveness, wagging her ass for him—she really liked him as a friend, she opened up her private feelings out of trust and regard for him. He still wanted to fuck her, but he liked her even more since then, in a different way. He didn't have many platonic girl friends, *real* friends. It was nice to see her face brighten whenever he came to her booth, knowing she didn't want to lure him to bed to prove her womanly power. So many of the beautiful girls and women he'd had during his days of intense popularity had thrown their bodies on him in a smothering avalanche, but just to say they'd fucked Del Kahn; if he, the exact same man, had met them before (or after) his fame, they might have sneered with distaste or laughed in his face.

Del wasn't tall, wasn't handsome. He had a very friendly, very pleasant face; he could look handsome in the right pose or light, and had been specially lighted and posed for publicity shots many times, but it was the pleasantness that made him seem handsome. He had short dark hair, thinning back from his forehead a bit (he liked the mature look and hadn't felt inclined to halt the progress yet), a not exactly delicate nose, a worried brow that made him look concerned and compassionate and also vulnerable. His face could register a lot of intensity, but the flesh never conveyed the extent of the intensity he actually felt. It came as a surprise to some just how strongly, or angrily, the pleasant Del Kahn could feel about things.

He had a muscular body, but his muscles were not the product of years of hard work (he had worked in factories, had drawn much of his song material from those early days, but he had usually performed light work), nor had they been hardened in the mean streets. He'd built them up during his touring days, working out and submitting to medical procedures, no longer content to be the skinny big-nosed kid turned down by the girls at the factories. His natural facial features, though, he had kept. It was, after all, *his* face. He didn't want to feel too phony, too synthetic, just happy about his physicality, strong and healthy. And Del had never cared for the garish or ostentatious costumes of many of his fellow musicians, had always dressed casually, in keeping with his image of being a regular man, an everyman, singing from the hearts of all the men and women who loved him and wanted to hear him express what they felt but couldn't articulate. After a while his casual dress had seemed like a costume to him, though, and he had felt trapped, obligated, as if he would be called a traitor, be accused of selling out, if he dressed up more often, dressed for the varied moods he felt.

Thus, now he felt liberated and gratified to wear this bright white dress shirt, a black string tie clasped with the turquoise-studded disc Sophi had given him, very sharp in his suit made from expensive Kodju silk, a dark greenish-black or blackish-green with a fly's eye iridescent metallic sheen. Sophi teased him that he looked like a Nevadan gangster lately, but that wasn't because he sometimes carried a pistol, since that wasn't so unusual, or unwarranted, in Punktown. It was just a stab of revenge, he felt. Not that she lived for revenge against him, but her little stabs let off her steam, and better that than a volcano. She wouldn't have bought the tie clasp if she hated his new look.

If anyone might now have still recognized Del Kahn, some old loyal fan, not as fickle as the rest, Del had himself practically erased the chance by deviating so drastically from the days of black t-shirts and jeans. He wasn't hiding, not at all; that wasn't the point, privacy aside. He simply had other moods to express. That had partly been his downfall. With his last few releases, Del had gotten more serious, adhered more closely to a unified theme each album. Less prevalent, and on *Heroes* absent, were the songs celebrating the freedom beyond the punch-out of the factory clock or the stale office, optimistic, fun and raucous. The Del Kahn who wrote an entire album full of gloomy portraits of true life characters wasn't the Del Kahn who had attracted all those eager fans, screaming girls, cheering men, with songs of liberty and love and passionate rebellion of the spirit against the chains of oppressive society. This Del Kahn bowed his head, defeated, under those chains. He wasn't an escape anymore. If Del Kahn had remained the t-shirted, grinning factory troubadour, he might not now be Del Kahn, the forgotten, who had sunk down in the murk of his own art. It wasn't so much that his audience had tired of him and drifted on. Many had, would have moved on no matter what. But the real thrust of it was that Del Kahn had tired of Del Kahn and moved on, and the general mass of fans had wanted him to remain as he was. He could understand that, as greatly as it disappointed him. He didn't resent his fans for needing that optimism. But he had other moods to express.

Of course, now people had magnetized to Chauncy Carnal of Sphitt, and Flemm and the Saliva Surfers and their kind, to find that raucous celebration of life. But it was a celebration in another tone, a mean-spirited, misogynistic, ugly tone, and his former audience's ardent embrace of these groups in his stead was what could inspire Del Kahn to resent them.

Del hadn't disowned his old work. But he had grown older, more experienced, more realistic, more sophisticated. He had matured. His old music was sometimes naïve. But people *wanted* to be naïve. They wanted to feel young, idealistic, passionate. Wasn't he meant to entertain them, rather than inform them of what the dismal VT news could already tell them? Didn't they want to laugh and cheer, rather than be moved to thought and tears? Why else had so many of Punktown's diverse people, male and female, human and non-human, lifted him as their spokesman on their shoulders in the first place? They had given him what he had, right? So who was he to betray their trust and need?

But Del Kahn wasn't a factory machine designed to churn out a stale product. That was what he had always rebelled *against* in his songs! He didn't feel that old burning optimism anymore. It made him as sad as any of his fans could be, but he had to be true to himself. He was an artist. He had hoped, in maturing, entering marriage, changing, that he could continue to express the feelings of his fans as they too matured and changed with the years. But they didn't want that. Their bodies were changing, their lives were changing, but their emotions still clung desperately to the safe, naïve dreams of youth. If they became dislodged they would fall into the black void of growing old and facing the unpleasantries of life, such as a greater responsibility to their jobs, paying bills, responsibilities to wives and husbands and children–and dying. Del Kahn hated drug abuse. He had smoked seaweed here and there, but he had never even tried gold-dust once. He had urged his fans years ago to turn onto his music, not to drugs, to expand their horizons. Well, it had happened. Del Kahn had become a safe, transporting drug, offering release and escape. And now he had taken the drug away, and the escapists among his fans had turned to other drugs.

Del stared into a pink whirlpool cloud of sugar, mesmerized. A hurricane spiral vortex. A paper cone moved into it, swept around the sides of the whirlpool, turning, gathering up a head of cloud sugar. Del's lips molded into a faint smile. "That looks sexual."

"Everything looks sexual to you." Too held up the finished cone of candyfloss, extended it to him. "A last cone for the year?"

"Oh, how sweet." Del took it.

"Ha ha."

"I'd rather bury my nose into something even sweeter."

"Ha ha."

"Can I dip my love cone into your sugar pit?"

"Someone told me somebody did that–she read it in a letter to a sex magazine," said Too, growing animated. "This guy put his thing in a candyfloss machine and his girlfriend and her sister ate it off."

Del laughed. "Oh, come on…the magazines write those letters."

"No they don't, do they?"

"*Yes!*" Del laughed. "Man." He took a bite of the cloud; it reverted back to a crunchy sugary liquid in his mouth. "Our last day together. You're going to school, and you may not be here next year. We may never see each other again. Your last chance to seduce me."

"Geesh, I'm heartbroken. I ought to let you have sex with me, and then suddenly pull my fake eyes out." It wasn't just anyone she confided in about her eyes. "How'd you like that?"

"Honey, you don't know me. I've had Tikkihotto girls. This one girl wrapped her eyes around my rod, pumped me until I thought I'd explode, and then used them to put me in her mouth."

EVERYBODY SCREAM!

"Well, all I have left is little stubbly ends, Del, sorry—but then, I guess that's all I need to handle your thing, huh?"

"I *told* you not to make fun of my penis. I happen to like single-celled organisms."

Loud rock music started up from the Screamer, off behind the booth. It was one of the first rides you saw when you came in through the gate, tucked in a corner of the charged fence. Del stared over at it through the glass of Too's booth. His manner grew subdued again. "I really will miss you, hon. You're a sweet, sweet kid—no pun intended. I really am fond of you, all sex talk aside. Write to me. Come back next year if you need work—I'll get you something better. Let's stay friends, alright?" He looked at Too and gave her that big, toothy, extra-pleasant Del Kahn grin.

"I'll write you, I promise." Too was embarrassed, averted her eyes. Luckily, a little girl had appeared, so that Too could keep her eyes on her whirlpool. "I may very well be back next year...God knows my mother and father won't give me enough money for a car."

"I'll buy you a car if you go to bed with me once."

The little girl paid for her cone, looked up at Del. "You pig."

Del laughed. "Sorry, honey, forgot you were there."

The child ran off. When Too let herself look at Del again, he was again looking through at the Screamer. "Decide what you'll be doing this fall?"

"Nope," he muttered. "Same old thing. I guess."

"I thought you said you might start writing some songs, and if you decided not to use them you'd give them to friends."

"Mm," he grunted.

The Screamer was a circular machine, with a full circle of connected cabs which rotated around a central axis, dipping and rising along with the dips and rises in the surrounding metal walkway as they spun. The cabs, base, and circular roof were white, but the sides of the roof, trimmed with colored lights which didn't show too well in daylight, were also covered with bright, crude paintings. Music was strongly associated with the Screamer. While there were far more complex, imaginative rides, it was the use of music and the very simplicity of the ride itself that made the

Screamer one of the most popular rides. Music blasted from speakers above the control booth attached to the left side of the ride at the highest point of the surrounding walkway. The Screamer's music was loud; it was the primary background music for a fifth of the carnival proper just by itself. And so, painted on the outside of the circular roof above the train which madly spun around the central cylinder, biting its own snake tail, were four or five music stars.

There was Magdilon Perimeter, naked as always (though looking over her shoulder to hide her breasts), with long dark hair and a hauntingly gorgeous and impassive face. She had committed suicide at the height of her career. There was Lotti, the Tikkihotto idol. He'd been assassinated. There was Zodiac Jones, still going strong today after over thirty years of performing; *his* style had changed considerably over the years, as he incorporated every popular new style that developed, without his fading into obscurity...but the partying exuberant *tone* had never varied in thirty-some-odd years. In his muvids, Jones–artificially young and smooth-looking–cavorted and pouted and panted and growled like the teenage boys and girls who played him.

Huge on the side of the circular metal canvas loomed the face of Del Kahn, eyes passionately squeezed shut, mouth wide as if to fellate, Sophi teased, the microphone clenched in his fist. On his head was the black beret he had taken to wearing for several years, at first because he wanted it but which he later maintained as a helpful visual identification symbol at the urging of his ex-manager. Men, boys, even women had followed suit with their own black berets. Del stopped wearing it when it had worn itself thin.

The painting hadn't been painted since Sophi had bought and assembled the carnival, ironically enough–it had already been there, and had been there since Del's great successful days. Del was embarrassed, had asked Sophi to have it repainted. "With who–Chauncy Carnal? You want that?"

"I feel like you're keeping this stupid dated thing for my sake. It makes me feel pathetic."

"Don't be stupid–you should be proud of it. Never mind if some kids think it's dated. I don't think they even notice or care."

Del thought it ironic that people were exposed to this huge portrait all day, and yet passing him on the midway had never identified him from it. Talk about embarrassing. Talk about salt in one's wounds.

"Oh well, should move along," Del muttered to Too. "I'll be around later, if I can."

"If you *can?* Thanks a lot."

"Have a nice day." Del raised his candyfloss in a salute, started away. Behind him, the Screamer yelled a song by Sputum as the first riders of the day filed up to the mounting ramp.

Noelle wanted to walk about first, get her bearings, but Bonnie said, "I want to spin around a little, get in the right frame of mind. Get the juices whipped up." She flicked a silvery "button" into her mouth, gulped it. Presumably, she saw the Screamer as a blender which would violently mix the blood and adrenaline and drugs in her body into one high energy fuel. The line wasn't too bad and they paid the man at the foot of the metal ramp a certain amount of the tickets from those they had purchased at a booth near the gate. Bonnie ran up the hollowly clanking ramp, lifted the restraining bar of a cab and slipped in. Noelle climbed into the cab ahead of Bonnie. The cab rocked from side to side. Noelle watched an insectoid alien, squat and tiny-headed, its naked body a lovely sky blue, pass her on the walkway and enter the car ahead of her. She couldn't see its cat-sized head over the backrest of the car but heard it chittering, maybe in excited anticipation.

Deafening music blasted; Noelle didn't recognized the group. Punktown's menu of music was as diverse as its inhabitants, and it wasn't until the song was half through that she noted the racing, growling vocals weren't in English, obscured as they were under bombastic layers of music like a multiple car collision, with flipping cars rolling over and over, while a further background layer was of pigs being slaughtered. "Noelle!" She twisted around in her seat. Bonnie was rocking her cab with her weight. "Get it moving–it'll be wilder when it starts running."

The last rider was locked in; an operator in an army jacket thumped down the walkway past Noelle, out of sight. A man's voice cut into the music over the intercom.

"Okay, we're just about ready to roll…rock and roll, that is. Keep your limbs inside the cars, please, and hold on tight." The music came back. The cars slowly began to turn around their axis. Noelle had ignored Bonnie's suggestion, scrunched down in her seat and gripped the bar as casually as she could appear. Her car rode up a hill in the surrounding metal catwalk, and as it came down the machine began to engage. Speed was picked up quickly.

With each revolution, the speed increased. The alien song ended, a new song started up, rousing and wild. Columns upholding the circular roof whizzed by like archaic telephone poles on a highway. Beyond, the whole world spun like a tornado around Noelle. A train of faces, the next batch of riders waiting in line, all seemed to be staring up at her as if to gauge her fear or dizziness, like scientists observing an astronaut in a training machine. The Screamer had reached, and leveled at, its apparent highest speed. Noelle rocketed up a hill, down into a gully, up again, and the cab was flying sideways in the wind, rocking without her intervention. Noelle didn't like the rocking and tried to stabilize against it, bracing her feet on the floor and firmly planting herself in the middle of her seat so as to maintain a balance. When the cab dove down into the gully her organs scrambled high into her rib-cage. When it climbed the hill the cab inclined more sideways and Noelle was a little afraid of it ultimately flipping upside-down to dump her out. The other cabs would slam over her body one after another.

It was exhilarating; despite or because of her fear, she loved it. She heard Bonnie scream her name and dared to twist around. Bonnie's pod was rocking madly, almost turning upside-down, but the restraining bar and centrifugal force held her in. She had one hand on the bar and waved at Noelle crazily. Noelle wore a big foolish grin, her hair snapping like tangled whips.

The young man in the army jacket, with a baseball cap over long greasy black hair, his face hard and grim, stood in front of the adjacent control booth, in which at least one shadowy man sat. On each revolution Noelle was afraid she'd bash into him, and flinched as he whipped past. He seemed to be standing there daring the cabs to hit him; Noelle could almost feel her car tick his clothing. Was this something he did to show off to the riders and impress himself or was he paid extra to add to the delicious mood of dangerousness?

The voice of the DJ or operator or whatever he was inside the booth came back in place of the music: "Okay...we're gonna pick things up a little bit...I think she can handle the strain. Are you having a good time? Let's hear it!" A few yelled "yeahs." The DJ had a slight Outback accent in his drawl, and he savored this like an actor playing a sinister role. "Now let's see how fast this baby will go. Y'all ready, now? I wanna hear ya. Here we go...everybody *screeeam!*"

This time there was a more enthusiastic response, and because Noelle heard Bonnie shrieking-laughing hysterically (and the insect being letting out a high cicada buzz) she cried out herself loudly. The man standing in front of the control booth was a blur indistinguishable from the zipping columns, and a siren wailing over the crazy beat of the music marked the climax. Soon the ride began to slow, slow, crawl to a halt.

The army-jacketed man trotted down the clanging ramp and put his hands on Bonnie's cab to keep it from rocking so profoundly. He then strode past Noelle. Noelle thought it was over and pushed at her bar but it wouldn't give; it had locked automatically, and a moment later the circular train of cabs began to rotate in the opposite direction–backwards. "Oh no!" she laughed, glancing back at Bonnie. Bonnie was exuberant. Maybe she should take a button from her, seeing as how she'd missed out on this morning's golden sunrise breakfast. Maybe that would help to disperse the gray shreds of fog which still crept between her and her excitement, still muffled her exhilaration and weighted her smile, a haunting distraction. Vague, but there.

The rotation increased in speed; now her car swept backwards up the hill, plunged backward into the gully, though her innards still piled up against her heart. The physical stimuli helped distract her from the distraction of the nameless, obscure fog and Noelle grinned stupidly again, squinting against the flagellations from her own living head of dark medusa-serpents.

The spinning having nearly reached its apex, the DJ broke in a last time. "Okay, we're about ready to call it quits. Hope you folks aren't too shaken up, now. Thanks for your time. I think we can still squeeze in a little more speed before you leave us, though. Are you ready now? Let me get my hands on the controls here. Hey, what's this red button? It says 'light speed', looks like. Let's give it a try." The speed picked up and the cabs surfed its highest crest. "Has anybody got a beer for me?" the DJ said to one side of his mic. "Oh–sorry–are we still on?" He chuckled with feigned embarrassment. "Okay, folks, looks like we're right there. Are y'all ready now? Oh-kay…everybody *SCREEEAM!*"

Noelle screamed at the top of her lungs shrilly.

"What's the problem here?" said Mitch Garnet even before he stopped walking up to the game booth at which he had distantly spotted some friction.

It was one of many games in the long aisle where most of the games were congregated, like close prison cells in which inmates were trapped by the bulk of cheap stuffed animals. At this one, two tall, heavyset boys in crew cuts and long black overcoats had been thrusting their jaws and words at the wiry shirtless Choom inside the booth. Mitch didn't have an advance idea of whom to side with so he kept it open. One boy had his hands in his pockets but they looked like high school or college jocks, all muscle, insulated at school, maybe, from the need for guns–maybe–but it was the way the Choom was sitting with his arms under the booth that had made Mitch intervene; he knew the Choom was even now aiming some weapon at the boys under the counter, ready to fire through the wood.

"Who are you?" growled one of the youths.

"Chief of Security–what's going on?"

"Nothing, man," said the Choom.

"This little snake cheated us, man–he said if you get the ball in the hoop you win a prize, right? I *got* it in the hoop but he says I leaned over the counter."

"He practically leaned over and put it in the basket," said the Choom, sticking to his casual pose of readiness.

EVERYBODY SCREAM!

"Blast *you*, twinkledink!"

"Alright, alright," said Garnet. "You—what's your name?"

"Rum."

"Rum *what?*"

"Rum Helsinki."

"Okay, Helsinki. A compromise. Give the kid another shot and I'll watch." The boy disapproved. "What if I don't get it *in* again. man? I had it in!"

"Don't push your luck, kid. I'm trying to be fair—alright? Take your shot."

Grumbling, the huge boy took up the ball, barely aimed, and casually tossed it. Right through the hoop without even nicking the sides, it seemed. He had made a point to step back clear of the counter.

Mitch gave the Choom a moment's long weary look. "Give the kid two prizes, Helsinki."

"Look, man, this is my game!"

"Do I have to come in there and take them myself? It's pretty crowded in there, Helsinki, you might get an elbow in the eye. Give him the fucking prizes, and it isn't your fucking game. The Kahns run a clean midway, they make a point to keep the games fresh. Don't think you're gonna make an extra profit because it's last night. I'm gonna keep you in my sights. Don't fuck with me. I won't even go to the Kahns, I'll deal with you myself—understood?"

"Sure, sure, don't get so rabid, Mr. Mauser." *Mr. Mauser* was a popular VT crime show. "Pick your damn teddy bears, college boy."

Mitch barred the boy's chest with one arm. "Wait a minute. What did you call me, Helsinki?"

"What's the big deal, officer?"

"You got a big mouth, even for a Choom, fuck-face. I said what did you call me? *Huh?*"

Helsinki looked a little closer at the human's eyes and small tight mouth. The face was a fist, wearing brass knuckles at that. It showed no compromise, and he wasn't so entirely stupid that he didn't know when to back down. "Nothing," he muttered, "sorry—alright?"

"Now give the kid his prizes. The next time I talk to you, you'd better take your hand off your gun or I'll blow your useless head apart—you got me, air-waster?"

"Understood."

Meanwhile the boy had picked out which hanging prizes he wanted. "Give me that pink unicorn, and that bumble."

Once the boys had left, Mitch moved on without another look at the Choom but felt his scalp ripple under a cautiously malignant stare. He continued on his beat, which would last all day and night with only a few breaks that he seldom expanded on or varied. Some of the game operators nodded to him and said hi. Finally at the end of the games he turned and at a snack stand bought his first food for the day—a bag of salty, tasty dilky roots, a native favorite, though treated and softened for human teeth. The Chooms had developed their heavy jaws and multiple rows of teeth to deal with the tough roots and vegetables of their world. An angry Choom—such as Rum Helsinki, for instance—might refer to a human as a "no-mouth."

Mitch strolled at a more subdued pace, juggling the greasy bag of roots and a *Candyjuice* soda. Until he heard the gunfire.

Mitch was good at tracing gunshots in a labyrinth, back from his days with Car Thirteen on Forma Street. The dilky roots scattered and bright *Candyjuice* splashed. He bolted, wove between people, bumping a few lightly as he passed, but he was good at avoiding that, too...since on Forma Street, if you bumped somebody it wasn't unlikely that you could be shot in the back as you ran.

Mitch was fast. People backed off and looked at the furious energy in his running as he shot past. He had chased down young, animal-quick car thieves and purse snatchers, gang kids and muggers, rapists and killers. Without exaggeration, Mitch could run down seven or eight out of ten runners, unless they were on a few buttons or something strong like purple vortex, that really gave them a jolt...and then they might reach hiding only to suffer a lethal heart attack or cerebral hemorrhage.

He could see them ahead in the open, in front of the lavatory shack, which looked like a small barn with a wooden divider to separate males from females. Peripherally, Garnet saw Roland LaKarnafeaux on his chair and his

EVERYBODY SCREAM!

men turn their heads and track him as he bolted.

The area was too open–dangerous. Mitch was already pulling his automatic pistol from inside his windbreaker. With his trained eyes he was able to slow down time and in a few seconds, computer-like, absorb and analyze information, to recreate the actions which had led to the outcome he would become a part of in another few seconds...

Five black men in their early twenties; they wore a variety of black clothing styles, but four of them wore the latest fashionable head gear for tough young black men: bright-colored rubber swimming caps. The mutant had one of them pinned by the throat in its single hand, and he was convulsing. Another had been hurled, it looked, a great distance and lay unmoving. The other three humans had pulled out guns, a pistol and two compact sub-machine guns, and were sending blazes of lead into the mutant. The mutant maybe had squat legs under the hanging, cracked folds of ossified gray flesh, but it only had one long arm (split and pus-oozing at the joints), the other a stump, and an elephant trunk for a neck with no head at the end. This madly thrashed. Greenish-white pus or blood sprayed and poured from tears in the silent creature's thick hide.

Mitch was firing his pistol from both hands even before he had finished running.

One of the two machine-gunners, the straps of his orange shower cap hanging unbuckled, took an explosive bullet in the side of the jaw. In police school, Garnet had been taught not to aim at a man's chest, for even hit there he could still keep coming long enough to kill you (even ruling out numbing drugs), but for the kidneys to lower blood pressure instantly or for the spine or mouth/lower face area to shut down the central nervous system, the only sure spots for immediate take down. But that Garnet hit the man in the jaw was mostly unnecessary instinct, with an explosive bullet. It turned the man's entire head into a red coleslaw.

The other machine-gunner started to look his way and caught two bullets in the chest. Even with a bulletproof mesh shirt the concussions broke his bones, split his organs, sent rib fragments ripping through his lungs.

The one with the pistol had fully turned and by now Mitch had come to a stop and aimed from his planted police stance. The black man's pistol had barely moved in his direction when an explosive projectile detonated on the man's left eyebrow. A mostly red splash flecked with bone, brain, hair, and pink rubber shot across the front of the wooden divider for the men's and women's toilets.

The mutant released its captive, who lay moaning barely conscious, and started to shamble away, disoriented, shaking. It only got a few steps before it fell, gave a few agonized heaves, and then lay still with its thick pus–blood oozing. Mitch came to stand over it.

"Elliot...*Elliot!*" a woman screamed, running. "Elliot! Elliot!" She flung herself down on the dead creature, mindless of the pus. Embracing it, cheek to the ossified hide, she sobbed hysterically.

"Who was he?" Mitch asked quietly.

"My husband," the woman groaned.

Garnet produced a hand phone and bleeped Del Kahn's code. A few moments. "Hello?"

"It's Garnet. We had a shoot-out by the toilet shed–four dead, maybe five. I killed three."

A long silence. Mitch waited for Del to ask him if it was necessary but he didn't. "Looks like tonight's not going to be as quiet as we'd hoped."

More wails, screams, chaos from off to the right. People were clustered around a boy of maybe twelve lying on his back, his legs crossed. In police school, the rule of experience was that if they fell with their legs crossed they would never get back up. A stray bullet from one of the machine guns. "Make that six–a kid got hit with a stray."

"Oh God...oh man," said Del Kahn's voice.

"I'll clean things up, take names. Then I'm taking an early break."

"Alright, talk to me later."

"Right." Mitch pocketed the device.

Last year there'd been a violent riot, like a cowboy movie brawl on a mass scale, mostly precipitated by a huge gang of bikers. But they had only been a catalyst. All it took was the right volatile mixture to set off a chain reaction in every direction. There'd been ten deaths, many injured, much damage.

EVERYBODY SCREAM!

We're only four deaths short already, thought Mitch. The riot had been at night. It was now just short of noon.

Yes, Mitch would deviate from his usual rigid schedule for an early break. Pearl made him agitated, but Pearl made him peaceful.

Far up ahead, not too distant from the barn structure in which the cows were penned, the toilet shed again saw normal traffic. From here as he walked, Del saw a man with a baby in a stroller standing next to the octopus-like dark stain on the front of the wooden divider while he waited for a wife or child to return from the ladies' room. Del slowed his walking pace down to a languid oozing. Mitch and the meds had cleaned things up fast. That was good. Carnage wasn't good for business.

"Hey," someone on his right said to him as he was scuffing past, wondering whether he really wanted to go to the morgue next. "You're a little late for the action, Del."

Del came to a stop, faced the speaker, hands in pockets. "So it would seem."

"Quite a mess. Your security man there is hot, though. Really cleaned house."

Del smiled tightly, shrugged. "Gotta have security."

The man with whom he talked was called Eddy Walpole. Tall, with neatly cut sandy hair, blonde eyebrows, steel-rimmed glasses, a constant little smile in his eyes, on his lips. He was reclining in a lawn chair with a cigarette dangling out of his fingers over the edge of the metal arm-rest, one sneaker hooked over another. He sat in the shade of a canopy that extended far out from the side of a huge hovercamper and was supported by rods and wires. A large van was a second wall to the enclosure. Two *Dozer* hovercycles rested off beyond the van. Under the tent were several long tables, one offering t-shirts and scarves and such, another new and used music chips, another table presenting a museum-like display of buttons, pins, jewelry, sunglasses, knives, handcuffs, metal seaweed pipes and related novelties under a pane of glass.

"He is good, but I couldn't help but question his handling of it a little bit. Do you know what happened?"

"A bit," said Del.

Eddy Walpole sketched out the incident. "The mutant was already dead on its feet...so why kill the three kids? If he wanted to put an instant stop to things, why not just finish the mutant off, which is gonna die anyway, plainly, instead of killing three other guys? See?"

"Well, they killed a boy–a bystander. Plus, if he shot the mutant they might think he'd shoot them next and the three of them might have fired on Garnet simultaneously. Also, by the sound of things they instigated the trouble, probably by harassing the mutant."

"He could have just let them finish the mutant and that would have been the end of it. He doesn't have to arrest people for crimes, just keep the peace. One life, instead of four."

"Well it wasn't a stray derelict, it was a woman's husband. If it were a human child, a little girl, would you still say Mitch should have shot the girl instead of the three men? Or that Mitch should have just let them kill her because she was only a little girl?" Del's tone was not argumentative; he knew Eddy well enough to know it was a sly little debate, but his solemn, forced tolerant tone must have been a bit revealing.

Eddy said, "I'm just playing courtroom with you, Del, don't worry...hey, he's a pretty tough trigger, that man of yours. Good man to have to step in for ya. I know it's no party when lives are on the line and there's no time to think, just act and hope you've judged for the best. I wouldn't want his job."

"Nor I."

"It's just senseless. Makes me a wee philosophical, is all. That three young men should have to die for shooting a degenerating sort of mutant who'd die in a few months or years. That a boy should have been hit by a tiny little chunk of lead that could have gone anywhere, and in the head instead of in the arm or something. Bad things domino. Ever notice that?"

"Yeah." Del's eyes, like parts of an automatic machine, parts of his robot self, shifted to two teenage girls who leaned over the glass of the museum-like

EVERYBODY SCREAM!

exhibit. They both wore Sphitt t-shirts but one's high feather-duster hairdo was dyed lime green and the other's was stark white like Chancy Carnal's hair. The trapdoor in the rear of one girl's black sweat pants was open fully, the other's trapdoor was still half buttoned, one flap falling aside in a cuter, more coy tease. No underwear. Young girls' bottoms were so smooth, so taut, like doll skin, no dimples or striations. But the costumes disgusted Del on another level. Sphitt fans, hardcore–a trademark outfit more like a uniform; the female branch of the cult. The green-haired, half-unbuttoned girl squealed over something in the case which pleased her and rocked her head madly from side to side, her feathery hair jiggling, as they did to the music when they listened. Seas of jiggling dyed hair at the concerts–Del had seen them on Sphitt muvids. Del called these ass-baring types "baboons."

When he overcame his robot and flicked his eyes back to Walpole he saw the knowing extra twinkle in the man's eyes and felt stupid, naked, his own trapdoor opened up. He resented the twinkle. He hated this asshole.

Walpole, however, stuck to their conversation. "Maybe I was a little hard on your man because I was chased down Forma Street by the Car Thirteen boys once. It wasn't Garnet; this was way back when I was a teen, but these guys were just as fast and just as tough. They beat me unconscious. One of them stomped on my hand and broke it because he said I was reaching for a wine bottle in all the trash–we were in an alley."

"That's terrible," Del said, half sincerely, though he would have liked to have known what the teenaged Walpole was running away for. "I don't think Garnet would have gone that far, from my knowledge of him."

"Well, you many very well be right. He was discharged, though."

"That's the pattern with Car Thirteen, he's told me. The force puts their toughest men in Thirteen on Forma Street to keep the people scared, but it's a real war and the forcers have to fight rough. So after enough complaints and charges and stink from civil groups and lawyers and whatnot the force discharges the man or men and starts over. Once you're detailed to Car Thirteen you know your career is in its last stage…it may be months or it might be five years if you're real lucky. But the force martyrs its Thirteen boys. I guess Mitch liked the challenge but he wasn't looking forward to the boot—he managed three years on the street. He gets a nice pension."

"And he must have so many notches on his gun handle it doesn't have a handle," twinkled Eddy Walpole. "I heard that some Thirteen boys take trophies; ears or hands or even heads."

"I'd say that's mostly talk. Maybe they start it themselves."

"You ever kill anyone, Del?" croaked a voice from deeper in the cool blue shade of the tent.

Again Del strained a smile. "Thousands. Does bad breath count?"

Roland LaKarnafeaux chuckled softly. His courageous lawn chair squeaked as he shifted his bulk. He was tall and huge, the great fat belly whale-like in appearance sheathed in its tight black t-shirt. Over that he wore his metallic purple windbreaker with the sleeves pushed up thick arms on which a dragon and a panther stalked through the underbrush of his forearm hair. His hair was long, frizzy, an even mix of white and black, his thick beard more white than black but eyebrows more black than white. Shiny black eyes, pouched and crinkled, his brow furrowed. He looked like a benevolent Santa Claus on vacation, a cigarette in one hand and a plastic cup of beer in the other. With his granny glasses low on his nose, he looked like he was waiting for someone...the baboons, maybe, or Del...to come sit in his lap. Though the shine to his eyes was dull compared to Eddy's twinkle, the constant little smile to the lips was oddly identical. It was this smile Del hated most, even more than the flaunted purple windbreaker.

"No, really, have you ever? I'm curious," LaKarnafeaux drawled in his molasses-thick monotone. It sounded drunk, but the eyes were a bit too focused. Some kind of drug maybe, or just too many through the years, but much of the glow in his eyes was currently a sober light, and he studied Del.

"No," Del admitted, his joking manner drained away already. "I'm lucky I never had to."

"You are lucky," said Eddy. "And of course you've been insulated a long time, being who you are. You've had guys like Garnet to watch out for you, be your walls. That's a blessing. I read somewhere that three out of five Paxton males will have killed a person either as a murder or in defense by the age of fifty."

EVERYBODY SCREAM!

"Well, I'm only thirty-seven, so I still have plenty of time."

Eddy laughed, and LaKarnafeaux chuckled softly in the shadows.

"I'm forty-three," chuckled LaKarnafeaux, who looked ten years older at least, "and I killed my first person when I was twelve."

"Show him the bat, Karny," said a boy of about seventeen who was sitting on a cooler back by the van, beer bottle in hand. He wasn't recognized by Del; just a parasite.

"The bat?" said Del, feigning interest.

"Oh, ah...ah..."

"Cod," said the boy.

"Sorry–Cod. Cod, go in the camper and get that bat."

The boy set down his beer, stepped up into the spacious hover vehicle.

"Pull up a chair–beer?" offered Walpole.

"I'm all set, thanks."

Meanwhile a third man had appeared, emerging from the van lighting a cigarette. Mortimer Ficklebottom, he called himself. Skinny, long-haired, and Del had never seen him without his rumpled black top hat or his black vest with rawhide fringe down to the ripped knees of his jeans. He wore granny glasses also. It was a thing of fashion, Del didn't doubt, since these men certainly had the money for corrective medical treatments, but he also wondered if the various drugs they took had a damaging effect on their vision. Of LaKarnafeaux and his men, only Johnny Leng ever seemed somewhat vital or fit...and then, not electric, just blandly purposeful.

"Nice suit," said Ficklebottom. He carried an aura of seaweed smoke; it still wafted in the air from when the van door had opened.

"Thanks." Del heard a young girl's voice coughing hoarsely in the van.

"Here 'tis." The boy Cod leaped down from the van. In his hands he carried a baseball bat made from a blue-colored metal, scratched with silver nicks and gouges, with a black grip. He handed it to the seated LaKarnafeaux with both hands almost as if reverently presenting him Excalibur.

"Mm." LaKarnafeaux sucked out the last of his cigarette, flicked the stub, handled the bat with his smile fond and pink in the nest of frizzy beard. "Yup...here it is...Exhibit A."

"What happened?" Del felt obliged to ask the wizened storyteller.

"Well," began Eddy Walpole, surprising Del into turning his head, "Karny used to live with an aunt and her husband in a little suburb of Diamondcrest–a beautiful place, but beautiful places seem to have the worst slums, ever notice? It was a tough little shack town by a moss marsh…"

"Everything was moss," LaKarnafeaux interrupted. "In the corners, moss in your toilet, all in the closets. You could wake up with moss starting to grow in your mouth. Moist dark places," he chuckled-wheezed. "I ended up sleeping with a painter's mask on."

"You couldn't kill it, very persistent," said Eddy. "Anyway, a neighborhood kid had this big mutant dog–no hair, all bald wrinkles, a real monster. One day Karny was down under a sand cliff batting pebbles out into the marsh when this dog came along and started growling at him. Karny swung the bat at it and pounded the dirt to scare it off but that made it lunge."

LaKarnfeaux chuckled and wagged his head, pulling at his beard, bat across his knees.

Walpole said, "So Karny smacked it, brought it down. He was a rough boy, lemme tell ya. Couple more bonks and he kills it–and who should come along but the dog's owner. Now this kid was fourteen and he was no slouch either–not in that neighborhood. He was not too pleased about Fido, to say the least."

LaKarnafeaux was red from his chuckling, pulling more and more on his beard.

"The kid took out a knife and they went at it. Karny caught him a good one on the wrist and he dropped the knife, and then a few good swings and it was over. Nobody had seen. The dog and the boy went into the moss, and by the time they were dragged out they were slime balls. Nobody ever questioned Karny about it. Twelve years old."

"And I still have my bat," said LaKarnafeaux, using it as a cane to help him pull his groaning hulk up out of his lawn chair. Cod skipped over to take his arm and help but Mortimer waved him back. Del saw the word *Dozer* embroidered in gold on the back of the purple jacket. There were clothing racks set up for display outside the tent, with black *Dozer* t-shirts for men and women, flame-eyed skulls and monsters and demons adorning their fronts, Mukas and Flemm and Sputum and Sphitt t-shirts, and clear rubbery jackets made from the leather of giant amphibians, and of course the bulky, many-zippered white leather jackets favored these days by most *Dozer* types. Two boys of about fourteen going through the t-shirts had stopped their browsing to listen intently to LaKarnafeaux's story. He grunted, "It's like a good luck charm…whatever. A piece of nostalgia." He held the bat up loosely in one fist, more a nightstick or truncheon to him now than a bat, and smiled over at Del.

"You had a rough life," Del said, at a loss.

"It's been interesting. Ups and downs."

"Yours hasn't been all ups either, has it?" Eddy twinkled.

"No."

"See? We're all the same. Fundamentally."

"Where's the lovely wife this afternoon?" drawled Mortimer Ficklebottom, popping a tab on a can of beer. He motioned to the two boys at the clothing racks; they came to him grinning. Passed them each a beer and they thanked him eagerly. "Last night, boys–enjoy."

Del watched the boys, breathing slowly. "I don't know where she is. Around."

"You're a lucky man. She is something."

"Thank you."

"She is that," agreed Eddy Walpole. None of them had ever had a real girlfriend around, from Del's observation, except for Johnny Leng for the first week or so of the season but she had disappeared. Sometimes a dourly pretty woman with two children had come around but Del didn't know to whom she and they belonged, if anybody.

"Nice being married?" asked Eddy

"To her it must be," smiled Mort.

"It has its ups and downs," Del said.

LaKarnafeaux chuckled, leaning the metal bat against the side of the camper. "But you wouldn't undo it."

"No," said Del.

"Sure. It's like kids. It's tough, but you wouldn't give them away."

"You have kids?"

"Oh yeah," answered Eddy for him. "A son fourteen and a daughter eleven in Diamondcrest."

"Good kids," drawled LaKarnafeaux in a fond monotone.

"No kids?" asked Eddy

"No."

"Why not, with her?" Mort grinned.

"We move around too much. We...ah...I dunno. Need to be more settled."

"Why have kids anyway?" mused Cod. "They just weigh you down."

Ficklebottom laughed and slapped him on the back. "You tell 'im!"

The van door slid open again, again releasing a genie of iodine smoke, and down stepped an exceptionally pretty teenage girl with wild dark blonde hair streaked with a few tendrils of pink, wearing only pink sweat pants. Her breasts were heavy for a teenager, and she could see to it with a little money that they never sank too much, lost their fresh ripeness. She sneered over at Del with a disgruntled twisty pout which looked like it might be her constant expression, eyes half-lidded. Sixteen, seventeen?

"There's my wife," Mort snickered, swatting her on the bottom. She grumbled groggily and went to LaKarnafeaux the vacationing Santa Claus, who had lowered himself wheezing back into his lawn chair, a fresh beer and cigarette in hand. The girl curled cat-like in his lap, drawing her legs up tightly, tucking in her head. "Aww!" teased Mortimer.

"Shh," smiled LaKarnafeaux, stroking her tangled mane.

"She's a sweet one," Eddy smiled.

"Cute," Del said quietly. Cod stared enviously, hunger...a dog waiting to be tossed a scrap. It wasn't inconceivable. Del had seen some real tasty females around this tent, and with some of the biker gangs that came through, many of them ranging in their teens. Not often as stunning as the models or model-like beauties he'd seen on the arms of business executives in Kodju silk, or Chauncy Carnal and his ilk (riding in their luxury cars, sports cars, instead of on the backs of *Dozers*), but still very impressive. It sickened him.

"Hey, Karny!" Two boys had shambled up to the tent, the speaker wearing a black wool ski cap with a pom-pom, a Sphitt t-shirt and black sweat pants with the trapdoor open in back.

"Later, later." Eddy shooed them away like flies. The boys skulked away, tossing glances back at Del.

"Fucking twinkledinks," Mortimer sniggered. "We should take that jacket back—bad publicity!"

One of the two had been wearing a purple *Dozer* jacket. A good number of them hung on the clothing racks. *Dozer* didn't market them—LaKarnafeaux had them made specifically for him, Mitch had informed Del. A kind of trademark. His own line of clothing, it seemed, despite *Dozer's* embroidered name and logo.

"Let them be," benevolent LaKarnafeaux wheezed sleepily, still stroking his napping kitten.

"I should go," Del said. "I'm holding up business."

LaKarnafeaux's eyes lifted over the tops of his granny glasses, met Del's, containing that glow again behind the black fog. Del regretted his jab for a moment, embarrassed, but then didn't. The bearded man said, "Don't worry—stay and have a beer. It's last night."

"No thanks—I don't really drink."

"Your lovely wife came by a few nights this season and stopped in to have some beer, with Johnny Leng and the rest of us," said Mortimer Ficklebottom, smiling. He was twisting a piece of rawhide fringe around and around a finger.

Del stared a long moment at him. Inside he groped blindly for a casual response. They were having fun, watching him squirm—he was the boss, in their perception. The authority, with Mitch as his fist, the police. He was Kodju silk and they were white leather. He had had fame, and money, but he had never killed a man, as if he had thus earned his power dishonestly. They didn't respect him. He might have respected them if they respected him, all else aside. Not liked them, but at least respected their individuality. What was it Fickleasshole was prodding at now—his wife's drinking habits? Or more of his sexual innuendoes? Either way, Del bubbled with lava inside, but held onto a cool facade. Waxen but cool.

He flicked his gaze to Walpole. Twinkling. They were always glad to see Del, always welcomed him...because they clearly sensed how much he despised them. Perhaps they even realized what Mitch Garnet didn't–that Del hated Roland LaKarnafeaux and his friends even more than he did.

"Well," the words finally came after this too-long pause from a dependable mechanical portion of his brain, "Sophi really runs the show and she likes to...get to know people and foster good relations."

"I guess she does," Mortimer smirked, now drumming the fingers of one hand on the top of his top hat. Mortimer glanced over Del's shoulder. "Nice shoes," he said.

Del glanced over his own shoulder but only saw a boy in black clothes swept along amongst other people. He thought, they despise me too, in their amused way. Because Del had spoken out against drugs. Not too often, as often as he might have, because the recording company heads, his own producers and business managers, had strongly advised him against alienating too much of his potential audience. But he was still known for his stance. These men despised him for denouncing their god–it was nearly a religious conflict. It wasn't that Del considered himself superior. He had tolerated his own wife's occasional seaweed smoking. His brother had briefly been a small-time gold-dust seller, and it hadn't made him happy but he hadn't disowned him either. And Del had friends who had even tried snakebite and other extremes, who smoked weed constantly. But they had *souls*, they had respect for others and themselves–it was an attitude, a set of values and ethics and honor beyond the subject of drugs. Though he had firmly enforced a rule of moderation on his band during work and tours, his fellow band members all partied to some extent or another (but none extremely). He had fired some road crew people for extremes or for dealing, and this too had been publicized, maybe encountered by these men. But he didn't feel superior for not taking drugs any more than he would have felt superior to a man who shoots himself in the temple with a pistol. It just wasn't for him. Even little by little, the bullet of drugs could finally reach the brain, draining away too much life blood in the meantime. In his mind Del called back the horrifying face of the girl dead from vortex that Mitch had shown him, the insides of that shotgun-like wound still glowing with living, triumphant poison.

He looked at Walpole's face. Gold-dust, cocaine and vortex corroded the mucus membranes first—how did he know what work these men might have had done behind their smug masks to clean out, repair, rebuild? At least they had the money for it. Del switched to the girl curled fetus-like on LaKarnafeaux's ample lap. Peaceful smooth face, lips parted (though still with a disgusted curl of teenaged beautiful insolence).

"Where you headed this fall, if not down south?" Walpole inquired amiably.

"No place special. How about you?"

"Maybe to Diamondcrest for a couple months this winter. Lie in the sun, do some marsh fishing."

"Don't sleep with your mouth open."

Everyone chuckled or laughed, though it looked like LaKarnafeaux was beginning to doze, his great shaggy head sagging.

"Why don't you come down for a week this winter?" offered Eddy. "We have the room."

"You and your wife," said Ficklebottom.

"That's a nice offer. I'll mention it to her."

"Del." LaKarnafeaux lifted his head suddenly. "You had a song years ago—*Spirits on Wheels*."

"Yeah, I remember it. Goldy oldy."

"I liked it. It really caught the...ah..."

"The spirit of freedom," Eddy completed. "The *Dozer* spirit. Moving around, not letting your roots take hold, staying *alive*. Damn good song."

"Thanks. It was my first real hit. A little naïve, maybe, though."

"Naïve? Why should alive be naïve?"

"I don't know—maybe I just don't feel the same way anymore."

"You're only thirty-seven, Del—I have an uncle a hundred-forty-two. He's alive."

"Well, then I have plenty of time left to work on it," said Del.

"Well it's last night, why don't you get up on stage and do a song? Make a come back, man, do it tonight. Don't think about it—if you think about it too much you won't do it. One song. Do *Spirits on Wheels*, man–you'll feel *alive*, I'll guarantee you!"

"The kids would look at me and say, 'Who the fuck is this joker? Why isn't he wearing crotchless pants?'"

"So open your fly! Just kidding. Hey, the kids will look and say, 'Hey, who is this new guy? He's great! This guy is gonna be big!'"

"Sounds fun. Maybe next year."

"Aww, Del." Eddy pouted, but still smiled simultaneously.

He's mocking me, Del thought. He knows how I feel. He knows I can't do it. They love that I fell, they love my failure. I fell, they prosper. Their god is supreme, hardly scorched by my brief flare. They're so observant. Why did I stop to talk, why am I still here, why did I leave my pride in the trailer this morning?

Could Eddy Walpole read his mind a little? It wasn't that he spoke for LaKarnafeaux, finished his sentences, related his stories for him–he was simply the boss's representative, front man. Business manager, agent, publicity man. Either he was just very perceptive or he took some kind of drug which boosted telepathy a little. Rumors about were that one of LaKarnafeaux's other men, Sneezy Tightrope, who wasn't present, could see the future in dreams, see things in your past and read your mind, and had even been a carnival fortune teller for a brief while. A sensitive, no doubt aided by some illegal military drug. The memory of such rumors made Del squirm inside his waxen skin-case. He had to flee. He tried to shut his mind's emanations off, focus on Sophi or something. Mitch.

"Well, I'd better head over to the morgue and look into things."

"Okay, Del, nice talkin' with ya. You and the wife come by tonight at least for a minute, will ya?"

"We'll try–things might be busy."

"Try."

"Don't forget the wife. We'll all be here. Johnny and everyone," said Mortimer Ficklebottom.

Del ignored him, looked to LaKarnafeaux. He was deeply asleep. Reverently, the boy Cod took away his smoldering cigarette and his beer.

EVERYBODY SCREAM!

Perched atop Pearl Mason's small, egg-like pink plastic trailer was a nicked and worn pink plastic lion, resting on its belly with its maned head held proud above its front legs. The two, trailer and lion, looked to have been formed as one, but in actuality the pink lion was one of two which had once flanked the entrance of pink plastic stairs that led into the apartment building where Pearl had spent much of her childhood. The old tenements were to be torn down, Pearl had found, to make way for a parking garage, and she had purchased the better of the two lions–the other, more battered and spray-painted, went to a playground. It hurt Pearl to have the two separated–they had been brothers, to the child. But one could save only so many discarded animals. She'd already owned the trailer, but it was pale yellow; she'd had the new pink coat of plastic applied. It had since buckled in a few places and two seams had split open to show the yellow inside. That bothered her, she'd have to tend to that. This was her home, it was her. She had to be happy with it, proud of it. Yes–a person's home was a reflection of who they were.

Pearl let Mitch in. There were only attempts at partitions; except for the toilet it was all pretty much one room. A chipped old horse from the miniature merry-go-round hung on the wall of the livingroom section, a birthday gift from Sophi and Del Kahn. Pearl made Mitch a coffee at the kitchenette counter, her back to him.

She wore a loose-fitting, short-sleeved and knee-length dress, soft pink covered with a black web-like cracked pattern. Her skin was the smooth, unblemished white of alabaster, her upper arms plump and soft and hips and bottom ample inside the dress. Her shoulder-length hair was a thick and crazy nest of frizz and tight curls, a sparkling dark-blonde–natural, amazingly enough, though maybe courtesy of a recessive gene from some ancestor who had had their blonde hair chosen for it by its parents.

"I heard a lot of shooting earlier," she said. Her voice was a high, cutesy squeak, but not affected, and not inane-sounding, with an additionally cute stopped-up nasal quality. Natural, like her hair, like her skin, her full bottom, but she had put them all to her advantage. One had best utilize one's inborn qualities.

"A bunch of punks killed a mutant and accidentally killed a little boy with a stray shot. I had to shoot three of them."

"Great. Was that absolutely necessary?"

"Absolutely necessary? No. No. I could have smiled and walked away. I guess it's not necessary to stop anybody from killing somebody, so long as it isn't you...and hey, you don't even have to stop that if you don't want to, right? We're all gonna die anyway, right?"

"Me and my big mouth."

"I've got a twelve-year-old raped and strangled in the ice box and everybody thinks I'm the fucking psycho mad-dog–even you. That's what I get for risking my life for other people, huh?"

"I'm sorry, I shouldn't have said that. I trust your judgment, okay?"

"Then why'd you give me the old clichéd, 'Great–was it necessary?'"

"I just don't like to hear it. It's scary."

"Then don't bring it up next time. You don't want to hear it? Nobody wants to hear it...that's why they'll have to go on and on hearing it. 'Cause they don't wanna do anything about it. That's the thanks I get. I always hoped people would be proud of me."

"It might be necessary for you to kill, but we're supposed to be *proud* you kill?"

"No–proud of my job, of which killing is a part at times."

"I am proud of your work."

"Then don't start on me. You're in a cold mood. Why?"

"I'm not in a cold mood. I'm a little blue. It's last night; it was a good summer, I had fun, now it's over." The coffee was ready and an herbal tea for herself; she turned to face Mitch and he took his drink. Pearl leaned her back against the counter while she dunked her tea bag in her mug. Mitch tried not to let his eyes drop but they half-flicked–it was a near unavoidable instinct even now. She had kept her back to him an extra prolonged time, until it was no longer feasible–a habit she took on when she was in a cold, or angry, or blue mood.

EVERYBODY SCREAM!

"You have all these club dates lined up."

"I know, it's exciting, but I'm sacred. It reminds me of the old days."

"Fuck the old days–they're over. Nobody up here knows about the old days...that was another life."

"And your old days are another life, huh?"

Mitch started to get mad, but broke a smile and had to look sideways away from her eyes. "I know, yeah, yeah. But it sounded good."

"I'm excited but I'm scared. Here I've got so many people I know around me, so many friends. I'm part of a big thing. In clubs I'll pretty much be alone."

"I can understand that–it's always weird starting a new part of your life, it's traumatic...starting a new job or moving or getting married or whatever. It was hard for you giving up your old life and coming here, but now look."

"It wasn't hard giving up my old life," Pearl corrected, "it was just hard starting my new life. *Stage* of life," she corrected again.

"It was hard for me giving up the force. I loved my job–what I hated was the fucking disrespect and apathy and lack of compassion and fucking *evil* I encountered. No thanks, we got, no thanks. I had friends die in front of me...and no thanks. They say Car Thirteen men are martyrs. *All* forcers are martyrs now. Being a forcer in Punktown is the most thankless job around."

"So what'd you love about it–getting even?"

Garnet gave Pearl a long cold look. "Getting even? I was *protecting* people, not getting even. I can't even bring up my work a minute without you jumping on the mad-dog thing again, can I?"

"I just can't imagine what you *loved* about it."

"The challenge of doing good. Okay?"

"Okay–sorry–you sure are touchy about it."

"About getting my head shit on for doing good? Damn right I'm touchy. I don't apologize for it."

"I'm not shitting on your head, Mitch. Get the chip off your shoulder. Fuck the old days–remember?"

"Alright, okay, enough about that." Mitch sipped his coffee. "It's just that it kills me, though. Everybody loves Mr. Mauser on VT and he blows away scum left and right…the girls worship him. They love that macho stuff. But I'm real–I scare them."

"There are girls who're drawn to violent men–punks, gangers, bikies, mobbies, beaters, apes. If you want a girl like that go ahead and find one. You have more to offer a girl than violence, Mitch, but it's you who doesn't seem to realize that."

"That sounds good but it's stools."

"Then stop moping about how nobody's giving you medals for blowing people's heads off."

"You know what it is? People are always so concerned about dealing too harshly with criminals. People are afraid to *hate* criminals. I've had them shoot at me, look at me with the desire to kill *me* in their eyes. If everyone could know that feeling they'd realize you have to hate them in order to stop them."

"You said you were finished."

"That's right, you don't want to hear it. Hey, Pearl, it wasn't your twelve-year-old son who got shot by a stray bullet from some mindless fucking waste product, was it?"

"Your adrenaline is still up too high, I think. Why don't you go away and come back later? I'm agitated enough as it is."

"I'm agitated, too–you're right. That's why I came to you, to help me mellow down. But instead you question my actions."

"I'm sorry, I told you, I'm sorry. Accept my apology or leave, please. I have a show soon and I'd rather not have to take a relaxer to do it."

"Sorry, sorry, sorry," Mitch grumbled. "Forget the whole thing." As he sipped he spied upon her over the rim of his mug. His eyes lifted to hers; she had caught him peeking at the strange, pointed and bent projection which pushed out the front of her maternity dress. He, quick killer of men, had to pause and suck in the air for extra weight to ask her, "Will you make love to me?"

She rolled her eyes and sighed. In coming out of their roll her eyes looked hotly past him.

"Good. Fine." Mitch's voice shook a little. "I just wish you knew what it was like to need help, to ask somebody to make love to you and have them roll their eyes. It wouldn't make you feel too nice, I think."

"I don't ask people to make love to me."

"But I do, so I'm a freak. I'm sorry—I guess maybe I should leave after all."

Pearl looked at his eyes again as he started to move. "Wait."

"No. You'll give in because you think I'm bullying you with a guilt attack. I'm not. I'm just saying the truth I feel."

"I know. I'm sorry. But you know how I feel."

"That goes without saying, Pearl. I understand your problem."

"I'll be okay. Let's go to bed. We'll both feel better. I'm sorry."

"Are you sure? Now I feel stupid."

"Don't feel stupid. What do you expect from me? You say you understand my problem, and I told you I feel blue…"

"I'm sorry. I'm too impatient. We'll both feel better, like you say. Okay? Are you sure you don't mind?"

"I'll be *alright*," Pearl sighed. "I want to—I like it. I'll be okay once we do it…" She set down her mug on the counter. He set down his mug on the stove and followed her through the parlor section into the open bedroom section. Pearl was opening a vial of pills, popped one in her mouth and swallowed without water. Shook the vial. "Almost out."

"Don't buy them from LaKarnafeaux yourself. Send somebody. If I ever heard one crack from any of them about you buying sex drugs I'd have to kill 'em on the spot."

Garnet tossed his windbreaker on the parlor love seat and laid his pistol on it before following her. Near the bed she turned to face him. He ran his hands up her mushroom-cool arms, down again, took a step closer. The irregular bulge inside her maternity dress pressed into him a little. He took in her face and she took him in as he did so. Pearl was thirty-seven, but younger looking; she took good care of herself…no gold-dust in almost a year, and she rarely even smoked iodine, as seaweed was nicknamed. Her eyes were dark brown, narrowed when she smiled, looking almost mournful. Her predominant feature was the smallness of her mouth in her rather pronounced, but not overstated, jaw—the corners of her lips barely extended beyond the edges of her nostrils. When she smiled and bared her teeth the lips hardly stretched, the upper seeming only to lift–along with her narrowed eyes giving her the aspect of being in discomfort or slight pain. But she was beautiful; her face seemed unspeakably old-fashioned to Mitch, aided greatly by her fair complexion and hair. She would have turned many heads even without the projection from her mid-section.

A little nervous with her eyes on him, Mitch broke his gaze free on the pretense of kissing her forehead through some corkscrews of gold hair. He began bunching up her dress gently in his hands. The projection snagged a moment inside the dress, as if gripping it.

Both naked in bed, he lay half on her, kissing her throat and upper chest, spreading his fingers around a plump breast, softer than any substance he could think of, semi-amorphous but heavy. Pearl had the classic female body, Mitch felt, the body immortalized by Earth's ancient artists before the age of machines, and to which men were drawn even as women starved themselves in competition with each other. Pearl was an alabaster statute come to soft, moving life–she had stepped down from her oil-paint divan or idyllic pastoral scene. She was not long-necked, long-waisted, long-legged; she was short, compact, as plush as some Victorian divan herself, richly upholstered. Mitch gently swirled his tongue around her pale nipple. He kissed lower, down her belly. She turned her head to one side as if sleeping, eyes closed, and parted her legs for him. The drug was starting to effect her.

She wore soft makeup, she smelled of soft perfume–sweet, but not chemical. She did, it seem, endeavor to always remain stereotypically feminine to an almost inhuman degree. She had seen to it that she no longer had to menstruate, and the acidic inner smell which arose from intense, sweaty sex never rose strongly from her, even now with his lower face pressed into her secondary soft gold nest. She had had the dimpled or rumpled cushions of her divan reupholstered, firmed to a youthful smoothness, though without becoming a uniform plastic. She never crossed the line into glaring artificiality, but her care to hide her natural, animal aspects was telling. Her underarms were a perpetual soft bruised yellow from sweat against her so-white skin, a human detail she had missed but which clever artists like Renoir hadn't.

EVERYBODY SCREAM!

She moaned slightly. His tongue tired, Garnet switched to his fingers for the moment, every part of his body a prodding creature that wanted entry. She squirmed, moaned again, tossed her head to the other side. He used his tongue and fingers in conjunction. She was there; the sex drugs had liberated her. Mitch's hunger rose to a frenzy; he had never so weirdly, crazily wanted to engulf a person, consume them, take in every ounce of them. He kneaded her belly with a free hand. Rubbed his face from side to side. The pressure against his head tightened and relaxed alternately, she would arch and buck but he was a rodeo star, he wouldn't be thrown. Pearl began to coo steadily in her cute, high nasal voice. Together, they were frantic. His hand switched from her belly to the leg of her parasite, which all this time had been lying across the back of his neck. He ran his hand up and down the small bent leg, up over the buttocks which projected from Pearl's mid-section. He squeezed them.

Pearl thrashed to a climax, rolled onto her side to close and draw up her legs–shutting him out as she did at her pinnacle, abruptly, sometimes pushing him away as if afraid she would topple over some cliff edge. Her breathing began to slow but her eyes stayed shut. Mitch always liked to bring her to climax first; then he was free to finish off in his way, at his pace and rhythm. With her closed to him, he kissed her outer thigh and hip. Worked his way up to the parasite.

It looked as though a child or small being had dived or tripped head-first into Pearl's plush body and become stuck inside. Protruding from her mid-section on her left side were one arm and two legs of an undeveloped parasitic twin, not even as much as a conjoined twin. The arm was bent and unformed, the hand more a hairless dog paw. The legs grew from a set of buttocks, these smooth and round but a bit less than adult in size, the thighs also nicely shaped but undersized. The lower legs, however, rapidly tapered and the rigid feet were rudimentary like the hand. The legs were bent at the knee and could be unbent a bit, but had no independent motion other than the occasional twitch. Pearl could tell a person where she was being touched on the surface of her parasitic twin, and could feel pain if it were inflicted.

She had once menstruated from the secondary vagina hidden under the hanging protrusion, passed urine (but not feces, as she had no secondary anus) against her will, necessitating a kind of diaper, but had had her need to urinate as well as her menstruation surgically done away with.

Mitch kissed the smooth thighs, gently licked and squeezed the miniature of Pearl's bottom. Pearl didn't open her eyes or squirm; he went on. Gingerly, as if afraid to rouse her from sleep, he shifted and rubbed himself through the groove between the buttocks. The tiny unmoving hand brushed his belly. The twitching inside him became too much–he nuzzled under the buttocks at the door to the supernumerary vagina...pressed against it.

Pearl opened her eyes, twisted her body away; not abruptly, but meaningfully. "No, Mitch," she moaned.

"Sorry," he sighed, embarrassed. "I'm sorry. You wanna roll over?"

She did, dreamily, still recovering, and positioned herself on hands and knees while he mounted her from behind. It wasn't impossible to lie on top of her but it was easier this way. From this view her anomaly was much less visible, and there had been those men in her life who could only have intercourse with her this way.

Her own, natural buttocks spread out wide before him, against his belly, a white expanse he ran his hands over. He reached under her to knead her belly. His left hand dared to run up and down the outer buttock of the parasite. This much Pearl tolerated. You had to be careful. Her moods dictated her protectiveness, the sanctity of her sister...

Most Earth colonists were non-European in origin. Asians, Blacks and Hispanics formed the vast majority, or mixes of these, and what White blood did surface was again usually mixed with one or more of the other types to a lesser or greater extent. There were those groups who steadfastly remained closed, shut off, jealously fixated on an ethnic identity–some Black groups, some Hispanic groups, White or Asian. Other people were so mixed that even their great-grandparents wouldn't have known if they were more Black than White, or more Middle-Eastern than Oriental, and weren't really one thing more than another–all physical and cultural identification obliterated, except as Punktowners. In the end, whatever the case, most human Earthers were darker-skinned, darker-haired. White-Whites might be sought after as novel, but also scorned or mocked, called "Anglos" or "lily-whites" or "ghosts." This last seemed the most fitting.

Pearl's family had been intimidated by this situation–though they lived in a southern colony, far from a concentration like Punktown–largely due to their faith in a distant branch of Christianity. Genetically, her grandparents had had all previous traces of non-European characteristics, as were discernable, avoided in the design of their two sons and their two daughters–a clean slate to begin with afresh. Red hair and blue eyes. Some people were reviving blonde hair, but red hair was the forgotten color. It took: of Pearl's parents' children, two were redheads and she was a blonde surprise. But there were other surprises.

Pearl's mother had been having trouble conceiving due to all the pollution in the air, a common problem in her area, and had acquired an illegal fertility drug in view of her narrow chances of an inexpensive legal route. Pearl was the first child, and maybe because she didn't seem too bad–so pretty, so blonde–they had the next two, but even though her mother quit the drugs after Pearl the poison remained with her. After the third child Pearl's parents realized they couldn't successfully bolster the White population, and her mother had had her womb removed...a harsh action, but the part now offended her; she didn't want it in her, Pandora's box that it was. Despite this, however, she loved her children–all three, or ten, of them.

Helen, after Pearl, was also born with a conjoined twin, but this was a head, shoulders, and two arms emerging from Helen's mid-section, dangling down. Helen had another, even far less developed parasite growing from her back, and had confided in Pearl how she felt *outnumbered* in her body by the other two. Pearl had never felt overwhelmed by her twin, but then her twin had never attacked her. At sixteen, Helen's lesser parasite had to be removed due to a dangerous, degenerative virus throughout it. This wasn't easy for her mother, who'd had every parasite baptized along with their hosts. Thus it was that Helen's mother refused to have the remaining parasite removed even after it began having strange violent fits, longer and closer together, in which it became more active and seemingly more sentient, biting and clawing whatever part of Helen it could reach. Her legs became a raw mass of wounds. Only as the severity increased did the parents finally relent and allow the parasite to be drugged, in such a way as not to affect Helen.

At seventeen Helen ran away from home. She had the parasite removed with Pearl's financial help. She could now never go home again, killer of her own red-haired twin named Violet. She had married at seventeen, divorced, now lived with a man. She had been fixed so that she would never have children of her own.

The other child, Eve, was unluckiest. Four parasites of various development and sentience shared her tormented host body. She was insane, and lived in a special bedroom at home.

Pearl had left home around the same time as Helen, at twenty-one. Her dream was to become a singer. Pearl's mother was a wonderful singer, had often sung the pretty blonde child to sleep with lullabies...

It was in a brothel's lounge that Del and Sophi Kahn, having come down south last fall with the carnival, saw Pearl Handles, as she was called, sing on a little stage. They were impressed. *Del* was impressed. The husband and wife conferred, and approached Pearl Handles after her performance.

Pearl hadn't stripped, although she was by now a prostitute to support her gold-dust habit, which in turn, ironically, was destroying her voice. She did, however, while performing wear a lace black bra and skimpy panties cutting into her succulent white flesh, a garter belt and stockings, heels. The parasite wore similar panties, stockings, and miniature heels, other times a ring or a frilly red garter band. But when Pearl came to meet with these strangers backstage she folded herself away inside a black satin cloak. Del had been disappointed, but tantalized.

After Del had introduced himself, Pearl recognized him, God bless her. At their offer she wept. Del had to pay off the slimy brothel owners but it was a good deed, not that he expected Pearl's singing to double the carnival's take. Del brought along Mitch and the KeeZees—that helped keep the owners' greed in check.

Del and Sophi had been great friends this past year, so supportive. They had sent her to a therapist. She'd quit dust, cut down on weed. Not since leaving the bordello had she given in to accepting money for sex, though some had tried. For sex, however, she had to take stimulating drugs in order to feel aroused.

Life had been good, of late, but now she was apprehensive, afraid. This fall and winter she would start doing nightclub shows. Sophi's people, and Del and his of course, had lined some up for her already, for a slight agent's fee. But she had grown accustomed to the open air of the carnival stage, to seeing old people and children, people who didn't want to fuck her, fuck the parasite hidden inside her dress, unrevealed. Now it would be back into dark rooms of adults in the night. Drinking. Lust curling up from them like cigarette smoke. But never the stockings, heels, red garter again...never. Only once had Mitch asked, and he wouldn't dare again, though he ached for it, having also caught her old bordello stage act. Never would Pearl *Mason* humiliate herself and her sister, baptized Betty by her parents, again.

Because, despite running away, despite her horror at what her two sisters had experienced at home, despite leaving the church, despite becoming a prostitute, Pearl could not bring herself to have her parasite removed. She hadn't kept the parasite in order to join Tragic Beauty, the name of the so-called "freak whorehouse"...without Betty she might have just as easily, being white and blonde, joined a "straight" brothel. Whatever notions, beliefs, prejudices she had rejected when she left home, she couldn't cut away the idea, the *feeling*, that Betty *was* her sister. "No, *might* have been," some would say. But Pearl would lift a bent, stunted leg. "This isn't might have been. This *is*. This is as much Betty's leg as if she was a Siamese twin. She's my retarded sister. She's my sister in a coma. But she's my sister."

Garnet grunted loudly as he ejaculated, pumping hard. Sometimes Pearl would climax massively twice; this time she didn't. She had stretched out on top of her twin at the end, but taking the pressure off by leaning on her elbows, her head down and eyes shut. Finally Garnet rolled off her, lay panting on his side. His eyes closed, now Pearl lifted her head and opened hers. She stared at him. Just how fixated was he on her parasite? It couldn't be more than he was on her natural vagina, or breasts and ass, which he lavished attention on. She wouldn't rather that he be repulsed, would she? It was just that his tongue or penis, or hands or eyes, kept magnetizing back to it, again and again. Am I paranoid, or what? she would wonder. She did now, because of his prodding with his curious dissector's scalpel, eager to pierce the freak. Every man's dream—the extraordinary in a jaded world, the extra-endowed. Two vaginas in one body, two women in one, with only one head, one mind to trouble with—what a deal!

Except that this was Pearl's sister Betty, and though she couldn't really say she loved her—despite the fact that sometimes she cried and stroked her (feeling the sensation herself), thinking of the blonde twin that had almost escaped her—she did try to respect her sister. And yet she had broken down and let Mitch copulate occasionally with the parasite. With Betty, who had no say, could make no protest. Pearl felt it, and it felt good (though not great), so it was *her* body too, wasn't it? Her vagina, her nerves linked eventually to her brain? Betty had no brain. But Betty was her sister regardless of all. And Mitch had made love to Betty, also. Sometimes it made Pearl guilty, ashamed. Sometimes it made her feel something very close to angry jealousy. Cheated on. As if her natural body, *Pearl's* body, wasn't enough.

But maybe—since in a way Mitch made love to Pearl when he made love to Betty—Mitch made love to Betty even when he made love to Pearl. They were two and yet one. It was easier to let Mitch kiss, touch, even occasionally penetrate Betty than for Pearl to fully break up where she left off and Betty began.

All she could hope, staring at Mitch, was that he would have loved her even without the extra body, the extra vagina; he had grown furious when once she questioned this, but people could fool themselves. She hoped he truly loved her, as hard as it was to hope through the jungle of her fears and doubts and bitterness, because in the face of all this, even against her will, Pearl loved Mitch. Maybe it's Betty's will, she thought bitterly. Perhaps jealous again.

The day was well along. The progressively slanting goldenness of afternoon light, a warm flowing honey, gave the carnival a mellow nostalgic mood, metal and glass picking up the radiance and twinkling orange. Bern Glandston was a little bored but had kept himself occupied; there was a long, straight dirt track with full bleachers on either side and lined with walls of standing people, and for a while he had sat and watched a variety of activities. Tractor robots pulled great weights, spinning their wheels—an award given to the robot that dragged the heaviest load. A few farm robot tug-o-wars were quite amusing. The robot displays ended with a robo-demo derby, the garishly painted and numbered old machines going at each other with a mad, murderous mindlessness that was almost frightening, but comical, the arena crowd cheering the mechanical gladiators. Dust clouds swirled spore-like in the gilded light. The machines crashed and clanged, adding to the whole mechanized heaving pulse of the carnival.

Bern moved on, found the restroom shack and urinated, checked his spill of moussed spikes, with a damp paper towel wiped the dust from his scaled slippers. Under the door of the stall behind him Bern could see that a man was on his knees in front of another man. He casually listened while he wiped his shoes. It gave him a subtle deep crawling. Bern had gotten off with other boys at school a few times—no big deal. It was a chic treat, it delineated his sophistication. He thought he should quit looking so much, detached, and befriend some girl or girls around here. He had a touch of dust and a few iodine joints on him for added incentive. He'd seen quite a varied parade, didn't know which way to turn—they came and went so fast, a storm of butterflies and he a befuddled collector with net in hand.

He was tempted to snort some dust but forced himself to resist, save it, stepped out into the fresh air, a relief after the badly ventilated shack reeking of waste from dozens of varieties of life forms combined into one miasmic stew. The blood and brains had been mostly hosed off the partition. Bern set to wandering. He utilized his proud, confident walk. His dirty blonde hair, his blank blue eyes and blank good looks were taken in by girls he passed; peripherally he saw a young Choom girl look over her shoulder as he went by her. He didn't do Chooms, though.

He bought a candyfloss from a tall, pretty young woman and chatted with her flirtingly. "Don't you ever come out of that box?"

"No. I don't have any legs."

"Can I come in there and find out?"

"Ah, I don't think so." She smiled cautiously at his freshness.

"Come out and take a break—come *on*." He leaned across the counter and lowered his voice seductively. "Come and have a smoke with me…what's your name?"

"Toovish. Too."

"Come and smoke one, Too. Make your night go by easier."

"I don't smoke."

"Aww."

"Sorry, I don't. Thanks anyway."

"You don't smoke. What's the world coming to, Too?"

After a little more fruitless flirting Bern drifted on. It wasn't evening yet and he still had plenty of time before Pox showed up. So his sauntering stroll was as calm and confident as ever.

Eventually he came upon a ride which was novel and intriguing but he couldn't participate because he didn't want to undress or wear a shower cap, though he did observe it from the outside for a while, and what he could see of the line of people entering it. Grinning, he lit a cigarette. He wasn't alone in watching; this was a display in itself.

Noelle and Bonnie had joined Pearl Mason's audience late and left early, at Bonnie's insistence. "Borrr-ing," she said out of the corner of her mouth, leading Noelle away. "Life is too short to stand around listening to a pregnant woman sing mindless sugar songs. I tell ya, girl, you step out of the skyscraper shadows and you're in hicks up to your neck."

The ride called Jonah's Whale compelled them; compelled Bonnie, anyway, Noelle being a little timid, squeamish maybe. The great aquatic mammal lay on its belly, high and long, awesome and a bit scary to approach despite its trance. All this building-like bulk was one body, one life? The black, dully shining hide was dry, a little cracked in certain places, with some parasitic lesser animals still affixed but long since turned to a crust. Great white patches, also, from long-dead sea fungi. Kids had spray-painted on the whale creature in a few places, this graffiti yet to be cleaned off. Also, someone had stuck bumper-stickers on its hide, something about an animal rights organization. These were often peeled off, but stubbornly returned.

The cavernous mouth loomed open, toothless–Noelle wondered how they got it to remain that way. Two little boys drew near the mouth, the older of them suddenly pushing the smaller one inside. He screamed. The older one dove in after him, the huge mouth dropped shut and Noelle flinched, giggled nervously.

A balloon-like C-shaped structure lay parallel to the whale on its far side so as not to obstruct it, one end of the C at the mouth and the other at the end of the funnel-like tail. The line gradually advanced enough that Bonnie and Noelle could enter the balloon. Inside, a man gave them each a gym bag containing a shower cap and a plastic pair of disposable swim trunks. He chewed gum, bored, drew a curtain. Bonnie stripped down naked, tucked her hair inside the shower cap. "I'm not wearing the diaper–I'm not squeamish. Or shy."

Though rather less enthused, Noelle undressed, zippered her clothing and shoes inside the gym bag. She put on the shorts, their three openings elastic banded to keep out liquid. Bonnie drew back the curtain and passed the bored man their bags. Noelle wondered if she should have tucked her wallet in the trunks.

They stepped out of the balloon-like changing station and waited at the whale's closed mouth, in the plain view of those gathered about. A few whistles, two teenage boys applauded and hooted. Noelle hugged her chest, took two steps back into the balloon building's doorway. A few boos. Bonnie clucked her tongue at her.

From the massive animal came odd rumbling sounds that seemed to make the very ground vibrate, deep muffled gurgling noises like the simultaneous flushing of numerous toilets. Noelle's eyes followed some thick cables which ran from the animal's body back into the balloon, where the bored man stood. There had been a control panel, and monitor screens showing strange things happening inside the whale, which the machinery kept alive out of its watery environment. The machinery also kept the animal comatose, activated and manipulated its inner functions. The whale was a gigantic living, or semi-alive, puppet.

A final mounting gurgling, a loud liquid whoosh of expulsion, the great maw opened and Noelle instinctively hugged herself tighter. Bonnie didn't hesitate, squatted deep inside the mouth, sat herself down, stretched out on her back with one ankle hooked over the other. She hugged herself, but only out of fear of breaking a bone, wrenching a limb, though that wasn't common. She had left enough room for Noelle to gingerly step into the mouth (quickly, afraid it would slam down on her skull) and lie on her back in a similar pose, Bonnie's head just beyond Noelle's feet. Noelle hoped she didn't hurt her friend through their closeness, although that usually only happened when people went in side by side. "I wonder what it would be like to go through fucking?" Bonnie called back, excited.

The mouth slammed shut, the outside light was cut off but an interior series of artificial lights came on. What if it malfunctions, Noelle was thinking, fear approaching dizzy horror, what if the full digestive process goes into action? A yawning sound, the hideous slick surface under her naked back began to tremble. The whale abruptly swallowed, shivering pudding-like flesh closing around Noelle and a gush of liquid washing over her. She tried to cry out behind her clamped mouth, squeezed her eyes shut as she was violently sucked along. Ahead of her somewhere Bonnie was laughing-screaming through the fluid gushing in her face.

Feet-forward Noelle was sucked upwards through a dark chute, then down into a large artificially lit white room of roaring fluid, on through a twisty pipeline which conformed itself to some extent to Noelle's form. Her eyes were open but blinking, her mouth open a little behind her cupped hand. Amazingly she spotted one of those animal rights stickers stuck to the slick inside of one of the bladder-like lighted rooms she was whisked through. A black substance like shaving cream was suddenly extruded through the walls of the next chamber and enveloped Noelle, her eyelids reacting in time to protect her. She no longer heard Bonnie ahead, or anything but the sounds of the whale. To go through here while on heavy drugs, she numbly reflected for a moment, would drive one insane. And it was done, of course, every day and night.

EVERYBODY SCREAM!

She picked up speed. A new spray of liquid showered away the black foam, she rocketed through an underground river, the current powerful, and suddenly she was launched into the outer air from the dilated tail opening. Noelle found herself lying on her back in a net, staring up at the blue sky, people laughing and cheering or hooting. She was disoriented; it took a second or two to adjust back to reality. Embarrassed, she rolled over and shakily, awkwardly climbed out of the net. She spit fluid onto the ground, coughed, snorted at the fluid in her nostrils. Bonnie was waiting for her in the other opening to the balloon, laughing, twisting a finger in her ear. "Pretty wild, huh, girl?"

"Pretty something," Noelle murmured, and almost retched, gagged, spit out more of her own saliva, afraid that it belonged to the whale. She followed Bonnie inside where a second bored man, not phased by their undress, handed them their gym bags. Further in the C there were a few shower stalls, which some didn't employ but Noelle and Bonnie did. After drying themselves with towels, they encountered a young black-haired man, naked and dripping clear fluid.

"That's pretty great on gold-dust," he said.

"Are you?" Bonnie smiled, stepping slowly into her panties.

"Yeah."

"I wish I was."

"Well...why don't you take some and go through again? My treat."

"Oh, excellent–where?"

"My car? In the lot."

"Do you have to pay to come back into the fair?"

"You can have them stamp your hand, I think."

"Wonderful."

"How about you?" the man smiled at Noelle, who was dressing with less luxurious slowness than Bonnie.

Noelle didn't want to get in the way. "I'll pass. I'll be around."

"You sure, girl?" Bonnie breathed, still exhilarated. Her nipples stretched out hard like the heads of eager little animals. "I don't want you to get lost or bored or something. I won't be too long."

114

"Can I talk to you a minute?"

"Sure. Excuse me a sec, ahh…"

"Moussa. Certainly–go ahead," smiled the dark, charming young man.

Noelle drew Bonnie aside, whispered. Moussa ducked into one of the showers, luckily. "Bonnie, be careful. Is this guy alone or with friends? If he's alone that's kind of funny, isn't it?"

"Why? He's just looking to make new friends, like we are."

"Just be careful."

"Alright, *Mom*. I'm not stupid, Noelle."

The second bored man reappeared. "Come on, no loitering."

"We're waiting for our friend to shower, okay, bumpkin?"

"Don't mouth off to me, little girl, just move along."

"Blast off, hick."

"Bonnie," Noelle said.

The man glowered, eyes bulging in their sockets like balloons filled with rage. He was tall and wide and wore an army coat. Noelle became afraid. "Move along, you fucking fish. I won't say it again." And then he turned and stalked away, visibly shaking with fury.

"God," Bonnie muttered, a little cowed, "what a psycho. I thought he was gonna kill me."

"See?"

"See what, see?"

Moussa emerged, his smile ever beaming. "Good, I was afraid you'd sneak off on me."

"I wouldn't do that to you, Moose," Bonnie smiled seductively. She addressed Noelle. "Are you sure you don't mind, girl? Just an hour…maybe you'll run into the guys."

"Maybe. Alright." Actually, Noelle invited the opportunity to be by herself, out of Bonnie's overpowering aura. Only a tiny bit insulted to be discarded in favor of free drugs and an unknown penis. She had quickly grown used to that from Bonnie Gross. "I'll probably be in that mall building poking around."

"Great–I'll look there first."

EVERYBODY SCREAM!

The three of them left the balloon the way they'd come in, but Bonnie and Moussa went one way and Noelle went another.

Noelle thought she saw the glazed eye of the whale turn to follow her but after a second look dismissed it as her imagination.

A young man fell in beside her. He wore black. Noelle's downcast eyes took in his beautiful silver and black scaled shoes before she glanced over at his face suspiciously.

"Hello," he said, "I'm Bern. How was that Jonah ride?"

"Icky. Next time I'll just ride through the sewer system...at least that would be free."

Bern laughed. "I thought so–that's why I didn't go through. What's your name, anyway?"

"Noelle."

"Noelle, you must be hungry after your harrowing ordeal."

"Not really. I won't be eating for a while."

"Well I'd bet a nice cold beer would soothe your nerves right now."

"Um, no thanks."

"How about a snort to mellow you out, or a snort to pick you up?"

Boy, Noelle thought, Bonnie should have waited a few minutes to meet this one; he was better looking and dressed like a male model, black lipstick and all. "No thanks, I'd really just like to be alone right now."

"Alone? This is a *fair*, Noelle, you're supposed to be having *fun!*"

Yeah, Noelle thought, fun like getting your black lipstick all over my tits and your bone in my mouth, right? "I'd really just like to be alone. Anyway, I'm meeting some friends soon...I'd like to be out where they can see me."

"Aww–are you sure? Just a smoke. Half an hour."

She looked straight ahead as she walked. "No thanks."

Bern sighed. "Alright, Noelle. It was nice talking to you. Hope to see you around."

"Thanks anyway."

Bern stopped walking beside her, watched her walk away. Damn–she was a sweet one. She submerged into waves of people, out of sight. Oh well. Bern turned, eyes moving in a sweep, flicking from one female to another as if he were changing VT channels in search of one to settle on. Plenty of time, but he still felt a bit stung, discouraged, finally. Two offers of drugs, and nothing. What *were* things coming to?

Sophi sat at a battered plastic table in the screened-in beer garden, a mug of mead and paper plate of dilkies at her elbow, a newspaper spread before her on the sticky table top. There was a two page spread of photos of the fair, a visual summing-up of the season. Happy-faced children behind bushes of candyfloss, screaming teenage girls on the Double Helix, a prize-winning cow gazing uncomprehendingly into the camera. Pearl on stage passionately singing, her narrowed eyes mournful, mic in hand like the painting of Del on the Screamer, her twin wearing a special sling inside her maternity dress to hold the three limbs close to the buttocks, which made for a more rounded and less conspicuous kind of bulge.

Idly Sophi paged more toward the paper's front. An odd story caught her attention. Last night some strange creature of monstrous proportions had been sighted clinging to The Head, an orbital asteroid sculpture created three decades ago by the artist Cyrex Rendiploom, portraying on one side a human man's face (howling in outrage or dismay down at the planet Oasis, like the man in the moon with a missile in his eye in that silent film by George Méliès) and on the other side a corresponding gape-mouthed skull visage. Scientists were investigating. A photograph showed a spider-like animal, many-legged, barbed, black, clinging to the globe's skull side, its legs spanning the entire skull surface. My God, it must be gigantic! Sophi marveled. The Head could be plainly seen at night when it was fully catching the sun's rays...and tonight it would be full. And the skull side would be in view, the paper further related. So it was that the mysterious giant animal would be visible to the naked eye tonight as The Head climbed the sky, to reach its apex around eleven.

Had it been hurled through space by some distant exploding ship or planet, grabbing hold of the first object that came within reach, or had it placidly swum through space to this inviting resting spot, or materialized there from another dimension? Even before she read it in the article, Sophi remembered last year around the end of summer hearing about a strange secret colony which officials had broken up on that skull side of The Head. The camp belonged to a group of several dozen Bedbugs, as they were nicknamed scornfully, scorned because they had this aura about them that made people nervous. They were an extra-dimensional beetle-like race, which used a strange sort of vehicle on an odd track to move from one dimension to another, the dimension determined by the speed of the vehicle and the pattern of the track chosen amongst the many variations offered by their large train beds. They had one train bed here in town. Whether this secret group had come from Punktown or directly from their own dimension they never revealed, nor their purpose for beginning construction of a bizarre mechanical temple inside a cave burrowed on The Head's skull side.

Since then officials had twice arrested groups of affluent teenage humans who had had themselves illegally teleported to the cave, where they held wild parties and odd rituals. A security team on rotating shifts was ever present on the asteroid sculpture now. Except that since last night, all contact with them had been lost.

Sophi also thought of the mysterious giant leg which had appeared right out of the air here at the fairgrounds two years ago. It was somewhat similar to the legs of the spider thing; insect-like and jointed. It had remained hovering and unmoving in that spot through carnival season and empty cold season, and had become one of the carnival's attractions, the first year having materialized behind the Dreidel but later given more room to be viewed and wondered at.

A hand touched the back of her head, stroked her hair. Sophi started a bit and twisted around at the waist. Disgust filled her, and resentful anxiety, like the immediate opening and spreading of a parachute. Johnny Leng withdrew his hand as if warned by her expression, but his smile didn't falter. "Hi, doll."

"Hi, scum. Would you mind not doing that?"

"Doing what? Breathing? Speaking? Existing?"

"Touching me. But you can stop existing, too, if you want."

"Can we join ya?" With Johnny Leng was Sneezy Tightrope.

"You can, but I won't enjoy it."

"Life isn't always enjoyment." Johnny took a chair opposite Sophi and Sneezy sat at a table end. "Sneeze, before you get comfy wanna grab us some beers? Another mead, gorgeous?"

"No."

"Get her one in case, Sneeze. You should Sophi...you're more sociable when you've loosened up a little. You're a tense person."

"Quit fucking with me, Leng." Sophi watched Tightrope head to the counter. "I mean it."

"I have quit fucking with you–that's why I've been so blue. What's the problem, hon? Did your hubby start sniffing us out?"

"No. I just don't want anything to do with you, can your pathetic bloated ego handle that concept?"

"But where did our love go wrong?" Leng cracked. "What happened, what changed?"

"I sobered up. You must have sobered up before and found out you did something stupid and disgusting like vomiting on the rug, right?"

"It's been my experience and observation that when you're drunk you do things you want to do but are too inhibited to carry out otherwise."

"Look, I was depressed and drinking and I just wanted to be fucked by a mindless animal such as you. It was primal lust, pal, that's it. It was an escape, like drinking. I'm capable of such regretful overindulgence."

"Twice?"

"So I'm a slow learner. There won't be a third."

"Oh, so your depression is all cleared up then, is it?"

"My feelings and personal life are none of your business, ass-wipe."

"Are you guilty? When your husband is out here fishing every night right under your nose?"

"Mind your own business, Leng, I won't say it again."

"Let him go on making a fool of you. For a couple minutes there you had some guts, you were looking after yourself. What are you, a masochist or something? He doesn't respect you, he doesn't know a good thing when he has it in his hand."

EVERYBODY SCREAM!

"Oh, but you'd appreciate me, huh? You'd be a wonderful husband to me, Leng, and never be unfaithful, right? Let me up. What happened to that pretty little girl I saw you with at the start of the season, where'd she go? I heard tell she was sporting a swollen upper lip with a cut in it, at the end. Did you appreciate her a little too hard?"

Johnny Leng was not a gentle-looking man. Short, muscular, he was deeply tanned a reddish color from the sun rather than tan booths, with an outdoorsy roughness to his features. His mouth was broad and thick-lipped, his eyes narrow with an almost oriental fold, his black hair short and mussed. White t-shirt and jeans. He was brutish, primal. The sun, hard work as a young man, time spent in the military, time spent in prison had squeezed the weak milk of sensitivity out of him. He was looking even less gentle by the second. The tight compressed sneer to his lips finally let words past, having held them long enough to drug them into calmness.

"You're mad at me because you're mad at yourself and you can't face it. It's you you're disgusted at. Be a bitch to me. But what I did with you wasn't a fraction of what your husband is out there doing, right now probably. How disgusted are you at him?"

Sophi glanced past Leng at Sneezy, still in line. His eyes were on her and he was smirking. Pot-bellied inside his tropically flowered shirt, tails hanging out over his baggy white shorts, he was short and tanned but the too-dark shade popular among tan fanatics, with his high, balding forehead an unhealthy shiny red in patches. A little black mustache and a series of chinless jowls gave his smug little smirk more of an irritating self-amused quality, to Sophi. His eyes echoed the smirk, which in turn echoed the sly, smug expression so often worn by both LaKarnafeaux and Walpole. It was uncanny, the exactness in tone. Of the friends, only Leng ever appeared to show naked anger. But it was Sneezy Sophi felt the most disturbed by, in light of the rumors about his alleged extrasensory abilities. Some said he only picked up on general moods, emotions. Others said he could read your mind like a book, delve into your past, dissect your present, forecast your future. That big, burned forehead looked so heavy that it was this perhaps which bunched up his jowls.

Sophi folded her paper shut, polished off her mead. As she set down her mug and her rear left her seat Leng clamped a hand over her wrist. Sophi flared her eyes into his. "Let go of me, scum."

"Is your husband scum?"

"Leave my husband out of it. Husband or not, I wouldn't want you to touch me again."

"People's hungers don't change. And your husband's never will, so stop hoping for it."

"I don't."

"That's not what Sneezy tells me."

Horrified, Sophi flicked her eyes to the line at the counter. Tightrope's eyes and smirk were still trained on her. She jerked at her arm but Leng held it pinned. "Let me go."

"You don't have to love me, bitch...I'm not naïve enough to hope for that...and even though I'd love like hell to nail ya to the mattress again I can live without it–" he squeezed her wrist harder "– but don't ever call me scum again, unless you're willing to call yourself scum...and your husband, too."

"It isn't that you fucked me that makes you scum. You're scum anyway. For the last time, let me go."

Johnny Leng cocked his head and tried on a broad, leathery smirk in the general character of LaKarnafeaux's, but less whimsical. "I want one more fuck or else I'll leak it to your husband about us. I'm sure not afraid of him, so what have I got to lose?"

"Do it. He knows I've cheated on him before. Now let me go." There was a tin ashtray near her plate of dilkies, her cigarette smoldering in it. Sophi took up her cigarette and poised the orange tip over Leng's hairy wrist.

He didn't let up the pressure or the smirk. "You don't hate me as much as you think. You still want me. Lust and hate go hand in hand."

"You couldn't be more wrong, Leng–next time ask Sneezy for a more thorough analysis." Sophi pressed the cigarette tip into his flesh.

Leng looked down at his arm, pouted, released her wrist. He rubbed the spot calmly. "Next time don't stub the thing out; you hold it to the skin *lightly*, so it keeps on burning." Still smiling. "I know–I've done it before."

EVERYBODY SCREAM!

"Stay away from me. One more word to me about this subject, any trouble whatsoever, and you and your fellow pigs are out of my carnival for good. Understand–*scum?*" Sophi flicked the cigarette butt at Leng's face and whooshed out of the screened-in tent even as Tightrope finally made it to the table with a tray of drinks.

Sneezy said, "She's afraid of me. It's strong. More so than she is of you. Can you imagine? I never killed anybody in my life." He snorted-chuckled, beer foam on his mustache.

Sipping his own beer, Leng wagged his head, amused. Sophi would have been a lot more afraid of him if she'd known that his swollen-lipped girlfriend who had stopped coming around was right now an unidentified corpse at Paxton police headquarters' morgue with both her eyes shot out.

As the afternoon sun further receded the carnival increasingly made up for the loss with colorful lights, encrusting the rides like jewels, and drawing more and more people, more people than in the day, like mesmerized moths. Heather Buffatoni's father had dropped her, Cookie Zalkind and Fawn Horowitz off in the parking lot, to return and pick them up at eleven. At the sight of magical, multifarious colors against the lowering sky, at the crest of the hill like a mystical city, Fawn's spirits lightened and she put behind her the fight with her mother, her mother's refusal to give her any more than twenty munits, and ten of that to be her allowance for next week, in advance! She had borrowed ten more from Heather's sister's fiancé, a softy.

Though most of her friends were of primarily Jewish heritage, Heather was Fawn's best friend and she had other primarily Italian friends, because when their station in life was high enough to minimize what Fawn considered to be an innate crudeness, they were of a like nature in ways to her Jewish friends…aggressive, strong, determined to succeed in life. Heather and Fawn had met last year in the same high school Modeling and Beauty class, in which nine out of the thirty-five girls had been of mostly Italian blood, a high percentage considering the heterogenous nature and endless mixed-breeding of society. None of the nine were in any sense beauties and only two or three were by a conventional standard truly pretty, Heather being one. She had a round and pleasant face, with short curly hair dyed blonde and a sexy figure destined for plumpness if future diligence wasn't maintained. Oddly, perhaps out of relaxed confidence, it was Heather who was the least egocentric of the nine Italian girls, and the quietest. The greatest two differences between Heather and Fawn was that Fawn had only tried smoking seaweed, whereas Heather had embraced it (and maintained a separate group of friends to share this pursuit with), and Fawn had necked with a few boys but was a virgin (except for her pet bug Herbie), while Heather had many exciting stories to tell.

They paid their way inside, and immediately met another group of girls from school: Colleen Narcisi from Modeling class, and Rena Tushkin and Diana Talmud. These girls had already attracted a few boys from school who'd been roaming in a separate group, shaven-headed hulking sportsters. One of them whom Fawn had told Heather she liked smiled at her and she cringed against Heather's arm in pleasure, squealing softly in her friend's ear. But minutes later as they noisily, excitedly chattered Fawn grew bitter at the way Colleen kept punching the boy on the arm and wrestling with him, tickling him, making contact in every childish way to secure his attentions. Fawn was also jealous of Colleen's white leotard-tight sweat pants with the rear flap fully open. Her mother forbade her from wearing such pants even with panties on under the open or partly-opened flap. Rena wore red pants, also with the flap open and without underwear. Diana, prettier, was also more reserved. These three were too attractive, too much competition…Fawn wanted to get away from them now that Colleen had staked her claim on the cute sportster.

Fawn urged Heather to buy tickets with her so they could begin right away on the rides, and Heather accompanied her to one of the ticket booths near the entrance while small hyperactive Cookie lingered to chat animatedly with the others.

Mitch jogged his way to the front gate. One of his people, Dingo Rubydawn, a Choom, had bleeped him that there was a potential problem with a group of Red Jihad who wouldn't give up their arsenal.

EVERYBODY SCREAM!

There were fourteen of them, only three being females. The only obvious difference between the females, veiled and black-garbed like ancient nuns, was their height. Two were children, but from the age of four they were required to hide their hair; at five females were considered adult and at nine could marry...so these might have been wives taken out for a night's entertainment on the kiddie rides.

The boys, ranging from sixteen (when a man could take a wife) to about twenty, were not, Mitch was relieved to see, the army-uniformed bearded clones who wore the red martyr bandanas of the considerable warrior caste. The huge posters they left around town showed a mass of these types approaching the camera in waves, their faces turned in profile to look at something. At first glance this poster seemed to show the same man reproduced over and over again, until you saw slight variations such as the height of the gun barrel held in front of their chests. Mitch had seen more variation in the personality of cats, easily, and even in simple-minded cows, than he had in his experiences with the Red Jihad cult. This, he'd said as a policeman after a few dangerous near-confrontations, was what would happen if you gave insects a religion.

The boys were starting beards, all wearing white shirts and dark pants. The shirts, never washed, were thickly crusted brown with dried blood–their own. The Red Jihad had a religious ritual by which a wound was opened in the top of a boy's head at sixteen and the bleeding was a purification, a cleansing shower. "Miscreants," "unbelievers" and "infidels" jokingly referred to this as a holy hole, and it was reopened every year on the man's birthday. A complex machine which judged the man's height in order to safely deliver the automatic gashing had been developed to keep up with each day's steady flow. Herds of men poured through like cattle to be slaughtered, the smell of blood adding to the analogy. Islam was the fastest growing Earth-oriented religion, and Moslems numbered in the billions on Earth, but many of them disowned the extremist Red Jihad schism–which despite this fact was growing steadily itself. No one but Red Jihad members inhabited the harsh planet called the World of Faith. The governors of Oasis, both Earth colonials and Chooms, were becoming restless with the growing hordes of Red Jihad and feared that one day they would overwhelm Oasis as they had their World of Faith, or at least grow numerous enough to present the constant problem they presented on far Earth. There had already been acts of terrorism here, thus far mostly directed at extensions of the Canon, rather than political targets, over the past few decades. There had been a group of Red Jihad students occupying a tenement building on Forma Street, and although they had been fairly well behaved Mitch had learned to treat them as if they all wore explosives strapped to their bodies even when they didn't.

Dingo and two of the town-hired uniformed men from the Fog Agency had the group detained peacefully off to one side, their tickets already purchased. Mitch took inventory: five automatic assault rifles with grenade launchers and laser targeting scopes. Holstered pistols on all eleven males, plus one with a grenade belt. Rough kids, but still not one of the hover cycle-riding warrior bands. "I'm Chief of Security," Mitch said as he strode up to them, flipping open his badge. "What's the problem, folks?"

The apparent leader sneered at him, eyes bulging. Ants can't smile, thought Mitch. "I have seen others with guns go unharassed! We will not have our weapons taken from us and we will not be denied the right to enter!"

"Alright, now just listen to me a second. We just wanna take the rifles, okay? We're not singling you out...we confiscate what we feel to be unnecessary firepower...you still have enough for self defense. Automatic fire and grenades create too great a risk to bystanders; we already had a boy die today..."

"Our enemies are many—we will not go about as sheep." The leader, Garnet noticed, had some blood crusted in the channels of his ear, his hair stiff and matted. He'd had his birthday recently, and probably picked at the scab as these younger men were likely to do to keep the blood flowing. Maybe his ten-year-old bride, her dark and lovely eyes peering up at Garnet timidly over the top of her hijab veil, found his bloodied appearance sexy.

"Well look—why don't we collect all the rifles but one? You can take turns guarding one-another while the others are having fun. That sounds reasonable, doesn't it?"

EVERYBODY SCREAM!

"We don't have to bargain with you, demon ghost!" snarled a sixteen-year-old, bayoneting a finger at Garnet, his face more furiously stamped even than that of the leader.

The Red Jihad were said to be unafraid to die–to die for their God was the ultimate honor–but Mitch was willing to bet that he could easily make this scrawny punk *very* afraid to die if they were left alone together. Or at least, make him beg to die for a reason other than to serve his deity. Mitch wanted to spit in his face. To spit in a Red Jihad's face was to cause him to become sullied forever, unable to enter heaven. Mitch ached to find out if the rumors were true that the Earth government had robot satellites that could fly in and spray the cities of the World of Faith with artificially-produced but organic, actual saliva, in the event that such measures became necessary. That would dampen their passion for martyrdom. But Mitch contained his hatred.

"Look, you don't need all that firepower in here."

"People mock us, challenge us," the leader said.

"I know, that's what I'm afraid of. But we take their big guns, too."

"We do not surrender our guns!" snapped the furious teenager.

The leader raised a staying hand. "We will give you all our rifles but one. But the pistols and grenade belt stay with us."

"No grenades, please...come on. This isn't a battleground, it's a *carnival*."

"I will compromise only if you compromise!" the leader growled.

"Okay, okay, okay." Garnet held up both hands. "Fair enough. Just take it easy in here, alright? Everybody's here for fun, that's all."

Dingo collected and tagged the four rifles, locked them in the gate shed's large safe-like weapons rack. The Red Jihad members moved along, sullen and proud. Mitch met the eyes of the little girl again. He couldn't read them but they weren't hostile. Red Jihad women who refrained from wearing the veil or dressed indiscreetly, colorfully, often had acid thrown in their faces by bands of idealistic teenage boys such as this one. Mitch felt like gathering her up in his arms and running off. He had a ten-year-old niece who loved him and drew happy-faced horses for him and who smiled without a veil.

Red ants, he thought, scowling after them. They reminded him of the Bedbugs, who, though less violent, were just as mechanical, just as devoted to their mysterious faith, and just as closed off from all other thought, tribes and beliefs, even as they moved amongst them.

Some great philosophers, great religions urged that one must undermine their identity to liberate the spirit, to release the selfish hold on one's self. But if this were the way the spirit was liberated, then the spirit was a fanged murderous demon and he'd rather be obsessed with his own particular, idiosyncratic, individualistic/materialistic being. Not being a Christian and not meaning it in a Christian way, Mitch nevertheless thought that the Red Jihad branch might have spirits but they didn't have *souls*. Whether the soul was an actual existing energy or state, or else only an abstracted symbolic concept, he would leave to the Theta researchers, but the word still served its purpose for him...

Fawn folded up her long strip of tickets, counted off the amount needed for the Screamer, the first ride which had caught her attention, mostly because of the loud music and the DJ's chatter: "Okay, we're about ready to speed it up now...you look ready to me. Are you ready to go faster?"

A weak chorus of, "Yeah!"

"I didn't *hear* that! I said, do you wanna go *faster?*"

"Yeah!"

"Alright, then...everybody *screeeam!*"

Fawn looked up into the face of a passing boy in a dark-stained shirt, wide eyes blazing at her. He spat a glob of mucus in her face, then spat out the words, "Satan's whore!"

"Hey—oh God! You..." But Heather gripped her arm.

"Easy. Don't look at 'em. I'll get ya some water and napkins."

"Blasting freakies," Fawn moaned, horrified at the substance on her skin. "They should spit in Colleen's face if they want to get mad at our kind." The little ten-year-old glanced over her shoulder back at her and Fawn wanted to give her an obscene gesture but restrained herself.

After the Screamer, Fawn and her two companions rode in the hover bumper cars, and after that they found a double dissecto booth. Fawn fed a munit into a slot, one of the doors folded open, she stepped inside with little Cookie. One munit a minute. The dissecto booth was actually a variation on a medical scanner. As little as one's clothing could be made to disappear in the mirror-like full-length screen, or one layer of skin, or all the skin down to the muscle, every organ put on display, or the moving, giggling skeleton laid completely bare. Fawn and Cookie laughed giddily at their raw pink muscles, at their laughter-convulsed intestines. Fawn turned her skull from side to side.

Cookie fed more munits, punched keys, adjusted dials until only their two hearts floated free in space, or their eyeballs, or their breasts (what little they had), finally punching their skeletons back in and hitting another button which gave them a poster-sized photograph of their skeletons' pose. Cookie rolled it in a tube and as the screen went dead they stepped out to find Heather and Rena and Diana Talmud talking with a man, Colleen and the cute sportster having mysteriously vanished, maybe to practice their own dissection.

The man, in an expensive blackish-green silk suit and string tie, seemed to be flirting most strongly with Diana, while Heather and Rena looked on amused. The guy had this stupid friendly grin like he really thought he would get somewhere with Diana.

"If ya don't believe me then come on and I'll show ya," the man was saying. "I've never played that game without winning a nice stuffed animal. I'll win ya a big teddy bear, how about that?"

"I've got more stuffed animals than I know what to do with, thanks," Diana smirked dryly.

"Then I'll win ya a t-shirt."

"Blast off, huh?"

The other girls exploded into laughter, even Fawn, Cookie hysterical. Heather only smiled pleasantly. Del's grin drained away. He was mortified.

"Hey, I'm only trying to be friendly."

"I've already got a father, pal, I'm not looking for a father figure. I'm not stupid. Go pick up some other daughter figure."

"I think you mistake my intentions," Del murmured, straightening up grimly. A lie, but meant to preserve him a tiny bit of dignity.

"Yeah, yeah," Diana smirked. The others giggled, though Fawn was a little afraid he might turn psycho and pull out a gun.

He didn't. Without another word he walked away.

The girls broke up more loudly than ever.

"What a sleazy operator," Diana sniggered.

Hector Tomas wearily trudged up the path of the steep hill, a great plateau upon which the noisy carnival city was built. He had a full dark mustache and heavy-lidded mournful dark eyes, wore his old black plastic Theta researcher jacket but with his ID badge unpinned. Under that he wore a gun. It was a nice one: government issue special agent's sidearm with no report, no recoil, and fast-acting plasma bullets. The Theta research group he had worked with had been commissioned and funded by the Earth colonial government to carry out their explorations and investigations. He himself had never needed a gun such as this during his explorations, but in the explorations of some of his fellow researchers special weapons had been utilized, or else those researchers might not have returned alive to their own dimension or plane of existence. He had never been to the place nicknamed Meatland by his fellow researchers, from which only two of the first full exploration teams had returned (out of five), with one of the two teams now on permanent disability leave for mental trauma. But he had been to dangerous places, encountered dangerous *things*. And yet, one didn't have to cross over to encounter dangerous places and things...hence the gun tonight.

At the top of the hill, finally, he swooned–weak, and *tired*. That made him nervous. He had been rationing his illegal anti-sleep pills until he could make the buy tonight, and had also been cutting back on his sedatives due to this rationing, so the sedatives wouldn't smother him without the electric fence of the anti-sleep drug to hold them at bay. He had been foolish to wait so long...he couldn't wait any longer, whether the drugs had been acquired for him or not. The first thing Hector did once inside the gate was buy a soda and wash down his last two anti-sleep pills together.

The jolt came after only a minute. He found new strength and calm. He could go on now.

EVERYBODY SCREAM!

But he had to go to LaKarnafeaux immediately, get that errand and its attendant suspense over with–*then* he could relax, browse around, go to see what cows had won prizes, what grotesque gourds had been shaped in suburban gardens. Maybe even play a few games. Because Hector loved carnivals; they brought back his boyhood. More innocent times. The bustle of life, people squirming everywhere like bugs under a rock uncovered.

"La vida es un carnaval," he muttered to himself.

Hector's new enthusiasm dwindled somewhat. The seething life reminded him of the less material–but no less busy–seething of another sort of life he had witnessed in crossing over. There, too, he had encountered women, men, fast-moving children swarming in all directions, plus nonhuman things occasionally mixed in. He had talked with some of those people…

Hector stopped by a trash barrel to drop in his empty cup and to survey the loud activity around him, the firefly swarms of light, the tracer bullet exchanges, the neon lightning storms, the people illuminated by all the fireworks like a reflecting, rolling ocean, children scattering madly like billiard balls. The comfort came back a little. Blissfully ignorant they were, and lucky not to have seen what he had witnessed, lucky not to have even seen photographs of Meatland as he had. All the activity, noise, the tents and trailers and structures, though temporary, made them feel safely insulated; a fortress. No, it was best that the majority would never read the scientific publications or watch the programs on the educational channels which showed the terrain of Meatland, the gently rolling hills red and grooved like bare muscle, with red liquid bubbling in rotten sores, all under a sky of red with black clouds swirling like ink in water. An endless landscape of mindless but organic matter. And it was good they would be mostly ignorant of the denizens of Meatland, the quick things that had reared out of the bubbling sores to chase and catch those hapless researchers, all wrinkly folds of shiny crimson flesh with no faces but for huge mouths filled with saw-blades of yellow teeth.

And it was good that they wouldn't know that Meatland was right here, right now, in the same space as this carnival, this carnival built over it, hiding it with all the lights and noise.

But Hector knew. He moved on.

Pearl let Del in. They were happy to see each other. She made him a coffee.

They sat in the small parlor area of her trailer with the carrousel horse Del and Sophi had given her mounted on the wall.

"I missed your day show," apologized Del. "I'll make tonight's–I promise."

"I'm going to sing *Blue Blues*," Pearl told him.

Del smiled, nodded, looked at his coffee. "Thanks. You do it well."

"You don't mind?"

"No–I'm honored. Really. You do it beautifully; from me it sounds like I'm gargling gravel."

"Stop that. It's stronger if it isn't too pretty. It came from your heart. I could never compete with that. I can't even write lyrics–God, how I envy you."

"This is a really cute trailer." Del looked over his shoulder.

"I'm going to miss you and Sophi this winter."

"We'll come see you."

"I feel safe around you."

Del smiled at her. "We care about you. We want to help you."

"You have–you gave me a new life. I can't thank you enough."

"You gave yourself a new life–you have the talent."

"Del...can I prevail upon you for another favor? A huge, huge favor?" She could see the light squirm in his eyes. "I hate to...ask...after all you've done..."

"No, go on," Del urged with mock casualness and interest. "You want me to write you some songs, I know. I'll do it, I promise...this fall."

"Well, yeah–that. That would be fantastic, I can't wait...custom-written songs from Del Kahn. But, ah, what I wanted to ask is...if you might consider producing an album for me."

Del couldn't catch his eyes before they dropped into his coffee. Nor infuse much feigned enthusiasm into his voice. "Well I will, Pearl...I will, okay? I promise...but not just yet, okay? I need some time to get my mind…ah…you know, but we'll talk to my business manager and my old producer this fall, alright? We'll sit down and talk and see what we can come up with."

"Oh, that's great, that's fine–I don't mean to push you."

"Don't worry about it. You're good–I want to see you recorded and I think I could do a good job of it for you." But…thought Del. But what? But I'm scared right now to go near the studio? But I'm too bitter to put my love on disk again right now? But I'm afraid to be perceived as sneaking back but hiding behind the body of another, an admitted cowardly loser? "We'll do it," he said blandly, looking up to smile an anemic promise. "This fall you'll have those songs so you can try them on for size first."

"That's wonderful. I can't thank you enough. Don't rush–at your leisure."

She's a gem, thought Del. She isn't using me; she's a friend asking a favor of a friend. He could tell she really meant it about at his leisure. She wasn't hunger without a soul, like others who had sought to affix themselves to him, leech-like, always swarming thick out there in the pond of life. That was why her singing had gripped him. It was human. She was *real*.

And beautiful. Del could never get out of his mind, when he was with her, the mental image of her singing in that brothel lounge down south, in lace black bra, cutting panties, garter belt and nylons, the twin hanging out of her in nylons and heels also, the upturned smooth second ass glowing softly in the mellow lights. Del's penis was his own parasitic twin growing out of him, part sentient, with a separate hunger…moving out away from him, reaching, sometimes pulling him along after it, sometimes overruling his mind. His twin yearned for her twin.

Del knew that he had a possible chance, considering the favors she asked of him. But the idea of holding her dreams hostage and demanding a ransom sickened him. He couldn't blackmail her. I may be low, he mused, but even I have my limits. Also, there was another factor to bear in mind…

"How are you and Mitch doing?"

Now it was Pearl's turn to look edgy, avert her eyes. "Good."

"Are you two serious or what?" Even if she were just a fuck to Mitch, Del would be reluctant. Out of respect. And fear, too.

"I don't know," Pearl said. On Mitch's behalf. She knew how *she* felt.

"I don't mean to pry. I mean…I'm just…you know. I don't know Mitch too well, privately. When he isn't at work. He seems like he's always at work…"

"He uncoils, " Pearl murmured. "But he's very defensive about emoting. He's always on guard. He's afraid. Love makes him uncomfortable."

"Your love?" Del probed.

"His own." Pearl caught herself, flushed and laughed uneasily, reaching for her tea. "He may not even love me. I think he loves my body. My *bodies*," she corrected.

"That's an insecurity you've brought into the relationship, I'd be willing to wager," Del said. "It would be there with anybody…Mitch, another person, me."

"I'm aware of that," Pearl said in a husky whisper.

"Give the guy a chance. He's a little intense, a little fierce, but he has a good heart. He cares. He hates a lot, but that's because he cares so much."

Here I am aching to fuck her, Del thought, but I'm selling her another man. But that was because now Del knew, finally, for certain, how Pearl and Garnet felt about each other. He wouldn't have expected it, really–not with Garnet's hostile intensity, not with Pearl's dark and bitter past. But now he knew. It was his duty as a friend to both of them to help push their hopes closer together.

Pearl hadn't responded to Del's last statement. He said, "Speaking of Mitch, I've gotta go talk to him about something."

Pearl glanced at a clock. "Stay here. He's coming over for his break in five minutes. I'll make you another coffee." She rose from her chair, awkward with the extra weight and limbs of her sister.

Del nodded, but grew quite restless inside. Mitch had never come in on the two of them alone in her trailer before, and this new knowledge made him all that much more uncomfortable. Guilty, as though Mitch might read his twin's mind. He considered escaping while he could and casually meeting Garnet nearby, but didn't rise from the parlor love seat.

Del waited as if for a dentist appointment, and after ten minutes of this

EVERYBODY SCREAM!

Mitch came. Sure enough, upon spotting Del his eyes seemed (in Del's mind) to be seeing Del's naked erection standing up from his zipper. His guilt must have been a garish tattoo on his face. Or maybe Mitch only looked funny because he had kissed Pearl on the lips in the kitchen before he realized Del was sitting in the adjacent living room. Del stood up and came to him.

"I've been looking around for you. Can we talk in private?"

"In here." Garnet led Del into the little alcove of a bedroom; Pearl remained in the kitchenette.

The bed was in disarray. Del tried to ignore it as the two men stood facing each other. "I want you to cuff LaKarnafeaux, or at least one of his boys."

Mitch stared, and then grinned. Mitch wasn't one to grin. He held out his hand to be shaken, and Del shook it, grinning foolishly also, though embarrassed. Mitch said, "Why the sudden change? Today you and your wife told me to leave 'em be."

"I talked to them today. I hate them."

"What about your wife?"

"I don't know. Don't worry, you're just following orders. If she doesn't like it she can crucify me."

"I can hardly wait. I'll get right on it, myself."

"Don't go crazy. Just one of them would be fine. Karny doesn't do much of anything himself so I doubt you can cuff him, but anybody's fine. Just be careful with Johnny Leng and keep clear of Sneezy Tightrope." Del glanced at a framed picture on a bureau of Pearl as a child standing with her sister Helen and her parents. "Maybe I'm being petty, concerning myself with these little clowns. What are they compared to the syndy, or corrupt businessmen, or corrupt politicians, who rob and cheat and kill on a mass scale? They're just a few bugs compared to that."

"Well, enough bugs add up to a locust swarm, right? They all contribute. You can't squash 'em all but you squash what you can."

"It's what they represent to me," Del muttered. "I can't stomach them anymore."

"I think we'll both feel better for this," Mitch smiled intensely.

Del nodded. Only Sophi concerned him. This was her carnival...but he was her chief investor, right? "They mock our impotence," he observed. "Let's show 'em we can still get it up. And fuck 'em where it hurts."

Garnet grew serious again. A moment passed. Then he said, "Del...you haven't ever, you know...slept with Pearl, have you?"

Del was surprised at Garnet's frankness in his approach, and by his meek tone; sad, as if he expected a wounding answer. Del said, "No, Mitch, never. I'm not after her. I know how you care for her."

Mitch was restless, looking away. Del had never seen him so vulnerable. He squirmed, his emotions like tiny worms magnified under Del's microscope. "Sorry I asked that. I'm just paranoid. She was a prosty once–you know how it is."

"Forget about that. She was lost...now she isn't. And don't feel bad about asking me, Mitch. My reputation isn't so saintly either, I know. But you're my friend–I couldn't do that to you."

But I could do that to my wife? Del thought, wondering just how far he had gone, for Garnet to have to ask him that question.

There was a great selection of eye pins on display inside the cabinet; boys wore them on their jacket lapels and girls wore them as brooches. Mounted in metal, and sometimes trimmed with stones of a color matching the iris, were authentic human eyes, animal eyes, the eyes of aliens familiar and obscure. One ambery eye without iris or pupil was as large as a chicken's egg. Wes Sundry was admiring an eye (animal? alien? mutant?) with a huge red iris and goat-like, sideways oblong pupil when he heard Fen beside him say, "Wes–scope out that redhead."

Wes looked up, glanced about until his eyes settled on her. A tall young girl with some friends. She was trying on a white leather jacket with long fringe dangling from the arms. "Cute. Nothing special."

Fen Colon drew closer to his friend. "You ignorant goober–*look* at her."

"Yeah, so, red hair. Probably fake. Her eyes are squinty and she's got a big nose. Look, her lips almost touch it. She's got a bony horse face, and no milkers from the looks. All the dung you give me over the sushi I like and you get hot over *that*."

Fen glared at his friend." I don't know why I keep you with me. You have no refinement, man. You're a backwards mucoid waste product."

"The sushi we had back in town was better than her! I don't see it."

"Red hair. Look, it isn't fake. Her eyebrows, her *look*…"

"That doesn't mean dung and you know it. If a one-eyed four hundred pound mutant had red hair would you get hot over her, too?"

"Ignorant, man. You're really sad. You don't know class when you see it."

"She's looking at you," Wes smirked.

Fen jerked his head. Over the top of the rack of heavy jackets, the redhead and a friend with curly blonde hair were looking directly at him, close and muttering to each other. When they saw him looking back they giggled and the redhead whipped around, showing him her back. Her fit of bashfulness made Fen grin. "You see that?" he cooed to Wes.

"These little fishes are looking at *all* the guys, man…just like we look at all of them."

Fen's grin turned upside-down as he faced his friend again. "You're just jealous because they know better than to look at a goober like you."

"Jealous of what? The blonde is a lot nicer."

"Good. One for me and one for you. We'll lose the little one."

"Or share her," Wes grinned. He pushed a wad of chewing tobacco in his mouth in preparation. "What about you-know-who?"

Fen glanced at the van and camper which, with the projecting tent-like canopy, formed a sort of camp. Some *Dozers*, some lawn chairs. No sign of LaKarnafeaux (described to them by Moband as looking like a fat, aging bikie), and lights were on in the camper. Only two men sat out to tend to business; one in a top hat and fringed vest and the other balding and small, in a flowered shirt, who was eyeing Fen and Wes suspiciously as if he thought they might steal something.

"I don't know," Fen murmured, lowering his head and pretending to study eye pins. "We may not be able to get to the fat man himself. Maybe we'll take down one of his boys, but they have to have enough vortex on them to make it worthy. What we really need to do is get inside the van."

They had seen two boys buy some weed right out in the open of the camp, but hadn't witnessed a vortex transaction. Was it customary to be invited inside the camper or, more likely, the van? The purpose of this reconnaissance mission had been to find out. One good thing was that they hadn't seen any of the enemy Martians stalking about, sticking close to vortex as they usually did, the way hyenas would circle a dying antelope.

"You make me laugh, spitter," Wes chuckled huskily. "You tell me (imitating Fen's stern manner), 'No girls, no games, no fooling around'–and now you smell red bush and you forget everything."

"I haven't forgotten anything, no-brain. Come on, before we lose them." Fen nudged past him.

"That blonde is cute," Wes reiterated.

Fen worked his way closer to the three girls, pretending to examine a rack of t-shirts. At an explosion of giggling he glanced over. Tiny Cookie was lost in a huge, clear rubbery jacket. Fen and Fawn met each other's gaze. Fawn looked sharply away, then back. "Hi," Fen said.

"Hello."

"Oh God," Cookie muttered, spinning away.

"You better help your friend find a jacket that fits."

"I know," Fawn smiled, a little flushed.

"Ladies," Wes nodded, stepping up, chewing. Cookie giggled into her hand.

"Hello," Fawn said, and Heather in echo.

"Having trouble deciding?" Fen nodded at the rack.

"Oh, I can't afford one–my mother wouldn't give me the money."

"Try some on and I'll tell you what I think. Never mind whether you can afford it for a few minutes." Fen and Wes came around from behind the t-shirt rack. "Go ahead, play model. You look like one, anyway."

"Thanks." Fawn's face filled with blood; she hid her compressed smile under her nose as she lowered her head and inserted her arms in the sleeves of another white leather jacket. Her feathered red hair hung and swayed. Fen

EVERYBODY SCREAM!

drank her in. The carnival lights played on her milky skin like the iridescent colors in an opal.

"Fawn and Heather are in a modeling class in school," said Cookie.

"I believe it," said Fen.

"Me too," said Wes, though only encompassing Heather in his broad, apple-cheeked chewing grin.

"That's a nice jacket you've got on," Fawn managed, looking up.

"Thanks."

"Were you in the army?"

"Yeah," exaggerated Fen slightly. A military vocational school. But they'd taught him how to shoot, stab, blow things up–right?

"How about you?" Heather asked Wes blandly.

"Nope," said Wes, spitting out a blob of black saliva. "I'm my own army." Heather smiled, started to knead like dough under Wes's faithful charm.

"You look great," Fen said, taking a step back to eye Fawn from foot to head. She wore an oversized blue t-shirt, black sweat pants as tight as leotards on her long slim legs (but with no rear flap), and Heather was holding her faded denim jacket with its assortment of pins, brooches and buttons.

"Thanks."

"But then you'd look great in any of them." He wished he could spare the money to buy her one. *That* would be a slick move. Maybe it would be worth it, but he'd have to wait a little longer and see. "What's your name, anyway?"

"Fawn."

"Wow–Fawn. What's that, like a baby horse?"

"No, that's a foal. I have a friend named Foal. Fawn is a baby deer."

"That's pretty. Really. I'm Fen." He held out his hand.

Blushing again, eyes averted, smile still trying to hide, Fawn extended her hand. "Nice to meet you."

"Hey," Wes said, "why don't we all go somewhere and get something to eat? Our treat–right, Fen?"

"Certainly."

"Me too?" Cookie raised her eyebrows, pouting.

"Certainly."

Heather looked to Fawn and shrugged. Fawn fought a smirk, turned back to Fen and said, "Alright." She peeled off the white leather jacket and slipped back into her denim one.

"Hold on a minute. Stay here." Fen returned to the cabinet where he and Wes had been browsing before. Fen called to the top-hatted man to assist him. Mortimer Ficklebottom pushed himself out of his chair with a lazy groan.

A moment later Fen returned, and handed Fawn a little paper bag. "For you to add to your collection, there." He pointed to her chest.

"Oh–thanks." Fawn dug into the bag. Cookie giggled. Fen felt his face flush hot. It was the red-irised eye pin which had also caught Wes's fancy. "Oooh," said Fawn, also red-faced again. "Thanks, it's beautiful!" Her pleasure was genuine; her delicate narrow eyes sparkled. She was beautiful.

"Can I pin it on for you? A medal of honor."

"For what?" She passed it back to him.

"For being so gorgeous. Where do you want it?"

Fawn whipped her head into profile, gazed up at the darkening sky. "I can't *believe* this!"

"Believe what?" Fen grinned.

"Pin it where you want," she said, hooking Heather's arm.

Fen stepped to her, positioned the scarab-like piece of jewelry at a bare spot close to Fawn's collar, just above her left breast. "Will the heart area do?" he smiled.

Fawn made a high squeaky sound and buried her face in Heather's neck, stomped her foot. Heather grimaced and shoved her away.

"What's wrong?" Fen smiled more broadly, eating it up.

"Nothing," Fawn said, and bit her lower lip. "Go ahead."

Fen pinned the strange red eye to Fawn's jacket. He appraised her. "Perfect. What do you think?"

"Thank you–I love it!"

"My pleasure. Are we all set to go?"

Affirmatives. They moved on. The balding man with the flowered shirt in the lawn chair watched after them, frowning, not sipping his mead.

Mortimer noticed this. "What's wrong?" he asked Sneezy Tightrope.

Holographic nudes hung on the walls of the van, a large vidscreen played a chip featuring nothing but blue waves on the white sand of a private beach in Diamondcrest, over and over, the same waves and same swooping birds repeated every hour if you could catch the pattern. The smell of seaweed had insinuated itself into the very substance of the van's interior like grains of sand into its cracks, corners and pores. Eddy Walpole came to sit on a fur-covered fold-out sleeper sofa beside Hector Tomas.

"Sorry, man, I just called our contact and his hand phone's turned off. He was supposed to be here with your package hours ago."

Hector blinked at his host numbly for a moment. "You have no idea where he is now or another way to reach him?"

"Well, I can try a few places. I'm sure he's still coming, he's a reliable source. He's probably on his way now, is what it is, most likely. Probably just forgot to put his phone on, or bumped it, you know. Why not go grab a burger and come back in an hour or two?"

Hector's hands were knotted on his thighs. The jolt of his last anti-sleep pills, without the calming sedatives to balance them out, crackled through his veins like blood turned to electricity. Corpuscles raced on laser beam tracks, screeching around corners, ricocheting off walls. Colliding in explosions of flame, everywhere throughout him, vehicles piling up...

"I suppose I'll have to," Hector breathed, slowly rising.

Eddy rose too. "Again, sorry. Normally our man is pretty punctual. I know this isn't professional. We'll throw in a bag of weed for ya, how about that?" Smile.

Hector had never tried that in lieu of sedatives. "Whatever. Thank you. I'll come back later, then."

"Good." Eddy clapped him on the back on the way out.

Outside, Eddy watched the tall man walk away with stiff movements, for a moment disoriented before choosing a direction, buffeted in that second by waves of people like a buoy. "What a burn-out," Eddy smirked to Mort.

"We have a problem," said Mortimer Ficklebottom.

The mall building looked like a hangar: a windowless collapsible building, long and high-ceilinged, although there had been no upper story assembled as there had been for the crafts show structure. The lighted interior drew a somnambulistic Hector inside. A bustling interior, crowded with people but more so with color, with items, with many tiny individual *things* all seeming to scream out for his attention simultaneously. A clamoring pawing at his senses, a cacophony of merchandise.

He made the mistake of paging through an encyclopedia on a counter, and subsequently listened for fifteen minutes as a pleasant but driven ex-teacher described the various sets of encyclopedias she was selling. Hector agreed that they were very impressive, and also that it was important children should have a set in the home and be encouraged to read…but finally managed to get in that he was divorced and had no children. Regrettably, he didn't add. He loved children. Their innocent enthusiasm was the very stuff of life. But their innocent enthusiasm depressed him. Better it was that he had no children to ache over. He extricated himself at last, eager to return to his spectral anonymity.

Fifteen minutes earlier Noelle Buda had fallen into the same trap, but younger and more energized, climbed to freedom more quickly. The woman let Noelle out of her grip reluctantly. She was zealously committed, as if she alone could save the neglectful masses from their illiteracy. Noelle had moved to a table that displayed cheap jewelry, a mixed and staring audience of eye pins.

She had played a few games half-heartedly, won a poster of the group Flemm which she had left on a table under a food pavilion for some younger girl to find. Riding rides alone had no appeal for her–especially since this carnival employed the practice of incorporating into some rides the dead bodies not claimed by the town morgue after the official waiting period. Two rows of actual human and humanoid skulls, six to either side on poles, flanked the path which led to the Vomit Comet. Purple lights glowed in their sockets now that it was dark. For most this added to the excitement of anticipation. It had no such attraction for Noelle.

Nor did the notion of signing waiver forms for the Vomit Comet, Double Helix and the Puker. Noelle had sought out quieter distractions. The great structure which housed the cattle, not far from the mall, had been smellier inside than she had expected from her visits to sanitized zoos, her only previous encounter with such large animals. Those cows that weren't standing lay in their own mud-pools of excrement; it caked their tails. They were too close, too–living walls, a few leaning out their dinosaur necks in slow motion to sniff at her. This species of cattle had great bony heads much like that of a hammerhead shark, their white-lashed eyes at the far ends of the hammer. Noelle didn't stay long.

She found the bumbles and such in a smaller structure, off to one side of the lavatory shed, more relaxing and enjoyable.

In order to qualify for judging, these bumbles had had to be bred, crossbred, mutated within what was considered unprofessional, limited boundaries, though the original species of bumbles was a completely artificially designed one. In corridors of cages were dozens of bumbles, to Noelle's delight. Huge–a few as big as lambs–or as small as guinea pigs. Most with floppy ears, a few with erect ears. Most black and yellow striped, but some black and tan, or black and white, or all black, or albino. These ghost-like bumbles had pink eyes with red pupils that unsettled Noelle, who preferred the warm darker eyes.

Prize ribbons for the various categories were pinned to the stacked cages. There were other kinds of animals, also; a variety of native aquatic birds, most of which had tiny sharp teeth for the eating of fish and laid black eggs which absorbed the sun's warmth, very tasty, the feathers of the birds ranging from gray to blue to green, so as to blend in with the water from predators, and maybe from hunters, these water colors having been noted to be on a slight increase in the years since Chooms had invented the gun, the Chooms later having had their knowledge updated by the Earth colonists.

Jeffrey Thomas

There were some Tikkihotto beetles that tasted to Noelle like salty chicken when cooked, and were in fact the size of chickens, plucking at the insides of their cages. Their chitin armor was white with black spines, their legs were barbed and black. They had three antennae-like ocular organs on either side of their heads, not unlike the tentacled "eyes" of the Tikkihotto. These insects and the humanoid Tikkihottos could see in ways beyond the capacity of humans. Auras, emanations, colors outside the human spectrums. Certain kinds of "dimensionals"–that is, creatures or beings from dimensions or planes other than this one–which were invisible to humans could be seen moving about by the Tikkihottos.

The feelers wavered at Noelle through the cage mesh. What color was her pretty brown skin to them? If she saw this image electronically relayed onto a screen (possible) would she find her visage beautiful or nightmarish? She didn't care to know what other auras, emanations, colors she secretly possessed. She had trouble enough with the things she already knew about herself.

Now, in the mall, she browsed at a stand rich in tackiness. Toys, t-shirts, souvenirs, gizmos. It could have been a museum exhibit of chintz. In contrast, a few tables opposite displayed crafts made by people at home, or in personal workshops. This was novel and quaint to Noelle; she was intrigued. Wooden plaques and key holders, hand-painted with *Welcome Friends*, *Home Sweet Home*, other platitudes, or else empty, waiting to be personalized by an artist in residence behind the table, hopefully but unobtrusively eyeing Noelle. She bought a beautifully scented wooden key holder cut in the shape of a cat, with her name painted on in soft blue while she watched. What would Bonnie say, she wondered uncomfortably? The artist and those others behind their craft tables made her shy. They were older, generally...some Choom, some human, quiet and calm and alien to her. Though she admired their work she couldn't imagine spending the time and effort to create such things herself. Thus she admired them all the more for their humble, apparently peaceful concerns, as one might admire the simple devotion of monks or nun but still be intimidated–maybe even feel inferior or lacking–in their presence. They were like serene animals, to Noelle, like those lazy-eyed cows she had seen (also a little eerie in their slow motion placidness).

EVERYBODY SCREAM!

Unassuming, closer to nature. But she couldn't live that way. It would be dull, she was afraid. Unstimulating. Still, the notion was distantly nostalgic, maybe a race memory type of thing, and romantic. Part of her envied their perceived lack of evolution.

Hector also felt uneasy moving in close to particular tables, solidifying to flesh in the gaze of the craft makers, but there were still material things capable of calling him out of his shadows. As much as he eyed the crafts and products, however, he studied the milling people, endless in their diversity, and yet like many, many kinds of insects, *all* insects in a way.

For one thing, he had never before seen these tight sweat pants with trap-door rears. Not once. And then suddenly he was surrounded by them, as if overnight teenagers (and older people aspiring to be teenagers) had conspired in an underground complex, toiling long and hard to create them, then emerging today. That abruptly could a new fashion appear, sometimes with no clue to its evolution, and just as abruptly vanish. Material things, but ephemeral.

Distressing to Hector was that there was too little or sometimes no distinction between the current teen fashions and the dress of young children. It used to be that once a fashion was discarded it passed on down to the children, while the teens adopted a new one. Now the fashion occurred simultaneously. Though he saw no *open* trapdoors among them, he did see girls of nine, ten, twelve wearing those sweat pants. The teens dictated fashion, the children and adults emulated them.

Despite the recurring, more unifying signs of fashion trends, however, there were too many kinds of people from too many origins to keep up with. It was as if the many varied dimensional planes which coexisted simultaneously in the same space had all materialized into view, though Hector knew better, knew that such a revelation would shatter one's mind.

A cacophony of lives. Even within this dimension, separate dimensions coexisted in endless layers, their beings elbow to elbow with each other but invisible to each other. They were capable of seeing each other if they really looked, their dimensions capable of being touched, entered, explored–though often one ended up wishing they had never entered the world of that other person.

In the physicist's overview of the universe and its kin, people–ruled by their chemical components–*were* chemicals, moving in fragile phials, separately enclosed from one another but waiting to crash and interact, either mixing or reacting violently, exploding. Phials spinning in the centrifuge of life, as in some carnival ride.

But were Hector's fellow humans and humanoids *only* chemicals, governed by electrochemical programming, "Personality" and "Identity" merely a matter of chemical variations or anomalies, with the extra physical influences of heredity and environment to help shape the self? What could be left, after all that, to call a soul, a spirit?

That had been Hector's job as a Theta researcher to find out.

That research work and the new perspectives it had lent to his world, when he returned to it, had proved a strain he couldn't deal with.

Even the new job offer that had come to him from another research group had made his flesh crawl. This group was funded not by the government but by a major corporation, and thus was making great strides, and they had a new idea for a company, a service to the public.

As a Theta researcher Hector had on various planes studied various kinds of trace-energies of "dead" humans and humanoids. In one place, the "dead" were shoulder to shoulder, mostly unmoving, only a few shifting in slow motion, eyes staring, unable to communicate. A *vista* of these beings, like a sea, so thick that Hector's team had had to float above them, though this was easy since there was no gravity, and the space suits they wore were a welcome insulation.

In another world–of endless moors of strange translucent gray grass, black cliffs rising in the distance, a world with gravity (though not with breathable atmosphere)–Hector and his comrades had seen only *one* being, a dark-garbed woman, drifting across the moors far away. They got close enough to yell to her and she stopped and glanced back at them a moment, so she was at least part sentient, but she vanished into a fog which curled up at all times from the rubbery grass. They did find a kind of cottage, later, apparently made from weird colorless materials from this world, and some dark robes inside, but no one showed up...

EVERYBODY SCREAM!

And then he had met dead people on other planes who were only too capable of communication, only too eager to talk. Chattering, babbling. Hector had spent most his time here, observing…interviewing. The identities of some of his subjects had been investigated and confirmed. He would be happily greeted by some of his subjects when he returned. But they varied in coherence for all their talkativeness. This realm seemed a kind of lunatic asylum for lost, disoriented or waylaid souls.

The burgeoning company had offered Hector a job relaying messages to the addled dead from their living relatives, and from the dead to the living. A desk job, they assured him, no personal excursions; a remote probe could be sent to collect these video impressions.

Hector had declined.

His last investigations had been into a plane much like this last kind, but here the "trace-energies," whatever they were in a physical or metaphysical sense, were unhappy. Desperately unhappy. Sobbing, groaning, moaning–all at once. Wailing, *screaming*. Pleading with Hector to take them away. And as if their surroundings weren't miserable enough, there were things that *preyed* upon them here…

Hector had been dismissed from his job shortly after these last studies, for "fatigue," "work-related stress." He had no idea what he was going to do with the remainder of his life.

His body bumped hard with another's. Dazedly he said, "Sorry," though he didn't know if he were at fault. A few yards beyond he fell into a short line at a Haww candy counter. Haww fudge was a favorite of his. He could see the Haww busy behind the counter, a floating red cone, with a blue ball floating two inches above the cone, rotating, and a second blue ball two inches above that rotating in the other direction. Three limbs were on level with the cone but not physically connected, and there was also a break at every elbow and digit joint. A peaceful race. To be a Haww, just concerned with extruding their delicious candy from the holes at the ends of their claws into intricate, lovely shapes. They only lived to be four or five years old, however. Would Hector rather live a hundred years–two hundred if pollution, ever-new diseases, his fellow beings didn't get him sooner–and suffer pain, anxiety, anger, depression, stress, when all the bliss and good in his life might possibly be condensed down into four or five years? He thought that he would be too afraid to give up his longevity, pain or no. He rationalized, too, correctly or not, that bliss and calm alone might be too boring, that pain was needed to know pleasure. Still, for their comparative lack of pain the Haww looked awfully, awfully content. This one whistled happily out of the holes in its one unoccupied arm while it bustled.

The pretty black girl ahead of him in line bought an intricately woven flower of candy on a stick, and then Hector bought a few pieces of various kinds of fudge, and a coffee. He drifted on, his flesh heavy, the floating being behind him light and quick.

Not every display in here was a shop. At one table there was a scale model of a house, bubble-like and cute, very affordable (comparatively)…but not so durable or well-made, naturally, for that money, Hector knew. Brochures, pamphlets, a vid screen showing such a house under construction. Another display ahead was one by an organization for animal rights. An animal lover, Hector moved toward it.

A man and woman sat on chairs behind the display chatting, hardly taking him in, giving him his privacy. He liked it that way; if he wanted assistance from people he would ask them for it. Perhaps, sensitive people as they must be, they sensed his desire for invisibility.

There were countless pamphlets representing the work of a variety of groups from the town of Paxton, from elsewhere in the province of East Kagin, from elsewhere in the country of Duplam, elsewhere on the planet Oasis, even one or two from Earth, devoid as it was of most animals except pets. But even pet animals, very often pet animals, had their natural rights horribly abused. In fact, it was the abuse of pet animals Hector was most horrified by, because in the victims he saw his own past pets, and because pet species are generally chosen for that purpose by their very gentleness and capacity for love. To see a photograph of a big-eared tiny beagle lying in a cage, its moist eyes half closed in its resignation to pain, and its flank a black and red raw crust from concentrated radiation burns inflicted to test their independent healing, not only appalled him but filled Hector with a bright hot fury that cut through much of his fog. His mother had owned a plump, loving beagle.

In glossy stills, scrawny watery-eyed, cross-eyed kittens, cute even with spinal cords severed, dragged useless hind legs despite having the tops of their heads uncapped and exposed, electrodes poking up from their skulls. One yellow cat, shaved and covered with strange wounds, glared at the camera, or maybe it was just his brow lowered over his eyes from those weighty electrodes driven into his head. A "before" photo showed the litter of kittens sleeping together, as yet unmutilated, in a nest of fuzzy, fragile innocence. Hector thought of his boyhood kitten Fluffy, who had loved to ride on his shoulder, up until her death in her teens. An animal *loving* a human. Humans *not* loving animals.

Monkeys, goats, other animals subjected to lab experiments. So senseless. The technology was there to outdate such medieval torture! Computer graphics, training films, cadaver dissection, the creation of cultured cells, tissues, even with bogus but realistic pain receptors if need be, all rendered these experiments unnecessary. But it was cheaper to buy the dogs from an animal "shelter" than to culture tissue with nerves, pain receptors. Money mattered more than life. If governments allowed big businesses to pollute and contaminate countless humans and humanoids, how could one realistically expect much to be done about these hidden-away mute prisoners? Well, sometimes governments did make some gestures. Little gestures of mercy could pamper people, distract them from the greater, more elusive evils being done elsewhere...or to them.

A pamphlet told how stubborn cows were unloaded at a stockyard. If a cow were too weak or recalcitrant to move from the truck she might be kicked, beaten with rods, cattle-prodded in the ears, poked in the eyes or vulva or anus. If this were unsuccessful, a rope might be tied around her neck, another to a post, and the truck would move forward. The cow would be dragged from the truck and fall, breaking her legs. There she might lie into evening, lowing in misery in the baking sun without water, savaged by the stockyard dogs. Such a case was presented. A representative from this particular animal rights group had protested at the scene, demanded that the animal be put away. She was scoffed at. The police were called but could do nothing. She gave the cow water but when she returned later it had been removed, out of spite. Finally, that evening, a butcher came and killed the tormented thing.

A photo of this cow showed her staring at the camera, her front legs under her and rear legs splayed, her white-lashed eyes half-closed, one of them swollen, blood welling from under it where a human had savagely kicked her. Savagely. Savages. Hector had once seen a vid of two scrawny black teenagers in some blighted colony throwing large stones at a dying, sickly cow. And their equally scrawny, nasty dogs snapping at it. The cowards darted in to club it once the stones had brought it on its side. The cow did not complain. Cows seemed to know their place. Hector could still hear the sickening distant *thump* as the stones smashed into the cow's face, making the huge lazy head turn, but the head just returned resignedly to its former position, obligingly, as if this were just another process like being milked. Those cattle-prodders were just like these stone throwers, who were just prehistoric humans hurling crude spears at mammoths. The only evolution came in the weapons, or the clothing, or language. Not in the heart.

What about those like Hector, though? He wasn't poor, was well fed, basically healthy. But what if he had lived in that arid, blighted colony? What if he had been uneducated and had to take a job in a stockyard? Well, he'd never do that so long as there was a toilet to be scrubbed, but still, the point was: was it too easy to stand back smug and superior and point a finger from where he lived? Was it, sadly, that money and comfort gave one the luxury of mercy and compassion? Old women in silk gowns could gather, kittens in laps, and bemoan the slaughter of dogs by the dirty peoples who ate dogs, but they didn't have to worry about feeding their families. They could afford the luxury of alternatives, were warm enough to stand back and notice the cold of animals. Okay, Hector could forgive those scrawny bastards their blood sport–their's was a harsh, benighted life. But scientists uncapping kitten skulls were not loinclothed Neanderthals–outwardly. The swaggering, guffawing assholes who kicked crippled cows in the face could buy plenty of beer to sustain themselves; no threat of hunger or cold justified their ethical and spiritual underdevelopment.

EVERYBODY SCREAM!

The cow stared at the camera both mindlessly and yet also as if, tired and agonized, it accused the human race, a splayed and bloodied martyr for its kind. It accused Hector. Hector, who loved steak. Whose wristwatch's band was proudly inscribed, "Genuine Pigskin." Hector felt guilty, unworthy to join those people sitting behind the display table, who were doubtlessly vegetarians. He was weak. A hypocrite. He had alternatives. He could seek them out. Synthetic meats, just as good. Cultured animal tissues without brains. But it was often cheaper to raise and kill animals than to build plants and pay workers to produce these alternatives. The local businesses jealously maintained their industry. *Later*, when animals were more depleted, outdated, as on Earth, would technology replace them. No act of mercy would decide this. Plastic might eventually fully replace leather. Cows might die out. Pigs. The like. Eventually become outmoded at every colony, become unnecessary and thus ultimately extinct species. But better that than slow torture, right? For now, here, it was cheap. I'm a slave to their morality, to my upbringing, to my community, Hector countered his conscience. He had tried quitting flesh a few times. He was addicted to his barbarism; not eating meat would be like celibacy. But he still loved animals, respected them, he did! He could not squash a spider–at his apartment he caught them in cups and put them outside. Would these two chatting people understand, forgive him? As a boy he had seen cows in books and imagined them grazing endless fields. He had had no realistic comprehension of the origins of his hamburgers. Why couldn't cows graze contentedly, and then one day just be sneaked up on, shot in the head, if people *had* to eat animal flesh? Why did baby calves have to be penned, unable to even move, and fed only milk solutions so as to become veal? Was he evil if he still loved to eat meat and asked only for mercy and compassion instead of absolute liberation for these creatures?

Still, looking into that photographed cow's face, he'd decided to try becoming a vegetarian again. The alternatives were available. Laziness or frugality did not excuse his patronage of these animal concentration camps.

Everything we do is evil, he thought. We can't eat, can't even dress without slaughtering other lives. The cruelty, the misery. What must it be like in a slaughterhouse, some pigs actually dying of fright before they were touched, he had heard—just as he had heard that pigs were more intelligent animals than dogs. What must that sound be like? Probably like that last world he had crossed over into…with its moans, groans, bellows of fear, screams of endless desperation.

Life was hideous enough. Was there no escape beyond it? In some world beyond did the souls of cows and pigs rend and eat alive the souls of shrieking humans through all eternity while monkeys gleefully cavorted? There, the scientists would be caged in fortresses built of white rat skeletons while white rat souls gnawed on their spectral flesh. There, human heads were mounted on the walls of mazes which once-beautiful women stumbled through blindly, groping, wailing, their skins ripped raw from the bared muscles, their eyes eaten away by those rabbits once blinded to test cosmetics. It would be a hell. But it would only be this hell turned inside out.

Hector drifted on, pamphlets in his inner jacket pocket.

At the back of the mall building there was a mini shop selling only clocks with decorative photographs as their faces. Some were portraits of Lotti, the legendary Tikkihotto, the clock's arms tucked down by his shoulder. Some showed cute little kittens or puppies on green grass. They were tacky, but they soothed Hector a little. The kittens should anger him after what he'd seen. These clocks were naïve things. It could be bad to be naïve. But it felt good now to be amongst these images; glorified oceans where no whales were harpooned, the placid farm scenes where no cows hopelessly moped inside those pretty blood red buildings.

Next to the clock display was a taxidermy display, irony of ironies, within sight of the animal rights display. Before he had realized it Hector was standing at it, admiring a lamp which incorporated a pretty-colored, fascinating fish, even considered buying it. Then he looked up at the pelts hanging over his head, the antlered trophies, a few large fur rugs behind the counter on the wall. He was horrified that people at the animal rights booth might this instant be drilling their hot eyes into his back. He moved out of the mall through its rear opening. But he still would have liked that lamp.

Though she had felt bad for the cows tied to their stalls all day by two feet of rope, shitting on their own tails, Noelle hadn't reflected on the teriyaki sticks she had bought earlier, and she didn't even consider stopping at the animal rights booth, avoided glancing at it a second time, flicked past it as one might embarrassedly flick channels past a VT commercial asking aid for skeletal, starving children. Too depressing. Earlier, alone in a tent which contained sheep in pens–their coats stained with shit, too many of them not covered in blankets against the growing chill of night, wearing bright ear punches–she had failed to detect the sad irony in the whimsical artwork hanging on the insides of the tent, a series of facts on sheep presented in questions and answers, showing cute cartoons of sheep acting like humans, which probably anthropomorphically inspired more delight than the dumb beasts themselves. "Can You Eat Them?" it was asked. "Oh Yes!" And the many ways were related. A smiling lamb was shown seated at a table wearing a bib, knife and fork in its hooves. Noelle had only absent-mindedly given one of the animals an obligatory pat on the neck, more to feel the scratchy shorn surface than anything. The sheep had been sheared in a contest earlier that day. The uses for animals were endless.

Noelle was growing restless. Sorry. She had *already* grown restless. She had bags to bring back to the car; she hated carrying them around. She was bored. This had gone on too long. How could even Bonnie be so self-concerned? Noelle sighed. She'd wait a little longer only, and then...and then what? Drive home, in Bonnie's car? This was ridiculous.

Well, the least she could do for now was to go get her hand stamped so she could return through the gate, then go down to the parking lot and put her bags in the car...except that she didn't have a key. Fuck!

Maybe Bonnie and Moussa-whatever had gone to her car. She could only hope. She had no idea what his would look like, or where amongst the desert of vehicles to look. The guys from school had apparently never shown up. Bonnie had dumped her for drugs and a fuck. And Kid was still standing in a dark corner of her mind, arms crossed, glaring at her. Such fun tonight.

Noelle retraced her path through the long mall building, exited the way she had come in. Just out of the huge threshold she numbly, not yet comprehending, watched the snipe run at the teenage boy like a phantom greyhound. It leaped, and was on him. The screams of others inspired Noelle, finally, to scream. She couldn't see much between the bodies of other people, through the rising dust–just frenzied movement as the weird bluish dog creature savaged the boy. It wasn't even this boy who had noticed the creature lurking under an empty animal trailer nearby, and had pitched a few rocks at it, some others then joining it. He was simply the one the aggravated scavenger had focused its rage on. Maybe it was his bright white leather jacket. Now red. The *screams*...

Noelle had dropped her bags, palms pressed to her ears, but watched–mesmerized. Of course it had only been a matter of seconds before someone with a gun took aim, a Choom man in a wide stance, pistol in both hands, but he roared in frustration because he was afraid to hit the boy. A black boy darted in with nunchakus and swung them. The chained club cracked across the snipe's back, and in a flash it was on him instead. It had him by the throat, its jaws widely unhinged like those of a snake. The black boy stumbled backwards, remarkably staying on his feet, but his useless hands fluttered like electrified moths. Only when the snipe hurled its entire body back and forth like a fish hooked on a line did the boy go down–to die. The snipe didn't let go.

Now the Choom squatted on his haunches and chanced a shot. It struck the beast on the right side of the neck. It released the boy, its wide mouth open in an uncanny banshee howl. A twisty, billowing cloud of black smoke poured into the air from the wound like a squid's ink unfolding under water. Two more shots. One missed, due to the smoke screen, one plunged into its ribs, out the other side. It furiously bolted away.

The phantom greyhound tore down the midway, trailing smoke behind it from three holes like jet streams. It leaped over a child, not even touching her head. Finally, however, mad with pain, it crashed into the side of a target shooting game. It crawled agonizingly up and inside the booth, where it challenged the panicking man behind the counter for this shelter. He went down under the creature. Both sorts of blood were seen rising from behind the counter.

Some teenage boys came to lean over the counter and lash its back with the heavy chains they wore around their waists. Whirling, it seized on boy by the wrist and yanked him over the counter. Others were rushing to help, all races and ages united in this battle. A man seized one of the machine guns mounted on the counter like a helicopter gun. These fired B-Bs at paper targets with red stars on them—if the star were totally obliterated you won a prize. He had just been ready to try for this when the snipe came along and now he returned to the loaded gun, swivelled and opened fire.

The streams of tiny silver balls tore into the snipe's clammy blue flesh, and from each a new puff of smoke escaped, then a thin stream. The snipe released the boy (whose arm was hit with some BBs, too) and flipped crazily into the air, twisted in mid-air, fell and flopped in circles as if to chase its tail. The smoke screen began to obscure it. The wounded boy clambered over the counter top, babbling.

Dingo Rubydawn, Mitch Garnet's Choom security man, stepped up to the counter and took patient aim into the stinking black whirlpool of cloud.

Back at the mall, Noelle heard the detonations of the two explosive bullets. This was enough. She wanted to go home. *Now*.

"Blast *me*," breathed Bern Glandston, blindly inserting a dilky into his mouth, then chewing it unconsciously. He stared, mildly awed, at the leg.

It was a free attraction; putting a tent around it and charging admission had been considered but would detract from the effect of the great spider-like appendage emerging out of empty air. Lights illuminated it and there was a sign nearby with information. Two years ago it had appeared, at first just the mechanical-looking claws at the end and a bit of leg, high in the air. Slowly, imperceptibly, more had emerged as the foot lowered toward the ground. After two years the foot was still two inches from touching ground. It was as black, glistening and reflective as obsidian, with cruel barbs, odd mechanical joints, tough bristles, and the words "Toby Fucks" sprayed on the upper part of the leg in the nearly impossible to remove paint favored by graffiti artists.

Bern stepped around to the back of the leg. He craned his neck. He thought the cross-section where the leg emerged from thin air might show an actual cross-section; bones, nerves, veins, whatever. The surface was just a flat black disc. Bern moved around front to read the sign further. It had been suggested that this extra-dimensional creature had been drawn to the site by the color, noise, or activity. "By the smell of dilkies," Bern muttered to himself, cramming one in his mouth. The sign went on that the leg was seven feet in length this year. Scientists had taken samples of this one, and in the air over a certain bank here in Punktown two hundred and forty-three of these legs had materialized. They had been fitted with lights to keep helicars from striking them at night, and a disintegrating unit had later been attached by brackets to two legs to catch a dribbling liquid which had started to rain out of the blue sky onto the bank, and which scientists later identified as a kind of waste product. The dribble had stopped after four months. It still remained to be seen whether or not those legs would have to be sliced away by the authorities in the future, pending further developments. The origin or nature of the creature was still unknown.

"Two hundred forty-*three*," muttered Bern, wagging his head, chewing. Staring. What kind of thing loomed above him now, cloaked in invisibility, standing in this same space but in some other dimension? What did it want here? It was enough to make even Bern Glandston ponder a few more moments, even if nobody else seemed interested, too busy rushing from ride to game to food stand.

But he did sense a presence close behind him now, and he turned.

Though he had never seen an alien of this type before he was more curious than startled. It was huge, almost as tall as the leg, and sturdy, muscular. The head was like a hornless cattle skull with intelligent human-like eyes set in the deep cups of the sockets, the teeth devoid of gums and covering lips. It was naked, its muscle definition thus clearly displayed, and this showed that while the helmet of a skull was entirely turquoise, around the jaw and neck there began a pebbly chainmail of tiny smooth scales, turquoise and black in various sizes and patterns which changed in accordance with the area of the large body. The scales and their patterns were beautiful. The towering being was staring down at the ground in front of Bern, not at the mysterious leg or the sign discussing it. Though not afraid, the proximity and size of the being made Bern want to say something to get on its good side. But then, it wasn't looking at his face, and in another instant Bern might have walked past it if he didn't notice something he hadn't at first for the darkness the creature glistened in. There was a large area of dullness which did not glitter with lovely scales on the being's chest, extending up over one shoulder and presumably down the back. This area was deeply indented. The scaled skin had been removed from the area.

Those cow-sized but human eyes lifted from his shoes to stare directly into Bern's eyes. Even without brows to lower or lids to squint, the eyes glared. And Bern felt a silent bomb of horror explode inside him, its cold tingling fallout spreading through his limbs, as he realized he was for the first time staring into the eyes of a Torgessi.

It clearly didn't matter to this particular Torgessi that Bern's shoes were *silver* and black, and couldn't have been made from the hide stolen from its own body. A low, ominous rattling rose from deep in its throat. Some of those distinct muscles shifted in its chest and shoulders like a restless sleeper under a blanket.

"Hey!" said Bern, and he spun on the heel of his slipper, and bolted.

It was after him. Bern wasn't sure how speedy a cold-blooded Torgessi would be but he held nothing back. It had stopped rattling so he couldn't judge its nearness by that and he didn't dare look over his shoulder. The suspended leg had been a little removed from the thick of carnival activity, and it was toward this that Bern ran, hoping the monster would be afraid to pursue him in public.

He plunged into a wave of people, bumping them, shouldering past some roughly, who glowered after him. He plunged between two game booths, jumped over a coiled drunk lying in the alley, and on into another corridor of the carnival labyrinth. Now, at last, he risked stopping to turn around and look for the creature. He panted, his heart somersaulting down the staircase of his ribs over and over.

The Minotaur stepped into the alley he had ducked into, its smoldering eyes falling directly on his. "Dung!" Bern cried hoarsely, bolting again.

Bern ran up to a group of apparent college kids who might prove sympathetic. "Hey," he wheezed, holding onto a boy's elbow, "you've gotta help me." The boy jerked his arm away but Bern hardly noticed as he watched behind him for the monster. He wiped the back of his hand across his mouth, smearing his black lipstick. "There's an alien chasing me...a Torgessi...it wants to kill me."

"Well don't lead it to us," one of the girls in the group sneered.

"Tell a security guard or something, will you? Call the police." Bern made ready to flee again, seeing that this was no shelter. "Has anybody got a gun?"

"No."

"Come on, please, I'll buy it from you."

"Learn how to handle yourself," the sneering girl hissed, disgusted with this groveling display.

"There it is!" Bern took flight. The security headquarters, where was it? He had to look for the administration trailers. He couldn't very well leave the fair, with Pox yet to meet, his big deal to be made, especially with so many people already promised for tomorrow.

As he moved Bern patted his clothes for his hand phone, so as to call the three-digit emergency number for the police, but his frisking of himself became more frenzied as he realized he couldn't find the device. Dung! He must have dropped it, or had it stolen from his pocket, while barreling through the throngs of carnival-goers...

Bern stayed in the main thoroughfares, hoping to become totally lost to the monster in the flood of people, but this also slowed his progress. At times it was like swimming upstream against a strong current. He came to a full halt, tangled in the knot of people gathered around an open tent in which men were arm wrestling. Moaning in despair, Bern glanced behind once more, and cried out. The towering alien was calmly but implacably striding toward him, its head above most of the bobbing heads, those eyes ever fixed on him. Bern panicked, tried clawing his way through the knot. "Hey, slime!" a man growled, elbowing him in the ribs. Bern grunted but persisted. He was almost through...

"Hey, kid." A huge, uniformed security guard loomed up abruptly, taking hold of Bern's arm sternly. "Take it easy."

EVERYBODY SCREAM!

"Thank God!" Bern gasped, and pointed crazily as the guard drew him a few steps away from the knot of people. "Help me...that Torgessi is chasing me...it wants to kill me!"

The guard looked. The alien had stopped in its tracks, a pillar around which the waves of people lapped, so multi-colored as if the carnival lights reflected on their watery surface. Its eyes hadn't left the boy. "Why?" grunted the guard.

"I have Torgessi-skin shoes...but hey, y'know?"

The guard glanced at the dusty slippers, back up at the Torgessi. "Hey you," he called. "You. Move along. Get lost. We don't want any trouble." No response. "Hey! Torgessi! Look at me!" At last, those eyes slowly rolled to the right to acknowledge the guard. "Be on your way...I'll have you expelled! Do you *hear* me?"

If it didn't understand the words, it understood the meaning. Slowly, reluctantly, the Torgessi turned away. Moved off in another direction. It didn't look back. The guard and Bern watched after it a long while until no sign of it remained. The guard released Bern's arm and grumbled, "Fucking aliens. This is an *Earth* colony. They've got no respect for us. You'll be okay kid...any more trouble just report it, okay?"

"Oh thanks...thanks so much. I thought it was gonna snuff me! Is there a pay phone I can use around here?"

"On the side of the piss shed, down by the mall. Go on, you'll be okay now. That lizard makes trouble with you again I'll personally make you a jacket out of him." The barrel-bellied guard chuckled bitterly.

"Thanks again, man." Bern wearily walked off in the rough direction he figured the mall area must lie.

Bern was correct, and the guard was correct that he was not attacked along the way. He waited his turn at a pay phone fixed to one side of the lavatory shed, punched Pox's number out. The vid plate came on but was malfunctioning, showed only a colored blizzard. The voice of Pox's beautiful girlfriend came on, groggy. She was perpetually groggy.

"'Lo, this is Bern Glandston—is Pox there?"

A long, barely tolerant sigh. "*No*. He's out."

"Out? Out where?"

"Out–I don't know. He's going to that carnival tonight."

"Yeah, he was going to meet me here–I'm at the carnival."

"Well look around."

"Did he tell you where abouts he'd be?"

"He doesn't tell me anything," said the blizzard of snow, for a moment almost coalescing into a beautiful but unpleasant face. "He just said he had a few errands to do and then he was going to the carnival..."

"A few errands to do first? Like what?"

"I don't fucking know, alright?" The line went dead.

"*Whore*," Bern hissed, punching his phone dead also.

Sighing, he turned to survey the carnival. If Pox were here already it still might take all fucking night to find him. What an arrogant, unprofessional scumbag. Disgusted and exhausted, Bern moved into the lavatory shed to fix his hair and makeup and wipe the dust from his shoes.

"Three dead," Del breathed. "From one snipe."

"And one kid with his hand half ripped off," Dingo added, handing Del a coffee. They stood in the security headquarters trailer–for the carnival's security team, not the town's commissioned team. Behind a desk a female security team member was making out some reports on the snipe attack. Mitch Garnet, not in attendance, was occupied elsewhere.

"They're mostly scavengers–if you leave 'em alone they'll keep their distance. Sometimes they'll prey on a drunk in a subway, but..."

"Well, you can never be sure. They say some kids were throwing rocks, though. There's gotta be a nest around here."

"Scary thought."

"I sent the KeeZees to look around where it first appeared. I don't know who I'd less want to be if they meet, the KeeZees or the snipes. I sure as hell wouldn't want to be the one to find their nest," Dingo chuckled.

Someone entered the trailer, both men and the woman behind the desk

EVERYBODY SCREAM!

looked. A young girl. Dingo Rubydawn's wary eyes relaxed a little. "Can we help you?"

"Yeah, ah, excuse me, but can you help me with something? I've been looking around for my friend for a couple hours now and I can't find her, and we didn't bring hand phones. Do you think you can page her...do you have a PA system?"

Wow, Del said internally. She had to be in her late teens. Mostly black, racially. Her skin was a lovely dark honey, her eyes–under full brows, half-lidded–made bedroom eyes look bulging wide awake; maybe the dreamiest dark eyes Del had ever seen. Her nostrils had an ethnic spread but not too wide and her cheekbones were well-shaped. The lips were thick and sensuous, despite the way shadow tended to fall over the upper lip and make a faint fake mustache.

"Yep," said Dingo. "What's her name and what's yours?"

"My friend's name is Bonnie Gross, and I'm Noelle Buda."

"You want to get on the mic yourself and say, 'Bonnie, where the blast *are* ya?' or should I do it and be more discreet?"

"Ah, I would like to say that," the girl laughed, "but I think you'd better do it if you don't mind."

"No prob."

She had a great smile, as heavy and drunken as her eyes. Her voice, too, had a thick, weighty sensuality in its slow, soft coos. Her eyes moved to Del a moment and gleamed, the honey-thick smile on him before she turned her attention back to Dingo. Man, that contact. She wore a tight-fitting black sweater, a lacy and ruffled multi-layered black skirt probably best called a tutu over black tights ending a little below her knees, black sneakers. A thin red ankle ribbon. She was small and slim, a child-like young woman; her dense mass of tightly-curled black hair looked to be a fifth of her body weight. Del loved women's hair. Once again, he could see why the Red Jihad made them keep it covered so as not to tempt men (though, not why they had to throw acid in women's faces to enforce it). Candy, man. She was fucking candy for the eyes. All the sugar and sweets of this carnival poured into a human mold...

Dingo got on the PA and said, "Bonnie Gross, please report to the security trailer...your friend Noelle Buda is waiting for you. Bonnie Gross, please report to the security trailer...your friend Noelle Buda is waiting for you."

"Thank you."

"No prob. You just wait here, I've got to get back to work. You want a cup of java while you wait?"

"Java?"

"Coffee," Del said for Dingo quickly.

"Oh, ah, sure. Thanks."

Dingo gestured to one of the office robots to tend to her. He made for the door. "Good luck, kid."

"Thank you."

Del and Noelle were left alone; the woman at the desk again immersed herself in her work. Noelle was smiling softly, drunkenly at him. "Crazy time tonight. I saw a snipe kill people, I got swallowed and pooped out by a whale..."

"Oh, you saw the snipe kill those people?"

"I'm afraid so. Not what I had in mind for a night of fun and entertainment, exactly. That shook me up. And now my friend deserted me for some stranger...Moussa-something. What next?"

"Maybe it'll be something nice, next," said Del.

"I hope so–I've used up all my bad luck. Two months of bad luck in advance. I've *earned* something nice."

The robot handed her a coffee. "Cream? Sugar?"

"No, this is good." Noelle didn't care much for coffee in any form. It was good for studying late, but so were pills. Mostly it was a social prop.

"More coffee, Del?" asked the machine.

"Oh–my *God!*" squealed Noelle. Del was startled, looked at her. She had spilled a little coffee on the floor; at first Del thought she had burned her mouth. Her free hand was clamped over it and above her hand her sleepy eyes had bulged awake at him. Only as she lowered her hand and began to speak did Del finally recognize this forgotten sort of behavior. "You're Del Kahn, aren't you?" she said in breathy awe.

EVERYBODY SCREAM!

A huge stupid grin spread across Del's face; he was unaccustomed, ill-prepared, and embarrassed. "Well...I guess I still am."

"Oh my *God!*" she laughed tremulously. "I don't believe it! I was looking at you and I thought it looked like you but I didn't really think so, with your suit and everything!"

Del shooed the robot away. "Well, I'd still be Del Kahn even in a dress, wouldn't I?"

"God, I can't *believe* this!"

"So...what, did you hear somewhere that my wife was running this carnival?"

"She is? No, I didn't hear that, I had no idea!"

"Really?" If possible, Del's grin expanded further. "God bless you, my dear...you made my day. A woman after my very heart."

"I love your music, I really do. I have three of your chips."

"Are you trying to get me to write you into my will, now? How old are you, anyway?"

"Eighteen. So what? I used to listen to you when I was thirteen–my brother had two of your chips. He gave them to me when he moved out and then I bought one, too. I have *Loud Secrets*, *Fossils and Fireworks*, and *Heroes*." There was a considerable gap in years and in work between those two early albums and his last. At least, God bless her yet further, she had bought *Heroes*, not limited to dwelling solely on his optimistic, rousing, passion-of-life stuff as so many tended to do.

"Well, Noelle, for patronizing me to such an admirable extent in the past the least I can do is treat you to dinner. Have you eaten?"

"Oh...well...yeah, just junk. I could eat a little something." Though her eyes no longer bulged she hadn't gone totally back to sleep. They shone. She was more child-like now, less darkly sensuous, but still lovely.

"Good, well let's go sit and talk while you wait for your friend to come. I've got nothing else to do, myself. I can help you salvage something nice out of the evening, I hope."

"Um, but what if I'm not here when Bonnie comes?" She looked distressed, she looked like she wanted Del to sweep away that problem–like she now wanted to shake off her friend, not locate her.

"Gola," Del said over Noelle's shoulder, "will you give me a call on my hand phone when her friend comes in?"

"Sure," said the woman at the desk.

"And try paging her again in a half hour if she doesn't respond."

"Right."

"Thanks." To Noelle, "Does that sound okay to you, kid?"

"Great! Believe me, Mr. Kahn, you *have* helped me salvage something nice out of the night."

"Likewise, and glad to hear it. Come on, I have an interesting place in mind–hope you haven't seen it already. It's a favorite."

"I remember seeing a few things when you got married," Noelle said as they strolled side by side.

"Used to be if I blew my nose you saw it on all the news and headlines."

"She's pretty, though I can't remember what she looks like."

Del chuckled.

"You know what I mean," Noelle grinned, embarrassed.

"I do. You're right, she is pretty," Del reluctantly admitted.

"I never heard about her buying a carnival, though."

"Well, I bought it, mostly. But it's hers...it's important to her." Now Del chuckled at himself. "Yeah, like she'd run a carnival if it wasn't important to her, huh? She loves it. She does a good job–there's a lot to juggle, a lot to organize. She has a good mind for business and management. I myself would rather leave that to others. Her real fantasy, though...or should I say goal...is to start a circus."

"A circus? With, um, flying trapeze and clowns and all that?"

"Yeah. She's been doing research into old, old Earth circuses. I don't know, though. I don't think Sophi is the circus type. She fits in better here. Carnivals are gritty. She's a gritty woman."

"Is that good or bad?" Noelle meekly asked, afraid to get personal.

Del didn't hesitate in replying, however. "Good and bad, like anything. Mostly good. It's good to be tough so long as you can still be soft, and she can." Despite his openness, though, he didn't want to talk about Sophi

EVERYBODY SCREAM!

anymore. He asked Noelle about herself, and she told him about school. She was open, too—except that she didn't bring up Kid.

Zebo's Saucer was actually a large trailer, not a space craft despite its saucer-like form and the fact that it hovered above the ground when traveling. A mobile diner. Inside there was a half circle counter and a few tables. On the walls were framed photographs and articles from newspapers and magazines. One recent photo showed Del Kahn and a smaller person, his gibbon-long arm around Del's shoulders. It was Zebo.

Zebo came to Del and Noelle's table for the exchange of introductions. He was barely five feet tall, a skinny disproportionate child with long arms and long hands, an oversized head with white skin as smooth and hairless as that of a fetus. No ears, a tiny slit for a mouth, two pinhole nostrils but two huge, wraparound lustrous black eyes with blinking translucent lids. Zebo had smiled and rushed over the moment Del entered.

"Did you get a look at Zebo's pictures?" Del asked Noelle.

She twisted in her seat against the wall to peer at a few mounted near her. One was just a copy of an old photo showing a fringe of pine trees and a white saucer craft, presumably much larger than this one, hovering in the sky.

"That was over Oregon in 1964," beamed Zebo, pointing. "Us, I should say. We had a crew of, ah, thirty-four on that one."

"Oregon?" said Noelle.

"Earth. Nineteen sixty-four A.D." Zebo clarified. "Beautiful country in Oregon at that time, all trees. No humans except for clones or the time-travelers are alive to remember that beauty, but I saw it. The things I saw of your world," he reminisced wistfully.

Noelle, granddaughter of a colonist and never having set foot on the planet this being called *her* world, turned to Del uncomfortably in hope of more clarification than Zebo had to offer. He was grinning. "Zebo made several trips to Earth long ago, to study us from a distance. A couple of times his ships were sighted or photographed."

"I made the *National Inquirer* on that one," pointing out a framed article. He laughed and wagged his head, related how scared those blubbering farmers had been in his monitor screens. And the time his team took a man and his wife aboard and performed examinations on their prone bodies. He playfully flopped the man's big penis this way and that. It was this kind of activity, and getting caught on film one time too often, he told Noelle, that had gotten him expelled from further visits. His memory of his voyages and missions had been erased, a procedure commonly used by his people on human specimens before release, but much of his memory had gradually come back.

Or so he believed, Del confided in Noelle when Zebo took their orders to the kitchen. "I think he thinks he did a lot more than he really did. If you believe him he was on half the unidentified flying objects reported in Earth's twentieth century. He says one of his teams helped ancient Earth people build some kind of temple or structure–I forget what he said it was exactly. They also supposedly seeded humans on various planets as an experiment. The Chooms evolved from Earth specimens they seeded here, for instance."

"He probably gets a kick out of seeing how much he can trick people into believing. Or he does it to make himself seem important. He's just another alien."

Del pouted in Zebo's defense. "I like the guy. And he makes some really odd, tasty munchies. They're out of this world."

Zebo brought their food, returned to the counter, read a magazine, though occasionally Noelle glanced over and he seemed to be spying on them, studying them. He would quickly return to his reading. An eerie thought came to her. What if he hadn't truly been expelled from his scientific team...if, in accordance with the passage of time, his studies had taken on this new kind of guise so as to move in close to the subjects? Del had said that Zebo's race had never fully approached the Earth colonial network. Stupid, she thought, chewing a tasty morsel. Now the little clown's got me believing his tall tales.

She focused, with a fresh surge of giddy inner excitement like a flood of drugs through her blood, on the man chewing opposite her. He crinkled a grin at her, eyes twinkly. She had to voice her feelings. "I really can't believe this–sitting at a table eating with *Del Kahn!* My brother will never believe me. I hope you can give me an autograph before you go."

"Only if you give me yours. I'd never have expected to be sitting at a table eating with Noelle Buda."

"Oh–huge thrill, I'm certain."

"I rather enjoy it."

The earnestness of his words and the way his words pressed down on her made her flush, her gaze diving to hide amongst the colorful food. "So, um...do you think you'll do another album anytime soon?"

She didn't see his grin stumble, slow its pace to a mere wobbly smile. "Who knows?"

"Oh," she looked up suddenly, "you have to record again."

"Why?"

"*Why?*"

"Why do I *have* to?"

"Because you have a talent! How many people have that kind of talent?" She wondered if he could be simply teasing her. Joking and wittiness seemed to be his charming way. But his reply, slow in coming, was unsmiling and somber.

"My last chip, *Heroes*, sold less than any of my previous chips–my first one included."

"Well, you know, it's the quality of your fans, not the quantity."

"Quantity matters, too. You needs sales. Who's the quality, anyway?"

"Well, you know, people who really listen to the lyrics, understand your meaning. Wouldn't you rather have a million listeners like that than ten million who just want music to drive to or dance to? It would seem to me the more people you try to please the more you have to sacrifice your, ah, you know–vision."

"Yes and no. There are some themes and meanings large enough to touch almost everybody–if they only chose to listen. It's stupid of me, since the people always come before the critics for me, but maybe if the critics had been kinder to *Heroes* I wouldn't have been so disappointed. But they weren't.

Bosley Simon said, and I quote verbatim, 'Del Kahn's self-serving pretentiousness is exemplified in his attempt to align himself with heroes more or less familiar, including Choom rebel-leader Mooa-Ki Fen in the dirge-like ballad *Rust*. His name-dropping seems to be an endeavor to glorify himself by association, to sell himself to us as a hero in the company of heroes.'" Del gave a bitter smirk. "Boss used to give me great notices. But I was lean, then. Now I'm a big fat lazy rich sacred cow and Bosley and his kind are the jackals. Same with the audience. They loved me when I seemed like one of them, lean and driven to make it–I *was* them. If I made it they made it. But I made it and they saw me as a cow, too. They didn't savage me, but they left me to starve."

Noelle looked sympathetic, even sad. "I didn't," she said, "Not everybody did." She made him less regretful of his self-pitying analogy. "I loved *Heroes*. It was so deep. I, for one–though I'm *positive* I'm far from alone–would love to see a new album. You know your song *Candy Apples*? Man, I love that song! That's a real carnival song. It's perfect for this place. I know the lyrics by heart. Want to hear?"

Del leaned forward, planted his jaw on his cupped hand. Smiled. "Sure."

"I'll say it, I can't sing it...

'The smell of french-fries is in the air
And the smell of popcorn everywhere
We'll risk the haunted house, my dear
Rest your head on my shoulder and ride out the fear
Tonight will be as sweet as candy apples
Tonight will be as sweet as candy apples.'"

She giggled. "Go on," he urged her, enchanted even in his melancholy, as if seduced by his own words.

"'Well, the thing we saw in the House of Freaks
Reminds me of the horror film we saw last week
I'll win you a cheap plastic teddy bear
That'll end up in a drawer with your underwear

EVERYBODY SCREAM!

And the things that we'll see
And the things that we'll do
Will come back in memories
And seem brand new
Tonight will be as sweet as candy apples
Tonight will be as sweet as candy apples

The stars are ferris wheels spinning in the sky
Tonight I'm glad to be the apple of your eye
I'm sorry that the target range hurt your ears
You say you want to risk the haunted house again, my dear?
Tonight has been as sweet as candy apples
Tonight has been as sweet as candy apples.'"

"Very good. No mistakes. That's an old one–from my first chip." Cute. But did Noelle know by heart the lyrics of *Blue Blues*? That reminded Del (glance at a clock) that he had best attend Pearl's final show shortly–no doubt she would expect him to be there.

The lyrics to *Candy Apples* pleased him but also embarrassed him. Same thing, now, with *Rust* or *Blue Blues*. Too bad. There lay the greatest sin of it: that as much as he hated them he ached to be valued by the critics, to please them, and they had made him doubt, at times, the worthiness of his creations. His value as an artist.

"You ever listen to old music? Pre-colonial pop?"

"No. Not really."

"There's a line in a song by a man named Elvis Costello, a far better lyricist than I could ever be. It's from a song called *Watch Your Step*. It isn't about carnivals, but I think about it a lot. It says, 'Ev'ry night go out full of carnival desires.'"

Noelle pouted in exaggerated appreciation, mostly just catching the pun. And then a particular meaning she sensed was intended for her by Del, via Elvis, dawned in her. Actually it was transmitted more in the way Del eyed her–drank her. His clinging melancholy, consciously or unconsciously, aided him by giving him a romantic sad dreaminess. Noelle's heart was a bird carried upward in a strong air current. It frightened her a little but exhilarated her much. She wasn't a stupid woman. She could see and feel what it was that this man, Del Kahn, desired of her.

And why should she deny him, or herself? Could the sex act with this relative stranger really be a sin when it was just an unfamiliar penis inside her instead of a familiar one? She had sucked her friend Jackybuns off in a bathroom. But then she knew Jackybuns. Then again, through his vids, his voice and face and especially his lyrics, might she not know Del Kahn as well as she knew Jackybuns, or Kid, or anybody?

"You're very attractive," Del cooed, softly so Zebo wouldn't overhear. "In fact, you are truly gorgeous."

"Thank you," Noelle said huskily.

"And what's more, you're sweet. I like a sweet girl. They're not as abundant as everyone would have you believe. If I were a wee bit younger and a wee bit unmarried I'm sure I could fall in love with you."

Wow. The air current was whipping faster, and higher than she'd imagined, the air becoming rarefied, the spinning scenery below obscured in clouds. It was disorienting. The flesh of Noelle's face felt molten.

What he'd said about being younger was wrong. What he'd meant was if he could go back in time. Age difference in itself meant little to him...he had, in his thirties, gone to bed with teenagers, even a few precociously younger teenagers, but he had never devirginized or even had to seduce any of them. There had been no effort; they had fallen to him easily, quickly. Like now. This was like the old days. Thus it was not only Noelle's perceived sweetness that enchanted, moved him.

"I find you very attractive, too," she croaked under her breath, squeezing her palms together between her knees under the table. "Needless to say."

"I want to go to bed with you."

Noelle swallowed the bird back down as it sought to fly up her throat, out her mouth. "I want that, too."

Her fear made her face more sensuous than ever, brittle with emotion ready to leak out at the first piercing. It made him a little afraid. This would be no mere mechanical exchange for either of them. So what, then, might come of it?

"We can't go to my trailer–I have no idea where my wife might be. But I know a safe place." He didn't add that he'd ascertained its safety by having used it before.

"Alright," Noelle said, and again swallowed...an almost comic gulping sound. She watched as Del meaningfully lifted his hand phone between them and shut its ringer off.

They were obviously finished eating; Del went to the counter to pay the check. Tossed a tip on the table, then gently took Noelle's arm to lead her out of the saucer.

Zebo watched their backs intently as they left, jotted some notes in the margin of his magazine, and then resumed his reading.

The first ride Fawn went on with Fen was a circular wheel with many individual open cells along its outer edge, facing in. Wes and Heather took cells beside each other (and Cookie, now a muttering tag-a-long, beside them) and Fawn and Fen crossed to the opposite side. Fawn stepped into her cell, pulled down her own restraining bar. At no point did the glum, wordless operator come in to see if these bars were being employed.

They were the entire group of passengers but for someone to Fawn's left separated by one empty cell, the first aboard. The wheel began to turn...slowly...picked up speed. Fast. The black sky overhead was a whirlpool. The carnival lights were being mixed in a food blender. Her hair dancing crazily, a snapping tattered war banner, Fawn cried out to Fen on her right, "This is great–I love it!"

"And I love you!" he grinned back at her, leaning over his restraining bar so she could see him clearly.

The wheel began to lift at an angle. It tipped more and more until finally it seemed it would become totally vertical, but it stopped tilting at a steep angle. Far across from Fawn, Cookie laughed crazily and waved. Behind Cookie the whole world was a whirlpool now, earth blended into sky. The wheel whipped Fawn up at the sky, then swung her down at the ground. This was the greatest point of the spinning—when you hurtled at the ground, the lights illuminating the people below like fish in an aquarium. Standing just below the ride was a woman eating something, a baby stroller in front of her. Upon each rotation and plunge Fawn imagined the wheel would become unfastened and she would crash directly into that woman with her stroller, they were placed so perfectly below, like sacrifices, or as if mocking the precarious power of the great machine whirling down at them. Turning her head against the heavy g-force was difficult, but Fawn watched Wes and Heather for a few moments. Heather was laughing appreciatively as Wes showed off by pushing his restraining bar up and away, simply holding on by planting his feet and gripping two poles. Then just one pole. His army jacket was flapping open and she was sure she could detect the black presence of a gun beneath.

Cookie, too physically stimulated to feel sorry for herself at the moment, went on laughing insanely. Sky and earth were a flicker behind her, a yin and yang spun into blurred motion. They had been sucked into a black hole. It was exhilarating, but scary. Fawn glanced over at the person on her left, who had said nothing, didn't laugh or cry out. Long dark hair streamed, writhed, but the person was too dark behind the mesh of the intervening cell for Fawn to see, at first. But as the wheel hurled them once more toward the ground as if to impale them on the glowing knives of light, Fawn saw greenish illumination pass over a woman's face. The naked grimace was not due to the g-force. The greenish light made distinct black pits for eyes, and as it left poured into and then out of one of the empty skull sockets. Fawn shuddered. This passenger never tired of the dizzy spinning, and never had to pay. But she didn't look too happy about it.

Fawn staggered down the steps, Fen pressing in to help her. Fawn looked for the mother and her baby but they were gone. "How do you feel?" Fen said close to her ear, his lips brushing it.

"Great," her voice trembled. She could barely look at him since what he'd said. Exhilarating, but scary.

EVERYBODY SCREAM!

New people scrambled up into the wheel to replace them. Fawn and the others moved along, and so Fawn didn't hear one of the new passengers cry out in recognition, "Oh my God–Jeanie! Jeanie! Jeanie!"

The second ride they entered together also gyrated in a fast circle, but there were branches growing from the center, with two carriages pointing in opposite directions at the end of each, which would rotate around each other as the entire machine rotated. It had an exact twin close by, actually the same ride, and the spinning path of their branches overlapped at one point. Were the mated machines so perfectly timed and calibrated that the whipping carriages of one would never collide with those of the other? Such a concern was the whole purpose of the thing. Fawn and Fen squeezed into a carriage.

The sadistic machine hurled them gleefully, cracked them in its whip, jolted them from side to side. Fawn screamed as their car seemed about to crash into those of the twin machine upon which Wes and Heather rode, but the car wove out just in time. Upon every full rotation their car also flew at the young man who collected the tickets and stood so still and calm watching their frenzied hurtling. He was grim, homely, tough-looking, a deep scar on a pocked face, the many colored lights pooled in the pocks like rain water reflecting neon. He seemed to be showing off to Fawn in particular (his eyes would appear to meet hers as she rushed at him) but she was sure he always did this...standing so close that the carriages brushed his shirt. Fawn resented him for making her nervous.

The solitary man in the other carriage at the end of their branch wore an expensive business suit, secured with a more complex harness than the others, perhaps of his own devising. He typed intently at a keyboard on his lap. Fawn didn't know, but he would ride this ride all night, had paid to ride this ride all day every day this season. He had a disease. Sometimes he had to go into constant spinning motion to find relief. He was having a device built into his home and one in his yard. He would allow his children to ride in them once in a while. This was the only way he could currently work at his job.

The force of the spinning pressed Fen painfully against Fawn, squashing her, pinning her. He had taken her hand; she squeezed it back. Shortly before the ride ended he leaned even closer to kiss her lightly on the lips.

The third ride was the Screamer, back toward the entrance. She, Heather and Cookie had ridden on it earlier, but without the company of the boys. Its loud music crashed in Fawn's ears, the wailing force which seemed to generate the spinning of the ride. She and Fen ran up the clanging metal ramp, squeezed together in one tiny rocking car. Wes and Heather, and Cookie alone, took cars on the other side, and were soon out of sight and out of mind.

Chauncy Carnal of Sphitt lustily rasped out *In Your Face*. Though the song was from a man's point of view, Fawn sang along softly and bounced in her seat to the beat as the last cars loaded up. She smiled to Fen as she sang, and he grinned. She became shy, stopped singing. He took her hand again and squeezed it as the circular train pulled out of the station. "Man, you're so blasting gorgeous," she could just barely hear him say to her.

Again, they were in a whirlpool of black night smeared with colored light and watching faces painted with glowing pigments, also blurring all together as if to create one huge hideous staring being. The Screamer blazed with bulbs from every available railing, support beam, rim and edge, and the lights flickered and fluctuated, pulsed and throbbed in time to the blaring, deafening, raucous music.

"Do you want to go *faaast*-er?"

"Yeahhh!" came the giddy chant.

Fen had released Fawn's sweaty hand, and rested his own on her leg above her knee. He gave it a light squeeze, then began rubbing his hand slowly up and down the length of her long slim thigh. Fawn's hands tightened slickly on the metal restraining bar…

"I *said*, do you want to go *FAST-ER?*"

"*Yeahhh!*"

Fen's hand caressed the inside of her thigh, damp with perspiration through her black sweat pants, the heel of his hand pressing into her crotch at the end of each heavy stroke. And, inevitably, his hand continued in its stroke, cupped her crotch, the fingers moving. Without even thinking Fawn moved her legs open wider, but she didn't look at Fen's face. She knew, uncomfortably, that he was watching hers, his gaze weighing more heavily against her than his pinning body.

"Alright...everybody SCREEEAM!"

Voices rose. Fawn made not a sound. Like a spider burrowing, his fingers teased the elastic waistband away from her soft belly. The spider scurried into the dark out of view, dug at the scantier inner layer. Fawn sank down lower in her seat. The legs of the spider slid lightly over her red crinkly hair, brushing it. Then proceeded lower. Teased at a more intimate layer. One leg made a reconnaissance mission into the dampness of this final burrow and found it inviting. Two legs hooked inside it, and the spider moved rhythmically as if in hopes of squeezing its entire bulk inside. His thumb rubbed at the tiny protuberance over the top of the cave like some kind of emblem.

Fawn arched her back violently, arched her neck back, clenching her eyes shut and grimacing like the trapped rider on that hurtling wheel. The music had plunged inside her through this opened hole, and crashed around madly, gleefully inside her body. The whole carnival had been sucked into her. She *was* the black hole. She squirmed and jolted in her seat as if this ride had finally revealed its true purpose to her, and was a torture device she was strapped into, electrified.

But, masochistically, despite the drug-like dizziness, the reeling disorientation, the shocks through her body, she welcomed the torture. She wanted to reach over and take him in hand but didn't dare let go of the bar. If she let go she would be flung off into space.

Fen's grin and gaze hadn't left her. Though he didn't share her rocking orgasms he loved just watching her face, knowing that *he* was doing that to her...it made him feel powerful; he had her fully in his hand. Anyway, he had no doubt whatsoever that his time would come soon now.

Del wove his way alone through the carnival, more a living ever-shifting maze than an inorganic one, the volume of flesh perhaps outweighing the volume of the inorganic materials which composed it. Del moved quickly. He had a slight fear of losing Noelle before he could get to her. He had sent her along ahead of him; luckily she knew the spot he'd chosen for a rendezvous, although she had expressed confusion.

He had been afraid to have Noelle accompany him. God only knew where Sophi might be. But even alone he dreaded seeing her pop up. Thus it was that he moved swiftly, furtively. Guilt drove him as much as his hunger.

She was there behind the Screamer; she hadn't changed her mind. She didn't look any less confused, but smiled nervously. Del did also, relieved to have made his destination without obstacle. And no kids were back here smoking iodine joints or fucking on the ground. "Stay here one more minute," Del instructed her, and gave her a light kiss on the lips.

Here? Noelle thought after Del had gone around the Screamer. She didn't see him go up to the elevated control booth with the shadowy figures inside behind its glass. Noelle glanced around at the trash on the ground, sensing sex that had taken place here previously as if she could still smell it. It was one of those places, like the back of a cemetery, where you could almost see the sperm wriggling all over the ground and onto your shoes.

Del returned again, and moved straight past her to a metal panel at the base of the ride. Keys jingled. Noelle understood. Del slid the panel open. "Go on in," he invited. He looked more than a little embarrassed, but still undauntedly hungry. His smiles were more shy, uncomfortable now than flirty and charming. It was dark in there and Noelle had to hunch down.

Once inside she could stand easily; so could Del, who wasn't tall anyway. He locked the panel behind him. It shut out the music a little, but it still poured in through some spaces above, as did the whirling lights, flickering across the vibrating walls, shadows of the train fluttering like the wings of huge birds. The inside of the Screamer rumbled. Del moved to two mechanic's lamps hanging from the support frame, and now the interior was well lit.

There was a plastic mattress in the center, of course. For a few moments she watched as Del removed a dark green plastic sheet from a cardboard dispenser and covered the bed, as a doctor will pull down new white paper on his examination table. Her eyes strayed to a number of empty beer cans, some tools spread out on a sheet of cardboard, a dog-eared skin

EVERYBODY SCREAM!

magazine tossed almost out of the pool of stark light. The sperm she had felt crawling across her shoes must have actually come from in here.

But hunger is honest, hunger isn't proud. Far stronger than the kind of mild disgust she felt was a fresh surge of desire at the bald purpose of this chamber. Straightening, Del turned to face her. He had been avoiding her eyes and she his but now they held contact. He slowly approached her and his aura of lust almost pressed her back; she had to put one foot a step behind her.

His hands sliding up under the bunched material of her lacy skirt, Del held Noelle's ass inside the taut smooth skin of her tights while their mouths locked. She let her tongue into his mouth first. He seldom kissed or fucked with closed eyes because he liked to watch the bliss, but he didn't always like to be looked back at unless it was that dazed grateful adoration when they (*if* they) reached their plateau of ecstasy. He ran his hands up and down her ass, cupped it, squeezed it. He unclamped his mouth to burrow into her neck, which she arched, her wide lips puffed wider as if swollen with lust, parted open. He kissed her throat, licked her neck just under her jaw line and she groaned shudderingly, holding on to him. Her hair was heavy with the smell of shampoo, her skin had the powdery aftertaste of perfume, chemical but clean. His hand whispered up the skin of her back under her sweater.

More of her body had the scent and taste of applied perfume as it was revealed to his hands, eyes, nose and lips. Like most young people without a lover, Noelle prepared herself each day as if that day she would meet one, and go to bed with him. A person might wait for years but still conceivably make sure to be so prepared. Only in one place–at which he thirstily dwelt like a man in a desert lapping at mud in a hole he's dug, dwelt until she squirmed as if to kick or buck him off, though she held his head there until he couldn't breathe–was she not so perfumed, but he was used to this.

He moved up to mount her after she'd finally pushed his head away, grimacing with eyes closed, and now she cried out and climaxed within moments of his furious pumping. She had been so primed that he had barely felt himself enter. Her slim legs greedily rose up to hook him like the jaws of a giant beetle, her toes curled from the intensity of her gripping. Del's contrastingly white buttocks pumped like a bellows. He was panting, sucking down air greasy with the smell of machine lubrication, holding her head in both hands and staring fixedly at her face, her head thrown back, upper chest and throat and bared forehead filmed with sweat. She pursed her lips out at the air, eyebrows lifted and twisted over her capped lids as if in pain. Staring at her face now, more than anything else, would bring him to his zenith.

She cracked her eyes open a little, smiled faintly at him. Though past the orgasm peak and below even the plateau, her smile looked grateful. But after a few moments Del looked away, twisting atop her body to draw a tiny brown-nippled breast into his mouth. So Noelle stared up at the dark ceiling as her body was rocked on the slick plastic sheet.

The train had stopped earlier, started again, stopped, now started again. Above, the DJ or operator or whatever you'd call him drawled, "Okay, we're just about ready to roll…rock and roll, that is. Keep your limbs inside the cars, please, and hold on tight…"

Mm, it was good. She knew another train of orgasms was coming around slowly. He nuzzled her neck and she inclined her face away, hoping he wouldn't kiss her, not liking her own smell on his breath. She stared beyond the pool of light into the dark where colored ghosts of light flitted around and around them. She could almost see all those people lined up out there, so close, for the next ride–staring at them, an audience.

The storm of wild music raged outside, the ceiling above rattled, clattered, the walls rumbling as the train picked up speed. They were inside a volcano. The speed increased, perhaps inspiring her lover, who had been slacking off to catch his breath.

Maybe she thought he was simply making it last, but Del was experiencing difficulty. He couldn't coax his own orgasm toward release; it would climb but elude him, then snaking out of his grasp.

"Just worry about what you do, pal," Sophi had said this morning after he had gingerly approached the subject of her drinking.

He lifted Noelle's left leg under the knee, held it out and up away from them as he pumped, stared at it. He would do this to Sophi or to anyone, not so much to admire the lovely shape but for a stimulus when orgasm was distant, either because the body had been under him so long that he

EVERYBODY SCREAM!

needed to see some of it to renew his drive, or when he was preoccupied, troubled, needed a focus other than an uncomfortably gazing face to arouse himself to release. It was also a way to fantasize that the leg belonged to another. This wasn't as possible with Noelle, however; her flesh color was a little too distinctive, and the red ribbon he insisted she leave on, ever the aesthete, was even more distinctive. Still, he held her leg out by the calf now to straighten it, his eyes basting its length.

This was curious to her but Noelle closed her eyes again, submissive. Above, the DJ called, "Okay...we're gonna pick things up a little bit...I think she can handle the strain. Are you having a good time–let's hear it!"

Fuck–why did this have to happen now, *now*, with this gorgeous creature, after so many others who hadn't roused him beyond casual hunger? Could that be it? Her extra appeal was actually blocking him?

He slipped out softly. Gently rolled her over. She complied but was alert for trouble, relaxing when he merely reentered her vagina. He propped himself over her, staring down at her brown buttocks against his pale belly, the way her lower back dipped and swelled abruptly into their bisected mound. He would admire Sophi in this way. But her ass was fuller, and white, with that brown dot of a freckle or birthmark near the crease. Idly he wondered how many days it had been since he and his wife had made love. Not too many. But he was too distracted to remember.

Del lowered his chest to Noelle's back, held her hair, his eyes tangled in it, all that he saw. He had this exquisite brown child-like being below him, supple and compliant, eager clay, and here he was staring into a dark nest of hair that could have belonged to anybody. To Sophi. Like Sophi's thick mass of hair. He visualized Sophi beneath him...her bottom with its telltale brown freckle squashed tightly against him...

The climax was finally mounting; he knew it. Just as it bubbled toward eruption he glanced at the girl's wrist watch in alarm. Ohhh–Goddamn. He'd missed Pearl's show. What the fucking hell *next?*

Her next train of orgasms had never pulled into the station but Noelle wasn't bitter and let the man atop her dig gravely for his. Far above the DJ went on with his ever sinister enthusiasm, "Okay, we're about ready to call

178

it quits. Hope you folks aren't too shaken up, now. Thanks for your time. I think we can still squeeze in a little more speed before you leave us, though. Are you ready now? Let me get my hands on the controls here. Hey, what's this red button? It says 'light speed', looks like. Let's give it a try." The rumbling increased to an earthquake. What if the ride collapsed, crushing them, grinding their skeletons into one tangled being? Noelle dug one hand under herself to finger her clitoris. Grunting, sobbing out, Del bounced crazily against her back in climax. That helped her. Yes, her train would come in again. The DJ said, "Has anybody got a beer for me? Oh–sorry–are we still on?" It was then, as she began to peak again, that distantly Noelle remembered the DJ having said all this so long ago earlier today–*all* of this–and it wasn't a script. She realized it was a recording.

"Okay, folks, looks like we're right there. Are y'all ready now?"

As she couldn't see Del when he–and then she–climaxed, it could have been anyone other than the famous Del Kahn inside her. It was just a sensation now devoid of identity. It could have been Kid she had given in to again.

"Oh-kay…everybody *SCREEEAM!*"

"I don't know, it looks a little green," said the boy, a mutant, with a glossy black oval growth bulging from a bloodless rent in his white forehead, pushing his eyes too far apart.

"It's fresh, that's why," said Mortimer Ficklebottom, standing with the boy under the pavilion of his camp. In a lawn chair lazily watching was a sometime associate, Crosby Tenderknots, just arrived and mead in hand; smirking.

"Yeah, well isn't it better ripe?"

"Are you telling me my business or what, kid? What do you want for the price? Hey, I can get you better weed, my friend, but it will cost."

The boy shrugged, pulled two crumpled bills from his front jeans pocket. The sandwich bag of seaweed was rolled in a tube he slid into the same pocket. The ungrateful punk didn't even say thanks.

"What the fuck do you think you're doing?"

EVERYBODY SCREAM!

The mutant kid bolted, dove roughly into the underbrush of people. Mitch barely glanced after him. He stood with hands on hips staring at Ficklebottom.

"Beg your pardon?"

"What did I just see?"

"I don't know, what did you?" Mortimer wasn't being facetious; he really wanted to know how long Garnet had been standing there–he hadn't seen him until he spoke.

"Don't play games, pal. I saw you sell that kid some weed."

"Come on, what is this, man?"

"I saw you sell that kid weed."

"Oh? He's gone. So is the alleged weed. It wasn't weed. Right? Where's your proof?"

"In my memory. 'Hey, I can get you better weed, but it will cost.'"

"Look, man, this isn't Forma Street. Right? Don't harass me. Go chase that kid; he's got the weed, now."

"And you sold it to him. You're the dealer. *Right?*"

"What is this, huh? Is this a joke? Don't you have better things to do, man? People have died tonight, you know?"

"Yeah, and a girl died last night. From purple vortex."

"Look, I sold a kid a ten munit bag of *shit* weed!"

"I'm sick of air-wasters like you thinking they can stand out in the open and sell drugs under our noses. I'm not harassing you, moron, I'm doing my job."

"What about everybody else? Go after everybody here, why don't you? Everybody sells drugs."

"Not everybody. But I will go after everybody who does, when I see it. And I saw it. I'm sick of punks like you giving our carnival a bad name. I'm taking you in."

Mortimer had to laugh in disbelief. "Taking me in where?"

"To the holding cells until I can have you taken to town after the fair closes up."

"What? To town? What the blast is this?"

"Big boy," smirked Crosby Tenderknots.

"What did you say, fuck-face?" Garnet snapped, turning on him. Crosby went on smirking and held his gaze but didn't repeat himself. "You keep your mouth shut." Back to Ficklebottom. "I'm empowered to take you in and I'm taking you in, loser. You fucked up, not me–blame yourself."

"The forcers will laugh you right out of the station!"

"What they do is their business. I'm just doing my job." Mitch stepped forward, but stopped when Ficklebottom moved backwards.

"Come on!" He was really agitated now, no vestige of a smirk.

"Why are you so afraid, Fickle-anus? They're just gonna laugh me out of the station, right? You act like you got something to hide."

Tenderknots, also no longer smirking, got out of his chair and moved toward the big camper. Mort tried to distract Mitch. "Look, man..."

"Yeah, go tell the fat man, ass-wipe," Mitch said after Crosby. Then he advanced on Ficklebottom again. Ficklebottom backed off. Crosby disappeared into the camper. Mitch lunged at Ficklebottom abruptly.

The skinny man tried to dodge to the right but Garnet caught him at the elbow, spun him to his knees, pinning his arm high behind his back. The rumpled black top hat he was never without toppled from his long-haired head. Growing from the top of Ficklebottom's lumpy head were stalks of pink celery, several over five inches long with others just emerging. At the end of each was a knot of flesh covered with dark hair. Some kind of infection or the aftereffect of some kind of drug? Mitch kicked the top hat away and pointed the muzzle of his pistol an inch from the nape of his prisoner's neck as Eddy Walpole stepped down from the trailer–also, miraculously, not smirking–followed by the dour-faced Johnny Leng, with his somewhat oriental eyes darkly intense.

"There's no need for that kind of shit," Leng purred ominously.

"He's resisting arrest."

"He sold a kid a bag of *weed*," Walpole said.

"Yeah. So I'm bringing him in."

"If there's a fine to pay we'll pay it to you now."

"You pay your fines downtown, pal, not to me."

EVERYBODY SCREAM!

"Uhh! Okay, okay!" Mortimer blubbered at the pain.

Garnet eased up, re-holstered his gun. He was confident that the others wouldn't attack him, not in front of a growing crowd, who munched their snacks as they looked on, momentarily interested as if they had drifted into another tent display of animals being manhandled. Garnet produced some handcuffs and secured Mortimer's wrists behind his back with no more resistance. Ficklebottom did plead to Eddy, though, "*Do* something, man! Come on!"

"Stand up." Garnet lifted his prisoner by the upper arm.

Walpole was more grim by the moment, and Leng could apparently no longer trust himself to enter into the conversation. Walpole said, "It won't happen again, Garnet. This is the last night, right? Why get so excited over nothing?"

"Why are all of *you* so excited over nothing?" And Mitch put his hand into a pocket of Mortimer's long-fringed vest. Nothing. He moved to the opposite pocket.

Down from the camper came Sneezy Tightrope. He tried to look inconspicuous as he stepped back beside a baseball bat leaning against the van, but Garnet wasn't afraid he'd use it. Only the crumpled munits the mutant boy had given Mort in this pocket. Mitch pocketed them for evidence. He patted down Mort's sides, started digging into his jeans pockets.

Finally down from the van came Crosby Tenderknots and, puffing, Roland LaKarnafeaux. He looked befuddled, as if just awakened, polishing the lenses of his granny glasses on the front of his black t-shirt, baring his hairy prodigious belly. Mitch worked between two attentive audiences now. Nothing of value in these pockets. Mitch shoved Ficklebottom around to face him and opened one side of his vest to its silken lining, where there was a slit.

"I want to talk to Sophi Kahn," Walpole said.

"So go talk to her; don't bother me, I'm busy."

"Johnny!" Mortimer whined, but Leng didn't speak or move. Or blink those black eyes.

From the inner vest pocket, Garnet's fingers emerged pinching two small clear packets. Inside the packets was a fine-grained purple sand which seemed to glow softly. Gripping his prisoner's elbow, Garnet turned to hold the packets up for Walpole and the others to see. "Boy, I'll bet you guys are surprised, huh?"

"Great," mumbled Mort.

"Of course," Walpole said. "Okay, Garnet, you've had your fun. So take him."

"What are you gonna *do?*" Mort cried at them, ridiculous with his hairy celery.

"Mortimer," said Johnny Leng. Mort looked at him and stopped whining. Leng said nothing else, kept his mouth shut. The meaning was obvious; he was ordering Mort to do the same. That Mortimer Ficklebottom knew Johnny Leng well was evidenced by his sudden, if reluctant, silence.

"I *am* going to talk to Sophi Kahn," Walpole said.

"Go ahead, man. It's your right." Garnet pulled at his prisoner's arm. "Come on, let's go."

"My hat!"

"His hat."

Crosby covered the celery-like growths with the top hat, and without another look back Garnet walked his prisoner away. The crowd broke up. The last to linger was a human boy of eleven in a camouflage army uniform and cap, who stared hard at Eddy Walpole.

"Don't worry," Eddy reassured the Martian. The boy said nothing, walked swiftly away to rejoin his unseen others. To Sneezy, Eddy sighed, "This smells like corpse pussy. Did the forcers set us up?"

"It was Sophi Kahn," Leng breathed.

"Neither," said Sneezy. "I *think*. Behind Garnet I saw Del Kahn standing. It's not bright, but that's what I saw."

"Sophi told him about us," Leng said.

"Whatever it is, it's trouble once Mort makes it to the station." Walpole turned to Leng. "Can you get in the holding cell?"

"No. Too risky."

"Boys," wheezed LaKarnafeaux. They all looked. He was putting his glasses on, positioning them delicately. "Mort's a good friend, he'll sweat it.

EVERYBODY SCREAM!

Don't talk like that." He gave everybody a mellow Santa Claus smile. "Just get the vortex and the rest and Crosby can ride it out for us. Tonight's the last night. So tonight we don't make any more money. Tomorrow we move on for Diamondcrest."

"The Martians will be very upset if we don't fulfill their business," Walpole grimly advised.

"Our last transaction. But everything else goes as quick as possible in case we get another surprise."

"What about those two boys?" said Sneezy Tightrope. "The ones who want to rob us?"

"Don't worry about them," said Johnny Leng.

LaKarnafeaux yawned, turned back toward the camper.

Pearl hadn't asked Del to come see her sing tonight, this last time for the season—it was he who had promised—but she had pretty much expected it of him. Especially after his promise to write for her and maybe soon produce for her; you would very reasonably assume to see him in attendance. But as she was introduced and began he still hadn't appeared to watch her from the side, as had been his habit previously. Still, she wasn't immediately distressed; maybe he was late. Also, sometimes she knew he had watched her from amidst the audience, and although her audience was very modest compared to what Del Kahn must have known, she could not be assured of finding his face in that profusion. So it was more a feeling than anything that told her he wasn't out there.

Her disappointment was an undercurrent which rose to a distracting tug when she approached the end of her performance with Del's song *Blue Blues*. She introduced it. "This song is a personal favorite of mine, written by a good friend–Del Kahn. It's called *Blue Blues*..."

The applause was a bit more obligatory than born of enthusiastic recognition. Closing her eyes against her distraction, Pearl sang:

"They say it's black and white

Jeffrey Thomas

And red all over
They say no news is good news
but what if it's all bruised?
My heart is black and blue."

The synthesizer unfurled a mournful hum from the speakers, out over the audience's heads like a rolling mist.

"The artists have elected it
The cheeriest spot on their pallet
And the poets have embraced that hue
Worship sea and sky of blue
But in ocean depths swim sharks
And planes crash from the sky
Singers sing a different tune
We know the dark side of the lovers' moon.

They say love is a glittering jewel
You wear to match your smile
But what should you wear to go with your fears?
Those sapphires you once gave me to wear
Are now my solidified tears."

Pearl had altered those last lines from Del's "Those sapphires *I* once gave *you* to wear are now my solidified tears." Faking, a bit, the emotion she liked to call up for the end, Pearl concluded:

"There's a yang to the yin of things
A black band of shadow under our wedding rings
For every inch a tree grows
Another inch a glacier flows
And though each thing is really two
It's still not simple black and white

EVERYBODY SCREAM!

Both yin and yang are blue."

The response from the crowd was impressive but Pearl's smile was strained. She felt hurt, and angry. She tried to tell herself that Del was out there somewhere—but another voice insisted mockingly that he wasn't. It made her doubt his promises, his enthusiasm; she remembered the way his gaze dropped into his coffee when she asked him if he'd produce her, and was disheartened as if she hadn't seen the significance the first time. He was only helping her because her friend Sophi wanted him to, she told herself. Maybe he didn't even care for her singing.

She avoided looking at Sophi, who had appeared during the second song, on the side just behind the curtain. Alone, as if in confirmation of Del's absence. The audience couldn't detect Pearl's pain but Sophi might, and she squirmed inside under her gaze.

Pearl might have been less shaken, less resentful, however, if Mitch had been there on the side with Sophi. But he wasn't. Her last show and he wasn't. One or the other she might uncomfortably swallow, but not the absence of both men. Pearl felt stupid singing the next song. As if her singing were not respected, not of value. This herd had gathered only out of a blind instinct to find out what the noise was. They would have congregated for nearly anything, and their applause was the salivating of programmed dogs.

But this was only the nauseous drifting on the black sea of a troubled dream. In a few moments a storm lashed out, waves rose, the dream became a whirlpool of nightmare. Later, Pearl would reflect that perhaps it was her own agitation and insecurity that generated the nightmare, and not, as it seemed at first, the appearance of the strange moon.

Actually it wasn't a moon but an asteroid set into orbit, the carven sculpture by the artist Cyrex Rendiploom called The Head, two-faced like a stamped coin, depicting on one side a human man's wild-eyed, wide-mouthed face and on the other an empty-eyed, yawning skull. There had been some Choom opposition to the depiction of a human rather than a Choom double visage but just the expected grousing, nothing to thwart the project. Tonight the skull face was turned to the planet Oasis, and it was also full, a bright mirror. Bright except for a huge bullet hole in the mirror, cracks spreading out from it. A bullet hole in the skull. It couldn't have been fear that made Pearl react as she did because she hadn't read or heard the news and didn't realize that this dark marring of the moon's face was a vast spider-like creature, and that all contact with The Head's two-man security team had been lost. But her eyes did happen to be on the moon as it poked its great glowing skull over the tops of distant trees and houses and the mountain range of city beyond that, some of its towers and pyramids a mile or more high, the skull not yet above these but peering between.

Pearl was near the end of this, her final song of the night, of the season—pain still knotted within her, bitterness and sadness churning, insecurity gripping her insides—when the moon caught her eye, a ghost leering out from the graveyard of silhouetted skyscrapers, and Betty kicked.

Her sister had kicked before, but on those occasions it had been a quick, mindless spasm. This time she *kicked*. You might even say she thrashed inside Pearl's loose-fitting maternity dress, fighting against her restraining harness as if to break free and rip herself from Pearl's body and scamper madly away.

Pearl gasped out involuntarily, stepped back a few steps from her microphone, almost losing her balance. The synthesizer music stumbled on a few moments more in the opposite direction. The audience gasped out involuntarily also. That is, some of it did. Too many people, mostly young but not necessarily, burst out laughing or yelled.

"What happened?" Bern Glandston asked the tittering teenage girl beside him. He'd been looking at her naked breasts and hadn't seen the wild convulsions inside the singer's dress, now already over.

"The singer's pregnant and her baby just went crazy for a second," she snickered. "Pretty disgusting. I don't know why the pig is up there singing and making everybody sick. Freak show."

Gripping her bulging middle in her hands, Pearl ran offstage, sobbing. Sophi caught her, struggled to hold her, Pearl fought a moment but gave in. Sophi embraced her, feeling the strange third body pressed between theirs. She expected it to try to kick her away, and felt creepy with it against her, but she wouldn't let Pearl go. Pearl herself was convulsing, now, sobbing almost

EVERYBODY SCREAM!

hysterically. Sophi felt angry–but at what? The creature? If such it was? It didn't matter if it was or wasn't, where Pearl left off and her sister, if it could be called that, began. It was no different than if Pearl herself had had an epileptic seizure. It was Fate's fault, and it was at Fate with its sadistic perfect timing that Sophi was furious. But as with Betty, was Fate a thinking, willful force or just a mindless nonentity, mindlessly destructive?

"I want to rip it *out!*" Pearl sobbed, desperate but defeated. "I want it out of me I want it out of *meeee!*" But she knew she couldn't do that and it was no use saying it so she went back to just sobbing and hitching and Sophi held her through it.

Go away, Sophi told the crowd in her mind, hearing them behind the curtain still. The show's over, can't you see that? Go the fuck *away*. But she knew what they wanted. To see and know more. Sophi knew bitterly what Pearl knew. That now they were intrigued more by Pearl's sister and her performance than they had been by Pearl and hers.

When Bern looked back for the shirtless girl she was gone, swallowed up in the moving, confused crowd which was reluctantly preparing to break up. He did see something else of interest, however. And it saw him. It was like a turquoise cattle skull without horns but with huge human eyes, now baleful, floating atop the sea of bobbing heads.

"Dung!" cried Bern, and he flung himself at the wall of people blocking his escape. A teenage girl toppled, swearing. Her boyfriend, larger, did not. He shoved back.

"Hey, you rancid little mushroom!"

Bern glanced over his shoulder. The Torgessi was having much less trouble in parting its wall. The eyes blasted steam onto him. Bern dove into the crowd at a new point and squeezed through the crack he made. The Torgessi reached but missed, and it became tangled a moment in the living slats of the rickety, splitting fence. Bern, meanwhile, was running.

He wove, he dodged, he ducked down alleys and into new avenues. He finally leaped behind one of a row of turquoise plastic capsules which were portable lavatory units of the kind used on construction sites. They looked like drums of toxic waste, and he knew they smelled like that inside. You had to cup a hand over your mouth. Inside they were pitch black, also—you had to aim by luck. Bern resisted the urge to lock himself inside one. It might prove his coffin.

Gingerly, he peeked around the capsule, expecting to have a giant hand seize him by the throat. No sign of the Torgessi, however. In relief he subdued his gasping, and also to stop gulping down the poisoned air. His side ached, a dagger blade of pain driven up under his lower ribs.

Behind him was a chain link fence, and beyond that the outside world, calling him to escape. The fence must have been charged, but Bern imagined himself climbing atop the lavatory capsule and leaping over the fence to the ground beyond.

No. He couldn't. He also thought about paging Pox over the intercom, but of course he couldn't do that. Unless he phrased it like, "Would Bern Glandston's friend please meet him immediately at the Double Helix?" That might not be so bad. Or he could seek out the security guard who had helped him before, or any guard for that matter, to have the creature tossed out. *Tossed* out? Escorted out, rather.

It hadn't given up, though, that was certain. So he couldn't expect that it would on its own. Bern didn't know who he resented more…Pox or the Torgessi.

His gun was in the car…so near. And there were guns nearer still, all around him, even openly displayed. He must try again to buy one from somebody.

If only Bern had known that all he need do was have his hand stamped and he could go out to the parking lot, then return. But then, even the idea of going to his car and buying a new ticket of admission barely occurred to him. He had to be here to meet Pox. And he didn't really want to have to shoot the Torgessi and thus call attention to himself; no, not at all. That would ruin everything just as surely as leaving the carnival would. Couldn't he just stick it out a *little* longer?

He would try to page Pox. He had to do something, and as long as he didn't mention Pox by name that didn't seem so terrible an idea.

All he had to do was get to the administration building, whatever and wherever that was. And if he encountered a security guard on the way that would be fine, too.

But he was reluctant to emerge from his shelter. All those people out there, all that noise and activity, but he still didn't feel safe. He was as alone as if the Torgessi waited out there for him somewhere in the rocky maze of a desert wasteland.

Still, after a few more deep breaths of air heavy with foulness, Bern ventured out.

Sophi called Mitch so that she might meet with him in the security trailer, but it turned out he was already there. Just a minute later, in the flesh, she asked him, "Did you hear about Pearl's show?"

Mitch looked a little breathless, a little pumped up, a little cheery in a hard, mean kind of way. Now he looked wary. "No–what?"

"Don't worry, she's okay now, but her parasite had a strange convulsion during her last song. She doesn't seem to know why. She's in the med trailer now for some scans."

"God..."

"Has this ever happened before, do you know?"

"No–never. Are you sure she's alright?"

"She seems to be. Except that she's very upset. They've sedated her. It was very embarrassing for her."

"Goddamn it–of all times for it to happen...during a *song*."

"Her last one, too. Have you seen my husband tonight?"

"Earlier. Not for awhile. I'd best go to her. I've just got to finish this report."

Sophi nodded grimly. Her eyes drifted to a computer screen at the table over which Mitch had been leaning, typing at a keyboard, when she came in. She said, "I hope it's not physical."

Mitch resumed typing. "Maybe it's nerves. She's been a little funny lately about the fair closing up, and the nightclub shows..."

"Hey." Sophi took Mitch by the arm to move him away from the screen. Uh-oh, thought Garnet.

The name at the head of the arrest report read: FICKLEBOTTOM, MORTIMER.

"What is this?"

Mitch touched a finger to the screen, calling her attention to more keyed words: PURPLE VORTEX. "I saw him selling weed to a kid, I cuffed him and he had vortex on him. A girl died of vortex just last night."

"You cuffed him for selling *weed?*"

"Seaweed's illegal. He did it right in the open. I saw him. I cuffed him. What am I supposed to do, be a lookout for him?"

Sophi wasn't used to Garnet talking back to her this strongly. It seemed to her, correctly, that he was being extra defensive. "I seem to remember this morning you asked me to let you run LaKarnafeaux and the others out of the fair. This strikes me as being a wee bit coincidental."

"I saw a crime committed."

"How many others have you cuffed tonight for selling *weed*, Mr. Garnet? How many kids for smoking it?"

"I knew he would have vortex on him, too, that he was selling *that*...the weed wasn't the main point. I *know* iodine is small by comparison."

"Do you have a personal vendetta against those people, Mr. Garnet? Are you trying to instigate something, some kind of confrontation? Because I'm not happy about it. I don't need trouble! Make ugly confrontations on *your* time on your property."

"I was doing my *job!* Do I have to ask your permission every time I see a crime take place?"

"Do you think I'm stupid, Mitch? Because that's what makes me madder than you exploiting your position for personal reasons. You think I'm stupid enough to believe your fucking lies."

Garnet stared hard at her but inside felt a slight tremor of shame at the truth in her words. Yet he didn't want to bring Del's name into it despite Del's assurance that he could if need be. He didn't deny Sophi's accusation, but maintained his defense. "Doing my job isn't making trouble. My personal feelings didn't put vortex in that asshole's pocket."

"It's the last night! We don't need this!"

"Why are you getting so upset over this, Mrs. Kahn?"

"You work for *me*, do you understand? For me!"

"I know that," Mitch said, almost too soothingly. "Why are you so upset over this? It's..."

Sophi whirled and slammed out of the trailer.

She had to find Del. This rabid asshole seemed to listen to Del more than he did to her...

No! That was precisely why she shouldn't go to Del. This was *her* carnival; rightfully Del had nothing to do with it.

Sophi was lost for a moment as to where to go. She wouldn't go back to Pearl; she didn't want to be there when Mitch came in. It was Johnny Leng who decided where she would go. She turned and he was standing there in front of her. Disoriented as she was, she gasped. She expected him to smirk at that but he didn't.

"Can we speak in your office?"

"No–why?"

"You don't know why?"

"I know. We've got nothing to discuss."

"Oh? I think we do. And I'm sure you'd rather not discuss it out here for anyone to see."

Sophi glanced around them. Where might Del be out there? "Hurry up," she snapped, taking the lead. Mitch might come out at any moment. She danced up the steps to her office trailer's door. What if Del were in here?

He wasn't. No one was. Sophi closed herself inside with her guest.

"What is it?" she growled, not looking at his slanted eyes, in which she might catch a mirror glimpse of her shame, Dorian Gray-like.

"What happened–did your *husband* find out?"

"Find out?" Sophi looked. "Why?"

"Your husband sent Garnet to cuff Mort. What do you know about that?"

"My husband?"

"Nothing?"

"No, I didn't know that. How do you know he did?"

"Sneezy."

"Why would he? Del doesn't want trouble any more than I do...it's Garnet who's the ex-forcer."

"He must have found out about us."

"Then why cuff Mort and not you? I don't believe it."

"Find out. And what can you do to get him *out?*"

"Get him out?" Sophi nearly had to laugh. "Hey, pal, you take care of your own. What am I, one of your sleazy gang? It's your game, you take your losses. It doesn't concern me."

"Will you be concerned if I tell your husband about us?"

"You won't."

"Don't challenge me."

"I told you, that won't work on me."

"Oh, you just don't care if I tell him, huh?"

"Look, what am I supposed to *do?* Garnet found vortex on him!"

"You own Garnet. Tell him to forget it!"

"I can't."

"You can."

"I won't. You fucked up. Live with it."

Leng's left hand slapped onto the front of Sophi's throat, a clamp. The other hand rose to level a pistol in her face. The muzzle of the gun almost brushed the lashes of her right eye. Sophi squirmed only a moment. She almost called out but gurgled instead, anger frustrated into fear. This final humiliation, this final helplessness brought tears into her eyes. For the first time, Leng had pried under her rock, flipped it over, to see fully where the soft, helpless things dwelled. They writhed in her eyes; one dribbled down her cheek. "Go ahead," she croaked.

"I'll kill your husband if he makes trouble with us. I don't care about Garnet and his KeeZees and your pot-bellied uniform boys. I'll kill him. Do you believe me?"

"That would be stupid."

"Self-defense isn't stupid. If he threatens us he'll die. If he backs off we'll forget it. He's lucky. We wouldn't forget about Mort for just anybody."

"Let go of me. I won't agree to help you if you threaten me. You're just making me hate you more than I already do."

"True. But I'm also making you fear me more than you already do. Fear me as you should. A minute ago you weren't being exactly cooperative, so I think this is working pretty good."

"I'll ask Del why he did this. I'll tell him to stop. Alright? Now let me go."

"In a minute. As long as you're being so cooperative, I want you to get down on your knees and suck me off."

"Go to hell!" Sophi sobbed, fury trying to swim up through the tears. Her hands lifted to fold around his clamping arm but didn't dare to actually push it away.

"I'll kill your husband if you don't."

"You'll have to kill me now, first, then."

"I will."

"People saw us come in here."

"I don't care. Look in my eyes." He squeezed, shook her, and was gritting his teeth. "*I said look in my eyes!*"

Sophi sobbed, and looked. She saw her Dorian Gray portrait there. Shame made it ugly. But uglier was the decay of her strength. The shame came mostly from that. She had never seen anything more hideous and disheartening.

"You know I mean it. I will kill you, and then your husband, and you know I will, don't you? You know I'm not afraid."

"I'll get Mortimer out for you."

"And you'll suck me off."

"No..." It wasn't a statement, but a ragged plea.

"This gun doesn't make a sound. You know I mean it. I wouldn't be holding a gun on you now if I wasn't serious. Do as I say and we'll be finished with our relationship, Sophi. We won't be back next year. Do as I say and it will be all over. If you don't, you lose. And you know I mean it."

Whimpering, shaking, her face red and wet and contorted, Sophi hated herself. She knew he meant it. And when the clamp began to lower her, she didn't resist.

Jeffrey Thomas

Del had sent Noelle back to the security trailer; he would rejoin her shortly. He wanted to be alone for a few minutes. The cacophony of music and machine all around him didn't disturb his thoughts–he was used to deafening music, the roar of an audience machine that he played directly like an instrument. *Had* played. That had been one of his greatest trademarks: his *closeness* to his audience, his talks to them, his stories, his intimacy with them in quiet and his involving of them when loud.

He could weave them all into *harmony* with him. All he had to do was clap once in one part of a song and thousands of people would take the cue, clapping along just the right way at just the right time and rhythm, in unison. In fact, those who didn't clap, at the height of his fame, were so few as to seem nonexistent. The image, particularly in a surrounding arena, of thousands upon thousands of hands clapping along with him was uncanny. Sometimes, *without prompting*, the audience would chant out his chorus for him and he wouldn't even have to sing it, just smile and wait for his turn. They were zealots. It was scary to have such power. Would they all have burned a cigarette tip on their foreheads if he suddenly did this on stage at the height of the concert? Not as many as chanted, but many would, and did such things at the concerts of other performers.

Well, he was exaggerating in this, though. Another performer, these very same people might do it. But if Del Kahn burned his forehead with a cigarette the arena would probably gasp out in shock, because that wasn't the Del Kahn they knew. They had an image of Del Kahn locked in a cell in their minds. It was unthinkable that Del Kahn might cry after a fight with his wife. That Del Kahn might want to play a villain in a movie, a dream of his, when everyone saw him as a heroic figure. The pedestal his publicity people, the media, his audience placed him on, in fact, became for a time so dizzyingly high he wanted to climb down from it but couldn't. There had been times when he had wanted to admit in public that he cheated on his wife, had taken young teenagers to bed, whatever other blackness he could dredge up and vomit out, just to shatter the prison of his guilt and feel human.

On the other hand–yin/yang–he loved the adulation. *Fed* on it. The feeling was most strong in an arena, when he was surrounded by them–*thousands* of people all around him, one man in the middle of a tornado of enthusiasm (his band, though much loved, seen merely as an extension of him), thousands pouring positive energy down on him, all simultaneously focusing love and gladness on him, a blasting light, giving him the energy critics then marveled at, to run around the stage exultant, dancing and leaping and clowning. It was like their energy mirrored back from him, because they had chosen him the mirror of their lives...

Now gone. All gone. They had all left him like thousands of wives losing interest except for maybe a vague fond memory, finding bright new lovers. Why shouldn't he mourn that? Why shouldn't that hurt in the very fiber of his soul? It was like an addicting drug wrenched away. A job lost. A child dead. As if Sophi had divorced him.

Del picked up the discarded porn magazine. One of the articles advertised on the cover, so glossy it felt slimy, was "A Summer Guide to Gashes!" He paged through it but his mind was elsewhere as his eyes trod the anonymous flesh.

How had he lost them? Why had he lost them? The questions haunted him always, as if he were the parent of that lost child, wondering, *if I hadn't let her walk to the store alone*...the husband wondering, *if I had paid her more attention...*

On the one hand, making new music in the newest style, like the relentless showman Zodiac Jones, could win new, young fans, a fresh audience, but they weren't familiar with the old work. *Too* new. Too trend conscious. On the other hand, one could stay the same. This could be a positive thing, if personally stifling–in that, in this world of constant speed and change and uncertainty, it was reassuring to have something solid and consistent to rely on. Children might die and marriages break up but the music of this person stood strong like a fantasy father. And Del had been that reassuring father for others to love, a voice of encouragement, urging people to find their strength. Until he changed, and his reliable near-constant optimism eroded to an introspective solemnity, and even bitterness at life with its sins against its children.

But couldn't he have sacrificed his desire or need to express these feelings, or express them instead in a book of poetry or such, and instead dig deep for some morsels of unsullied happiness to be placed under the spotlight for the sake of others? Didn't people know the sins inflicted on them by life well enough? Wasn't it happiness they sought to know better–happiness that was the rumored thing they wanted to hear about, as Vikings might have sung of Valhalla?

Yes, yes, of course all this. But most performers already sang chiefly of happiness. There was no shortage. He had to be true to himself. It always returned to that uneasy conclusion.

"I'm sorry, Del, but that song *sucked!*"

Del had somehow heard that one shout amidst all the cheers and applause. It had been an arena. He kept mostly to the front, of course, as there was only a comparatively small crowd behind him, but he did run to the back of the stage to play directly to them also. The voice came from the floor, in the first rows. At the height of his fame, no one in the first three or more rows was a teenager in a Del Kahn tour shirt. He saw business suits, high fashion, jewels, he smelled their perfume of money and drugs. Images stuck in his mind, snapshots in his scrapbook. Of a grim little man and his stiff, prim wife standing in the second row like rock in a sea which bobbed and wriggled, clapped and danced along with him. Of two homely men in expensive clothes in the front row, one obnoxiously drunk and melting all over his date, both dates tall shapely blondes in tight black dresses, one with her midriff revealed, the other with a hole revealing one entire breast.

A friend had once watched him from the fourth row and in a conversation about the concert told Del about the five youngish, well-dressed men without dates who had occupied the row ahead of him (all tall and all directly in front of this shortish friend, as fate would have these things). Before the concert began they had stared way up behind them at the people in the furthest seats near the ceiling. "Look at the ants," one laughed, waving. One said, "Can

EVERYBODY SCREAM!

you believe some poor bastards stood in line eight hours for tickets?" They had paid, probably, five to seven hundred munits for these twenty munit seats.

"I'm sorry, Del, but that song *sucked!*" The shout came from the third row, it seemed. Close. It had been a new song, not yet recorded. Now, Del didn't ask for blind reverence. But still, he thought about this jeer, the five fashion boys on the town, the two young business men with their whores, the grim little man and his stiff little wife. They probably couldn't name one song off of any of his first three albums. He was hot, he was an event, they could tell their friends they had scored six hundred munit seats the way they might brag about a painting they had bought (though they didn't actually *love* it), or about some high class drug they'd acquired. Del hated them. He wished he could have had them teleported right out of their seats and traded their places with the kids behind his back near the arena ceiling. Those kids knew the words to his most obscure songs, danced and clapped wildly. He loved them all the more for the venom he felt toward those others primarily directly up front. He played over their heads, ignoring them as he would his security guards.

If he played such an arena now, stuck to all his old popular favorites, who would show up? Was it too late, had his old loves remarried? The idea was too scary for him to implement. Right now.

He ached for the old harmony. There had been a unity, a focus stronger than in a church. That harmony with them had been his harmony with himself.

A harmony with Del, but had the audience members been in harmony with *each other?* One clapping man might accidentally bump into another and their grins would turn into instant snapping glowers of defensive warning. Had he ever done anything to bring them closer together than just physically? He could only hope.

Looking up at the myriad faces in his mind's eye, indistinguishable ant faces, he thought of the high percentages of those who murdered and wondered how many killers or future killers had grinned and applauded him in those arenas. Hundreds and hundreds at a time, in a place like Paxton or Miniosis. Murderers for whatever reason, offensive or defensive. Millions of them, maybe, had bought his albums.

But Del had never killed a man. Despite the statistics. He had lived an insulated life for much of his adult years, safe behind the walls of his profession, his guards. He still had guards, in a way, but not specifically. Not like before.

He saw Sophi in his mind. Somehow he was losing her, too, he felt sometimes–like now. He had changed, and in changing had done something to alienate them from each other. His most loyal fan of all, and still he could lose her.

But was that something he had done to alienate her really such a mysterious something?

He tossed the skin mag away from him into the darkness. The Screamer rattled above, the hurricane of light and music whirled around this still eye, the DJ's recorded ravings chanted mindlessly. Del felt sticky and disgusting under his clothes, and decided he must take a shower immediately before checking back with Noelle at the security trailer. He wasn't in such a hurry to rejoin her anyway. His previous desperate enthusiasm now drained from him, he even hoped she would be gone when he got there.

The group Johnny Bland and His Girl Friday Mona Blasé played their latest song *Exploring Your Cavern of Love* on the car radio. This was not so remarkable a coincidence, as nearly any popular radio station at this moment might be playing a song appropriate for Fawn to lose her virginity by.

Fen had deftly broken into this large car. In her weak-legged excitement Fawn had no room for concern. The possibilities of being caught or simply seen by passing people were just minor distractions. Fawn swooned moaning under Fen as soon as they entered the back seat, and wrapped her legs around him as he ground his pelvis against her pelvis through their clothes, grinding his mouth on hers. She didn't resist when he fully undressed her; she helped pull his shirt off. He was big inside her but didn't hurt going in, her maidenhood gone and a small trail blazed already by her love bug, and she was drenched with preparation.

EVERYBODY SCREAM!

Now she held his intense, working nakedness against hers, her long white legs clenched around him. She was in bliss, didn't care about sperm; Heather had given her a pill before heading off with Wes Sundry deeper into the dark sprawling parking lot. She wanted those sperm inside her, dying glorious kamikaze deaths. She gulped down her own enclosed smell, too desperately hungry to be self-conscious.

"Oh...oh...I love you...I love you," she chanted, her writhing under him mounting.

She was lucky that she climaxed first, bucking under him. A moment later he groaned shakily, drove a few times with extra violence, his stabbing coup de grace, and then melted heavily over her as if unconscious. Whether he would have immediately kept on going for her sake was questionable. The entire actual sex act ended a moment before the song by Johnny Bland and His Girl Friday Mona Blasé ended. He was still inside her. Fawn kissed her soporific lover's neck and smiled as she listened to the next song begin–*Fuck an Angel*, by Bruised Lips. It was a wrenching teen ballad. She forgot about childish joys, of dolls, of friends, games, dismissed such memories of happiness, by thinking to herself that she was the happiest she had ever felt in her life.

Smiling, she moved her eyes to the window at their feet and cried out, gripping Fen. A man was out there gazing in at her. How long? Now that their eyes met he rapped on the glass. Fen twisted around and out of Fawn, cursing, hurting her legs heedlessly.

Muffled voice. "Open up–security."

"What do you want?" Fen dragged his pants to him. "This is our car."

"I don't care, open it."

"Let my girl put her clothes on!"

"Open it *now*."

"You *fuck*," Fen hissed under his breath. Fawn clawed on the floor for her panties. She heard Fen open the door. She heard a *poof* sound, then a second, and a wetness spattered her back. She lifted her head, swept aside her curtain of red hair.

She cried out again, but not too loudly. The gun muzzle was only inches from her face. It smelled burnt. Through a thin blue mist came the unfamiliar face of Johnny Leng, and compliantly Fen slipped rubbery to the floor to make room. Fawn didn't look but peripherally caught sight of darkness splashed on his nakedness. She began making incoherent sounds. But not too loudly. She backed nakedly against the door but didn't attempt to open it.

"Shhhh," Johnny advised pleasantly, pulling his door shut behind him. It might take a while to build to a third climax after Sophi and Heather, but he could take his time now, and Sneezy was out there leaning against the car to keep watch, smoking a cigarette.

"I'm not with him, I'm not with him," Fawn sobbed hopelessly.

"Sorry, but you were. And now you're with me."

There was a boy of seventeen lounging in one of the lawn chairs. He told Hector with a smirk, "Sorry, dad, we're not doing business tonight." The boy must have been related to that man he'd dealt with before, Hector thought, taking in that familiar smirk, though Cod wasn't related to Eddy Walpole. "You can buy a *Dozer* t-shirt, though."

"I'm expected. My package wasn't ready an hour ago. I was told to come back."

"Oh?" The boy looked amused, as if by a disheveled drunk.

"Yes. Now do you think you might go inside and tell him I'm here?"

"Well, I guess I can do that." The boy got up. He moved to three teenage boys and a girl nearby who were standing drinking beer. They all five looked at Hector. The girl, in a black *Dozer* t-shirt meant for a child and bikini panties, very pretty and with a lovely body, smirked. Apparently the boy had asked these others to keep an eye on him. Cod disappeared into the van.

A bit uncomfortable under the gaze and soft chuckles of the drinking teens, Hector turned his back to glance into the flows of people. A dwarf black man waddled by, his head twice the size of Hector's as if that was where his missing height had hidden. A tall and spindly alien couple in sparkling gold robes glided along, their skin as white and glossy smooth as porcelain, their heads only as large as Hector's fist, their black hair braided into one thick connecting bridge to signify their marriage. A pack of Hispanic boys came sauntering along from the other direction. They wore white leather jackets, and in a few moments Hector saw that the words *Hispanic Panic* were emblazoned on the backs, no doubt their gang name. From their collars down their chests hung girls' panties like a tie or bib, probably belonging to their girlfriends or a trophy from a gang rape–a new fashion style for rough teenage Hispanic gangs. The girls with them were aged between eleven and fourteen, Hector judged, and were all dyed-blonde Anglo types but for one Hispanic girl. The boys and girls alike were loud and boisterous, with proud intimidating lawlessness screaming from them.

Hector wasn't surprised when they blocked the path of the tall linked couple. It was natural; he had anticipated it perhaps before the gang did. Hector's heart pounded for the couple as they tried to move around the boys, who fanned out to block them. One boy of about nineteen, probably the leader, flashed open a switchblade. Of course–how could they resist that silly, stupid braid? Some of the boys closed around behind the frightened, passive couple. God forbid they should have to flee connected like that. The boy brandished his knife in the air, grinning his huge white grin. The others laughed, taunted the couple, began snatching at their matching purses. No one passing by stopped to help.

The blade hovered high in the air, as if in some ritual the boy, an evil priest, would unmarry these two–as if he were waiting for his dark god to bless the knife before he struck. Hector faintly acknowledged an approach behind him, and Cod's voice. "Alright, dad, you're clear to go in." But Hector walked away from the voice.

"Hey," Hector said as he drew his gun from inside his black plastic Theta researcher jacket, that nice government agent's sidearm with no recoil and no sound and plasma bullets that could dissolve you without a trace in less than a minute. "Hey," he said again, and now took a two-handed firing stance despite the lack of recoil–to keep his hand from shaking.

"Whoa," said Cod, backing up. Fast.

One of the boys looked over, cried out sharply. The others looked. One jerked his hand toward his underarm.

"*Don't!*" Hector boomed, more out of fear than anger, training the gun on this boy. The kid raised his hands above his head. "I'm a forcer," Hector said. "Leave those two alone or I'll have you taken in."

"Hey, Officer Bato, ease up," the leader laughed, clicking his knife shut and slowly pocketing it. No sudden moves. "We're just playing, you know?"

"I'm not playing. Move along."

"Oooh," mocked one of the fluffy blonde pre-teen girls.

"Stop drinking so much coffee, huh?" laughed the leader. He said something to the others in Spanish, which Hector wasn't really fluent in despite his heritage. They began to move along, but nice and slow and unhurried. One still purposely bumped against the giant couple as he passed.

"I see any more trouble with you and you've had it, amigos," Tomas said after them, straightening up, lowering his pistol. He did feel like he'd drank too much coffee. Several too many gallons.

"Oooh," said that girl over her shoulder again.

The married couple stood staring down at Hector. Without eyes or even mobile features, he could still read their gratitude. They both nodded their linked heads, then resumed their gliding away. Stuffing his handgun away, Hector let out the air that had ballooned his heart and turned to see Eddy Walpole standing there regarding him alongside Cod. Hector moved to them.

"Hello again–officer," Eddy greeted him gravely. No smirk.

The horrible realization came over Hector, and his heart ballooned again. Fate was the clown at tonight's carnival. Giggling, prancing, spraying water from a lapel flower into people's faces. "I'm not really a forcer," Hector said hollowly, as if he himself didn't believe his own words. "I just said that to scare those boys off."

"And why would you want to do that–unless you were a forcer?"

"I was concerned for that alien couple."

"Why?"

"Why?"

"I'm sorry, sir, I don't have anything to discuss with you tonight." Eddy began to turn. Hector saw his own hand shoot out and he caught the man's arm.

EVERYBODY SCREAM!

"Wait...please...I'll pay you double."

"You must think I'm pretty brainless, huh?"

"I'm not a forcer...I'll show you my I.D....I used to be a Theta researcher, that's all..."

"Your credentials don't mean anything to me, sir." He set us up, thought Eddy Walpole. He's in this with Kahn. If only Sneezy was here right now.

"Look in my eyes."

"Hypnotism won't work, sir."

"I need your drugs, can't you see that? You know what it looks like." Hector took a step closer, still holding Eddy's elbow. "Look at my eyes."

Eddy did look. And then he slowly nodded. The knot loosened in Hector's belly. "Alright," Walpole said softly. "Come inside. But leave your gun with the kid."

"Of course."

Hector half expected the invitation to become a trap, felt defenseless without his gun, but Walpole produced the drugs...even the promised bonus of seaweed for the inconvenience of waiting. Hector thanked him sincerely. Smirking inside, Walpole thought, how could I have doubted him? "You're a lucky man. We're shutting down our business for now. You're our last customer."

"I appreciate it." Hector slipped the six pill dispensers into various pockets outside and inside his jacket. "Thank you."

Eddy smiled, clapped him on the back, showed him to the van's door. Hector glanced over his shoulder at a bearded fat man who hadn't said anything. This man smiled at him pleasantly, peering over the top of granny glasses low on his nose. Beside the fat man throughout had sat a boy of eleven or twelve in a camouflage uniform and cap, his hair a crew cut stubble beneath, his eyes on Hector like blade points. Hector didn't know much about the Martians other than that they exiled their members when they reached thirteen, and had a code of honor that restricted them from shooting a man who wasn't armed with a gun–though Hector suspected this law had more to do with impressing themselves than anything else, considering their reputation for being one of the most violent and ruthless of Punktown's newest, or even established, gangs. He seemed to remember reading something about a drug they all took to stay pumped up. Vortex…purple vortex. That was it.

The door slid shut behind him. Mission accomplished. He felt as he had when returning from some of his trips crossing over. Relieved, and shaken. He had to find a place now to roll his weed in the papers they'd given him, smoke it and calm down. Well…maybe it was better to just sit down finally and have a few beers.

He was so relieved that it made him happy and ashamed of himself at the same time.

Hector hadn't gone too far before he saw the Bedbug.

It was moving along in the crowd, weaving purposefully but not rudely through the generally taller beings. Black, bipedal, beetle-like. Two of its six, pincer-tipped tendril arms–the lower two–had been removed and replaced with mechanical arms with four fingers and opposable thumbs, an artificial adaptation to a humanoid-oriented world. It wore no clothing or jewelry, but slung on a kind of neck strap was a small black device of some sort. A camera? A translator, maybe. Or a weapon.

Hector sort of began to drift along after it, eyes fixed on it.

They lived in another dimension, passed in and out of dimensions in their strange vehicles called trans, locomotive-like things that before disappearing traced intricate patterns on odd beds of tracks, hence the appellation Bedbugs–a derogatory nickname to indicate the negative feelings many had for the race, best called a prejudice. But why this abhorrence, when there were stranger, uglier races? That another of Punktown's most feared street gangs was a gang of Bedbugs was not a sufficient answer. Maybe it was a feeling people couldn't put a finger on.

Where was this one headed? To buy some candyfloss? To toss some darts at balloons? To climb aboard some madly circling ride that reminded it of a tran? Hector was thankful that the being was so intent on its destination that it didn't swivel its tiny head around to see him sort of following it.

A man held his nose after it had passed. Hector felt, if not sorry, at least sympathetic toward the loathed beings. But stronger was the horror, the terror, that made him want to both follow it to its destination, and get as far away from it as possible.

EVERYBODY SCREAM!

He almost lost sight of it, but it reappeared far ahead and he quickened. Then it turned into an alley between trailers and was gone. Hector began to press forward insistently through the flocks. He reached the alley, moved through it to its mouth, and halted there. Not far ahead, the insectoid had obviously reached its destination.

It was a great spider-like leg growing out of the empty air. A lighted sign explained the attraction as best it could but was too far for Hector to clearly read. Something about an extra-dimensional being reaching into this plane of existence, like a swimmer testing the water temperature with his toes. Something about two hundred and forty-three legs identical to this one having appeared out of the sky over a bank in town. Yes, yes, he remembered the story. Remembered that dribbling liquid fell from the sky near those legs for four months and had to be caught in a disintegration unit to prevent those who used the bank's heliport from requiring umbrellas.

There was a dribble from the air here, too, he could see. It puddled a little but seemed to be mostly absorbed by the dirt.

The Bedbug swivelled its head and Hector drew back sharply, but it didn't swivel far enough behind to see him. He relaxed. Now in its feeler-arms it raised and pointed that device hanging from its neck. It did seem like it was taking pictures with a camera–though a complex-looking one. No one passing took but a casual notice. But Hector stared raptly. His horror, undiminished, and curiosity were one and the same.

No lights blinked on the black device, there was no flash or sound from it. There was, though, a thin bluish smoke as from a cigarette which came twisting out of a grille in the side of it.

Hector remembered reading how the odd mechanical temple built illegally in a cave on The Head by a small group of Bedbugs had produced bluish smoke from various openings and grilles. Someone sucked ice water up the straw of Hector's spine.

Most people, even scientists, had no real idea why the Bedbugs should be so disdained. But then most people, even scientists who had dissected a few Bedbugs, had no idea how, or if, or *what* they ate to survive.

Hector knew. He had been told about it, and once toward the end of his career had even seen it. No, not here. Not in this dimension.

It had been in that place he had crossed over into, where the "trace-energies" of human beings such as himself were in constant woe, ranging from brooding melancholy to all-out hysterical anguish. The *screaming*…thousands, all in a wretched harmony, a unity of fear. They had begged him to take them away, would have clawed him to pieces in their desperation had they had physical limbs.

"They *feed* on us!" they told him, over and over. "Stop them! Save us! They bring us here…the Gatherers…"

Maybe his associates had learned since his dismissal where the Bedbugs had collected all these tormented souls from, to be kept penned shoulder-to-nonmaterial-shoulder in this place until *needed*, but Hector didn't know. He ached to know and to never know.

The government was currently insistent on keeping these findings a secret. Debates were underway. Did they have a right or obligation to protect these souls, trace-energies, reincarnations or whatever they chose to call the tormented beings? They didn't have legal jurisdiction over the world where these entities were penned and harvested. In fact, they were trespassers there, since the Bedbugs had actually artificially opened or created this great space to store their rations in.

All debates aside, Hector couldn't help but wonder when he read the obituaries. Read that some child had drowned. When he considered his own inevitable end. Where would he go? Was there no peace beyond? And even if the predators caught him, caged him for a decade or an eon, and then consumed him (the *screams*), would something of him survive on another plane? Or would his soul, if such it could be called, be reduced to the violet gas that escaped from the rear apertures of the Bedbugs, the noxious smell which caused some to scornfully hold their noses?

The insect-like creature at last lowered its device and moved on.

Hector did not pursue it further. He did, though, cross to the leg, a skeletal accusatory finger, to stare at it and read the accompanying sign. The dribble from the air made sounds in the muddy puddle. He had no idea that no one had ever observed a liquid dribbling from the air before this.

EVERYBODY SCREAM!

They were back. Eddy stepped out of the van to see what was keeping Sneezy. The small balding man in the flowered tropical shirt stood just beyond the awning smoking a cigarette, looking off, it appeared, into the sky.

"Sneeze–come on in."

Sneezy Tightrope mumbled something. One word.

"What? Hey–Sneeze. Come on, wake up."

"Huh?" Sneezy turned around. He looked perplexed, distracted.

Eddy looked up to where his friend had been gazing and saw the bright coin of The Head still low in the sky but rapidly rising.

Mitch's always tight voice was tighter over the public address system. "Del please come to security immediately. Del please come to security immediately." Del had just stepped down from his own trailer, fresh again but wearing the same greenish-black silk suit, white shirt, string tie...like nothing had happened. He wasn't far from the security trailer but hurried even so, feeling guilty that he had shut his phone off earlier.

Several separate bits of information were absorbed simultaneously when he entered the large mobile building. Noelle was indeed not here–had her friend been located? She hadn't stayed to say goodbye? He was relieved and hurt.

Mostly relieved, because his wife was here. And it was Sophi he focused on, despite Garnet's extra-grim intensity. Sophi was sitting and looked up into Del's eyes, shocking him for several moments. Her face was pallid, setting off the redness around her eyes. She looked shrunken, turtle-like, inside her violet sweater and half hidden behind her hair. Her cigarette trembled. Del decided that this matter had to concern her in some way. Not much could reduce his strong, tough wife to this. He felt dread.

Dingo Rubydawn, Mitch's Choom man, was also present, and spoke first. "Del, you know that girl who came in here looking for her friend? Noelle Buda? Well, she came in here about an hour ago and asked me if her friend had answered her page. No, she hadn't, so I paged again. No show. So I figured, why not go down to the parking lot to see if she's partying in one of the cars. Right? Well…"

"What?"

"I found a dead boy and girl in a car. They'd been partying. No clothes on. He'd been shot twice in the head. She'd had her eyes shot out. He had a gun with him but didn't use it, I guess. I thought I'd found the Buda girl's friend, but when I looked at their wallets it wasn't her. They'd broken into the car, too, apparently—we just paged the owners so we can talk to them."

"So who were they?"

"His name was Wes Sundry. Looks like a punk. She was Heather Buffatoni. We tried calling her parents but can't reach them. High school kid, looked fairly respectable. I called Mitch."

"I sent the KeeZees to run a search of the whole lot," said Mitch. "It didn't take long to find the next one…just a few rows over. Same deal. Car broken into. A boy shot twice, once in the face and once in the throat. He was naked, had a gun he didn't get to use. Same make of gun as the Sundry kid. This one's name was Fernando Colon."

"And a girl?"

"There must have been. The boy was naked. But no sign."

"Maybe she escaped. Or maybe she's the one who did it. Could that girl have been Noelle Buda's friend? That Moussa guy she went off with might have made his name up."

"It wasn't her friend," said Dingo. "We found her."

"One of the KeeZees found her. And Moussa. It was his real name," said Mitch. "They were in a third car. This time it was registered to the guy—Moussa Habash. He was dressed and behind the wheel. He had a gun—not the same brand as the other two—and there were gold-dust traces on a hand mirror on the floor, some seaweed in a little container, and a bottle of booze. He was a law student. Rich father; he's on his way."

"The girl," Del said, impatient.

EVERYBODY SCREAM!

"In the seat beside him, naked. Bonnie Gross. He'd been shot once in the forehead. The girl had been shot twice in the face and once in each breast. We've got a serial killer at the fair. A psycho," said Mitch.

"Does Noelle know?"

"She identified those two, but didn't know the others from their I.D.'s–she's over in the med trailer having a coffee."

"Okay," said Del, shakily, strangely feeling in charge. He hadn't looked at Sophi again but knew she was in no shape to take control. "All the bodies are in the cooler?"

"Yes. Gross and Habash just came in ten minutes ago."

"Are you running time of death tests?"

"All the standards. I put in a call to the force, too. They'll be sending down two detectives to look into it and a cruiser to patrol the lot."

"Check to see if the same weapon was used at all three scenes."

"Even if it wasn't, the killer could have two guns. But that's another test we're running. The cars have been print scanned. We're running the scans through the police files open to us. We tracked down Bonnie Gross's people and someone is on the way. Nobody to contact, yet, for Sundry or Colon."

"We've got to find out if that Colon boy was with a girl. She could tell us a lot. If she didn't do it."

"If she's alive," said Dingo.

"Sounds like a psycho who can't stand seeing a girl and boy getting to it. A repressed fanatic," mused Del. "Jealous."

"I don't want to limit myself to a speculated motive just yet," said Mitch.

"Three scenes of killings, two with naked boys and naked girls, and one with seaweed that wasn't taken? Looks sexual to me."

"Well, we'll see."

Finally Del turned his attention back to his wife. "Are you alright, hon?" he asked. He didn't feel dread toward her now, only concern, and still a little confusion. Even when their fights were so bad that she cried she never looked this battered.

"I'm alright," she croaked, not making eye contact. "I looked at the bodies, that's all."

"Oh." He'd thought so. Still...she'd seen plenty of bodies in their morgue before. And what about the mummified bodies incorporated into some of the rides? He thought he could smell drink from her, now.

He said, "Would it be too great a risk of scaring off the killer if we paged the carnival for anyone with info on the five dead people to come forward?"

"A real sickie or someone bold like a gang of punks would stay, page or no page, if they really wanted to stay. But if he's smart, a mobbie or a pro, he's already left anyway, so I'd say page."

"Page their names," Del told Mitch. "Anyone with information on these murdered people please report to the security trailer immediately. Then list the five names."

"Could be bad for business," said Gola, behind the desk.

"Well, this is more important," rasped Sophi. That was the final word. She was boss. If she didn't mind, no one could say much.

"I really hope we can do this ourselves," Mitch said. Involved investigations weren't his strong point; with Car Thirteen on Forma Street he'd dealt mostly with "in progress" conflicts. "I don't want the town boys to think we need them to hold our hands."

"It isn't a fucking contest, Mitch." Sophi stood, faced Del. "Can we talk alone in a few minutes? At home?"

"Yeah–sure." Del glanced a Mitch, who shrugged, on the way out.

They didn't talk along the short walk, or even until they were alone together in the turquoise and pink kitchen of their trailer home. Sophi lit another cigarette and Del asked her again, "Are you alright?"

"It's been a long, bad night and I'll be glad when it's over."

"A few more hours. We're getting there. Why don't you lie down awhile and let Mitch and me worry about this? You look bad."

"Del, why did you have Mitch cuff Mortimer Ficklebottom?"

"He was selling purple vortex, that's why!" (So Mitch had told her.)

"Are you trying to make trouble or what?" (So he didn't know about Johnny–it wasn't revenge.)

"Trouble? I said he was selling vortex. *He* was selling vortex but *I'm* making trouble?"

EVERYBODY SCREAM!

"Yes, he was selling vortex, they *all* sell it...is this some kind of revelation to you, suddenly?"

"Look..."

"You're out of line, Del! This is my goddamn carnival, do you understand? *Mine!* And I didn't want trouble tonight. Why this sudden concern over LaKarnafeaux's people?"

"I hate them."

"So do I. Another big revelation? Did you love them yesterday?"

"No, but I had enough of them tonight, that's all." He knew it was her carnival, but he had bankrolled most of it, hadn't he? He had to live here with it, *in* it, didn't he? But he didn't want to open that can. She'd say, "Oh, so you bought it and you own it and I'm really just the manager for *you*, is that it?" She must have said that to him before half a dozen times. It wasn't true–he respected her leadership most of the time. Sometimes he felt like a part of management, sometimes he detached himself, just sat back and watched. But tonight he couldn't watch any more.

"Why, did you have enough of them?" Sophi pressed.

Del avoided her glaring green eyes. Leaned his rear against the sink, hands in pockets, eyes on the swirly pink plastic marble of the floor.

"They're laughing at me. Greasy smug scum who sell drugs that kill kids, and they're laughing at me. But that I could live with. Alright? Look at the source. Do I respect their opinion? I know better. It's the kids. The kids who come and hang around all day with his people. They flock to that fat pig like he's Santa Claus. Beautiful girls who want to grow up like Mortimer Ficklebottom and Johnny Leng. They emulate them."

Sophi saw Del's meaning. His motive. *Jealousy*. You got me raped in the mouth at gunpoint for *this?*

He said it. "These kids worship him, but me they won't listen to. Me they don't know."

"My God."

He looked up. "What?"

"How petty you are."

"Petty?"

"You make it sound like every single one of your millions of fans has deserted you so they can hang around with Roland LaKarnafeaux."

"And with Sphitt. And with Flemm. And with the Saliva Surfers, and Mukas, and the Upchucks, and Ming and the Mongoloids, and all the other fuckheads who have so much wit and wisdom to share."

"Del. Kids do like to have fun, too, you know?"

"Fun? Living for drugs is fun? Treating women like meat is fun?"

"It must be–you've done it."

"I never *used* women. They enjoyed me and I enjoyed them."

"Yeah, yeah, whatever. Anyway, do you think that if Sphitt and Flemm retired today all their listeners would flock to you? They'd find some other buffoons."

"Maybe with less buffoons around kids would give more serious stuff a chance. I had them for a while."

"You never had all of them. You never had all the Sphitt-lover types. And you never lost all your fans, for God's sakes. One of the dead kids in the parking lot had a chip of *Heroes* on him, Mitch told me. That Fernando Colon kid. What you want is to hit the mainstream again–that's all. You had a taste of the big, big time and now you can't accept less. You got spoiled, Del. But don't worry…you were big enough that in a few more years you can be rediscovered as the next nostalgic fad, and then you'll only be forty or so and you can make a silly full-blown mainstream comeback. All you need is to have a good firm to market you."

"Fuck you, Sophi. I don't have to make a 'comeback'–I didn't go anywhere. My audience did. And as far as my 'loyal fans' go, their only loyalty is to a few early albums, but as soon as I tried to experiment and grow they weren't so loyal any more, were they? I grew up and they didn't."

"You lost your faith in the joy in life and they didn't."

"They want to stand *still*, nice and safe. You'd think they'd be intrigued to watch an artist grow and change, but no."

"You got too serious. Your early stuff had more humor. It was more fun."

"*Fuck* fun. I'm sick of hearing *fun*. Fun is fine, but fun alone is like living on drugs–it's empty. It doesn't build you. Pretentious, they called me.

EVERYBODY SCREAM!

'*Heroes* is one dirge after another, even when the pace picks up. It's like a droning funeral,' so said Bosley Simon. I guess the critics can't be pleased, huh? I'm pretentious, Sphitt are morons. How can you win?"

"By not trying to please everybody."

"Fuck. Fucking critics. Fucking audience. Yeah, they love to see a nobody rise up, they want to boost you—you're one of them who's making it. Then when you're up there they're jealous and alienated and they pull you back down so you can be a loser like them."

"Fuck your audience, huh? Losers? No wonder people don't want to listen to you. What do you want, immortal celebrity? You still get *played!* You had a time of glory. You can look back on that. You made friends, you were loved, many still love you. Some people starve to death in alleys."

"Yeah. You ever seen an old man drunk in an alley? Starving, cold, sick, demented. Am I supposed to see that and feel content that at least at one time he was young and vital and loved and appreciated? He's still alive! *Now!* He should *still* be loved!"

"Ohh, Del, you poor neglected derelict. You're some real pitiful prima donna to *dare* to compare yourself to a person as tortured as that."

"It isn't just *me!* That's not the whole thing, damn it! I heard a teenage girl once say that Frankie Dystopia was a gagger. Frankie Dystopia—the most brilliant lyricist around! I've heard young girls call Bellerophon a bunch of gaggers. They don't do drugs, they sing about social injustice, they represent causes, but they're not *cute*, see. Like Sphitt allegedly is. Sphitt, who would fuck those stupid baboons and then leave them in the dirt and laugh about it. I'm worried about a future where less and less Bellerophon is played, when people would rather grow up to be cute like Chauncy Carnal and not a 'gagger' like Frankie Dystopia. Yes, I am hurt—but it isn't just me!"

"It's always been like that, Del," Sophi told him dryly. "Don't be so naïve. You're obsessed, and it will destroy you. And it will destroy us."

"Don't put that guilt on me, Sophi. Don't. You know how much my work means to me and you knew from the start what it would mean. People come here to enjoy your business. But it isn't your *art*, and they aren't your *audience*."

"Del, you talk so much about your audience, but you don't know who or what your audience is. It's gotten to the point where your audience is every girl you take to bed. That's the audience you've found to go on feeling desirable and appreciated. Can you see that, Del? You're playing to them one at a time."

His eyes had something like hatred in them, and they were fixed on his wife's, but her eyes were hard, unflinching–it was his that shivered and dropped. He turned to the sink, held its edge.

Sophi pushed it deeper. Pounded the stake into the vampire, as if to make him dissolve to dust. He felt it starting. She said, "You need that adoration somehow. Just that short, concert-length period. I know you don't love them, except how you love an audience. It's anonymous. But it isn't impersonal either, is it? It's intimate. It's still love."

"I'm sorry," he mumbled.

"It shouldn't hurt like it does, I suppose. I'm never too afraid you'll leave me for one of them. So what am I losing? It doesn't take so much time. Well, the act. The cruising does. Is it the secretness of it? Am I old-fashioned, to take my vows seriously? To have believed that romantic intimacy would be kept just between you and me? It is romantic, Del. It isn't just cold business, like with a prosty. You charm them, you seduce them, you play them–they're your fans. You're obsessed with them and you're focused on them. They mean more to you than me."

"No, Sophi. They don't."

"How stupid do you think I am? How unobservant?"

"I'm sorry. You're right about everything. I'm selfish and self-pitying. I neglect you. I've humiliated you. But I never cared more for them than you."

"More for yourself, then."

"No. I'm selfish, but I love you. I'd die for you."

"You're killing me."

He spun, glared again, but tears were condensing. "Oh, I'm killing you, huh? It's a premeditated murder, yes, you're right–I hate you, I've meant to destroy you from the beginning. That's why I married you. That's why I helped you build this damn place."

"You're killing my spirit, Del. And you're killing your own."

EVERYBODY SCREAM!

"Oh...God." He hid his face in his hands. And shook. "I'm sorry," he moaned through the bars of his fingers. "I'm sorry. I'm sorry."

Sophi released a ragged exhalation. She felt good to have let it out, and she didn't cry. She felt her strength returning. Her doubts loosened their grip. She had done the right thing in not resisting Leng. She couldn't take chances. Yes, she would have Ficklebottom released. As much as she had wanted to take Del's gun and go find Leng and shoot him herself, it could be all over if she just let them go. Things could return to normal. Yes, she knew Del would listen to her. He'd stop cruising shark-like for victims. For now, at least. There was no doubt. She had known all along that if confronted so bluntly, if told that he was killing her spirit, as she indeed felt, that he would cry and beg her forgiveness. The only problem had been that she had hoped she wouldn't have to say it. That he would let himself see it, and say it to himself. But he hadn't. He was a man, and weak, like all men. She couldn't expect him to be a hero, as his fans had seen him, just the good man that he basically was. He could be a very good man. She loved him very much, and wanted to go to him now, but he had to suffer for a while, even though her anger had dispersed with her sigh. It was done. She had said it. She was like Mitch. Emoting too much was like bending a joint the wrong way. But she had opened a door and it had let in some air. You had to let yourself be vulnerable. She had said it. And she still felt strong, after all.

"Del...come on, we'll talk about it later." She tried not to sound too soothing despite this wash of tenderness. "Alright? It's in the open, that's good. We have a lot to think about right now."

"I'm sorry," he sniffled, averting his face.

"Listen to me. I'm going to order Mitch to let Ficklebottom go, alright? I don't want trouble. I don't want any of them seeking retribution against us."

"Did they threaten to make trouble?" Now he looked at her.

"Not directly," she lied. "But I spoke with them. They spoke to me. I just don't want to risk it. I was assured they wouldn't come back next year and that's good enough for me."

"That's all I wanted, too."

"Yeah—well next time don't play games."

"I'm sorry."

"Mitch won't like it but he'd better not give me any grief."

"I'll back you up," Del promised her. Now he let out a ragged, hitching sigh. "You believe me? That I love you?"

"Yes."

Eddy Walpole turned from the phone. "Mort's on his way home–they just let him out. What happened with you two, Johnny?"

"Don't question me like that. Mort's out. Why are you upset about that?"

"You didn't endanger us, did you?"

"I had her let Mort out so we *wouldn't* be endangered, alright? I have my own way of doing things, alright?"

"Your way of doing things can affect all of us, Johnny. You're part of a team."

"Boys, boys," chortled Roland LaKarnafeaux. "Don't sweat, Eddy. All Johnny did was slip her the cyclops, I'm sure."

"Exactly," Johnny said, and laughed uproariously. "You're getting like Sneezy now, Karny."

"It's a good thing it's our last night," Eddy grunted, mostly to himself. Inside the camper, they hadn't heard the five names listed over the PA system. Eddy would have worried that much more.

"Gatherers," said Sneezy Tightrope.

"What?" asked Eddy, looking over.

Sneezy sat watching a blank space of inner camper wall. His eyes were unblinking, his mouth a little open. His gaze was aimed almost at the ceiling. "Gatherers," he repeated in a faraway voice, breathy as a ghost's, and the plastic cup of mead in his hand fell from his fingers to splash the thick carpeting.

"Hey, man!" Leng jerked his feet away. "What are you on?"

EVERYBODY SCREAM!

Mortimer Ficklebottom was returned all his belongings–except, of course, his drugs–at the desk. A smile for Mitch. "Better luck next time, Mr. Garnet."

Mitch wasn't about to let him leave until Sophi and Del came in, despite her orders over the phone, but just then they did. He didn't waste a moment. "Why are we letting this air-waster go?"

"Don't question me, Mitch," said Sophi. "They won't be back next year...isn't that enough?"

"No, it isn't. You're afraid they'll retaliate somehow, someday when we don't expect it? You're afraid of that? Then we might as well never arrest anybody. We might as well let everybody do like they want. What's the fucking *point?*"

"Just this once," Sophi told him with surprising patience, a reassuring tone. "I just want tonight to end calmly."

"I don't see it. He'll laugh at us. He's laughing at you."

"I'm not laughing–you hearing things?" Ficklebottom pouted.

Dingo was quick and caught Garnet before he could reach the prisoner. They fell sideways to the floor. Del dove at them, as did one of the uniformed town-hired guards who was present. Mortimer had backed off, bald terror coming over his face. He straightened his top hat as Dingo, Del and the guard hoisted Mitch to his feet. "Okay, alright, alright!" he shook them off.

"We have more to worry about with these killings, Mitch," Sophi tried reasoning.

"If you let him go I won't be back next year either."

Sophi held his gaze. Del cooed, "Mitch..."

"I mean it."

"Don't threaten me, Mitch. That won't change my mind. I can't stop you from leaving...but I'm boss here and my authority holds. Leave or stay, that's your decision, but I won't be threatened."

Oh? she thought. *Oh?* Wasn't that it? That she *had* been successfully threatened?

"He's nothing," Del backed her up, as promised. "We made our point, Mitch, they'll be gone next year. That's enough."

"Do what you want." Mitch stormed from the trailer.

"Thanks, folks." Ficklebottom pocketed his tattered wallet.

"Don't thank me, you pathetic slime," Sophi replied. "Get the fuck out."

"He's out there," Mort realized.

"He won't touch you. Get out of my sight."

He did. Dingo came closer. "New developments."

"What?"

"Mendez here came in with a girl named Cookie Zalkind right after we read off the names. A few minutes later some other kids came in...Colleen Narcisi, Rena Tushkin and Diana Talmud. They were schoolmates of Heather Buffatoni. Zalkind says she saw Buffatoni go off with Sundry. And all four girls say they know the girl who went off with Fernando Colon. Her name is Fawn Horowitz. A classmate, too. They haven't seen her since. So we were right about that. Mitch called her mother and told her that her daughter is missing. She's coming down. He didn't tell her about Buffatoni being dead, yet."

"Is she bringing pictures of her?"

"Yeah. Her lawyer, too, probably–she said if anything happens to her daughter she'll stomp this place into the ground."

"Better call Max down," Del told Sophi. Max Schenkel was their attorney. Tonight would keep him busy for months, but the carnival had never lost a case.

"Okay, more lab results," Dingo went on. "No print match-ups to police files. The only blood in the Colon car was from Colon. Nothing from Fawn Horowitz–a good sign. On the floor of the Colon car we found a red shocker tablet but none on him or in his system. No shell casings. No report yet of gunfire, but people might mistake it for firecrackers or even ignore it. With all three vehicles the shots were not fired *through* the glass. The doors must have been opened for Sundry and Colon. For Habash the windows were open. No one even drew a gun in defense. Maybe it was someone they all knew. *However...*"

"Yes?"

EVERYBODY SCREAM!

Dingo sighed. "Habash and Gross were killed with a different gun, and had been dead for two hours in their car before the other three were killed."

"Great," said Sophi.

"So that's where we stand. The town boys have arrived, they're at the morgue. You might wanna go talk to them."

"Would it be dangerous to page Fawn Horowitz?" Sophi asked gravely.

"I don't know."

"Does that Cookie kid or the others have a picture so we can start a search?"

"They've gone–sorry. Zalkind's people came right out and got her."

"Mitch must have gone over to see Pearl. Do you know how she's doing?"

"Good, I guess. Okay."

"What about Noelle Buda?" asked Del softly.

"She's lying down–they gave her a sedative or whatever. She's pretty shook. I guess she's stranded for now too but we can worry about that later. I don't know if she's called her people."

"Let her rest. Thanks, Dingo, you're doing a good job."

"Some last night, huh?"

"Mm," Sophi grunted in bitter agreement.

"Let me see your hand."

The face hovering high over her was washed with wave after wave of colored light. A sliding red light would pool into the eyes of the face and then pull itself up and out and slide off the other side of the face. The black helmet on the head of the face was a seething mass of swirling nebulae of light, and myriad glints were stars. The expression was harsh.

"Let me see your hand." Someone took her wrist, twisted her arm. Vacantly she looked. There was a dark mark on her hand, which looked so far away and didn't feel like part of her, her nerves not reaching that far. The face was satisfied with this mark, nodded. Let go. "Go on."

She stumbled along, her body only a dragging string dangling from the balloon of her head. She was pushed along by those swelling behind her, until she washed onto a small patch where she stood watching the tides and eddies all around her. She swayed. She lifted her head and stared at a machine rising above some trees nearby. It had long arms that rotated, dipping up and down, and in each palm twirled a little box, like some octopus juggler. It was a glossy black with green lights running along the arms, dispensing a green glow to the foliage of the trees and to whatever or whoever else was near. And above this pirouetting monster hung a full moon. It bled tatters of ectoplasmic clouds. A violent shiver went through Fawn. She hugged herself, turned sharply away and blundered into the ocean again.

She shot a glance over her shoulder. It was following her.

She collided. Hands shot out and gripped her. Her heart was jolted as if a cattle prod had been touched against it. Whipping her head, she bugged her eyes into a new hovering face. It was darkish-skinned. The beginnings of a beard. Long filaments of flesh were being pinched away from the face like stretched strings of bubble gum until they snapped and new strings were drawn out. Fawn's eyes lowered to a white shirt. Strings were also being pulled out of this reflective mass. Fawn saw colors that she had never seen before in opalescent swirlings on that white surface. Much of the shirt, though, had been darkened–mostly about the shoulders–with thick dried stains. The man shook her by the arms so that she would look at him again. He didn't seem to be really any older than she. Maybe she could appeal to him, in that light.

"Watch where you are going, Satan's whore!" A violent shake. Her arms hurt. She heard laughter and saw others like this young man close at hand.

"Help me," she said. Her voice sounded absolutely alien to her and yet, also, the only familiar and reassuring sound in this loud place. "I'm...I must be drunk..."

"She is on drugs," sneered a voice close at hand.

"You knocked my drink on me–look!" A hand had switched to her hair, clenched it. Her head was jerked low and she whimpered. She was meant to see a stain amidst the opal swirls but only saw the dark dried stains–was that what he meant? She did see a cup and spilled ice on the ground.

EVERYBODY SCREAM!

"I'm sorry," Fawn mumbled, wanting to cry. But tears would never be able to climb up out of this smoke-filled abyss. Her head was lifted for her. Now red sparks were leaping out of the man's glaring eyes and she recoiled in his grip, horrified, afraid that if the hot sparks lighted on her face they would sear her. She saw his mouth form as if to speak but a liquid thing leaped from it, a glowing red projectile of lava. It struck her face.

Fawn screamed, thrashed. The agony was unbearable. The flesh of her face bubbled, hissed, spat like frying bacon. She clawed the man's shirt. People passing glanced at her, she noticed through her shrieks. A hand struck her face. Wasn't it afraid to be burned on her skin? She fell, and hitched with sobs, the pain beginning to subside. Didn't severe burns stop hurting once the nerve endings were destroyed? Multiple hands hoisted her roughly back to her feet.

A half dozen passing black boys smiled at her. They wore black graduation robes, open over their street clothes, and mortarboard hats with red tassels–the next fad, maybe, when the rubber swimming caps and clear ruffled shower caps died out. A brown and white mottled mollusk with eight heads and one thick tentacle floated by, a few of the heads seeming to regard her for a moment.

The man wouldn't let go of her. Were he and his companions going to rape her? A rogue memory slithered inside her in many small broken worm-like pieces and she shivered violently. She retched. The man held her farther out from him.

"This is a typical female infidel," said the man who held her. "Look at her. They are all like this. You see this?"

Fawn looked toward where he was directing his voice in particular. Three figures in black robes, their hair and lower faces hidden. At first Fawn took them to be nuns. Dark eyes solemnly staring. She felt on trial.

"Someone will see us," said a voice behind her. "Let her go."

"She spilled my drink on me. I want her to pay me for it!"

"She isn't worth the trouble. Look how drugged she is."

"They would have our women become like this wretched *thing*." A twist of her arm. Fawn staggered, groaned. The young man regarded her, and now grinned. His teeth gave off white sparks...cool, but they smelled. "You have taken more drugs than you had intended, haven't you? Does it make the colors brighter and the rides faster, to take your poisons? How much brighter the colors are now, eh? And the rides must surely be faster eh? Well–we must help you! We can help you have fun!"

The others laughed, but for the grim women, and the one dissenting voice behind her. "We mustn't make trouble for ourselves."

"She has made her own troubles." The man looked around him, settled on something. "Over there–that looks fun. Eh?" He tugged Fawn by the arm and she stumbled after him. Another man took her other arm to help her along. The rest trailed behind.

This machine stood out through the fog in the swamp of her mind. It was a great wheel, with many individual open cells along its outer edge, facing in. The fetus of a memory stirred in her. They approached a glum, wordless operator. Someone gave him tickets. A few tongues of electricity played between the two hands as the tickets were exchanged. The glum man had a dim blue aura and blue sparks spilled out of his nostrils, bouncing down his shirt and bouncing on his shoes until they faded.

"I'll put her on," offered the man who held her arm. "She's a little sick." She was escorted to a cell. Electricity from her contact with the metal mesh floor coiled vine-like around her legs. Ahead there was someone already in a cell. Two purplish, gaseous beams were being shot from this person's eyes. Or *drawn* from its eyes. Long, dim, stretching off high into the black sky until they were lost.

Her escort locked her restraining bar in place. He had, it seemed, purposely chosen the cell next to the being with the beaming eyes. Cool sparks from his teeth, again–smelly. "Have a nice ride." Then he clanged away, electric tongues lapping his legs.

There were a few others on the wheel but their eyes didn't beam. Shortly, the wheel began to turn...

She tried to make out the faces on the people across from her. Did she know them? It seemed that she did. Names hopped like grasshoppers away from her grasping hands. Cookie? Cookie. That was someone's name...

EVERYBODY SCREAM!

And to her right the cell was empty, though she thought sure that someone had been there before...

"*And I love you!*" a voice cried out remotely from that cell.

She felt a pain inside. Not of loss, because she hadn't really lost anything. It was the pain of fear. Because she had opened the door to a nightmare and was locked in its cell, like a prisoner in a burning prison unable to escape, no one to rescue her. The flames of unknown carnival color leaped and lapped all around her.

The wheel spun faster. It began to tilt at an angle. It tipped more and more and seemed it wouldn't stop until it was fully vertical, but did stop just short of that. Lights like tracer bullets whizzed all around her, pierced through her. She hurtled at the ground, a flesh meteor. Faces down there stared up at her from the bottom of the ocean. She hurtled at the sky, at the stars. Veered. She was plunged to earth, reborn, whisked to heaven again, reborn again, an endless cycle of reincarnation, life after life lived out in seconds.

But tattered memories of her previous lives would bob to the surface and float like dead fish.

"Can I pin it on you? A medal of honor," said a disembodied voice.

"For what?" her own voice echoed.

"For being so gorgeous."

"You're too cute to shoot."

"I can't *believe* this!" her memory laughed.

"I'll make you feel good. You'll be so high you won't come down for a week. You might not be the same person when you do, but that might not be so bad, and better to be changed than dead, right?"

"Please," her memory sobbed.

"Don't beg me. You're lucky enough already. You should see your blonde friend."

"Please, please, God..."

"Ha. You must have bought this eye from us, huh?"

"Can I pin it on you? A medal of honor."

"*Please*," Fawn said aloud, and gazed down at the eye on the front of her denim jacket above her left breast. It was red-irised, with a goat-like oblong pupil. It glared at her. Red sparks were whipped out of it by the wheel's spinning but the air took them safely away. Some bounced off the floor of the cage like an arc welder's torrents of sparks. The eye was alive, hateful, drilling. Fawn screamed.

She looked away. The ground rushed up at her. Faces. Figures. They watched her. The men in the stained white shirts, their three nun-like women. Others. One figure, not a human, glowed with a purple aura. It was insect-like. It was watching her. She plunged toward it. It invited her. At the last moment she pulled out of her dive...up and up.

She rocketed toward the full moon. It had the harsh glowing face of the security guard. Its edge rippled, shot flares into space. There was a great *thing* across the face. It was not actually the moon which regarded her, but this thing that sprawled across its cold cratered mattress. Fawn howled, shrieked, rattled her restraining bar. She was flung down at the waiting insect thing. Shot up at the moon. Again and again bounced between the two.

All this time those two smoky purple rays had beamed from the eyes of the being in the cell to her left, strafing the people below and then plunging off again into the sky. When they raked across the moon the flares from its rippling edge leaped further, shone more brightly. Now Fawn leaned forward to see into the next cell and beg for help. Maybe they could escape together.

The smoky beams emanated from empty skull sockets. Vomit rained on people below. Someone cried out, pointing. The glum worker touched a keyboard blandly. The wheel began to slow and lower.

The Red Jihad disappeared. So had the insect thing.

Two uniformed men clanged up into the wheel. They unlocked the restraining bar and lowered the flopped figure to the mesh floor delicately. One rolled it over while the other called first for a med emergency unit and then to the carnival security headquarters.

The med team arrived first. Dingo, Del and Sophi came after.

"Let me see her wallet," Sophi droned, and took it.

"Dead," said one of the med team.

"What was it?" Dingo asked.

"Drugs. She had a half dozen kaleidoscopes in her, I'd say. Hallucinogens.

EVERYBODY SCREAM!

And some red shockers, too. Bad combination. Brain damage—she blew her fuses. It was a miracle her heart didn't give out first."

"Great," said Dingo. "Fucking great. And her mother's here with her lawyer."

Del stared down at the splay-legged corpse in horror. He had seen this girl tonight. Alive, vivacious, without the open-mouthed expression of terror, the thick blood from her nose. He had been flirting with a group of teenage girls. One had told him to blast off and the others had laughed, including this one. Heather Buffatoni must have also been one of them. He hadn't viewed her body—would he have recognized it with the eyes shot out?

"Do you think she was overdosed on purpose?" Sophi asked.

"I don't know that," said the med team member, crouched by the body still.

Del felt a tremble at the horror in the corpse's open eyes. They stared up at the star-littered sky. They were afraid.

The gold-dust was inside an oversized toy bumble that Pox had won. It now sat beside Bern Glandston on a bench at a sticky picnic table where the two men drank beer. Pox had just lit a black-papered herb cigarette and squinted out of the tent-covered area at the throngs of living beings. They had heard gunshots a few minutes ago but someone had told them that it was a demonstration of police dog training, hostage situations, and the like, and the shots had been blanks. Not that they had really been concerned, just curious. Bern said, "There was a lot of activity at the security trailer; somebody killed a bunch of people in the parking lot."

"Drugs," said Pox, as if in disgust.

"Probably."

Bern had made it safely to security headquarters and paged Pox several times. Finally a teenage boy Bern had never seen came to bring Bern here. Pox had then paid the boy for the errand and dismissed him. Bern had felt somewhat safer coming here with the boy, at least less alone, and now that he was with Pox he felt so relaxed, so relieved, that all his bitterness was forgotten. He hadn't exploded at Pox as he'd planned lately–he couldn't really afford that anyway, could he? But he had told Pox about the Torgessi. Pox had chuckled. In his relief, Bern had chuckled, too.

He didn't like sitting with his back open to the passing throng, though, and glanced over his shoulder once in a while, half consciously.

"Hear about The Head?" asked Pox.

"The Head?"

"The Head." Pox pointed his cigarette.

Bern twisted to glance over his shoulder. "No–what?"

"That giant critter they found on it?"

"No–what giant critter?"

"You can't *see* it? It covers the whole fucking face."

"Is that...that's an *animal?*" There was a shadow, like a dark hand over the carven jack-o'-lantern face.

"They sent some scientists and soldiers out tonight to see what happened to those security guards."

"Something happened to some security guards?"

"Yeah. Lost contact. So they sent some probe ships–guess they didn't want to teleport just yet. Well, on the way down here I heard on my car radio they've lost contact with two of *those* and so the other two turned back."

"Holy stools."

"I don't know what they're doing now, but I'll bet they're gonna be ready to fight next time. But from here, look how far away and quiet it is. Who knows what's going on."

"Just blow the whole thing up." Bern swigged his beer, smacked his black-painted lips. "Well, I got what I came for. I've had better days at carnivals. Guess I'll be heading home."

"I'm not sticking around, myself–got a few other appointments yet tonight." The mobbie polished off his beer. "Don't let that lizard turn you into a pair of shoes, boy." Chuckle.

"Ha, ha."

"I can walk you to your car, if you're scared."

EVERYBODY SCREAM!

"I'm fine."

"You sure?"

Some of the bitterness was on the way back. "Positive. I'm gonna have another beer," Bern grunted. He hadn't really intended to, but...

Chuckling, Pox rose and clapped Bern on the shoulder. "Let me get it for you, Bernie. Sorry to keep you waiting tonight. I'm a busy man, though, you know that."

"No problem," Bern sighed.

With a new beer in front of him and the stuffed bumble beside him and Pox gone and the moon behind his back, Bern sat.

Outside, Eddy found Sneezy Tightrope standing at the edge of their camp, gazing at The Head. Cod and some other teenage boys were passing a bottle of pink milky wine and an iodine joint back and forth with a batch of teenage girls. Eddy intercepted and squashed the joint, hissing to Cod, "Are you crazy, after what happened with Mort?" Cod muttered an apology. Eddy moved past him to Sneezy.

"Maybe you should take some detox pills, Sneeze."

"I'm not juiced," the small balding man mumbled, distracted. "I just need the air..."

"Are you getting transmission overload again?"

Many advertisers now bought time on wavelengths which the brain could pick up without a mechanical receiver. As if the commercials breaking into rented vids, into theatrical movies, weren't enough, commercials were also often run *on top* of the movie on a subliminal, superimposed wavelength and beamed out into the world indiscriminately to be received in a telepathic way beyond the ability to switch off, to escape–though quiet, slipping into the back door of the subconscious, not making their influence known even as you reached for that jar of *Monkey-See Peanut Butter*. But too many voices cramming one radio could create static, clutter, chaos, and especially with someone of Sneezy's sensitivity. There had been times he had gone into maddened seizures, until doctors began prescribing him blockers. He had eventually found a blocker that kept out much of the open-air transmissions but which didn't hamper his ability. However, there were those times when he still had trouble.

"I...it's something like a transmission. It's like...I can hear Bedbugs...talking through a machine..."

"Bedbugs?" Eddy was interested in this topic. Bedbugs were significant.

"There are a few of them here. It's...it's strong. What they're..." Sneezy trailed off. Just stared at the sky.

"I'm sure it doesn't concern us. They don't deal directly with us." Walpole kept his voice low. "Come on inside, man, take something to sleep." Eddy didn't like the way Tightrope's temples were moving as if he were chewing, though he wasn't. *Pulsing.* You normally didn't see that with him. Eddy followed his friend's eyes to The Head for a moment.

"I need air. I'm going to take a walk."

"You don't have anything on you, do you?"

"No, I told you, man, I'm clean." Sneezy took a few plodding steps out of the camp. "I have to take a walk..."

Eddy grunted, made back for the camper. Bedbugs, huh? They could be up to anything; even those who dealt with them secretly found out little about them. Their strange activities never seemed to hurt anyone, though, except for that one vicious gang, and they appeared to be on their own. Eddy found it hard to believe that Sneezy's sudden odd behavior had been brought on by anything the Bedbugs were doing. It was probably a kaleidoscope or two, despite what he'd said.

At the camper's step Eddy glanced back but Sneezy was gone.

The black girl's mouth was open a little bit and her full lips squashed against her thin pillow. Her hair was a thick blanket. Despite the rubbery deformity of drugged sleep she was beautiful, and Mitch knew that Del had made love...had sex, rather...with her. He regarded her dispassionately a moment

EVERYBODY SCREAM!

more before rejoining Pearl, closing the door. Pearl had largely cleared her way through the mists of her own sedation, enough to talk. "I'm going to go home to my trailer," she croaked, forehead in her hands, gold hair hiding her face in shame.

"No, I want you here. There's a mass murderer out there–you won't be safe."

"It's too bright, it gives me a headache. I feel queasy."

"I'll have them sedate you some more."

Pearl stood. Mitch took her arm to help her. He began to rub her back. "No one's going to break into my trailer–I'll lock it. You can walk me over if you have to."

"No, damn it, can't you at least wait until the place shuts down? I worry about you. Alright?" He moved to embrace her.

Pearl stepped back. She was sure he would begin stroking Betty's crouched form through her dress, gently, romantically, seductively, if she let him embrace her. She was sure she would jump if his hands touched that shape.

"What's the matter?"

See? He's getting mad. Betty is my oversized breasts. He wants *them*. I happen to be attached to them, she thought. It was okay to love breasts, but in proportion. Out of proportion breasts attracted out of proportion interest. Betty was her attraction. A sideshow attraction.

If she cut off the big breasts, then who would woo her?

"I'm going to have Betty removed."

"What? Why?"

"You can ask why. You don't have to live like this."

"Hey, don't start with that. I know it isn't easy. But why this sudden impulse? You always said you were against it the same way you're against abortion."

"Do you know what I went through tonight?"

"You're embarrassed. You'll get over it. You did great, I hear–this is *nothing*."

"This," Pearl gestured at the shape, "is nothing?"

"People are worse off."

"Yes, but they're not me. I'm me, and I'm like this. I've had enough. If you don't like it, I'm sorry." She wanted to add *if you don't like it find yourself a new freak* but didn't.

Mitch sighed. He watched a med robot that sat at a console dabbing at a lighted keyboard. A screen relayed the scan findings of the team that had just responded to the death of Fawn Horowitz, their missing person. Kaleidoscopes, red shockers. A heavy-duty police scan could locate these drugs amongst the people here, but so many of them were bound to have these common drugs on their persons that it was nearly pointless to rouse the police to such a project. "Whatever you want, Pearl. I know how you must feel, and I know you mostly kept Betty for your parents' sake..."

"Not just for them."

"Whatever. Just think it out, don't be rash."

"And how will you feel about it?"

"How will *I* feel? Ethically, you mean?"

"About *me*."

"What about you? That you're being selfish? I don't think you're being selfish. If Betty has a soul tangled up in you, maybe you'll be setting her free. Look at it that way."

"Will you still...will I still be attractive...to you?"

"What? Of course! What do you think?"

Pearl looked suspicious, vulnerable. Hugged herself above Betty. He really did seem angry, insulted at such a question. "You like Betty."

"Well...you know. I mean, I like your legs. They're attached to you. I want you to keep 'em. But if, for whatever reason–good reason–you needed to have them cut off, I'd still...be attracted to you." He'd almost said love, in front of the robot. "Right?"

"You like me better with Betty?"

"Well, it's unique. It's more body to touch...more flesh, more limbs...more...you know. Is that so terrible a thing to desire? If I had two penises you'd probably be intrigued."

"I'm just..."

EVERYBODY SCREAM!

"Insecure, I *know*, I understand. Betty is what they wanted when you performed, when you hooked. But I'm not those men. Cut her off. I'll stay with you. I promise."

Pearl looked down at her plump crossed arms. "I don't think I can," she murmured. "I think I was just saying that...to test you."

"Don't test me, Pearl."

"I *had* to."

"Alright–whatever. Are you satisfied now?"

She looked up, imploringly. "You didn't suspect I was testing you, did you? And just say that to humor me?"

"No." Mitch was patient, this time, not insulted. "I meant it. I thought you meant it. Don't keep Betty just for me, Pearl."

"I wouldn't...I wouldn't, believe me."

"Maybe we should stop calling it Betty. Maybe we could have a funeral service for her. Would that make you feel lighter?"

"I might just as well cut her off, then. What would be the point in carrying this? I'll keep her."

"I'll try not to touch her beyond what's necessary."

"Never mind that. It's Betty, but it's my flesh, too. Things have been fine as they are all along. You just have to talk it out in the open, that's all. I feel better already."

"Good. Man–give me the benefit of a doubt next time, huh?" Mitch approached to embrace her but this time she didn't step back. Sandwiched between them, Betty seemed to be both cuddling to them like their child and also straining her legs against him to keep them apart. But the legs were weak. Pearl hugged Mitch against her and whispered so the robot couldn't hear, "I love you, Mitch."

"I love you too, honey," he said quickly, to get it over with, like a tough little boy to his mother, but meaning it thoroughly.

Of course, however, this squashing close contact made him physically aroused, too.

When Del, Sophi and Dingo returned to the security trailer they found that Mitch was there, having convinced Pearl to remain in the medical trailer to rest in case she suffered a reoccurrence of Betty's seizure. She was more inclined to listen to him since their talk, and didn't want to be alone anyway. She felt disoriented and creepy in having to be a little bit afraid of Betty right now, she admitted. And Betty was hard to get away from.

There was also a scene of hysterical pandemonium to greet the Kahns and Dingo. Dolly Horowitz's face was a red knotted thing wringing out tears, and she clung to the arm of her attorney Aaron Novis for support. She was currently shrieking at Mitch Garnet.

"…you fucking apathetic ass-wipes don't give a shit about innocent pee-ee-ee-ople," she sobbed, out of control. "You don't care, you don't care. Who are *you*?" She whirled at the newcomers. "Who runs this shit-hole?"

"I'm the carnival manager," Sophi introduced herself. She had already guessed who Mrs. Horowitz was.

"Why is my daughter dead? *Why?*"

"She died from an overdose of drugs, Mrs. Horowitz, I'm terribly sorry. Kaleidoscopes and red…"

"I *know* that, god damn it, but my daughter never used drugs! It wasn't like her!"

"We believe she was forced to take them. There was a boy with her in a car. He'd been shot."

"Oh…God…why? *Why?* All these people shot and where the hell were all of your fucking security people?"

"They were shot with a silenced gun," Mitch said, assuming, but two-thirds correct, "in a dark parking lot, all six of them inside cars, their bodies then slumping down out of sight."

"Why is the parking lot so dark?" asked Aaron Novis. "Don't any guards patrol the lot?"

"Mostly they just direct traffic in and out, sometimes they walk through the lot to see if people are milling about drinking or whatever, but they don't make car-to-car searches. We've never really had much trouble in the lots. Some drinking, some fist fights. Mostly people just go there to fuck."

Del winced.

"My daughter wouldn't do that, damn it! For God's sake! She was drugged and raped! I can't believe this, I can't believe this…oh, God, Fawn, my baby, my baby…"

Three people entered the trailer as Aaron Novis told Sophi, "The security situation in your parking lot sounds woefully negligent, and you can expect an appropriate lawsuit from my client."

"We already did expect it," Mitch said.

"Mitch," Sophi said evenly.

"I'm going to own this place, you'd better believe it, I'm going to own your fucking slime-pit, lady," Mrs. Horowitz spat at Sophi.

After tonight I'm inclined to just give it to you, thought Sophi.

The three newcomers were the chief guard from the Fog security team hired by the town, and two Paxton police investigators in street clothes. They introduced themselves to Mrs. Horowitz and the lawyer, and then suffered a fresh onslaught of her agonized wrath. Del was glad to see the focus shift from Sophi, and from Mitch, who he'd been afraid would really begin to lash back. Del took his wife aside.

"Maybe we should shut down early."

"Oh come on, Del."

"Come on what? Sophi, Horowitz has money. Buffatoni, probably. Gross and Habash. This is going to be hotter than when some bikies or gang punks shoot each other up."

"We've had it before, just not so focused into one crime. The town will take the bulk of it. This is their event, their people do the parking lot."

"Do you want more dead people on your conscience, then?"

"Hey, Del…I've never bothered counting up the bodies we've had since we started. It's a part of it. I don't kill them, they kill each other. Why not shut down early so a few more people don't get killed? Well, then, why even open next season? Imagine the lives we'll save! Why not shut down every parking lot and alley in Punktown? Why not shut down the whole town? Huh? Because wherever people get too close they end up killing each other."

"That's true, but tell it to her lawyer."

"The town wouldn't go for it anyway, Del, believe it. Either way, they'll look like they can't control their fair, but closing early is admitting too much to the fact. They'll stay open–that's less memorable for next year than closing would be. Rich or not, these people will blend in with the other killings, mostly. We might even end up with a riot, like we did last year–a big mess. The people know what time they have to leave by, they accept that and gear to it. But cutting short would be like ending a movie before the climax and telling everyone to go home. The people you want to protect by sending home don't want to be sent home."

"Well...at least call the town people, to say that you tried. It will look good for us." Over Sophi's shoulder Del saw Mitch approaching.

Sophi sighed. "*Alright*."

"Dingo says some Red Jihad were seen putting Fawn Horowitz on the Spinnet," Mitch said tightly, as if accusing someone of something.

"Yes," Sophi admitted. "The Spinnet operator gave a description. They left after she began vomiting on people, looks like."

"Well, blast, man, that's it! It was those fucking monsters! Habash...Moussa Habash. Arabic, right? And Horowitz and Gross were *Jewish*, right? Maybe somebody didn't like seeing them together. You follow my thinking?"

"Hey," said Del thoughtfully.

"Why would they drug her up and put her on a ride?" said Sophi. "And then wait around in the open until she died?"

"Well why would they even put her on the ride and then watch at all? I saw those creatures come in, I *talked* to them, I convinced them to leave some of their firepower at the booth...they're not friendly types who'd buy a kid a ride on the Spinnet."

"Maybe it was them, maybe it was other ones, maybe it was someone else...why would R.J.s drug a girl and then shock her to death? They don't take drugs; where'd they get them?"

EVERYBODY SCREAM!

"Off Colon, maybe. She still might have had them herself, too."

"Why wouldn't they have just shot her with the rest?"

"They're sadists! They throw acid in their own women's faces! Let's find these bastards and grab 'em if they're still here!"

"Mitch. We can't cuff Red Jihad. I'll put a call in about the possibility and let the authorities contact their embassy."

"Are you *insane*?" Mitch snarled at Sophi, not even seeing Del through his rage-inflated eyes. "Why not stand around and watch 'em slit babies' throats, next?"

"I'll *call*, Mitch. I hadn't considered the significance of Habash...it's a possibility, alright? But I don't want you cuffing them–it's too dangerous."

"You're afraid!"

"Next year we'll open up and the first night a bomb will level the fair. Then what will the body count be, Mitch? I will call the authorities, alright? And you will respect my judgement. You work for me."

"Not any more." Out of his rear pants pocket Mitch Garnet pulled his billfold like a gun, slid out his security badge and flicked it past Sophi. It clattered. From another pocket came his hand phone. It clattered onto a desk, bounced off onto the floor to clatter some more. Del almost expected the gun with its explosive bullets to follow but should have known better.

"Mitch, come on," he said, "calm down..."

"I don't want your impotent, meaningless job. I'll call my grandmother–maybe she'll do it for you." And Mitch stormed past the others on his way out. Even Mrs. Horowitz paused from her wails and accusations to watch him slam the door.

Sophi and Del looked at each other. "He'll mellow down," said Del.

"He's a cement-head fucking fanatic."

"He cares."

"He isn't being realistic. Look how he talked to me! And you didn't say anything!"

"Hey, you're the boss, as you so often remind me."

"And I'm your wife!"

"Oh-ho-ho."

"Blast you, Del. Alright?"

"Everyone's wired. We'll all calm down. Just stay mellow yourself, will ya?"

Dingo approached them now. "The latest developments. I called down to the gate guards about the Red Jihad. No one saw them come or go around the times the victims would have been killed. And they've left...right around when Horowitz died."

"See?" Sophi told Del, lifting her chin defiantly. "That scared them off. Why didn't shooting the other five scare them off, if they did it?"

"Hey, it's Mitch's theory, not mine."

"Also," Dingo continued, "I described Horowitz over the phone and one of the gate boys thinks he remembers her; red hair and all. Disoriented, he said, like she was drunk. He asked her to show her hand stamp so she could come back in. He's not sure on the time but it was shortly before we got called down to the Spinnet. I asked him to come to the morgue."

"Good."

"Thing is, she came in alone."

"No Red Jihad with her?"

"Alone."

"Good work, Dingo, stay on it," said Del.

"Couldn't have been the R.J.s," said Sophi. "Mitch is shorting his circuits. Looks like you'll be my new top security man, Dingo."

"What?"

"Sophi," said Del, angry.

"He quit."

"Give him a chance to calm down, will you? Man!"

"Mitch quit?" said Dingo.

"He's just frustrated—we all are. Too bad you were a few seconds too late, Dingo—Mitch is sure the Red Jihad did all this. I don't know if he's gone out to look for them or if he's back at the med trailer but I'm sure as hell glad they left."

"I'll call him."

EVERYBODY SCREAM!

"He left his phone. Don't worry, he'll calm down...he just needs to get away from all the screaming."

"So do I," said Sophi. Now one of the two police detectives approached, having slipped away from the blast furnace of Mrs. Horowitz's anguish to find out what the latest developments were, and why Mitch had stormed out.

"Remind me never to marry a Jew," he said confidentially, smirking around the cigarette he was lighting. "She isn't gonna lose her daughter without some kind of reimbursement in money to make it worth something."

Del Kahn sighed irritably. He was primarily Jewish himself. Why shouldn't a bereaved parent want to lash out at something tangible? He would have wanted to own the carnival too. But then, only so he could burn it down.

Sophi called into town. It took twenty minutes to get hold of someone in authority. Her request to shut down the annual Paxton Fair early was denied.

At the edge of the grounds was a large building especially constructed for the fair, two stories high, which museum-like exhibited most of the entries in the various agricultural, craft, and art contests which had taken place throughout the season. There was a stage outside where some of the exposition and judging had taken place, and a few days ago a mind-reader/hypnotist (a telepath somewhat more gifted than Sneezy Tightrope) had entertained there, calling up members of a large audience seated on benches. At present the stage was a barren wharf, a few teenagers sitting on its edge or far under it, smoking and drinking quietly.

Inside, the mood was similar, if brighter. On the second floor Hector Tomas found much to engage his interest, but there were only two couples with him in this single, immense, barn-like room. Near the stairs where he had first come up were the framed, hanging prize-winners in the various art and photography contests. A fraction of it was impressive, most was pedestrian, several deserved ribbons but the prize-winning status of some of the artwork was incomprehensible to him. It wasn't a matter of style–he had very eclectic taste in art–but of talent, skill. All the people in Punktown and this was the best they could offer? Either not many people were to be bothered creating art these days, or else the deep Punktowners kept to their own galleries and had left this contest, less sophisticated, less chic, to the outer dwellers.

Much of the photography was so good as to be professional, but aside from composition and subject the technology took care of that. What most compelled him were the quaint displays of knitted sweaters, wood projects, floral arrangements, other crafts spread on nearby tables. A lot of the wood pieces were lovely and he would have liked to purchase them. There were tables spread with plastic-covered prize-winning pies and pastries, bread and various dishes. A tall bookshelf-like rack held a great many canned and pickled goods in pretty colors; red, pink, purple, amber, green, luminous with the gelatinous translucency of whatever it was inside them. This floor made him feel peaceful, gratified, as had the floor below with its agricultural displays: flowers, vegetables, fruits, plants. The care, the dedication. Who were the people who took the time to do these things? He didn't know them. Even the poor art was done with pride and love. Was it where they lived–on the periphery of the vast city–that inspired this patient dedication, or simply that in the deep of town there were too many stressful, loud distractions for him to notice this kind of thing? Both, probably. But he thought, seriously, that maybe the best thing for him now would be to move out this way. What must it have been like once, when these items were more commonplace, more utilized, than novel or decorative as they chiefly were now? He would have liked to have lived amongst the pre-colonial Chooms, he fantasized. That was a nearer daydream than Earth's ancient, similarly quaint and homey times.

Did the woman who made this prize-winning pie cheat on her husband, or snort gold-dust, or dress in leather and whip her nameless lovers? Did the man who made this bench molest his own daughter? Were these real expressions? Could he dare trust the hope they seemed to symbolize to him…of passions which didn't involve greed and lust and avarice?

By the time he decided to descend back to the room below, the second floor was empty but for him and a seated woman reading a magazine who was no doubt meant as a guardian lest someone steal a prize-winning cookie.

EVERYBODY SCREAM!

Previously below he had marveled at sunflowers from Earth, never having seen them before–taller than he was, with maned heads like lions. Children had painted or carved jack-o-lanterns out of pumpkins and native gourds, displayed on one table. Another held hideously warped and deformed gourds, like cancerous organs ripped out of giants for exhibition, in an ugly gourd contest. Fortunately, he reflected, this fair hadn't tolerated a contest to create the most hideous, mutated version of a rabbit, pig, cow or other such domestic animal as he had seen as a teenager at several other fairs. The person who could create the most absurdly grotesque creature which could remain alive without artificial life support would win, so long as the "artist" worked within certain nonprofessional technological limits.

Again, questions stirred in Hector's mind as he once more scanned the spread fruits and vegetables, potted plants and flowers, relishing the near empty quiet of this place. The *work*. The dedication. So important to these people, so meaningless to others. But then, even the greatest art, the greatest books, might be burned by some just to have something to toast wieners over to go with their beers. People would never agree on what was of value. And wasn't the growing of vegetables just as primal and mindless an instinct as the desire to do drugs, copulate and spin in a loud colorful machine? It was just a matter of quiet animals and wild playful animals, Hector thought. Animals. We are just that. He thought of the Bedbugs...and of their huge, horrifying stockyard...

Turning, he gasped out loud against his will. A bizarre coincidence, or had that thought been a weird premonition? Through the dangling vegetation of hanging potted plants, luckily shielding him, he saw them. There were three of them. One had the strange device he had decided was a camera, and was no doubt the same being he had watched photographing the mysterious insectoid leg. They were standing around a row of cages on a low table, each containing several birds of a kind that Hector had never seen before. Apparently they laid small but delectable eggs, yet that hadn't stirred his memory either. The birds had just flown into a crazed uproar, fluttering in their cages like moths in a spider web, honking frantically. Hector remembered them as being a little smaller than chickens, gray with iridescent wings, pigeon-like in that regard, but with tapir-like snouts rather than hard beaks. As he watched, the Bedbugs began to buzz and chatter in an odd clicking code to each other.

Hector had come here aimlessly, but wondered now vaguely if maybe some other instinct had guided him. Some submerged, half-formed knowledge...or linkage.

The three black, beetle-like entities moved on, briefly examined the display of mutant gourds, luxuriantly ghastly. The odd birds, however, showed no sign of calming down yet. One of the Bedbugs turned to look back at them, causing Hector to flinch and attempt to appear inconspicuous as its gaze swept across him. After some more clicks and buzzing the three beings made their way toward the exit. It was obvious to Hector that they didn't care to draw attention to themselves.

Why did he feel this strange *need* to follow after them–almost a desperate tugging? He started out from his shelter of leaves, but his eyes were drawn to a man he had barely acknowledged before–small, pot-bellied, dressed in a tropical shirt and white shorts, with a high balding sunburnt forehead. The man had also started a few steps after the Bedbugs as they left the building, coming out from where he had been standing previously behind the towering sunflowers, his shirt like camouflage...but now he stopped in his tracks dazedly, open-mouthed. Staring out of the building. Hector was oddly perplexed by him, but would have moved swiftly past him out of the exhibition hall (and where then?) had the man not suddenly collapsed limply. Hector found himself surging to him, crouching by him. An old Choom woman nearby glanced over sourly and clucked her tongue. The tapir-nosed birds still honked and fluttered behind Hector.

He saw thick, almost blackish blood running out of the man's nostrils, into his mouth. His temples throbbed visibly–alarmingly. The man's eyes rolled up to meet Hector's eyes, and a hand grasped Hector's wrist. Hector glanced longingly after the Bedbugs but they were already gone. Had they glimpsed him, had that been it after all, not the noisy birds? Had they seen his Theta researcher's black jacket and recognized it as such?

The man was mumbling, squeezing more urgently for Hector's attention.

EVERYBODY SCREAM!

Hector said to the old woman, "Could you call for an ambulance, please? There's a medical trailer here..."

"I *know* that, I work here." The old woman waddled toward the open door, clucking her cow-sized Choom tongue again.

"What is it? Louder," Hector urged the fallen man.

"Gatherers...the Gatherers...they're coming," the man croaked, trembling violently, feverish. His eyes blazed, insane.

But a violent tremor went through Hector as well, almost a thrill of recognition...though a nightmarish thrill. A thrill of unreality. The Gatherers. *They* in the dimension that was nothing more than a stockyard had spoken–wailed, in terror–about something called Gatherers. They couldn't explain what the Gatherers were...and it had simply been assumed by the researchers that this referred to those particular Bedbugs who were assigned the task of stocking the astral pen, though to Hector's knowledge no one knew how they accomplished it.

"They bring us here!" the man on the floor rasped in a deeper tone. Then, his voice altering again:

"They reach into our world!"

"They're coming...Gatherers...the one on the moon is just a *nymph!*"

Hector was filled with loathing and horror now–he wanted to tear free of this man and run. Run for his sanity. It seemed that several different minds were alternating in voicing themselves through this unwilling medium. Voices so familiar in their fear and desperation.

But he remained, and asked the man, "What are the Gatherers?"

"The Bugs call them..." The voice seemed to be the man's own now, but no less frantic. "...they call them. They were on the moon before, to call them. Three are coming through tonight. The nymph on the moon–it's through. The bank...the bank..."

"My God," Hector said, lifting his head.

"The Gatherers collect the harvest. They reach into our world and take what they can, but tonight three are coming through to take more. They want more. The Bugs...worship them. They pay them tribute. Then the Gatherers collect the harvest for them..."

"The leg," Hector said.

"We have to stop them! We have to stop...they're taking away the dead..."

"Listen to me...listen..."

"Vortex! Oh my *God*, don't you see now? I see it now! Oh...my God...and I've *snorted* it! I never knew! I don't think Karny even knows..."

"What do you mean?" Hector recognized the man at last. His aspect had been different before, but he'd seen him with the group from whom he had purchased his drugs. Purple vortex. It had entered his mind upon seeing a Martian inside the van.

"We don't get vortex from the Bugs...we get it from the Lobu. Everyone thinks the Lobu make it, but Karny found out. Karny found out. The Lobu get one of the main ingredients from the Bedbugs. No one knows. It's their farts." Now the man laughed crazily, tears streaming out of his eyes, blood running down both sides of his face into his ears. "They fart purple gas. The Bugs. That's what the Lobu buy and put in the vortex. That's what it is..."

"Jesus," hissed Hector. Not laughing. He looked out of the building again, as if to locate them out there somewhere. The leg. The smoking, camera-like device. The one on The Head. *Just a nymph...*

"They fart out the gas. The gas is from *them*...their harvest...after they eat it. And we sell it." The man blubbered, hysterical. "We've *snorted* it. And we never knew what they were *eating...*"

At least that much Hector had already known.

The hand crushed his arm in a convulsive return of strength. The man sat up a little as if jolted. "Don't let me die! Don't let me die–*please!* They'll take me...they'll take me! We gotta stop them! Hurry–*hurry!* Go tell somebody! Don't let me die–*please!* Pleeeease!"

He screamed, arched his back as if a greater voltage now jolted him, and shook. Hector fell onto his back in wrenching his arm free. The shriek rose to an inhuman pitch. The birds smashed in their cells, down puffing up into the air, straw kicked out by their electrified feet. Hector stood up in time to see Sneezy Tightrope die. His skull did its best to resist the inner explosion but his head cracked open a little in a few places nonetheless. The shriek gurgled away, the shaking took a little longer as the body gradually relaxed from its rigid arched position, sinking down like a parachute to settle. The thick blood pouring from the fissures was almost a peaceful thing–like a release.

A release?

A cage toppled off of the bench-like table, and as Hector scrambled to his feet he glanced over. The sight inside the cage transfixed him. He had to go and look closer, and at the other cages…even as his flesh crawled.

In various states of progression, each bird was painfully splitting, dividing, amoeba-like, into a new bird. Tangled wings and legs, agonized heads thrashing, honking.

Hector fled the building.

Bern had no idea how old the Lobu female was–they could naturally live to be a thousand or more on their home world, and even on polluted, violent Oasis they could easily reach five hundred. He didn't know much about them; their politics, their religions, their art or architecture. He did know, however, from a friend at school, that their kind had three distinct sexes, two being "male," so that accidental pregnancy was less likely to occur, since the female must copulate with both males, one sort always before the other, within a few hours in order to become fertilized. Thus, they had been free for many generations to enjoy their sexuality without fear or restraint or inhibition. Only generally known to the Earth colonies for a decade, they had already become highly desirable sex partners. They were well known, also, for their use of drugs. Their long life spans made it less pressing to raise children, and these were taken care of in boarding schools, largely segregated from the adult world, until they reached sexual maturity at the surprisingly early age of five. Theirs was a hedonistic, almost utopian lifestyle, without sexual repression, discrimination or fear, and thus they had few wars, their religions non-patriarchal despite the two-to-one ratio of "males." But they did, sometimes, become bored and discontented in their later years. Some branched to other worlds to combat this now that space travel had been introduced to them–not invented by them, due to a certain stagnation in technology. Others committed suicide...not uncommonly.

Bern didn't know much of all this, though he did draw comparisons with the Wedling Way, a similar belief system—religion?—practiced by certain humanoids and even Earth humans in which each member, or wedling, could have ten wedlings for mates, and each of them ten wedlings, and so on. Many wedlings were bisexual. Again, in the Wedling Way the members lived extra-long lives, though through artificial means, which in the Earth colonies was illegal to such an extent, as was cloning, but it was allowed here as an essential of a specific belief system. At a thousand, though, the wedlings by their own laws were required to halt all artificial means of prolongation and live out the remainder of their lives naturally. Bern did idly wonder if many, many years ago the Lobu had passed a variation of their belief system on to a humanoid group who came into contact with some of them, perhaps captured as sex slaves.

It was a highly desirable thing to be accepted into the web of the Wedling Way—Bern knew of a few famous actresses and singers who had been allowed into this lucky following. He had fantasized about it. Tales of wedlings committing suicide or breaking off from the order hadn't reached him and wouldn't have altered his fantasy. He had also fantasized about the Lobu females. One thing he did know, *the* one thing he had seized upon, was that they had two equally inviting vaginal openings, with a strange set of four mandible-like digits outside which they could insert into corresponding vents in the groins of their males so as to stimulate them. His friend had told of the expert use of these digits in the fondling and manipulation of the human scrotum and anus.

The Lobu female seated a few tables over from him was alone, delicately spooning herself ice cream, and casting glances at him, suppressing a smile (a stiff expression adopted from humans). She was taller than he, slender and hairless, her polished flesh a softly mottled green and orange, looking like pliable agate. Her very humanoid face was lovely and large-eyed, without a nose, the only unpleasant feature for Bern being the two large ear holes. She wore only a diaper-like piece to hide her middle area, her chest flat and without nipples but with two pink gill-like openings on either side which resourceful humanoid males had also discovered to be gratifying areas for penetration.

Funny she should be alone, but judging from that and from her subtle yet still obvious flirtation Bern decided she must be a prostitute.

She was nearly finished eating, and he was concerned that she would leave if he didn't act soon. He couldn't expect her to take the role of aggressor–a much sought after Lobu wouldn't have to, so wouldn't be likely to. And the longer he hesitated the greater the chances of someone else seizing the opportunity. But could he afford her? His friend had said that they didn't come cheap. He had his gold-dust now, though, he reasoned…if she had one of those tube-things his friend had said they inserted in their chest gills to inhale it.

Why be intimidated by this gem? He wasn't shy, and his beers also made him bold. She wouldn't be making eyes at him with those glossy pink-irised orbs if she thought him beneath her. He rushed down the last of his beer, mostly foamy backwash. His friend had said their skins were cool like forest-shaded stone, and that they had no offensive body odors–rather, a pleasant natural exhalation from their gills reminiscent of the warm cozy smell of hot apple cider. Bern was smiling as he rose from his table and started around it toward hers. The beer went to his head as he stood, so he kept one hand to the table for support. Her eyes were on him with a look of sweet, mild surprise…feigned innocence. Yes, he was going to get lucky tonight after all. *Very* lucky. From an extremely negative alien encounter to this…it had been worth it, and Pox's lateness…

Pox…the drugs…God! he turned and saw his gym bag still on the bench where he'd been sitting–abandoned. A couple with three small children were already taking his place, one of the children reaching for the handles of the bag to pull it toward him for inspection.

"Ah, hey, excuse me…excuse me." Bern almost stumbled in his haste to get back. "That's my bag, thanks."

"Can ya prove it?" said the boy, dragging the bag close.

"Ben!" his mother scolded, wrenching the bag from him. "Sorry."

"No problem–thank you." Bern accepted his bag. Man, that was close! But despite the acceleration of his heartbeat his good spirits hadn't much faltered, and he turned back toward the Lobu with a grin.

The agate-skinned, willowy Lobu was still coyly smiling at him, but the Torgessi standing a bit behind her wasn't–it glared, actually, making for an interesting yin and yang composition.

"Ohh–man," Bern groaned, then spinning away to flee. He met the eyes of the mother who had given him back his gym bag. "Help–get a security guard–someone's trying to kill me!"

"You'd better run," said the little boy who'd found his bag.

Bern looked. Here it came. The Lobu female had ceased to exist to him; he didn't even see her. Just the skull-visaged Torgessi, big and getting bigger. His gym bag tucked to him like a football, he took the boy's advice.

"Look out, look out, look out!" Bern plunged through a flock of girls in their early teens. He collided with one and the both of them fell, him heavily atop her. She screamed. Her friends yelled at him. He scrambled to his feet. His partner in collision kicked upwards at him. Her heel caught him in the crotch. He gasped, stumbled away from her and fell again on hands and knees. "Ahh...God...you *fish!*" he choked.

"Pollinate me, you gagger skiz!" the girl screeched, rising to give him a sharp kick in the rear.

Bern reared up, swung his bag in an arc, caught the girl in the head with it. She went down. The Torgessi was there where she had been. Hands. His shirt was snagged a moment in fingers but he was hurtling through, the one on the ground screeching in a near alien language.

The beers were a stew in his belly, the fear and the kick in his groin were the added meat and vegetables, and it sloshed sickeningly inside him. He would rather fall on his knees and vomit than run, but he didn't have that option. He wove in and out of people, his frantic eyes searching for a guard, a protector, a shelter, an escape. Ahead was a ride, beyond that a dilapidated house with people lined up at the front. Bern made for the ride, not daring to look back to see how near his pursuer was.

He vaulted the low metal railing surrounding the ride but his ankle hit the top bar and he fell, rolled. "Hey!" someone barked, but he didn't look. On hands and knees he scrambled madly under the whirling ride, dragging

EVERYBODY SCREAM!

his bag. The whooshing above him scattered his moussed coiffure.

Crouching low as if disembarking from a helicopter, he cleared the ride, reached the opposite fence and swung himself awkwardly over it. Still he didn't look back. He ran at the dilapidated house. It looked fake, its deterioration up close crudely rendered, a prop for a low budget movie. He plowed into the line, climbed through it like a ladder of bodies. Bounded up onto the mock rickety porch. "Hey!" the ticket collector, a teenage girl dressed as a vampire, exclaimed. The door was closed.

"How much? How much?" he panted, now risking a look behind him. He didn't see it. But it was around here somewhere.

"Three green tickets."

"Hey, blaster!" someone in line yelled up at him.

"Here!" Bern slapped a ten munit bill into the girl's hand, reached for the door.

"You have to wait until the last group is out–hey!"

Enough *heys*. Bern let himself into the house, slamming the door after him.

Black, but a purplish light ahead. He plunged toward it.

As he turned a corner a figure stepped out in front of him. A teenage Choom boy with black skeletal eye sockets and cheeks, but these hollows too neatly delineated. A meat cleaver half buried in his head, blood splashed across his shirt. Bern winced, pushed past him.

The walls, floor, ceiling of this narrow-halled, twisty maze were black, with occasional purple lights and signs with cryptic warnings that glowed fluorescent in the light. A room opened on his left. Green light. Papier-mâché gravestones, a skeleton in rags hanging from a gibbet. Another corner, and a yellow-lit room from a funeral parlor, folding metal chairs and flowers around a coffin on a draped table. Bern heard girls screaming somewhere in the labyrinth ahead. The lid of the coffin was flung open and a red-haired teenager sat up in the box screaming. Unnerved, Bern pressed crazily on.

A door opened. A figure leaned out, the hands grasping at him. He cried out as the fingers snagged his shirt for a moment. The face, however hideous and glowing in the purple light, was not the cattle head skull he at first thought it was. He escaped it. His skin glowed a radioactive purple against his blending black clothing, as if he were one of the denizens here.

Another open room on his right. Red light. It was an evil miniature church altar. There was a podium with an upside-down cross on its front and an open book atop it, no doubt some musty encyclopedia meant to represent a blasphemous, ancient ritual book. A pipe organ had been cleverly constructed out of crude materials and a sheeted dummy sat at it with immobile claws on the keys, recorded organ music playing over the howling wind, ghostly moans, rattling chains (and shrieking teenage girls) that had been present all along. Bern climbed over the wooden railing that was there to dissuade people from entering the exhibits, having seen no living beings around, though he kept an eye on that seated figure for movement. He ducked behind the organ.

Here he found a speaker, out of which the loud organ music issued. Not only that, but he saw that there was a trapdoor. He hauled it open. Without hesitation he took advantage of this act of providence. He pulled the hatch closed after him.

It was a sub level, just high enough to crawl through on hands and knees. Wires were taped to the walls, and here and there he saw red letters in luminous paint glowing on the walls, the one directly beside him being 4. The hatches. No doubt the ghouls and ghosts used this sub level as a means by which to pop up unexpectedly from exhibit to exhibit. Also, ahead, tiny green and red lights glowed, obviously from some machine either having to do with the sounds or lights. Though much of the sub level stretched off into inky uncertain depths, Bern felt that he was currently alone down here. Nevertheless, he wanted to find an area in which to hide where the ghosts wouldn't see him, where he could lie and rest, wait for the carnival to close...the Torgessi to leave.

There were support beams, but they weren't enough to shelter him. He crawled on, now sure he was safe from the real monster but afraid to be expelled by the teenage phantoms who had made this haunted house out of the shell provided them. Bern chanced across signs of previous activity down here: buckets of fluorescent paint, a rotting pumpkin, a girl's white gym sock. Here and there a little purple light bled down from cracks above, but it was into greater darkness that Bern decided to head.

He was rewarded. Against a far wall he found that some of the boards were just propped on the other side, not nailed in place. Taking the chance that this might lead him outside, or directly into the headquarters of the ghosts, he pushed the boards away. Blackness. He squeezed through and replaced the boards gropingly. There. Let it find him here! He didn't know if a Torgessi's sense of smell was sharp, but outside of that and telepathic ability, both of which he doubted they possessed, it could hardly track him down now! Just a couple more hours at the most, and the place would start shutting down, and he'd have beaten that blasting lizard and he would kiss his shoes and buy two more pairs if he ever got the chance, just to spite it.

Bern found he could stand here, and did. It was a space between inner and outer wall. Moving along a bit, he saw some outside light ahead near the floor, coming through a crack. Loud music, carnival sounds also seeped in, drowning out the banshee moans from inside. Bern edged closer to the light. Now the area he was in opened up according to the maze scheme of the inner network of haunted rooms, and Bern was grateful for a space in which to stretch out, to actually lie down while his nerves and stomach, a clamoring carnival inside him, wound down...the departing crowds of adrenaline filing out of his veins.

But it soon became apparent that in this open, dimly lit room between the walls he was not alone.

They had drawn up against the walls, had been listening to him approach and enter their dwelling. Their emaciated, cadaverous naked bodies naturally glowed a faint fungoid blue. Some had reared up flat against the wall on two legs, most were on four. They looked like starved dogs. The ghosts of starved dogs. Their waiting eyes glinted.

Though he wouldn't be able to share the information, Bern Glandston had chanced upon the nest of the ghastly canine scavengers called snipes, the existence of which Del and others had speculated on. He stood paralyzed with the import of this information. His bag full of gold-dust was of no bargaining value here, and was hardly a weapon...but he swung it anyway as the first ghost sprang.

Jeffrey Thomas

Had he had distant sight of them when he emerged from the building, Hector might very well have pursued the Bedbugs himself, but he didn't. Even so, for a few moments as he jogged for the nearest telephone he could think of, the one on the outside wall of the lavatory shed, he was torn between calling the police and then the government-operated headquarters of the Theta research group, or seeking out the floating giant leg personally. The plasma bullets in his gun were much more corrosive than those legally available to the public, but would they work? And even then, it had at least two hundred and forty-two more such limbs. Instead of withdrawing, what if—enraged—it came through more quickly? For two years it had been slowly inching into this dimension, but if it were to *come through* tonight as the tormented man back there had warned, then it must be capable of more rapid locomotion. These questions and considerations were what kept him on his course for the telephone.

Panting, he found it unoccupied, and tapped out the three digit emergency code for the police. The vid plate remained a mad blizzard of colored static, like a window into a horrid other dimension. An emotionless voice, perhaps a robot's, responded, "Paxton Police Precinct 54—can we help you?" The phone had put him through naturally to the nearest station.

"I'm at the Paxton Fair…I need help immediately…something terrible is happening…"

"Have you contacted the security forces at the fair, sir?"

"No, I haven't…I will do that, but…"

"I suggest that you first contact the fair's security forces, sir, and see if…"

The blow to the back of his head prevented him from spinning to face whatever it was he had sensed floating up behind him. The force drove his forehead against the vid plate. He grunted. His collar was seized, and his arms. All three of them had their tentacles on him.

He was dragged quickly backwards around to the rear of the lavatory shed, and two twelve-year-old boys there smoking a joint bolted. Hector was spun and slammed up against the wall to face his attackers.

The leader's name was Saturnino Azusa–to his friends, Saturn Boy. The ones who had pinned his arms were Angel Cajones and Jesus DeJesus. The other two boys present were Manuel Santos and Miquel Santiesteban. It wasn't their faces that Hector recognized, so much, but their white leather jackets, the girls' panties hanging down their chests like ties. Crucifixes, religious pins were affixed to their lapels. Saturn Boy was the one, he began to realize, that he had prevented from assaulting that alien couple. Then he had held a knife. Now it was a small silvery revolver the boy pointed at his face while Angel and Jesus held him tight.

"Why were you calling the police, Officer Bato, when you *said* that you *are* the police? Hmm?"

"Look...please...we're all in terrible dan– "

The kick to his genitals made him jack-knife as far as his secured arms would allow. In coming down, his forehead cracked against the barrel sight of Saturn Boy's pistol. Saturn Boy tucked the gun in his rear waistband and reached into Hector's jacket.

"Yeah...here is that beautiful gun of yours, amigo. I like this–want to trade? What? I can just have it? Hey, man, many thanks!"

The gang's girlfriends, all dyed blondes (but for one dark Hispanic girl) between eleven and fourteen, giggled and tittered.

"Look at this beauty, huh?" Saturn Boy weighed the weapon in his hand, then dug some more into Hector's pockets, coming up with his wallet. He took his remaining money. "I don't see no badge, officer." Saturn Boy flicked the wallet away, held something under Hector's nose. "Hey, what is this, man? Your birth control pills?"

The others laughed. Struggling not to vomit, through the colored blizzard of his mind's static Hector recognized one of his six pill dispensers. Oh no–God no. "Don't," he wheezed.

Saturn Boy pocketed it, dug some more. "Dung–look at this, huh? You stinking old junkie." One dispenser after another was discovered like Easter eggs. The others hooted, whistled. One by one Saturn Boy transferred them to his own pockets.

"Please, they're no good to you…they're just anti-sleep drugs."

"I don't care what they are, amigo–I'll find some use for them, right?"

"Please…don't. Look, I'm a Latino like you…"

Saturn Boy laughed uproariously. "Yeah? So what the blast do I care, man? Anyway, you don't look Hisp to me, man…you look like a blasting Anglo *pretending* to be a Hisp. You know?"

"Come on, everybody is in fucking danger, man!"

"You're the one in *danger*, lily-man." And Saturn Boy kicked Hector in the stomach with a great deal of force. He followed that up with a swing of his new gun, its barrel gashing the top of Hector's head. Hector vomited and his arms were released. On hands and knees. Other feet swung up into his mid-section now. A foot swung up into his face. He heard the cartilage in his nose crunch. He rolled onto one side, curled fetus-like.

"Please…please," he sobbed, as the kicks went on. He saw that one of the kickers above him was a grinning blonde girl. She actually jumped up and down on his ankles now, laughing. A black gulf was opening to him like the jaws of some immense hideous creature, yawning to swallow him. Panic was a landed eel flopping helplessly inside him but muffled through layer after layer of cotton. "Please…don't kill me!" The black maw. The laughing girl. The glinting crucifix pins, mockingly winking. The Gatherers…

"Please don't kill me!" he moaned hopelessly one last time before the vast black maw closed around him.

"I'm seeing some of the encephalic abnormalities associated with certain types of clairvoyants." The chief of the carnival's medical unit was a Choom woman named Regina Brass, youngish and small and thin and sharp. A walking, talking scalpel. Before her and Del Kahn and Dingo Rubydawn lay the naked corpse of Sneezy Tightrope, his head split as if from a great fall. His mouth was open, lids half closed over somewhat crossed eyes; he looked like a cat struck by a car. Mitch, so fond of touring Del through the morgue like a museum curator presenting his recent acquisitions, would have been

EVERYBODY SCREAM!

very interested in this particular specimen but hadn't returned. And Sophi knew of this development but was still occupied with Mrs. Horowitz, her lawyer, and now people connected with Heather Buffatoni, Bonnie Gross and Moussa Habash. No one had been discovered to weep over Fen Colon or Wes Sundry. Luckily Sophi's lawyer Max Schenkel was here now.

A blue light passed over Sneezy's pot-bellied, unevenly tanned body, according to Regina's directions. Monitor screens presented findings in a series of codes easily familiar to her but as incomprehensible as hieroglyphics to Del, who watched them intently nonetheless. "So how'd it happen?"

"I'm not sure yet. It's very strange. It certainly doesn't seem to be the result of a tumor or growth...I can't trace a somatic origin."

"Well it sure wasn't psychosomatic," said Dingo.

"Drugs?" offered Del. "A bad mixture? I can assure you, this guy was into drugs."

"Oh, I can see that." Brass touched key pads. New columns of cryptic characters. "I can see iodine, gold-dust, purple vortex, red shockers, buttons, beans, kaleidoscopes, even a little fish...from a longer while back. I could pretty well tell you how much of what he's taken over the past month, and a fair idea of his drug behavior over the past year, and even throughout his life, based on the condition of his organs and brain. What's left of that."

"Kaleidoscopes and red shockers," said Del, looking up at Dingo.

"Common drugs," Dingo warned him, but one could see the interest in the Choom's eyes as well. "Has he taken any shockers or kaleidoscopes tonight, Gina?"

"Ahh." Dancing fingers, one-handed. "I'd say yes to a few shockers...nnno to kaleidoscopes. Not today. But not distant."

"Could he have been murdered?" Del asked.

"Anything's possible. Lots of ways to murder people. I've never seen this way before, though, I'd say."

The old woman who had called for an ambulance had given a description of a man she saw kneeling by Sneezy. The man mustn't be a suspect, since he had asked her to call for the ambulance, but he might know something. Vague description, though–could have been anybody. What Dingo had, he had passed on to the KeeZees, in case they chanced across a person who matched the information. Dark-haired Earther, mustache, black plastic jacket.

Sounds beyond the room, a knock, a tech robot opened the door and past it pressed Johnny Leng, arrogantly muscular, and Eddy Walpole, increasingly smirkless. Where was Roland LaKarnafeaux, Del thought, the boss? Johnny was his body and Eddy was his brains. So what was there left of LaKarnafeaux? Del was reminded how inarticulate and lacking in charisma LaKarnafeaux was, like a senile Buddha. The fat man was a balloon filled with hot air of the past and legend. Why hadn't they overthrown him? Could they possibly be as mindlessly entranced as were the teenage boys who emulated that dozing sage?

"God!" Eddy gasped, staring over Leng's shoulder at the starkly dead form. "What happened?"

"We don't know," Dingo said. "It wasn't a tumor or anything like that."

"He'd been acting funny tonight," muttered Leng, grim. "Staring off into space. He dropped a beer out of his hand. Really fuzzed."

"I'm sure this didn't help," Del said, pointing at the screen. Leng looked. "What's that?"

"Iodine, fish, gold-dust…purple vortex. Kaleidoscopes and red shockers."

Leng matched Del's intense, probing gaze. "Yeah…a lot of people indulge. But their heads don't explode, do they?"

"Your friend was exceptional…clairvoyant. That's funny, though, huh? Two of your friends in one night connected to purple vortex; not exactly one of the most widespread drugs."

"Yeah, funny–hilarious. I guess you're happy my friend's dead."

"No…but I won't wear black tomorrow."

"You're a real smug fuck tonight, aren't you, Kahn?"

"Johnny," Walpole hissed.

"Watch your mouth, punk," snarled Dingo Rubydawn, doing a mild imitation of Mitch Garnet.

Walpole changed subjects quickly, placing his words as if they were his body between Kahn and Leng. "Sneezy told me that he was picking up some kind of transmission telepathically."

EVERYBODY SCREAM!

"Of what nature?" asked Regina.

Walpole hesitated. Should he mention the Bedbugs? He didn't want to voice the word, so intent was his group on keeping the secret of purple vortex–more secret than even he suspected. Sneezy wasn't coming back, so why bother? But then, what if the Bedbugs had murdered him somehow? Had Sneezy told someone that the Bedbugs sold the Lobu the main ingredient of vortex...and had the bugs then found out? Were all of LaKarnafeaux's crew in danger? It was best if they investigated that possibility mostly on their own, but maybe a few careful clues toward that end wouldn't hurt.

"It seemed mechanical. Voices, he said. Not a standard advertising wavelength, apparently–he took blockers for that. And he assured me that he had not been taking drugs."

"That'd be a first," said Del.

Eddy ignored him. "His temples were pulsing, man...you could really see it."

"Zebo over at *Zebo's Saucer* diner is a telepath to some extent, I believe," Del said to Regina. "We should call and see if he's alright and if he's feeling any strange vibes."

"Good idea," said Regina.

Del's voice was admirably even, considering the tremulous anger...nervousness?...vibrating inside him at his confrontation with Leng. They had spoken with Sophi about Mortimer Ficklebottom and she had agreed to let him go. She had assured Del that they hadn't threatened her. Would Sophi lie about that? Del felt as if somehow Leng knew that he had given Mitch instructions to cuff one of the LaKarnafeaux boys. Since Leng's curse at him he'd avoided those hard, almost slanted eyes. Maybe he did feel a little nervous.

Dingo phoned *Zebo's Saucer*. To Leng and Walpole, Regina Brass said, "I'm almost done with your friend for now, then I'll transfer him to the morgue. I'll keep analyzing my findings. I'll let you know when to pick him up–I may need to keep him around a little while."

"Well, ah, we'll be moving on tomorrow," said Walpole. "We won't be around."

"Is there a way we can contact you?"

"Ah...we'll contact you. I'll call a funeral parlor when I get back to the trailer, then I'll call and let you know who I choose. When you're done with Sneeze you can let them know to pick him up. Then they can cremate him and hold onto the ashes until we're able to swing by sometime...or maybe they'll mail them to us. We don't know when we'll be around this way again."

What would they do with the ashes, Del thought...scatter them? Snort them? Ha–that'd be an appropriate tribute to Sneezy Tightrope, he smirked inside.

"No answer." Dingo had given up. "Hope he's alright."

"You'd better stay here–I'll go take a look," Del volunteered.

"Ah, doc," said Walpole. "Could the transmission have done that to Sneeze, or could he even possibly have been purposely murdered with some kind of transmission?"

"I don't know at this point. I hope to be able to find out. This one's a little extra intriguing."

Del was outside, heard others leaving the med trailer behind him and stopped to see. Approaching him were Walpole and Leng, looking like they also intended to stop, and speak to him. They did. Del vibrated again as Leng's eyes skewered him like black pokers heated in a fire.

Walpole asked, "Mind if we come with you?"

"If you want. How come?"

"If Zebo was affected, then it's less likely it was murder."

"Do you have a reason to feel that someone would want to murder any of you?" Del asked in a provocative sort of tone.

"You ever feel like someone might want to murder you?" Leng replied.

"Johnny, smarten up," Eddy hissed.

Leng whirled on his friend–the instant ferociousness that distorted his face and neck so startling that Del was sure Leng meant to strike Walpole one massive blow that would kill him, and he almost stepped back from them. Leng snarled, "Don't you ever fucking tell me to smarten up in front of this smug little ass-wipe, Eddy–don't you fucking *ever*...you hear me? *Huh?*"

Walpole remained calm, perhaps in an effort to appeal to Leng's reason, perhaps out of self preservation. But he did say, with an understated firmness,

EVERYBODY SCREAM!

"You're out of control, Johnny. Better think about it."

"Think about what? I won't have you humiliating me in front of my enemies...I won't fucking stand for it."

"Your enemies?" Del echoed, before Walpole could respond.

The ferocious hatred swivelled to blast him now. Correction–directed at Walpole it had been furious *anger*. Now it was, however, hatred.

"Don't act so stupid, Kahn...Sneezy told us. You couldn't fool the Sneeze. You sent your dog-boy Garnet down to see us and make trouble..."

Oh God...so they hadn't avoided Tightrope's ability. Then LaKarnafeaux's people had approached Sophi. That was how she knew he had instructed Mitch, not from Mitch himself, who wouldn't have betrayed his boss...or pseudo-boss. Del felt naked. He was glad Sneezy Tightrope was dead.

"You hid behind your rabid little trigger-boy, huh, Kahn? What for, huh? You know something about me you don't like? *Huh?*" A savage smile. A tyrannosaur might have displayed such a smile. Johnny Leng's muscles seemed to extend beyond his physical body, forming an aura around him, tight and electric and dangerous.

"I know things I don't like about you," Del said softly, trying not to swallow, lest Leng hear it or see his adam's apple rise and drop; thus, perversely, he felt the aching need to swallow.

"Oh, is that right? Such as?"

"Let's go back to the trailer, Johnny..." Walpole tried to interrupt.

"Such *as?*"

"You sell drugs. Strong drugs."

"Interesting theory. Anything else? Anything more related to you, maybe?"

"I don't know what you mean."

"No...you really don't know, do you? You don't know much of anything, looks like. For one, you obviously don't know what's good for you, because you don't know what I'm capable of. You don't even know much about your wife, do you?"

"Johnny...I'm gonna talk to Karny..."

"*Talk to him!*" Leng hadn't taken his poker eyes out of Del's sockets.

"Huh? You don't know much about your own wife, Mr. *Del Kahn*, do you?"

"What do you know about my wife?" Del couldn't get much voice past his clogged adam's apple.

"Hey, did I say I knew anything about your wife? Hey, I don't know either. I don't know what her favorite color is, or what her favorite movie is...but come to think of it now, I *do* know she has this little freckle or mole or something right at the crack of her ass." The predator's grin was Choom-like in size, scarring deep crease lines in Leng's weather-worn face. "Ha–the first time I saw it I thought it was a smudge, if you get my meaning. Turned me off until I got used to it. You ever been bothered by it?"

"You scum...you fucking scum...what do you know?"

"Only what she let me know, Mr. Kahn, sir."

"Johnny, you're going to hurt us. Stop. I mean it."

"What did you do to her?"

"I did to her what she did to me. You want specifics? I wish I had thought to take a vid without her knowing, but I don't have a camera anyway."

"I don't believe you."

"Believe it, little man. Hey–why hold it against her? You had your friends and she had me. Anyway, like she told me, she's had others before me and you knew about that...so what's one more?"

"My wife wouldn't go to bed with a stinking monster like you."

"Your wife got wet because I was a stinking monster. Women like stinking monsters. They just can't accept it. They tell themselves they want nice little supposedly respectable moneymaking cowards like you."

"Tightrope read my mind...that's how you know about the mole. You can't fool me."

"You look like you're gonna *cry*, son...aw, don't do that. Look, if you don't want to believe, then don't. If you want to think Sneezy read your mind, then comfort yourself. But I'm not fooling you. You're fooling yourself. Alright?" Leng started past Del. His face passed close and Del fought the impulse to withdraw from it. "Give that luscious ass one last kiss for me, will ya? Right on the mole."

Laughter. Del took one step after him. Someone had his arm, suddenly.

EVERYBODY SCREAM!

Walpole. "Don't. He wants it."

"I'll kill him," Del rasped. Now he let himself swallow...it was, indeed, a very loud gulp.

"Forget it–he's lying. He's just intimidating you because of Mort, and he's upset about Sneezy. He'll get over it. I'll talk to Karny. Anyway, we'll be gone tomorrow so it's best to let it go. He's just taking out his frustrations. He's lashing out. Don't fall for it...he's lying."

A long shuddery breath rattled out of Del. Something like relief...but it was not something he could entirely exhale out of him.

Walpole let go of his arm as Leng's swaggering form receded, went on: "Go see Zebo, man. I'll call the med trailer later to hear what you find out, alright? Walk it off, man–it's nothing. Don't let him make a fool out of you. It's nothing."

"Right," muttered Del Kahn, and he strode away from Eddy Walpole.

Eddy watched after him, much concerned. Certain he would see Kahn veer instead toward his home trailer or into the security station, in search of Sophi Kahn. But he didn't...he seemed truly to be heading off for *Zebo's Saucer*. A sigh of relief, but only partial. Only temporary. He was bound to question his wife sooner or later. What if she broke down and confessed?

A good thing they had already sent Crosby Tenderknots away on his bike with the vortex and the rest...but still he didn't feel safe. Would Karny agree to packing it up tonight...*now?* Anyway, if the Bedbugs had murdered Sneezy that was another very good reason to get the hell out of here right away.

Had Walpole known how Leng had dealt with the threat of Fen Colon and Wes Sundry–discovered by Sneezy–and of the attention it was receiving, he would probably have been close to frantic right now.

But even then it wouldn't have occurred to him to hop on his big *Dozer* and head out alone. He wouldn't leave Karny.

The only customer in *Zebo's Saucer* was so strikingly hideous for a nonmutant that Del forgot his mission for a moment. He had seen the Mo-mo-mo-mo in books and in vids but never in person. They had hulking, dark orange carrot-like bodies, creased almost into fissures, with a droopy branch-like antenna dangling from the top knob, not really a head in the human sense since the functions of a head were dispersed or not in identifiable evidence. One leg was a thick, twisted club of wrinkly flesh, the other a veiny, scrawny two-toed bird leg. One arm looked like a giant penis ending in long, tactile hairs, the other wasn't really an arm but a huge warty barrel constantly oozing slime. The one large eye was situated at the barrel's root. This particular specimen had a diaper-like garment covering the open bottom of its barrel, as it sat at the counter with a coffee in front of it. The Mo-mo-mo-mo were among the most consistently vain races of intelligent beings, arrogantly obsessed with their own self-proclaimed beauty and glamour. To them, the perfect symmetry of humanoids was a ghastly, too mathematical, too mechanical, artificial-seeming arrangement–a perverted ugliness bordering on abomination.

Zebo wasn't dead. No cracks in his oversized, hairless head. He was closing up early, however. Though the tiny being never looked vivaciously healthy to Del, he did think that Zebo appeared a trifle wan as he came to meet him at the semicircular counter. "Howdy, Del," he said.

"Zebo–how do you feel? Anything funny happen tonight?"

"What do you mean? Did somebody tell you?"

"Tell me what?"

"I've been picking up some, ah..."

"Telepathic transmissions?"

"Yes, that's it. How did you know?"

"We've got a corpse down in the morgue. You know Sneezy Tightrope?"

"Yes."

"Dead. His brain exploded."

"Goodness. Well...mine didn't, as far as I know. Ha. Strange."

"I thought you might know something."

"My customer here told me more than I could fathom." Zebo nodded at the Mo-mo-mo-mo. "It's telepathic also...more so than I."

EVERYBODY SCREAM!

"Of course." Del took in the asymmetrical being afresh. It had its hairy penis hand in its coffee mug. "So what did it say?"

"Well, it came in earlier...shortly after you were here. Ate, and left. After a big jolt it came back, knowing I was telepathic, to ask me if I had felt it, too...as you're doing now."

"Big jolt?"

"I'd been receiving something for several hours, mounting but low...then there was a massive jolt. I almost lost consciousness. So did the Mo-mo-mo-mo. There's been a few lesser jolts since. I took some blockers after the first big one...I don't know if that's why the lesser jolts weren't as bad. The Mo-mo-mo-mo can shut down its perception naturally, like closing an eyelid."

"So Sneezy wasn't murdered. Why'd his head explode, though?"

"Either he was too weak, or too close to the transmission source. The same jolt I felt, no doubt."

"Do you think it's a malfunctioned advertising wavelength, or some kind of attack on people's minds, or what?"

"Oh, I know the what, and part of the why...as I said, mostly through the Mo-mo-mo-mo."

"So what is it?"

"Bedbugs. They're transmitting over a telepathic amplifier-projector device."

"Bedbugs. Is it a weapon?"

"No–a communication device. And it isn't their transmissions that are creating the jolts...but the *response* they're receiving. That transmission is coming from a creature in another dimension. Not a Bedbug. I can't tell what."

"God," Del muttered. Bedbugs. Yeah–come to think of it, maybe he had seen one or two lurking about; in their silent scurrying, easily blending into the shadows. He remembered that on two separate occasions, oddly enough, when he and Sophi had visited an art museum in town, they had seen a small group of Bedbugs clustered avidly around a certain ancient stone bas-relief portraying a tentacle-headed, winged mythical creature or god. Other times while riding subways he had seen some of the odd graffiti of that violent rogue gang of Bedbugs, and would think of a news story concerning a train that had been conveying a rival gang in the early morning hours, and which came to an unplanned stop in the dark of a tunnel. It was suddenly swarmed with Bedbugs, who left only two bulging-eyed innocent riders alive amongst the corpses to tell the tale. Strange beings, always conveying the mood of being up to something furtive and sneaky.

Zebo said, "They're chanting to it…mostly praises. How intelligent it is, whether animal or being, we can't tell. It's some kind of symbolic fertility god to them, apparently.…they keep referring to a harvest of some sort. It seems very near. It must be *here*, but in another dimension. Supposedly it's going to come through into our world tonight."

"How come?"

"It pertains to their harvest. The Mo-mo-mo-mo noted something odd. It told me it sensed the Bedbugs observing animals here at the fair…experimenting on them. Something about seeing if their energy could be drawn from them while still alive, rather than after they were already dead." Zebo chuckled. "I hope they don't mean to feed their god some cows and bumbles."

"They'd better not be experimenting on the animals here, the weird fucks. God…crazy. So that's what killed Sneezy, huh?"

"Has to be. I surely felt it."

"Of all things. No great loss, I mean…but man. Glad I'm not psychic." Del glanced at the Mo-mo-mo-mo. God, it smelled. Like baby shit. Sometimes they referred to themselves as the Perfumed Ones.

"Night's just about had it," Zebo said. "Another year gone. I thought I'd close down a little early…I need some rest."

"By all means. Well…" Del stepped back from the counter, watching Zebo tap a pen on his closed magazine. "That explains most of the Sneezy Tightrope mystery. I guess I'll have Dingo send some guards out looking for the Bedbugs to tell them what happened and to be careful what they're doing. And to see if they're messing with our animals. This will have to be reported to the police."

"Mm," agreed Zebo.

"Well." Del took a few steps toward the door. But his eyes were drawn once more to the vegetable-like hulk sitting at the counter. Zebo was watching Del's hesitance expectantly, it seemed...waiting for him to say something. He did. "Just how strong is that thing, telepathically? I mean, can it focus on one person far away from it...among many other people?"

"Perhaps. Why?"

"Will you ask it to try and do that for me?"

Zebo turned, stared wordlessly at the Mo-mo-mo-mo. The single whale-like eye lazily rotated to gaze back at the tiny being. Del returned to the counter. He leaned away, however, as the Mo-mo-mo-mo's drooping branch-like antenna suddenly began to lash and flick and spin crazily. He batted his lids in a protective reflex reaction.

Zebo faced Del. "It says it can try. Who do you have in mind?"

"My wife."

"Sophi Kahn. What was her unmarried last name? Her sense of self and identity will be very tied up in her name awareness. It can track her through her name."

"I have a picture." Del reached behind for his wallet.

"No, no, just the name."

"Her maiden name was Redshell."

Zebo turned once again to the Mo-mo-mo-mo...once again the antenna twirled like copter blades, snapped like a whip. Zebo and Del waited. Del felt nauseous. The baby shit smell was definitely not helping.

Zebo looked to Del. "It has her. What is it you require?"

It had her. Sophi's thoughts at this being's disposal, a buffet spread before it. She would never suspect, like a woman undressing under the gaze of binoculars. Del swallowed. "Can it dig...can it find the name Johnny Leng in my wife? Can it tell me if she ever went to bed with him? Had sex with him?"

Zebo looked at the Mo-mo-mo-mo. Then the tentacle spasms. Del's left hand pinched at the inside of his jacket's pocket, rubbed the silk material. Zebo turned to Del, his alien face expressionless, and Del's stomach rolled upside-down. Zebo said, "Yes, Johnny Leng is there...very strongly. There is much bitterness, much anger in your wife toward Johnny Leng. And fear, also. Yes...your wife did sleep with Johnny Leng."

Then the bottom dropped out of Del's chest. An insidious trapdoor. His heart fell end over end over end down a bottomless well, with a chilly vacant area left in its place, the whooshing tug of his plummeting heart sucking his spirit down after it. "How many times? More than once?"

"Yes."

"*Willingly?*"

"Yes."

"My God. My fucking, fucking God..."

"But not tonight. Not willingly tonight..."

"*Tonight?*" He wanted to cry. Her wanted to punch her. *Punch* her. She had confronted him about his cheating, made him promise to fight it, and now this. Words from their marriage ceremony hovered at the back of his mind, mockingly. *I am my beloved's and my beloved is mine.* Song of songs. He both liked those words for the circle of harmony they made and disliked them for the implication of one possessing another. Now they were a total joke to him. A joke. Johnny Leng. That stinking monster. It was true. Willingly. Johnny Leng...

"Why did she do it?" he breathed. "Why did she cheat on me?"

"No rational reason. Emotions of hurt, resentment, confusion. And the typical hunger of the flesh. But tonight was different."

"Why?" he was shaking. He would kill him. Kill that Johnny Leng...

"He forced her into a sexual act tonight. She didn't want to. She is guilty about her actions, Del...she's sorry. She resents herself. She wants to tell you about tonight but she's afraid that he will hurt her and you. He has said he would." Zebo's voice was grim. The Mo-mo-mo-mo's antenna was still spinning, flopping, relaying information. "He held her at gunpoint tonight."

Del was nodding. "Mm-hm. Mm-hm. Okay." His nostrils could be heard dragging in long, stench-filled breaths of air, letting them out long and slow. He slipped his hand phone out of his jacket. "I see now. Thank you, Zebo. Tell it I said thank you."

Zebo observed Del closely as he thumbed keys on the phone, and reached a robot tech on the other end. "Let me speak to Dingo," Del told it tremulously.

Moments. The Choom security man came on. "Del?"

"Dingo, meet me at *Zebo's* right away, understand? Right now. I want you to arrest somebody."

"Who?"

"Johnny Leng. He raped my wife tonight. She isn't there, is she?"

"No...she isn't...dung, are you *sure?*"

"Yes. Don't say anything about it to her if you see her. Just get over here quick before I go and do it alone." He signed off, pocketed the device.

"Del," said Zebo. Del looked. "She's sorry, Del. With all due respect, you had a young lady in here tonight."

"I know. I forgive her, Zebo. It's my fault, probably. But I don't forgive him. Thanks for caring."

While Del waited, the Mo-mo-mo-mo "spoke" some more to Zebo. "Foolish humans, so morbidly obsessed with their reproductive process. They should be asexual, like *my* people," it concluded proudly.

"Ooh, look at that, huh?" said Venus Bovino, spooning some ice cream into her mouth from a little cup. Her daughters Claire and Mallory stood by her doing likewise.

"What is it?" Claire asked, sneering.

"Read the sign, why don't you—what are you, blind? Nicky. Nick."

"*What?*" Venus's burly husband sauntered over with a sigh of disgust. Up ahead inside a tent men were arm wrestling on a raised platform, a crowd encircling it. Right now a human was up against a simianoid. The little ape-featured being seemed to be winning. Nick was sure he could take the creature.

"Look at this thing."

Nick joined his wife. "So what?"

"Do we have one of these in our back yard?"

"No–and I don't have a dead whale in my back yard either. Like I said, so what? Come on, huh?"

"I guess you have no interest in things."

"I guess you're interested in stupid dung. Now come on."

"I'm reading."

"Yeah? Fine. So read. I'm going on ahead."

"So go."

"I am. I'll be at the arm wrestling tent."

"Of course."

"You're lucky the girls have ears." Nicky swaggered on ahead.

Venus licked her plastic spoon, tossed her trash aside onto the ground, wiping her sticky lips and fingers with a balled up napkin which she jettisoned also. Two hundred and forty-three legs over a bank in town, huh? Wow. And here there was one touching the ground, two curling down toward it and the end claw of a fourth emerging from the air. There was a dark wet area below as if a liquid had spilled from that space but no longer came. Venus thought that if she stared hard enough at the two curled legs she could see their infinitesimal movement, as when one watches the mercury of a thermometer rise when their warm thumb is on it, or the minute hand of a watch move.

Venus wondered if one day a full two hundred and forty-three of these huge black insect legs would appear here, also.

Seventeen-year-old Cod had been getting rather drunk, rather foggy, and Johnny Leng had snapped at him, given him some detox pills. He was now sharp and alert. Two other boys lounging in the lawn chairs had been ordered away by Eddy Walpole. When Del Kahn, Dingo Rubydawn and Mendez of the Fog security outfit marched toward the camp they saw only Cod outside it…and two Martians. One was peering stonily into the showcase of key chains, buttons, eye pins, switchblade knives. The other leaned against one of the pavilion's support rods, rolling a cigar in his mouth…or the remnant of a

EVERYBODY SCREAM!

licorice ice whip–Del couldn't tell yet. Both had holstered pistols, but none of the bandoliers, grenades, or huge rifles (called assault engines) associated with them. The one leaning against the support rod, a boy of about eleven, had a camouflage-painted face to match his uniform and cap, however...and a necklace strung with a half dozen dried and shriveled ears. He was squinting as he watched the three men stride determinedly toward the camp.

Dingo was a little ahead of his companions, and ignoring the two loiterers addressed Cod sharply. "Where's Johnny Leng?"

Cod glanced from one man to the other to the other, then back. "Why?"

"That doesn't concern you, loser–which is he in? Van or camper? I want ya to get him out here."

"Why?"

"That doesn't concern you, I said, and I won't say it again. Just do it."

"I don't know if he's here."

"You lying worthless punk. Leng!" Dingo took a few steps under the wide canopy stretching out from the body of the bus-like hovercamper. "Johnny Leng!" he shouted. "Get out here now!"

The van door slid open and a door in the camper opened simultaneously. Mendez put his hand on his gun handle. Del's hands twitched, wanting to do the same but his gun was at home. His heartbeat was the steady rhythmic background of this composition, upon which all other tracks were being laid, these varied participants all constructing their own parts to the piece. An improvised jam session. It could go anywhere.

A few passing spectators had washed up on the shore of the living river, attracted instinctively by the tension on this island. Another. Another. In a few minutes it would almost be an audience.

Out of the hovercamper came Mortimer Ficklebottom, shirtless but still with his top hat, and a groggy, blinking teenage girl, her curly black hair in her face, pudgy but slovenly sensuous and large-breasted, wearing only black bikini panties cutting into her fungus-white flesh. Out of the van came Johnny Leng, then Eddy Walpole, and finally the slow-moving bulk of Roland LaKarnafeaux. Leng now wore an open, scratched and worn brown leather *Dozer* bike jacket over his muscular torso. The night was getting ever cooler...brisk. Del felt the bite of it through his silk suit, which seemed ever thinner, and he had to force himself not to shiver. He wasn't entirely successful.

"Is there a problem, guys?" asked Eddy Walpole.

"Johnny Leng," said Dingo, "you're under arrest."

"What for?" muttered Johnny Leng in a low, menacing tone.

"The sexual assault of a woman, under the threat of death."

"What woman?"

"You goddamn well know what woman, you slimy piece of dung," blurted Del Kahn, stepping up beside Dingo. Shivering had become shaking.

"I don't know what you're talking about, Mr. Kahn, and you can refer all questions to my lawyer tomorrow. I deny everything."

"You deny what you told me? You admitted to that...you admitted what you did!" Del was remotely mindful of the gathering audience.

"I never admitted to raping anyone or threatening to kill someone."

"We're going to take you in and let the court decide that, Leng," said Dingo. He came forward, but slowly...wary.

"Now wait a minute, here, boys," chuckled jolly Roland LaKarnafeaux, moving forward also, unhurriedly, as if this were all some silly misunderstanding. "Let's not get all worked up until we get our stories straight..."

"I *told* you, Del...he was only teasing you!" Walpole exclaimed.

"You lied to me...I have proof."

"What proof?" sneered Leng. He had taken a step back from Dingo but stopped when Dingo stopped.

"A telepathic being. We'll have it testify in court, under a truth scan to prove it's not lying," said Del.

"Come on, now." Uniformed Mendez started moving toward the accused man. Right hand on his pistol's butt, left hand fumbling out a pair of red plastic handcuffs. "We're not asking you, we're telling you..."

"I won't go in," muttered Johnny Leng sideways.

"Johnny," said Eddy Walpole. Then helplessly he watched as Johnny Leng's right hand plunged inside his scuffed leather jacket. "*Johnny!*"

"Hey!" Mendez yanked his pistol out of its sheath.

EVERYBODY SCREAM!

"Dung!" Cod hurled himself under a table spread with folded t-shirts.

"Come on–no!" wheezed Roland LaKarnafeaux, holding up two palms, as if such a gesture might stop two trains from colliding.

"Look out!" Del shouted to Mendez too late, and ducked, folding one arm across his face.

The Martian leaning against the pole didn't chance the possibility that Mendez's uniform might have a lining of bullet and ray-proof mesh, or mesh woven directly into the uniform material; he went for the head. His pistol was a ray blaster. The red bolt streaked the air like a flashing comet, briefly glimpsed. The full three foot length of it vanished into a new hole just above Mendez's right ear. His left eye burst.

Crouching, Dingo jerked out his semiautomatic loaded with explosive rounds. Leng also crouched as he fired. His gun made no sound. Leng squeezed the trigger so rapidly that it might have been a fully automatic weapon. One bullet drilled into Dingo's face just below his nose, one crashed straight on like a hot rod into the wall of his gritted Choom teeth. One struck his powerful jaw, one slipped into his throat and two missed altogether.

Dingo only got one shot off before he fell dead. The projectile impacted on the shoulder of Eddy Walpole and detonated. There was a wet explosion, and the whoop that leaped from Eddy's mouth might have been his soul startled into flight. His arm was torn completely off, with much of his shoulder and a little of his neck. The bullet had been meant for Leng and its nearby concussion, the splash of red paint across his face and body, sent him to the ground with a heavy grunt.

Del snapped his gaze from Mendez to Dingo. Mendez had fallen on top of his clenched gun. Dingo was sprawled with his arm cast out, his pistol loosely in hand, trigger guard hooked on one finger...as if in death he proffered it to Del.

Del snapped his gaze to the two Martians, pointing their blasters at his face. The one who had killed Mendez still chomped down on his cigar-or-licorice whip. Del held up his hands."I'm unarmed!" he babbled. He could feel the molten arrows from their guns piercing his body even before they pulled their triggers. Del Kahn knew he was going to die now.

They didn't pull their triggers. One looked uncertainly to the other. The other, the one who had killed Mendez, still stony, lowered his blaster. It was the code of the Martians. They could not shoot an unarmed man.

Del snapped his gaze to Johnny Leng. Leng's dark eyes blazed recognizable through a mask of blood and a plastered confetti of flesh and cloth. He was pulling himself to his feet, unsteady, his gun hanging limply, heavy. Only his gaze was steady. The strength of his gaze hoisted the rest of him up, a marionette. One string started lifting up the blood-speckled gun.

Del ran at Johnny Leng. The audience was yelling, screaming.

Mortimer shoved his girlfriend out of his way, broke from the camp in a sprint, his top hat toppling, left behind in the dust. His girlfriend staggered, hugging herself, blinking, head tucked into her shoulders. Roland LaKarnafeaux had slid along the outside of the van, fell to his side, floundered, came up on hands and knees to crawl…

Del tackled Leng, driving the air out of him. As one they crashed back into the open door of the van, Leng underneath. Del brought a fist down. It mostly glanced off a broad, well-defined cheekbone. Del caught the gun as it came up in Leng's left hand. The gun went off. The silent bullet zipped past his ear. He seized Leng's wrist in his right hand. With both hands he pounded Leng's forearm against the edge of the van's sliding door…again…again. Now the gun flipped over Leng's hand to dangle just by its trigger guard. One last bash and the pistol was dislodged, disappearing into the van.

Leng's free hand lunged, caught Del by the hair. Del cried out. He twisted his head to follow the twisting. Letting go abruptly, Leng cocked his arm back close to his body…then drove his elbow out into Del Kahn's cheekbone below his left eye. Del stumbled backwards away from Leng, unpinning him. Leng pushed himself out of the van's threshold.

The kick came up into Del's crotch. As Del folded the punch arced into his temple. His lapels were seized, he was hoisted up and his whole body was swung. Let go. He crashed limply against the side of the camper and slipped down it into a puddle of half-consciousness.

Taking a deep breath, Leng looked around him, and his searching gaze came to rest on the pistol proffered in Dingo's hand. He didn't take his time in going to it, but he didn't hurry either. Despite his fog and the pain pulsing within it, he felt in control again. He stooped (God, his *back*) and curled his fist around the gun. Explosive bullets. Loud, messy, but now there was no time or need for stealth or subtlety. Straightening up, Leng turned...

Del swung Roland LaKarnafeaux's blue metal baseball bat with both fists gripping the black plastic sheath of the handle, swung it from way back behind his shoulder, swung it with the twist of his entire body, swung it with his teeth gritted and his eyes insane with hunger. Leng's eyes had held only cold, determined intent. That wasn't quite enough at this moment.

The bat slammed against the side of Johnny Leng's head, and either Del felt something within crack or crunch, or else it was the vibration that gong-like traveled along the bat into his arms. Leng was thrown to the ground. His legs curled spider-like under him, his hair gray in the dust. A moan. Still the gun in his hand. Del stood over him. The bat with which Roland LaKarnafeaux had killed his first man–a boy, really...a child–killed his first person at the age of twelve, still rang with its vibration in Del's fists, his body ringing with its own vibration. LaKarnafeaux's Excalibur. Del had seized it from its resting place against the camper, had yanked the sword from the stone although he was not the king. Anyone could wield this Excalibur because it was only an old baseball bat, nicked and gouged, not mystical, not mythical.

Dingo's gun left a groove in the dirt as Leng dragged it toward him, his back arching. His arms pushed. His head left the ground. He was slow and patient; he moaned almost calmly. Del got closer by one more step. Executioner's sword or child's toy or vibrating extension of human rage, the bat lifted high and came down hard.

The audience cried out in the thrilled unity of horror, loathing, morbid fascination.

Johnny Leng splayed flat on his face. He didn't moan now.

Del turned, eyes still hungry, on Roland LaKarnafeaux, who on hands and knees rolled the large corpse of Mendez over onto its back, exposing the bright plastic and metal gun underneath it. LaKarnafeaux gaped up in shocked distress, a fat child caught with his hand in the cookie jar. Del covered the few steps toward him, swinging the bat up into the ready position once more.

"Hey—no! *No!* Come on!" LaKarnafeaux blubbered, tumbling onto his back, hands flailing, pushing his body along with his legs away from Mendez and the gun. "Don't, man, I give up! Don't, don't, don't!"

Del quit advancing, stood over Mendez. LaKarnafeaux was sobbing, tears actually running into his grizzled beard, his glasses dislodged, hanging from one ear. His t-shirt had rolled up to expose the hairy planet of his belly. He was too helpless and pathetic a thing to kill. Like the beast called Jonah's Whale, through whose body people rode, he wasn't even fully alive. Killing him would be more like pulling the plug on a life support machine. He groveled, whimpered, whined. Now Del carried the scepter of the blue baseball bat.

Over his shoulder, he glared hard and brightly at the Martians. The fiery triumph he showed was splashed with the cold water of fear as he saw the boy with the cigar-or-licorice whip lift his blaster to aim it at him once more." Hey—*wait!*" Del tossed the bat away. "Wait!"

Purple vortex, the Martian captain had decided finally, was more important than a code of honor...

"I'm unarmed, I'm unarmed!" Now Del was batless and groveled. Things could change so quickly. No one person could ever be the most dangerous, the most powerful. They could just take turns based partly on their skill and boldness, and partly on opportunity and luck. Del's opportunities and his luck had shifted badly. The deliberateness of the Martian's aim, the one or two ticks of hesitation, indicating a last vestige of reluctance, were all that saved him. The Martian, in that tick or two, in turn squandered *his* moment of opportunity and luck, of dangerous superiority...

The explosive bullet from Mitch Garnet's pistol transformed the neck of the Martian captain into a gushing organic volcano, his head obliterating like a shotgunned plaster bust. The pitiful rag of a body crumpled bonelessly. In his crouched firing stance, Mitch merely had to swivel a few inches to reduce the head of the second boy to a shattered clay pigeon.

"Get down, Del!" he roared. "Everybody *scatter!*" He meant that for the audience.

Del understood Mitch's meaning as he dove behind a display table.

EVERYBODY SCREAM!

Not everyone understood, or even had time to respond anyway, and most of those who tried collided with each other as the three Martians sprang out from their hiding places nearby and opened fire with their baroque, ridiculously bulky assault engines, bandoliers with grenades clipped to them criss-crossing their narrow chests. One Choom man in the range of fire absorbed an automatic blast of a half dozen ray bolts, and like a lasered St. Sebastian swooned in death. A teenage girl took a hole through her narrow neck. A man had his wrist lanced clean through.

Mitch rolled, came up kneeling, fired. His explosive bullet struck the boy on the gun. But the gun blew up. And the grenades blew up.

He had popped out from behind a trailer which was a dilky stand, and the chain of explosions which shattered the Martian to fragments like a vase blasted with a machine gun (each bullet shattering more, but all so close together that nothing was left for long) rocked the trailer, tore through the metal skin of it. The lights flickered inside. The Choom proprietor had ducked under his counter back when the first of the gunfire began, wiser than the gathered crowd, most of whom hadn't really fled until now, only moving further back or spreading out a little, confident in their role as observers, as if this were all some holographic VT program. A few pieces of shrapnel struck the proprietor but left only minor cuts.

The shrapnel freed from the grenades, however, was like ten machine gunners standing in a circle wildly spraying…a ravaging locust storm. Many of the frantic audience members went down thrashing, flopping, shrieking. Three would die, and a burly teenage boy would live the rest of his life as a glassy-eyed giant fetus hooked up to a machine.

"Fuck! You fucking *bastards!*" Mitch bellowed in outrage at having been forced by these monsters to himself make the nightmare even worse. You couldn't even fight back at them. They made you help them kill. Mitch shook with this madness, horrified at himself. He was a protector of the people. He was afraid to shoot again.

One of the remaining two strafed his gun toward Mitch, ripping through a blindly stumbling, shrapnel-pierced man to do so. Though he couldn't fire again, Mitch was able to dive at the ground, scramble for cover behind the table with its museum display of handcuffs, knives, iodine pipes. The glass shattered, the freed colorful eyes danced exuberantly, crazily, high into the air.

The other Martian moved to a more advantageous position. He saw a form hiding behind a table. A grenade rocket might hurt LaKarnafeaux at this nearness to him. He launched a huge capsule of military-grade plasma from his rifle instead.

The capsule hit Cod on the left of his chest and the quivering gelatinous plasma spread instantly over his writhing, flopping form like a blazing mantle of white light half solidified. It ran into his open mouth; no scream got past it. It poured into his ears, his nostrils, sank through his pores. In moments the quivering blob grew less and less human in outline and shrank away to nothing…no bones, no sludge, no stain.

The strafing Martian, seeing that the enemy was pinned, came running out from his station to close in on a clearer target, circling in to better see those display tables. Too frenzied strafing might hit LaKarnafeaux and they couldn't have that. Luckily, at last, most of the bystanders had withdrawn or lay dead or immobilized, creating less obstruction.

The Martian, however, ran past Shiv Mofo, who had ducked behind a trash barrel, a black gang boy wearing a hot pink rubber swim cap, who had never much liked the Martians and who was even more offended by having been caught in the middle of one of their gun battles. As the Martian ran past Mofo, ignoring him, Mofo simply extended his arm and shot him cleanly through the skull with two lead bullets.

The Martian continued running for a bit, but weaving as if dodging air fire, before he pitched forward dead across a moaning wounded innocent.

Garnet found a safe spot to peek out of, and maybe to fire from, in time to see the last of the Martian unit die. Two white humans and a Choom were shooting him, standing around him and getting closer as he dropped his rifle. They had decided individually, without the inspiration of Shiv Mofo or each other. This was outer Punktown, but it was still Punktown. The little boy's inner lining of bullet and ray-proof mesh seemed to be keeping him barely alive, except for some bone-cracking blunt trauma, but some gang boys of similar age dashed in with nunchakus to flail at his head, and finished him off and then some.

Wearily, warily, Del Kahn and Mitch Garnet stood up from behind their shelters. Del saw two scorched ray holes in Mitch's silver windbreaker but knew he had a protective mesh lining inside. They looked at each other for a moment, then Del saw Mitch scan the battlefield of dead and wounded with a look of horrified despair he had never seen on Mitch's tight, hard face. Rousing himself from his shock, however, Mitch went to handcuff the cowering, trembling, half insensate blob that was Roland LaKarnafeaux.

Within minutes, almost every weapon (and some wallets) had been stripped from the dead. One of the gang boys tucked away his nunchakus in favor of a Martian's hand blaster, another lugged away the Martian's trademark assault engine. Del watched a boy dash off with bandoliers from which a half dozen fragmentation grenades hung like fruit. Del himself bent to retrieve Dingo Rubydawn's semiautomatic from the hand of Johnny Leng…half to keep a kid from taking it, half for himself should more Martians attack before the inevitable influx of town enforcers.

Tucking the flat gun in his waistband, Del watched a bloodied, disoriented man, apparently struck by shrapnel, stagger away with the assault engine from the Martian killed by Shiv Mofo.

Once again a crowd gathered, a tide coming in, more people than ever…children licking ice cream, teenagers munching corn dogs, and toward the rear a towering, bluish-greenish scaled Torgessi, craning its neck with mild curiosity as it placidly chewed dilkies from a greasy little bag.

Nick Bovino's arm ached but his pride was more injured…that fucking little monkey had beaten him within a minute. Five feet tall and as skinny as his daughters. He cursed under his breath and rubbed at his arm. At least he'd seen a *human* man beat it, finally. A handsome young man had won against five contenders in a row, had been awarded a trophy…but those who had gathered and remained to watch him didn't applaud his victory, cheer, or clap his back. They were either too shy or reserved or unemotional or too used to watching life through their VT screens.

His wife and daughters had never caught up with him. Now where the hell were they? Probably watching those fireworks he had heard going off a little while back. Was that them up ahead? Christ, were they still gawking at those stupid crab legs? There was a small crowd there now but Nick saw his daughter Claire's bright pink Sphitt t-shirt and knew it was them; he quickened his pace and drew in enough breath to berate them.

"For Christ's sake, Venus, are you still here?" he began, arm aching, pride smarting, grateful for the opportunity to yell at someone.

"Look," she told him.

Nick looked. His brow furrowed. "What the blast are they doing?"

The three Bedbugs stood before the legs in a line, the one in the middle with some kind of black device on a strap around its head area which had no winking lights or lit screens but which exuded a thin bluish stream of gas from a grilled vent in one side.

There was a waterfall splashing out of the sky. It poured over several of the legs and had a faint pinkish tinge. A large muddy puddle with trash floating in it spread around the Bedbugs' pincered feet. Was that creature actually underwater in its dimension, having now torn a hole wide enough to let in its sea? How long might it go on for–long enough to flood the carnival until they could get some zapper under the flow to catch and eliminate it? Might the hole in the dam widen, the gush too violent to contain, until that alien sea flooded all of Punktown? Or was this a sort of amniotic fluid released with the birth of the creature into this plane?

Nick saw a curled leg uncurl and touch the muddy ground; he could see it sink and settle as weight shifted onto it heavily. He watched a pincered claw appear from the sky, then become a whole leg which also settled into the mud, all within thirty seconds. He counted fifteen legs in various states of advancement, with more claws appearing.

The moon-sculpture called The Head was nearly directly overhead.

"Let's go, Mom." Mallory clung to Venus's waist. "I'm scared."

"Wow!" said a little Choom boy who came running to watch.

EVERYBODY SCREAM!

Something else began to appear...not a leg. Its shape and identity were not apparent at first, particularly through the widening pink waterfall.

"My God!" Venus exclaimed, recoiling suddenly against Nick. "Look at those eyes!" And then she let out a scream...but at something new that had come into her vision.

Toward the crowd came a human man, pained but determined. Blood from his nose had caked on his face, in his mustache. He wore a dusty black plastic jacket and carried a frighteningly over-complex rifle with multiple barrels, heavy-looking for him to carry let alone the dead child he had taken it from.

"Look out," he croaked to the crowd firmly, and they obliged...had been obliging even before he spoke.

One of the Bedbugs noticed him and began to chitter excitedly, a cicada-like sound.

The man took a wide stance and red ray bolts sprayed from him.

The chattering Bedbug went into a crazed tarantella. Some of the bolts glanced off its chitin-like armor. Others cracked the shell, sent pieces of it flying like pottery shards, and a viscous greenish fluid spattered and ran from the punctures. It went onto its back, kicking and lashing its tentacle-like arms in the spasm of death.

Hector switched his aim to the one in the middle.

The black device, specifically. The blue smoke vanished, the plastic or metal or chitin shell dented, cracked, and from the cracks escaped flicking snake tongues of black electricity. The web of electricity spread from the device across the shaking Bedbug's body. The device didn't explode...the black current simply stopped, and released from its grip, the Bedbug dropped dead, its two prosthetic arms adapted to life in a hominid-dominated society steaming.

Hector ducked as one of the giant legs shot out of the air and swept at his head. Another–it caught his sleeve. He hurled himself to the ground, and from the ground on his back fired at the last Bedbug as it came leaping-scrambling toward him with maniacal speed and movements, chattering piercingly. Before the whipping arms could reach him the ray bolts drove it back, back, back. It fell, convulsed, the cicada-screams dwindling and green life fluid oozing.

Hector rolled away from the reaching arms through the mud, regained his footing and now faced the eyes of the Gatherer.

It made no sound, no cry, but despite the nonhuman aspect of the eyes, Hector could see and hear the roar of hatred in them. The chanting device was destroyed; it was wedged between worlds…pinned. But so long as it was reaching into this world it could still collect the energy-traces of the freshly dead. Hector leveled the muddy humming rifle and squeezed its trigger.

The ray bolts glanced off the thick external skull-like housing around the eyes, but one eye dented in, dented more, caved inward and a pudding-thick green blood came flopping out. Quick scribbles of black electricity also issued from the wound. The great creature did not cry out even now, but the legs had gone mad, all clawing the air and mud, tangling with each other, the many heads of a Hydra with a sword in its breast. Hector couldn't hit the other eye through that frenzy, or worsen the damage of the existing wound. Hot rays whined off the armored legs—one of them, the first one, still sporting the spray-painted words "Toby Fucks" like a tattoo.

A bolt ricocheted back at Hector, over his shoulder, almost hitting someone off behind him as well. This wasn't working. He looked down at the gun, read the tiny digital displays. Plasma launcher. He thumbed the switch and a green light came on. Again he pointed the rifle and squeezed the trigger. Nothing happened.

Someone from behind was coming forward, and took his elbow.

"Let me see that," said Nick Bovino, jaw set. "I was in the army."

Hector allowed the man to take the weapon from him, stepped to one side to numbly watch.

Nick fell into the wide stance of a rock singer, swivelled the gun, muscles bulging, and yelled as he launched plasma capsule after plasma capsule…

The white hot gelatinous material quickly encased a number of those limbs that pawed at the air like the legs of rearing demon horses. The legs blazed a trembling white, and the increased frantic kicking and stamping sent hot globules flying, dislodged, but fortunately no one was hit.

EVERYBODY SCREAM!

The audience grew—people came running, children with puffs of candyfloss—and some of its members advanced to plant themselves beside Nick. Two teenage gang boys spat at the creature and then opened fire with their revolvers loaded with a much weaker plasma bullet. A paunchy middle-aged Choom with a baseball cap blew off rounds on an old semiauto with lead bullets. A Fog security man arrived panting, then another, confused as to whether to break up the firing squad or add to it—but by then Nick had started punctuating his plasma onslaught with rocket grenades. This cooperation was not harmony. The audience and shooters shared a focus, unified in fear, and loathing, and hostility. On one hand it was encouraging. On the other, these people weren't sure why they were fighting this monster, except that they had seen one man, Hector, battling it. They only knew it was big and unknown to them and so they feared it and so they had to destroy it. Only by a dim instinct and by good fortune were they correct, this time, in their hostility…and so it was heartening to Hector nonetheless as he watched them kill the Gatherer. This time it was cavemen spearing a mammoth rather than big game hunters shooting an elephant. It had a good purpose. He could admire them—cautiously.

The rocket grenades were what did the trick, so it was Nick, really, who killed the monster, the others just adding their symbolic support. And even then they couldn't be sure the great animal was actually dead—both eyes gone, chunks of armor blasted away, the legs no longer thrashing, just quivering limply, dragging the mud, some finally melted to stumps by the plasma, the constant pink waterfall rinsing away the oozing green blood—as it slowly slipped backward into its own dimension. The head with the black electricity dancing from its shattered eyes submerged into empty air, vanished. Leg after leg. The waterfall decreased. The water stopped, the receding stopped, the portal clamped shut on two last legs, one of them reading "Toby Fucks." And these Nick blasted with plasma and grenades while the security men pushed everyone else back. The bombs shook Hector; he flinched. And it was over.

Shiny with sweat and grinning, exhilarated, Nick looked around for Hector as if he might hand him a trophy. He would make love to Venus tonight like a teenager. "Hey—you want this back?" He extended the bulky rifle.

"Keep it." Hector smiled tiredly, his bruised belly unknotting slowly, gingerly...but with pleasure, as if insinuating itself into a soothing steamy bath. "Thank you."

"Yeah...sure." Nick would have liked to ask the man some questions but he was already slipping away into the crowd, vanishing from sight like the creature. Nick was left standing confused, holding the assault engine, muscular and sweaty, and it was Nick who would appear in holographs and photos on the front pages of tomorrow's tabloids and newspapers: "The Man Who Beat the Monster," "The Hero at Last Night's Paxton Fair."

When he got home that night and listened to the news before taking a soothing steamy bath, Hector would learn that the government's attack on the creature affixed to The Head had been successful. The panning camera view of the corpse would make him shudder. *Only a Nymph.* He would count five pairs of various-sized eyes, some of a different color or shape. He had only seen a *fifth* of the Gatherer's immense face, he would realize.

The Gatherer above the bank in inner Paxton had come fully through, devastating much of that vast structure but not reaching the street below before various security forces could respond. Fortunately, at that hour the bank had been nearly empty and only a few people, mostly police, were killed (and drained of their trace-energies?) before the Gatherer climbed back into the sky and disappeared again into its own world.

It would soon develop that the Earth Colonial Network would send teams of soldiers, accompanied by Theta researchers, into the vast corral of the Bedbugs to guard those tormented inhabitants from the feasting, with orders to fend off or kill those Bedbugs that persisted. The souls would be claimed as kidnapped members of the Colonies, and it would be demanded that the Bedbugs release them to continue on the various roads they had been hijacked from, return them to the various places—where they might have come to a final rest—from which they had been abducted. Once in a great while drastic, decisive action did cut machete-like through the jungles of red tape. This was one such rare occasion, precipitated by the attempted invasion of the three Gatherers.

EVERYBODY SCREAM!

Until they could be freed, the harvested ghosts would slowly cease the idiot wailing of the damned...though still forlorn, disoriented, mournful, they would come to only sniffle or moan at the most. This change would make it easier for the Theta crews to question them coherently and learn from them. Their sense of waiting would take on another character, and though most wouldn't be sure where they were destined now, some would actually become high-spirited and optimistic. The shadow of Johnny Leng would not be one of these.

Hector would call his old workplace the next afternoon and admit his role. His killing of the Bedbug priests. And he would reveal the terrible secret of purple vortex. He would be anxiously invited down to his old workplace to talk, to help...

Even through all his own fear and loathing, however, Hector couldn't fully *hate* the Bedbugs. He could even identify with them, a little bit. He feared sharks. But he didn't hate sharks. Sharks had to eat, didn't they?

That night, or actually in the early hours of tomorrow, Hector would finish his bath, watch some more news reports on VT, shut off his VT with a tired smile, go into his bedroom and stretch out on his bed...and sleep.

His greenish-blackish Kodju silk jacket was tossed over a chair and he had removed his string tie and its clasp, loosened his collar, rolled up his shirt sleeves to his elbows, but Del didn't remove Dingo's pistol from his waistband, starkly outlined there against his white shirt. Sophi was holding him, crying softly, the pistol touching both their bellies at once like a cold erection between them. Del whispered to her, rubbed her back through her sweater. Stroked her thick mane of hair.

"I'm sorry, Del," she moaned.

"You don't have to say that. It's my fault. I didn't listen when you needed me. I was selfish. It's my fault." But Del knew it was his fault and her fault and Johnny Leng's fault and Roland LaKarnafeaux's fault and the Martians' fault and Mitch Garnet's fault and on and on. They were all interconnected, all gears in the machine. And so he knew better than to unduly take on much more than his share of the responsibility for tonight's carnage. Carnage. Funny word. From the Latin *caro, carnis*–representing "flesh." The same source for the word carnal. And for carnival. Del had read once, and it had stuck in his mind and strangely resurfaced now, that "carnival" came from the Latin words *caro* and *levo*, and meant "to take away flesh."

Awkwardly Del slipped free of Sophi, and she sniffled, not looking at his eyes. They knew it would take time to look into each other's faces without guilt and insecurity. Mitch came in now and they were grateful for having broken apart. Sophi made her breathing even, turning away to wipe the corners of her eyes with her palms.

Mitch still looked haunted, to Del, drained of his savage vitality…his buoyant swagger now a heavy plodding. Would it all come back as before, or would it be tempered from now on? Mitch addressed Del, since Sophi had turned from him.

"The forcers haven't caught up with Ficklebottom yet. They're going to take LaKarnafeaux with them tonight. It doesn't necessarily look good, though. No drugs on him, nothing much in the camp. Of course, every illegal substance in the universe is in his body. He says he'll submit to a truth scan to prove he didn't know anything about Leng…raping Sophi. That he didn't order it, anyway. We've got enough on him to put him away, but not for any significant period. *Except*…I took notice of Leng's silenced gun and ran a quick test that indicates it was his gun that killed Heather Buffatoni, Wes Sundry, and Fernando Colon."

"God…Leng did it. Why?"

"Who knows? So far no guns collected at the scene match up on Gross or Habash, though. Nothing in the camp. Anyway, if LaKarnafeaux can be convinced or bullied into a full truth scan session, maybe we can find out if he ordered those killings or at least was aware enough of them to hook him as accomplice. There's a lot to work with–it's not like he'll go free tomorrow–but I'd like to see him buried alive. We just don't have that yet. All we can do is hope the force goes all out for the case and doesn't just file it."

EVERYBODY SCREAM!

"Is Del going to have to go downtown?" Sophi asked, joining the men now, red-eyed but composed.

"No–your lawyer took care of that. Not until he's called to a specific inquest. There'll be no trouble, believe me. It was clean self-defense."

"So Leng killed those kids. He must have drugged Horowitz, too."

"When I got my results on the gun I looked at the scan on her and found semen traces of Colon and another that matches Leng. You can count her as one of his victims."

"Monster," Sophi breathed.

It hadn't hit Del yet. He had killed Johnny Leng. He had never ended another person's life before...

Sophi's lawyer and several other people entered the security trailer. Mitch seized the opportunity to draw Del off to one side. "Noelle Buda's parents are here for her. She asked to see you. I didn't want to say it in front of Sophi."

"Where is she?"

"Outside."

"Alright. I'll, ah...walk with her to their car. Thanks, Mitch." Del went to Sophi. Two of the people with her were from the town; white male humans who had introduced themselves as municipal administrators. "Excuse me. Sophi–I need some air I'm going to walk Noelle Buda and her parents out."

Sophi looked at him. She saw that this was his confession. Her red eyes were not entirely without hurt, and traces of anger remained like the redness. But after a moment or two of recovery she told him, "Alright–be careful. The Martians might come back in full force for revenge."

"They won't tonight with the place swarming with forcers and g-men."

"That might actually attract them."

"I doubt it. I'll be alright."

"What about next year?" one administrator fretted to the other.

"We'll just have to deal with that next year," said Sophi. "Next year is the Paxton Fair's twentieth anniversary. I hope you guys won't change your minds about that."

"We won't," said the senior administrator. "We hope you won't."

"No chance." Sophi looked to Del. He smiled tiredly and gave no objection...though right now the thought wasn't one he embraced with leaping enthusiasm.

"That's the spirit," the administrator told her.

Del left the trailer.

It was cold. He slipped back into his jacket but crumpled his string tie into one pocket. Three people were waiting for him nearby.

Noelle's father smoked a cigarette, flicked it away at Del's approach. He was tall, grim, black. Her mother was white, harsh-looking...at least now. Their eyes on him made Del feel as if he were Noelle's young boyfriend being introduced to her parents for the first time. As Noelle did introduce him he was struck once more by her beauty. So much beauty in the world. So little could one person have of it. But there was a reassuring sanity, sometimes, in accepting those limits.

Noelle's father shook his hand. "Thank you for seeing to our daughter's concerns, Mr. Kahn. I'm sorry to hear what's happened here tonight."

"We'll be alright."

"Still no word on her friend Bonnie?"

"Not yet, but it looks connected to a series of apparently drug-related executions that took place tonight." *Committed by the man I murdered*, Del thought.

"I just wanted to say goodbye," Noelle said meekly, drawing his attention.

"Come on, I'll walk you all to your car." Del lightly took Noelle's elbow–only for a moment.

The carnival had been closed for nearly an hour now. Over the loud speakers people had been asked to leave a little early. There had been a flood of people out and a new flood in. Firemen, paramedics, police to guard tonight against Martian retaliation. Government people to investigate the strange incident with the three dead Bedbugs and the vanished giant leg, the battle recounted by Nick Bovino and others.

The rides stood still...dark, skeletal, like winter trees against the distant bleeding glow from Punktown, where its sharp outline stabbed the night's

EVERYBODY SCREAM!

black flesh. The rides and Punktown's spires intermingled into one jagged horizon, both being structures built to lift people into the sky. No more colored lights. No more music by Sphitt and Flemm roaring from the Screamer. The carnival's flesh had been taken away. Patrols of town enforcers flitted through the ruins like ghosts.

Del was both irritated and relieved that the Budas did not walk a little ahead to let him talk with Noelle privately. She simply looked impatient, tried hooking his eyes at every opportunity, hers bright and sad in the dark. Mr. Buda was asking Del questions about the events of the night. It became apparent that he knew Del had killed Johnny Leng but didn't seem repulsed by that.

Some guards at the gate let them through without questions. They descended the long inclined path to the vast dirt parking lot, now empty in the dim moonlight and barely adequate flood-lights except for a few scattered vehicles, mostly close by and belonging to the recent arrivals...though one vehicle far off belonged to Moussa Habash, and its eerie remoteness in the lot made Del imagine that the slumped punctured corpses were still inside it.

Off near the lot entrance some police guards glanced over at them but kept on smoking cigarettes, automatic weapons slung over their shoulders.

The Budas' vehicle was near at hand and they stopped outside it. Mr. Buda unlocked the door for his wife and she slipped in. Again he shook hands with Del. "Thank you, Mr. Kahn."

"Nice to meet you, Mr. Buda. Take care."

Now, whether intentionally or not, Del and Noelle were left standing together outside the car as her father ducked into it and shut his door.

"I'm sorry about your friend, Noelle. I'm sorry about everything."

Noelle nodded. She glanced down at her mother's window. At this angle, near the rear of the vehicle, her mother couldn't see them well, and the windows were closed against the night. In returning to Del, her eyes were almost pleading. "I was wondering if, you know...we could get together again some time...you know, to have lunch or something."

"I don't think that would be a good idea, hon. I'm sorry. I'm sorry I took advantage of you like that," he whispered.

"You didn't. We both did it. Anyway, we don't have to, um..."

"I'm sorry, Noelle–I can't. I'm married."

"You were married before."

"I was being selfish. I was hurting my wife. I can't do that."

Noelle let out a ragged sigh, hugged her arms, gazed off toward the dark trees that bordered some of the lot. Bonnie's car, she noticed, had been removed by someone sent by her family. "Well, I knew you were married all along. I knew it was just some fun. It isn't like you promised to make me your mistress or anything."

Was that a hint? He side-stepped it. "You don't have a boyfriend now?"

"No."

"That's hard to believe. You won't go long without one, Noelle, believe me. You're a lovely, sweet woman." Del took one of her hands and her hugging arms unfolded from her chest. He squeezed it. "I enjoyed your company. I'll remember you. Don't be sad, huh? Who am I, anyway? I'm nobody extra-special."

"You're Del Kahn."

"Yeah? And you're Noelle Buda." He didn't know how much of her attraction to him was based on his being *Del Kahn*, but he didn't want to insult or hurt her now by pointing out that that had to be much if not most of it. What did she *really* know of him? Well–maybe she knew a lot, actually. She could recite his lyrics. And to know his lyrics was to know him. So maybe she really could love the true Del Kahn. But even that couldn't matter now. "I've got to go, hon. And your parents are waiting. "He gave her hand a firmer squeeze, and then she embraced him.

Her body felt good against him, the gun in his waistband again a cold erection. He almost stroked her thick mane of hair. He glanced down at her parents' car, his face hot, cheeks throbbing. He patted her back with one hand instead of stroking it, and after one extra-tight squeeze began to slip away from her.

Noelle's mother wondered what was keeping them, and scrunched down a little to peer into her door's rearview mirror. She saw the end of the embrace, their coming apart. Behind them, approaching, she saw another person. They

EVERYBODY SCREAM!

had not yet seen this person, apparently. Mrs. Buda knew this person, in fact, but in the dark hadn't yet recognized him. She didn't care for this person...

Now Del heard the crunch of dirt behind them and turned. A young man with tight thin lips and the short bristled haircut typical of a Choom. Del didn't know him, but Noelle knew him as she also turned. Del lifted his hands and cried, "Hey!"

"Is that your new boyfriend, Noelle?" croaked Kid Belfast, pointing the pistol he carried at Del and firing it.

The gun wasn't silenced. The lead bullet smashed Del. He went down.

Noelle screamed, scrambled around behind the front of the car. The driver's side door opened and Mr. Buda twisted partially out, a small semi-automatic pistol in his hand. Kid crouched a little and blasted off three shots in rapid succession. One bullet struck Mr. Buda on the base of the thumb, tearing it half off. Mr. Buda screamed now, his gun dangling by the trigger guard.

Kid started around the car to fire into it some more, as he had fired into Moussa Habash's car so many hours earlier. He had several times nearly given up hope that Noelle would reemerge from the med trailer tonight, and when the carnival had closed he had taken to hiding once more in the bordering trees, discouraged by the influx of forcers. But then this car had pulled in. Good old, wonderful, open-armed Mr. and Mrs. Buda. Kid was almost more intent on killing them now than Noelle. Almost.

Despite his wound, Mr. Buda had almost got his door closed. Kid pointed his gun into the crack. He heard forcers yelling, running. He fired into the car. A bullet shattered Noelle's mother's knee cap. Kid saw Mr. Buda switching his businessman's neat little, official-looking, antiseptic semiautomatic from his torn hand to his other. And the forcers would be here any moment. He quickly turned to head around to the front of the car. Noelle...

He wasn't crying. He had stopped crying hours ago.

Kid saw her legs as she scrambled around to the driver's side again. He had played this game with a friend as a boy...chasing each other around a car with battery-operated toy guns, watching for each other through the windows. He had still been a Choom, then.

He moved faster. Time was running out. He came around to the passenger's side of the car. She was on her back in the dirt, there, her eyes huge up at him. Del was on his back with her, also propped up, as if they had been caught in bed together, his shirt red and Dingo Rubydawn's semiautomatic at the end of his outstretched arm.

All the skillful cosmetic and structural surgery was swept away…the narrowing of the heavy Choom jaw, the implanted single row of puny human teeth, the adjustment of muscles and tendons, those thin tight lips. The explosive bullet was a sledgehammer swung into a plaster bust. A wet red explosion across the night sky. Del and Noelle stared up at this last display of fireworks.

Kid Belfast's headless body toppled away. The coroner would, upon a post-mortem scan, identify and record the body as being a Choom.

The forcers from the gate arrived. It wasn't long before two med helicars lighted nearby. Noelle had crouched by Del to hold his hand, weeping, but had been gently pulled away by a forcer to make room for the paramedics. She went with her parents in one of the helicars to the med trailer inside the carnival. Both had been bandaged and given pain blockers, were calm and coherent. She held both their hands and sobbed. And sobbed. "It's my fault," she chanted. "It's my fault…" Even though she was but one gear in the whole machine.

The paramedics attended to Del, lifted him onto a stretcher, into the other helicar. Sophi was there with him now, and she held his hand. Radio chatter. Activity. A needle being inserted into his arm, taped in place, colorful monitor screens. The pain blocker drained away the agony. Del smiled up at his wife weakly, drowsy.

"Too bad…looks like I'll be alright, huh? For a minute there I thought I'd be a star again. VT specials on my life. Collected retrospectives of my work. Black velvet paintings. I thought I'd be the next Lotto-ichi."

Sophi laughed through her tears. She thought of the plastic bust of that Tikkihotto musician-political hero she had given Del, with its realistic moving eye tendrils; a music box. "Oh well," she said. "You'll just have to settle for being mortal."

"I will be really famous again, I'll bet...for now. I was shot tonight. I shot a boy and clubbed to death the man who raped my wife." Del's tone had turned sober. "There's a VT movie in that. A mini-series."

"Maybe. But I'll be glad when it goes back to just the people who really appreciate you and your music. Won't you?"

"Yes," Del admitted.

Mitch Garnet clambered up into the helicar. "Del," he said.

"Sorry, sir, no room," a paramedic ordered him.

"I'll be okay. See you at the med trailer," Del reassured him.

Mitch reluctantly backed off. "Alright–see you inside." How much more pale and shaken could Mitch Garnet look tonight? He'd get better, as Del would. But he would always be haunted in some way by tonight. Those who had survived tonight, those who survived *every* night, were affected in little ways or big ways.

For Dolly Horowitz, tonight was the night her daughter had died. Tonight a Choom man had given his girlfriend an engagement ring while they were high in the triple Ferris Wheel. Mrs. Oggen, an elderly Choom woman who had submitted a jar of preserves to be judged, would proudly return tomorrow to retrieve it, and would remember this year primarily as the year she had won first prize.

The helicar lifted and bore Del Kahn and Sophi Kahn back into the carnival.

About the Author

JEFFREY THOMAS' first book set in his milieu of Punktown was the collection titled *Punktown*, from which a story was reprinted in *The Year's Best Fantasy and Horror #14*. It will soon be released by Prime with twice as many stories as the original edition. His 2003 Punktown novel *Monstrocity* was nominated for the Bram Stoker Award in the Best First Novel category. *Punktown: Third Eye* is a shared-universe anthology of stories written by other authors in addition to Thomas. He lives in Massachusetts, and every Labor Day weekend makes a pilgrimage to the Spencer Fair, which inspired him to write *Everybody Scream!*.

Printed in the United States
117160LV00001B/5/A